LOOK WHAT THEY'RE SAYING ABOUT NALINI SINGH
AND HER PSY-CHANGELING NOVELS

"BREATHTAKING blend of passion, adventure, and the paranormal."
—Gena Showalter, *New York Times* bestselling author

"A MUST READ for all of my fans. Nalini Singh is a major new talent."
—Christine Feehan, #1 *New York Times* bestselling author

"A COMPLETELY UNIQUE and utterly mesmerizing series."
—*Simply Romance Reviews*

"DOWNRIGHT FANTABULOUS."
—*All About Romance*

"YOU WON'T BE DISAPPOINTED."
—*Night Owl Romance*

continued . . .

continued . . .

Visions of Heat

"Breathtaking blend of passion, adventure, and the paranormal. I wished I lived in the world Singh has created. This is a keeper!"

—Gena Showalter, *New York Times* bestselling author

"This author just moved to the top of my auto-buy list."

—*All About Romance*

"Brace yourselves because . . . [it] will set all your senses ablaze and leave your fingers singed with each turn of the page. *Visions of Heat* is that intense!" —*Romance Junkies*

Slave to Sensation

"I LOVE this book! It's a must read for all of my fans. Nalini Singh is a major new talent."

—Christine Feehan, #1 *New York Times* bestselling author

"An electrifying collision of logic and emotion . . . A volcanic start to a new series that'll leave you craving for more."

—*Romance Junkies*

"Make room for [*Slave to Sensation*] on your keeper shelf."

—*Romance Reviews Today*

"A sensual romance set in an alternate reality America with just a bit of mystery to keep readers flipping pages."

—*Fresh Fiction*

Kiss of Snow

---◆---

NALINI SINGH

BERKLEY SENSATION, NEW YORK

THE BERKLEY PUBLISHING GROUP
Published by the Penguin Group
Penguin Group (USA) Inc.
375 Hudson Street, New York, New York 10014, USA

Penguin Group (Canada), 90 Eglinton Avenue East, Suite 700, Toronto, Ontario M4P 2Y3, Canada
(a division of Pearson Penguin Canada Inc.)
Penguin Books Ltd., 80 Strand, London WC2R 0RL, England
Penguin Group Ireland, 25 St. Stephen's Green, Dublin 2, Ireland (a division of Penguin Books Ltd.)
Penguin Group (Australia), 250 Camberwell Road, Camberwell, Victoria 3124, Australia
(a division of Pearson Australia Group Pty. Ltd.)
Penguin Books India Pvt. Ltd., 11 Community Centre, Panchsheel Park, New Delhi—110 017, India
Penguin Group (NZ), 67 Apollo Drive, Rosedale, Auckland 0632, New Zealand
(a division of Pearson New Zealand Ltd.)
Penguin Books (South Africa) (Pty.) Ltd., 24 Sturdee Avenue, Rosebank, Johannesburg 2196,
South Africa

Penguin Books Ltd., Registered Offices: 80 Strand, London WC2R 0RL, England

This is a work of fiction. Names, characters, places, and incidents either are the product of the author's
imagination or are used fictitiously, and any resemblance to actual persons, living or dead, business
establishments, events, or locales is entirely coincidental. The publisher does not have any control
over and does not assume any responsibility for author or third-party websites or their content.

KISS OF SNOW

A Berkley Sensation Book / published by arrangement with the author

PRINTING HISTORY
Berkley Sensation hardcover edition / June 2011
Berkley Sensation mass-market edition / November 2011

Copyright © 2011 by Nalini Singh.
Excerpt from *Tangle of Need* by Nalini Singh copyright © by Nalini Singh.
"Deleted scenes" copyright © by Nalini Singh.
Cover photo of wolf and moon by Photosani/Shutterstock.
Cover photo of man by Vojtech Vlk/Shutterstock.
Cover hand lettering by Ron Zinn.
Cover design by George Long.

ISBN: 978-0-425-24489-0

BERKLEY SENSATION®
Berkley Sensation Books are published by The Berkley Publishing Group,
a division of Penguin Group (USA) Inc.,
375 Hudson Street, New York, New York 10014.
BERKLEY SENSATION® is a registered trademark of Penguin Group (USA) Inc.
The "B" design is a trademark of Penguin Group (USA) Inc.

PRINTED IN THE UNITED STATES OF AMERICA

10 9 8 7 6 5 4 3 2 1

For you, my readers

CAST OF CHARACTERS

In alphabetical order by first name
Key: SD = SnowDancer wolves   *DR = DarkRiver leopards*

Aden Arrow, Telepath (Tp)

Alexei SD Lieutenant

Amara Aleine Psy member of DR, former Council scientist, twin of Ashaya, mentally unstable

Andrew (Drew) Kincaid SD Soldier, mated to Indigo, brother of Riley and Brenna

Anthony Kyriakus Psy Councilor, father of Faith

Ashaya Aleine Psy member of DR, former Council scientist, mated to Dorian, twin of Amara

Ava SD, mother of Ben, friend of Lara

Barker DR Soldier

Ben SD pup, son of Ava

Brenna Kincaid SD, tech, mated to Judd, sister of Andrew and Riley

Clay Bennett DR Sentinel, mated to Talin

Cooper SD Lieutenant

Council (or **Psy Council**) The ruling Council of the Psy race

Elias SD Senior Soldier, mated to Yuki, father of Sakura

Evangeline (Evie) Riviere SD, sister of Indigo

Faith NightStar Psy member of DR, cardinal foreseer (F-Psy), mated to Vaughn, daughter of Anthony

Ghost Psy rebel

Hawke SD Alpha

Henry Scott Psy Councilor, husband of Shoshanna

Indigo Riviere SD Lieutenant, mated to Andrew, daughter of Abel and Tarah, sister of Evangeline

Jem (real name: **Garnet**) SD Lieutenant

Judd Lauren Psy member of SD, Lieutenant, mated to Brenna, uncle of Sienna, Toby, and Marlee

Kaleb Krychek Psy Councilor

Kenji SD Lieutenant

Kieran Human member of SD, Soldier

Kit DR Novice Soldier, brother of Rina

Lara SD Healer

Lucas Hunter DR Alpha, mated to Sascha

Lucy SD, nurse, assistant to Lara

Maria SD Novice Soldier

Marlee Lauren Psy member of SD, daughter of Walker, cousin of Sienna and Toby

Matthias SD Lieutenant

Max Shannon Human, Nikita's security chief, married to Sophia

Mercy Smith DR Sentinel, mated to Riley

Ming LeBon Psy Councilor

Nathan (Nate) Ryder DR Senior Sentinel, mated to Tamsyn, father of Roman and Julian

Nikita Duncan Psy Councilor, mother of Sascha

Riaz SD Lieutenant

Riley Kincaid SD Lieutenant, mated to Mercy, brother of Andrew and Brenna

Rina DR Soldier, sister of Kit

Riordan SD Novice Soldier

Sascha Duncan Psy member of DR, cardinal empath (E-Psy), mated to Lucas, daughter of Nikita

Shoshanna Scott Psy Councilor, wife of Henry

Sienna Lauren Psy member of SD, Novice Soldier, sister of Toby, niece of Judd and Walker

Sophia Russo Former Justice Psy (J), works for Nikita, married to Max

Tai SD Novice Soldier

Tamsyn (Tammy) Ryder DR Healer, mated to Nathan, mother of Roman and Julian

Tarah Riviere SD, mother of Indigo and Evangeline

Tatiana Rika-Smythe Psy Councilor

Teijan Rat Alpha

Toby Lauren Psy member of SD, brother of Sienna, nephew of Judd and Walker

Tomás SD Lieutenant

Vasic Arrow, Teleporter (Tk-V)

Vaughn D'Angelo DR Sentinel, mated to Faith, jaguar changeling

Walker Lauren Psy member of SD, father of Marlee, uncle of Sienna and Toby

Xavier Perez Human priest

Yuki SD, lawyer, mated to Elias, mother of Sakura

X

1979.

    The year the Psy race became Silent.

    Became cold, without emotion, without mercy.

    Hearts were broken, families torn apart.

    But far more were saved.

    From insanity.

    From murder.

    From viciousness such as unseen in the world today.

    For the X-Psy, Silence was a gift beyond price, a gift that allowed at least some of their number to survive childhood, have a life. Yet over a hundred years after the icy wave of the Silence Protocol washed away violence and despair, madness and love, X-Psy are, and remain, living weapons. Silence is their safety switch. Without it . . .

    There are some nightmares the world will never be ready to face.

Chapter 1

HAWKE FOLDED HIS arms and leaned back against the solid bulk of his desk, eyes on the two young females in front of him. Hands clasped behind themselves and legs slightly spread in the "resting" stance, Sienna and Maria looked like the SnowDancer soldiers they were—except for the fact that their hair straggled in a wild mess around their faces, matted with mud, crushed leaves, and other forest debris. Then there was the torn clothing and the sharp, acrid scent of blood.

His wolf bared its teeth.

"Let me get this straight," he said in a calm tone that had Maria turning pale under skin that was a warm, smooth brown where it wasn't bruised and bloody. "Instead of staying on watch and protecting the pack's defensive border, you two decided to have your own personal dominance battle."

Sienna, of course, met his gaze—something no wolf would've done in the circumstances. "It w—"

"Be quiet," he snapped. "If you open your mouth again without permission, I'm putting both of you in the pen with the two-year-olds."

Those amazing cardinal eyes—white stars on a background of vivid black—went a pure ebony, which he knew full well indicated fury, but she clenched her jaw. Maria, on the other hand, had gone even paler. Good.

"Maria," he said, focusing on the petite changeling whose size belied her skill and strength in both human and wolf form. "How old are you?"

Maria swallowed. "Twenty."

"Not a juvenile."

Maria's thick black curls, heavy with mud, bounced dully as she shook her head.

"Then explain this to me."

"I can't, sir."

"Right answer." No reason they could offer up would be a good enough excuse for the bullshit fight. "Who threw the first punch?"

Silence.

His wolf approved. It mattered little who'd incited the exchange when neither had walked away from it, and the fact of the matter was, they'd been meant to work as a team, so they'd take their punishment as a team—with one caveat.

"Seven days," he said to Maria. "Confined to quarters except for one hour each day. No contact with anyone while you're inside." It was a harsh punishment—wolves were creatures of Pack, of family, and Maria was one of the most bubbly, social wolves in the den. To force her to spend all that time alone was an indication of just how badly she'd blundered. "The next time you decide to step off watch, I won't be so lenient."

Maria chanced meeting his gaze for a fleeting second before those rich brown eyes skated away, her dominance no match for his. "May I attend Lake's twenty-first?"

"If that's the use you want to make of your hour on the day." Yeah, it made him a bastard to force her to miss most of her boyfriend's big party, especially when the two were taking the first, careful steps into a relationship, but she'd known exactly what she was doing when she decided to engage in a pissing contest with a fellow soldier.

SnowDancer was strong as a pack because they watched each other's backs. Hawke would not allow stupidity or arrogance to eat away at a foundation he'd rebuilt from the ground up after the bloody events that had stolen both his parents and savaged the pack so badly it had taken more than a decade of tight isolation for them to recover.

Holding on to his temper by a very thin thread, he turned his attention to Sienna. "You were," he said, the wolf very much in his voice, "specifically ordered not to get into any physical altercations."

Sienna said nothing in response. It didn't matter—her rage

was a hot pulse against his skin, as raw and stormy as Sienna herself. When she was like this, the wildness of her barely contained, it was hard to believe she'd come into his pack Silent, her emotions blockaded behind so much ice, it had infuriated his wolf.

Maria shifted on her feet when he didn't immediately continue.

"You have something to say?" he asked the woman, who was one of the best novice soldiers in the pack when she didn't let her temper get in the way.

"I started it." Color high on her cheekbones, shoulders tight. "She was just defending—"

"No." Sienna's tone was steady, resolute, the anger buried under a wall of frigid control. "I'll take my share of the blame. I could've walked away."

Hawke narrowed his eyes. "Maria, go."

The novice soldier hesitated for a second, but she was a subordinate wolf, her natural instinct to obey her alpha too powerful to resist—even though it was clear she wanted to remain behind to support Sienna. Hawke noted and approved of the display of loyalty enough that he didn't rebuke her for the hesitation.

The door closed behind her with a quiet snick that seemed shotgun-loud inside the office's heavy silence. Hawke waited to see what Sienna would do now that they were alone. To his surprise, she maintained her position.

Reaching forward, he gripped her chin, turning her face to the side so that the light fell on the smooth lines of it. "You're lucky you don't have a broken cheekbone." The flesh around her eye was going to turn all shades of purple as it was. "Where else are you hurt?"

"I'm fine."

His fingers tightened on her jaw. "Where *else* are you hurt?"

"You didn't ask Maria." Stubborn will in every word.

"Maria is a wolf, able to take five times the damage of a Psy female and keep going." Which was the reason Sienna had been ordered not to get into physical confrontations with the wolves. That and the fact that she didn't have her lethal abilities under total control. "Either you answer the question, or I swear to God I really will put you in the pen." It would be the most humiliating of experiences and she knew it, every muscle in her body taut with viciously withheld anger.

"Bruised ribs," she gritted out at last, "bruised abdomen, wrenched shoulder. Nothing's broken. It should all heal within the next week."

Dropping his grip on her chin, he said, "Hold out your arms."

A hesitation.

The wolf growled, loud enough that she flinched. "Sienna, I've given you a long leash since you came into the pack, but that ends today." Insubordination from a juvenile could be punished and forgiven. In an adult, in a *soldier*, it was a far more serious matter. Sienna was nineteen going on twenty, a ranked novice—letting her actions slide wasn't even an option. "Hold out your fucking arms."

Something in his tone must've gotten through to her because she did as ordered. A few small cuts on that creamy skin kissed gold by the sun, but no gouges that would've spoken of claws. "So Maria managed to rein in the wolf." If she hadn't, he'd have kicked her right back into training. Losing control of your temper was one thing; losing control of your wolf was far more dangerous.

Sienna's hands fisted as she dropped them to her sides.

Looking up, he met those eyes of absolute, unbroken black. It was clear she was fighting the elemental impulse to go at him, but she continued to hold her position. "How far did you go?" Her control was impressive—and it irritated him in a way it shouldn't have. But then, nothing about Sienna Lauren had ever been easy.

"I didn't use my abilities." The tendons in her neck stood out against the dirt-encrusted hue of her skin. "If I had, she'd be dead."

"Which is why you're in far more trouble than Maria." When he'd given the Lauren family sanctuary after their defection from the cold sterility of the PsyNet, it had been under a number of strict conditions. One of those conditions had been a prohibition against using Psy abilities on packmates.

A significant number of things had changed since that time, and the Laurens were now an integral and accepted part of the pack. Sienna's uncle, Judd, was one of Hawke's lieutenants, and often used his telepathic and telekinetic abilities in defense of SnowDancer. Hawke had also never tied the hands of the two youngest Laurens, knowing Marlee and Toby would need their mental claws to defend themselves against their rambunctious wolf playmates.

But that freedom didn't extend to Sienna, because Hawke knew exactly what she could do. The instant Judd accepted the lieutenant blood bond, keeping secrets from his alpha had become a question of loyalty and trust.

"Why?" Sienna lifted her chin. "I didn't disobey the rule about using my abilities."

Naturally, she'd challenge him. "But," he said, reining in the wolf's snarling response to her defiance, "you did disobey a direct order in engaging in the fight—you said it yourself, you could've walked away."

White lines bracketed her mouth. "Would you have?"

"This isn't about me." He'd been a young hothead once upon a time, and he'd had his ass kicked for it . . . until everything had changed, his childhood wiped out in a surge of blood and pain and piercing sorrow. "We both know your lack of control could've led to a far more serious outcome." The hell of it was, she knew that, too—and still she'd let herself cross the line. That angered Hawke more than anything else.

"I could be confined to DarkRiver land," Sienna said while he was considering how to deal with her, "if you don't want me in the den."

Hawke snorted at her reference to the leopard pack that was SnowDancer's most trusted ally. "So you can hang out with your boyfriend? Nice try."

Sienna's skin flushed a dull red. "Kit isn't my boyfriend."

Hawke wasn't going to get into that conversation. Not now. Not ever. "You don't get to have a say in your punishment." He'd spoiled her. It was his own damn fault it was coming back to bite him in the ass. "One week confined to quarters in the soldiers area, one hour out per day." Psy were much better at handling isolation than changelings, but he knew Sienna had changed since defecting from the PsyNet, become far more intertwined in the bonds of family, of Pack. "Second week spent working with the babies in the nursery, since that's the age you've been acting recently. No duty rotations until you can be trusted to stick to your task."

"I—" She snapped her mouth shut when he raised an eyebrow.

"Three weeks," he said softly. "Third week you'll spend in the kitchens as a dish hand."

Her cheeks burned a hotter shade, but she didn't interrupt again.

"Dismissed."

It was only after she'd gone—the autumn and spice of her scent lingering in the air in a silent rebellion she would've undoubtedly enjoyed had she known about it—that he loosened his hold on the wolf who was his more feral half.

It lunged for her scent.

Sucking in a harsh breath, Hawke fought the primal urge to go after her. He'd been battling the instinct for months, ever since the wolf decided that she was now an adult and, therefore, fair prey. The human half of him wasn't having much success in changing the wolf's mind, not when he had to fight the hunger to claim the most intimate of skin privileges every time she was in his presence.

"Christ." Picking up the sleek new sat phone the techs had issued him four weeks ago, he put through a call to Dark-River's alpha.

Lucas answered on the second ring. "What is it?"

"Sienna won't be heading down to spend time with you cats for a while." Aside from the distance Sienna apparently needed from the den, from *him*, she'd been working with Lucas's Psy mate, Sascha, to understand and gain control of her abilities. But—"I can't let it go. Not this time."

"Understood." The answer of a fellow alpha.

Hawke sat on the edge of his desk, shoving a hand through his hair. "Can she handle it?" He knew she wouldn't break—Sienna was too strong for that, a strength that acted like a drug on his wolf—but the power that lived within her was so vast, it had to be treated as the wildest of beasts.

"Last time she was down," Lucas responded, "Sascha said she displayed an exceptional level of stability, nothing like when they first began to work together. They're not having regular meetings anymore, so that's not an issue."

Mind at rest on that score at least, Hawke said, "I'll make sure Judd keeps a psychic eye on her just in case." Sienna wouldn't appreciate the oversight, but fact was fact—she was dangerous, and he had to consider the safety of the pack as a whole. As for the ferocity of his protective instincts when it came to her, he wasn't about to lie and pretend they didn't exist.

"Can I ask what happened?" Lucas's tone was curious.

Hawke gave the cat a quick rundown. "She's been worse this past month." Prior to that, her newfound stability *had* been noticed—and approved of—by all the senior members of the pack. "I've got to start coming down hard on her or it'll cause discontent in the den." Hierarchy was the glue that held a wolf pack together. As alpha, Hawke was at the top of that hierarchy. He could not, would not, accept rebellion from a subordinate.

"Yeah, I get it," Lucas replied. "Surprises me though. She's the perfect soldier down here, doesn't ever give me lip. Got a mind as sharp as a razor."

Hawke flexed and unflexed his claws. "Yeah, well, she's not yours."

A long, quiet pause. "I heard you were seeing someone."

"You want to gossip?" Hawke made no attempt to hide his irritation.

"Kit and the other novices saw you with some drop-dead gorgeous blonde a few weeks ago. At a restaurant down by Pier 39."

He thought back. "She's a media consultant with CTX." SnowDancer and DarkRiver held majority shares in the communications company, an investment that was paying off big-time as even Psy began to search for news reports free of the crushing influence of their dictatorial ruling Council. "Wanted to talk to me about doing an interview."

"When's it going to be on?"

"Next time you see a pig flying past the window." Hawke didn't play for the cameras, and he'd made damn sure Ms. Consultant understood that SnowDancer wasn't planning to change its mean and carnivorous image to pretty and fluffy anytime soon. She could work with that or find another posi—

A sudden thought sliced clean through his remembered annoyance, had his hand tightening on the phone. "Was Sienna with the novices?"

"Yep."

It was Hawke who paused this time, his wolf taking a watchful stance, caught between two competing needs. "There's nothing I can do about that, Luc," he said at last, every muscle in his body taut to the point of pain.

"That was what Nate said."

The leopard sentinel was now happily mated with two cubs.

"Not the same." It wasn't simply a question of age—the brutal fact was that Hawke's mate was dead. Had died as a child. Sienna didn't understand what that meant, how little he had to give her, give any woman. If he was selfish enough to succumb to the unnamed but powerful pull between them, he knew full well he'd destroy her.

"Doesn't mean you can't be happy. Think about it." Luc hung up.

She hasn't slept with him, you know . . . Don't leave it too late, Hawke, or you might just lose her.

Indigo's words two months ago, speaking about Sienna and that cub who was stuck to her like glue whenever Hawke turned around. Aside from the fact the boy was a leopard, there was nothing wrong with Kit. He'd make the perfect ma—

A crunching sound.

His new sat phone bore a jagged crack through the screen.

RECOVERED FROM COMPUTER 2(A)
TAGS: PERSONAL CORRESPONDENCE, FATHER, E-PSY, ACTION
REQUIRED AND COMPLETED*

FROM: Alice <alice@scifac.edu>
TO: Dad <ellison@archsoc.edu>
DATE: September 26th, 1970 at 11:43pm
SUBJECT: News!!

Hi Dad,

I have the most exciting news. While I'm currently completing my thesis on E-Psy, I've just gained funding to do a second study on the rare X designation! The grant committee referenced my two papers last year and said that my outsider's view on Psy abilities had given rise to some unique conclusions—I suppose they're right. I'm not Psy after all. My Es never made me feel like an outsider, but that's their gift, isn't it?

George, who will soon be a colleague rather than my supervisor, says I'm setting myself up for failure with this project since the Psy Council has been getting harder to deal with of late. Plus, so little is known about the Xs. But that's the point of it, I tell him. I might not be an archaeologist like you, Dad, but I'm exploring my own strange lands.

Speaking of George, he's working on a paper about the development of the Internet. He's adamant it wouldn't have developed as fast as it did had we not had the PsyNet as an example and impetus, and I have to agree—funding alone came thick and fast in the early days because businesses wanted informational parity. He wants another anthropologist's take on it, so I said I would forward it to Mom (will you tell her?).

I hope the sands of Egypt are being kind to you both.

Love,
Alice

*File note: Covert scans of George Kim's mind show evidence of a subtle but total telepathic wipe in relation to the Eldridge project. Given the delicacy of the wipe, there is a high likelihood it was completed by an E-Psy. He has no useful or problematic knowledge. Terminal action not required.

Chapter 2

HER CALM FACADE shattering like so much glass the instant she was behind closed doors, Sienna kicked the back wall of the quarters she'd been assigned in the area of the den set aside for unmated soldiers. She rarely used this room, preferring to live with her brother, Toby; uncle Walker; and cousin, Marlee. But now she was stuck in this small, sterile space for the next week.

Sienna, I've given you a long leash since you came into the pack, but that ends today.

She flinched at the echo of memory. There'd been nothing but the most cutting anger in those eyes of a blue so very pale, they were those of a husky given human form. Paired with that mane of silver-gold and, most of all, that alpha personality, Hawke was a man who invited female attention without effort.

Her hand fisted. Because today, he hadn't seen a woman in front of him, but an unreliable member of the pack, one who'd put SnowDancer in danger with her actions. No punishment he could've given her could compare to her own self-recrimination. The ice-cold knot of shame in her gut was a chill reminder of just how badly she'd messed up. All this time and work, and when it came down to it, she'd allowed her temper to overrule her rational mind.

"Damn it, Sienna." Thrusting her hands into her hair, she grimaced at the dried mud that flaked down her face, and began to strip. It took her less than a minute to bare herself to the skin. Stalking into the tiny shower, deeply grateful that the pack-minded wolves had set it up so everyone had private facilities, she washed the dirt, grass, and blood off her body before beginning to untangle the long, mud-stiff strands of her hair.

It took a long time.

Through it all, frustration—at herself, at her inability to let go of something that was tearing her apart piece by painful piece—raged like a caged tiger within her. If the changelings had a beast inside of them, then so did she, and it was a far more vicious thing, far colder in its ability to destroy. Right now, that beast was focused inward, raking at her with searing claws. Lowering the water temperature, she shampooed her hair twice, then ran the conditioner through it, bringing it forward over her shoulder to make sure she got the ends. It was only when she was almost finished that she realized what she was seeing.

Grabbing a wet hunk of hair, she lifted it to her eyes and swore. The powerful resonance of her ability had neutralized the dye. Again. For the third time in a month. It spoke to a lack of control that worried her. She'd been so good since she began to spend a large amount of time in DarkRiver territory, her Psy abilities so stable that the fear that had locked around her throat since her defection had burned away in a storm of confidence.

Then she'd seen— *"No."*

Snapping off the water, she stepped out and picked up a large, fluffy towel Brenna had given her as part of a birthday gift. It was thick and luxuriant against her flesh, a sensory pleasure she couldn't help but embrace . . . just like she couldn't resist the compulsion that had led to her current situation.

She clenched her jaw so tight it shot a bolt of pain along the bone. But the sensory shock helped her shake off the gut-deep craving that never quite left her, and she concentrated on rubbing herself dry. The bathroom mirror, when she glanced at it, showed her a female of average height with hair of such a deep, deep red it appeared black when wet.

"Like the heart of ruby," Sascha had said the last time they'd put in the dye, the empath's hands gentle on Sienna's scalp. "Such a shame we have to cover it up."

Unfortunately, they didn't have a choice in the matter. Her

hair was too distinctive. Then again, Sienna thought—staring at a face that had become refined in a very feminine way, all trace of childish softness having melted away while she hadn't been looking—maybe it was safe now.

Her hair had in fact darkened in the years since her defection from the PsyNet. Aside from the changes in her face, her body was both noticeably curvier and more muscled. While she carried the muscle in a fluid way that didn't bulk her up, no one who had known her while she'd been jacked into the Net would recognize her now. Especially given the brown contact lenses she always wore outside of SnowDancer territory.

She hadn't worn them today. The bruised eyes that looked back at her were those of a cardinal, a genetic marker that set her apart from the world in a way that couldn't be explained, not even to another cardinal. Perhaps the only person who had ever come close to understanding the violence of what lived within her had been her mother, a cardinal telepath with her own demons. Sienna's brother, Toby, was a cardinal, too. Three in one family . . . it was extraordinary.

But not as extraordinary as a cardinal X surviving to adulthood.

A hard, rapping knock.

Jumping at the sound, she quickly pulled on underwear, a clean T-shirt, and the soft black pants she liked to wear at home. "I'm coming!" she called out when the pounding started again. Since her door had a note indicating she was confined to quarters, it could only be one of the senior members of the pack.

Damp hair tucked behind her ears, she opened the door to come face-to-face with a man who was unquestionably lethal. "Judd." It surprised her that he hadn't 'pathed to her instead of tracking her down.

Then he spoke. "Can you handle being confined?"

The edge of the door dug into her palm, a hard, cold bite. "He asked you to make sure of that, didn't he?"

Judd Lauren might've been her mother's brother, but he'd also been an Arrow, one of the Psy Council's most deadly assassins. He was better at maintaining a mask than anyone she knew, and now his face told her nothing. "Answer the question." His tone made it clear he was asking not as her uncle, but as a SnowDancer lieutenant.

She came to attention. "I'm fine." Her emotions were causing her shields to shudder as her thoughts ricocheted in a hundred different directions, but they were holding. That was all that mattered, because without her shields, she'd be a far more destructive threat than any man-made weapon.

Judd's eyes never moved off her, and she knew he'd made his own assessment of her status even before he nodded. "You know what to do the instant there's a problem."

"Yes." She'd 'path him, and he'd teleport in, shoot to incapacitate. If the shock of pain didn't splinter her psychic focus, he'd aim for her head next. It sounded barbaric and she knew it would break something in him to do it, but someone had to act as the failsafe, a backup in case she could no longer stop herself. Because the fact was, she was a cardinal with a martial ability. There was a high chance her shields would lock down the instant she went live. Not even an Arrow would be able to break through on the psychic plane.

A physical attack was the sole avenue left. Her certainty that Judd would strike that blow if necessary was the only thing that allowed her to live without constantly fearing for the safety of everyone around her. Though notwithstanding her current situation, she'd achieved near-perfect psychic discipline in the preceding months, something no one, not even she, had expected of an X outside Silence.

The reminder had her steeling her spine. "I'll use the time alone to augment and refine the controls you and Sascha helped me develop." Judd wasn't an X, but as a dangerously strong telekinetic, he understood the bone-deep fear that drove her to keep the vicious strength of her abilities trapped in the steel cage of her mind. It was also why he'd kill her if it came down to it.

"Good." Leaning forward, he cupped her cheek, the gesture no longer as startling as it once might've been—before Judd mated with a wolf who had survived her own nightmare. "I did wonder when you were going to push Hawke too far." Stroking his thumb over her cheekbone, he brushed a kiss on her forehead. "Take some of this time to think, Sienna, figure out where you're heading."

Her emotions a tight knot in her chest, she closed the door after he left and walked back to the bathroom to pick up the brush on the shelf by the mirror. "Hawke's mate is dead," she made herself say to the woman who was her reflection, her fingers clenching to bloodless tightness around the carved wood of the handle. "He buried his heart with her."

Even in the face of that harsh truth, the brutal compulsion inside of her refused to be extinguished, to be contained. Like the destructive power of an X, it threatened to consume her until only ashes remained.

LARA was on her way out of the den when she ran into Judd Lauren. "Here," he said, hefting the medical kit she was in the process of slinging over her shoulder.

"Thanks." Noticing the direction he'd come from, she said, "I heard Sienna and Maria returned from their watch hurt, but no one's called me. They okay?"

The Psy lieutenant followed her lead out of the den and into the searing sunshine and crisp air of the Sierra Nevada before answering, "Scratches and bruises, nothing major."

Her healer's heart settling, she lifted her face to the painful clarity of the chrome blue sky. "It's days like this that make me glad to be a SnowDancer." To be a wolf.

"Brenna and I went for an early morning run, when the mist was rising up off the ground." Judd's tone gentled in a way she knew he wasn't aware of when he spoke of his mate.

"I love that time of day." When everything was fresh, the entire world a hushed secret. "Which direction did you go?"

"The other side of the lake," he answered as they moved on. "So—who's injured?"

She rolled her eyes. "Two of the juveniles were doing God knows what, and now I have a broken arm and three cracked ribs to heal."

"You don't usually need this." He tapped the medical kit.

"Juveniles," Lara muttered, "occasionally need to learn a lesson about the fact that maybe they should take better care not to break their limbs. I'll do some healing to ensure everything is as it should be, then cast the arm, strap the ribs." It would take longer to mend than if she used her gift to fully repair the injuries, but would do the boys no harm.

"The peripheral benefit is it keeps my medical skills from getting rusty, plus it allows me to hold my healing abilities in reserve in case we have a sudden critical injury." While Hawke could share his strength with her through their healer-alpha bond, her own body could only handle so much before it collapsed.

"Here." Judd pushed up a branch so she could pass underneath. Which was why she was in front when they entered the clearing, where one of the injured boys lay propped up against a tree, cradling his arm. The other sat cross-legged, clutching at his ribs. Brace was tall and lanky, though Joshua had put on a bit of muscle over the past couple of months. Right now, however, both looked like shamed six-year-olds.

The reason, Lara guessed as her heart thudded hard against her ribs, was the man standing with his arms folded, looking down at the two miscreants. "Walker." She'd scented the dark water and snow-dusted fir of his scent as she and Judd neared but had put it down to the fact that he was often in this area with the younger teens—having been put in charge of the ten-to-thirteen-year-olds. A tough age for wolves, but Walker handled them without so much as raising his voice.

She could understand why—quiet, intense Walker Lauren had a presence akin to that of any dominant wolf. "I didn't expect to see you here." Her voice came out a little husky to her own ears, but no one else seemed to notice.

Walker's pale green eyes held hers for a long, tense second. "I was passing by when I glimpsed these two." His gaze shifted over her shoulder. "I'll carry it back."

"We need to speak—bring the kids for dinner." Judd melted away into the forest so fast, Lara didn't even manage to turn around in time.

"Lara, it hurts." It was an almost apologetic voice.

Wrenching away the suffocating web of want and anger and hurt that had wrapped around her, she went to her knees. "Let me see, sweetheart," she said, checking first Brace, then Joshua. "Hold still for a second." Using the pressure injector, she gave them each a shot of painkiller.

She was vividly conscious of Walker hunkering down beside her, his body big, the scent of him as cool and reserved as the man himself. As she worked, he spoke to Joshua and Brace. Whatever they'd done to get into trouble, the boys' wolves relaxed at once under his attention. Lara only wished her own wolf wasn't so hypersensitive to his presence, until its fur rubbed up against the inside of her skin—but sensitivity aside, the wolf maintained a wary distance. Both parts of her had learned their lesson when it came to Walker Lauren.

"There," she said a while later as both boys checked out Brace's high-tech cast, made of a transparent plascrete. "Any pain or discomfort, you come to me straight away, you understand?"

"Thanks, Lara." A brilliant smile from Joshua followed by a kiss from each teenager—one on either cheek—before they got up and raced off, as if they hadn't been fighting tears not long before.

Shaking her head even as her wolf did the same in affectionate amusement, Lara packed up her gear and watched Walker pick up the bag without effort. It took several attempts to get anything out through a throat gone dry as dust, but she was determined not to allow him to unsettle her. "Thanks."

A silent nod.

As they walked back, Lara's mind rebelled against her own resolution, drowning her in thoughts of that kiss the night Riaz returned to the den. The senior members of the pack had thrown the lieutenant an impromptu welcome-home party. The bubbles had been flowing, and Lara, who didn't usually drink, had had a little too much champagne. It had given her the courage not only to argue with the tall Psy male who'd fascinated her since he first entered the den, but to drag him into a dark corner, go on tiptoe, and find his mouth with her own.

He'd kissed her back, slow and deep and with that powerful body held in fierce check, his hands curving around her ribs as he pulled her into the V of his thighs. The strong muscles in his neck had flexed under her fingers when he angled his head to deepen the kiss, the slight abrasiveness of his unshaven jaw rubbing a rough caress over her skin.

Big as he was, she'd felt surrounded by him, overwhelmed in the most sensual of ways, his shoulders blocking out the world as he backed her to the wall. She might've been buzzed, but she'd never forget a single instant of that experience. Woman and wolf, every part of her had been stunned at her success . . . for the five short seconds it lasted.

Then Walker had lifted his head and nudged her back to the party. She'd thought he was acting the gentleman since she was a tad tipsy, but he would surely do what all dominants did when they wanted a woman, seek her out again when she was sober. He hadn't called her the next morning, which hadn't left her in the best of moods. But he had called her later that same afternoon.

They'd gone for a walk, her heart in her throat the entire time. She'd thought it was a beginning. Until Walker had stopped on the edge of a cliff that fell into a valley with dramatic suddenness, his dark blond hair pushed back by the breeze, and said, "What happened last night was a mistake, Lara." His tone had been gentle, and that had made it all the more terrible. "I apologize."

Ice crawled through her veins, but not wanting to make a mistake, she'd asked, "Because I had too much champagne?"

The answer had been absolute, the rejection crystal clear. "No."

She thought she might've made some smiling remark before excusing herself to walk back to the den alone, but all she could remember was the crushing black of her emotions. God, this man, he'd *hurt* her. However, if it had been a simple case of unrequited attraction, she'd have forgiven him—as she knew too well, you couldn't control who you fell for.

No, what had hurt and angered her was that it hadn't all been in her head. She knew when a man wanted her, and Walker had wanted her . . . enough to kiss, apparently, but not to keep. If that was the case, he was plenty big and strong enough to have stopped her kiss before it ever touched his lips. He hadn't. He'd held her as if she mattered before breaking her heart. And that, she couldn't, wouldn't forgive.

"Lara."

Glancing up at that face drawn in rough masculine lines, she shoved the memories back where they belonged: in the past. "Sorry," she said with a smile built out of pure pride. "I know the kit's heavy. I can take it the rest of the way."

Walker ignored her attempt to keep the conversation casual. "We haven't spoken for several weeks."

She knew he was referring to the late-night conversations they'd had before the kiss. Walker was a night owl. Lara often stayed up late with her patients. Somehow, they'd ended up having coffee around eleven most nights—with Walker keeping a telepathic eye on his daughter and nephew when Sienna wasn't able to stay with them. They hadn't talked about anything of particular note, but those nights had given her the courage to do something that didn't come easily to a wolf who wasn't a dominant.

Healers never were—though they weren't submissive either. Normally, her packmates' dominance simply didn't affect Lara, though her wolf had the ability to put all of them, young or old, at ease. However, things didn't work the same with Walker. Still, she'd made the first move, chanced that kiss that had led to her humiliation.

Since his rejection, she'd made sure to be busy or not in the infirmary around that time; the wound was too fresh. But time had passed, things had changed; she wasn't only surviving, she was holding her own in this encounter. That didn't mean she was about to allow Walker to make his way back into her life, not when she was ready to move on at last.

"Have you forgotten? We spoke when I patched Marlee up after she skinned her knee," she said with a laugh that sounded natural. "Actually"—she held out her hand for the kit—"if you don't mind, I'd prefer to walk the rest of the distance alone. It'll give me some thinking time."

Walker stood unmoving, pale green eyes locked on her. "And if I do mind?"

An uncomfortable heaviness gathered in the air.

She didn't understand why he was pushing this, but what she did know was that she wasn't going to open the lid on that box. Not today or any other day. "If you're okay to carry it back," she said, misunderstanding on purpose, "then thanks." With that and a cheery wave, she headed off into the woods in the direction of the waterfall.

There, she thought, it was done, that excruciating chapter of her life closed.

Chapter 3

COUNCILOR HENRY SCOTT had made the decision to sacrifice San Francisco two months ago, regardless of the economic and financial upheaval such destruction would cause. Now it was simply a case of putting the final pieces in place.

With that in mind, he turned away from the view of the busy streets visible through the window of the office he kept at his London residence, and to the man he'd placed in charge of coordinating his military resources—all of which had now been integrated into the streamlined structure of Pure Psy. The original civilian personnel had been quietly moved out of command positions.

Henry didn't need a political party. He needed a weapon.

Which was why Vasquez was now in charge of all Pure Psy operations. There was nothing prepossessing about the man—he stood a bare five feet four inches, with a build more akin to that of a gymnast than a soldier, and a face so unremarkable people forgot him within minutes of meeting him.

"How long," Henry asked, "before we can move on San Francisco and the surrounding changeling-held areas?"

"A month." Bringing up the files on the main comm screen, Vasquez gave Henry a précis of their current status as regarding men and weapons. "What the wolves call 'den territory' will be the most difficult to take, but I'm working on a possible solution."

Henry nodded, left it at that. Vasquez would be useless to him if he didn't think for himself—something Henry's "wife," Shoshanna, would do well to emulate when it came to her own advisors. She surrounded herself with flunkies, none of them with the intelligence of a gnat. Which was why Henry was running this, while Shoshanna thought she held the reins. "Are there any problems I need to be aware of?"

"No."

"In that case, we'll meet again in a week's time."

It was only after Vasquez left that Henry brought up another file. It was his investment portfolio, and once again, it was in worse shape than warranted. He didn't have to be an expert to realize whose hand lay behind the slow, untraceable strangulation of his finances—Nikita Duncan was a master at manipulating money. However, while her actions were certainly problematic, the losses were nowhere near enough to stop him. He'd take San Francisco soon enough, obliterating the base of her empire.

As for the changelings . . . they could not be allowed to live, not after their constant and continuing defiance. They believed themselves immune to the Council's reach to the extent that they'd encouraged the conception of a hybrid with changeling blood, a fetus that, if it came to term, would result in the dilution of the psychic abilities that made the Psy race the most powerful on the planet.

Henry wouldn't permit it.

It was time the world went back to the way it had been for over a century, the way it *should* be, with the purest of Psy in power, and the other two races allowed to exist only so long as they followed Psy rule. When people thought of Snow-Dancer and DarkRiver, Henry wanted them to see the blood-soaked cost of noncompliance.

Chapter 4

THREE DAYS AFTER the situation with Maria and Sienna, Hawke found himself looking down at a small, big-eyed face. Going down on his haunches to meet that wildly curious gaze, he said, "Looking serious, Ben."

The five-and-a-half-year-old, who happened to be one of Hawke's favorite people in the den, nodded. "Didja really put Sinna in jail?"

Hawke bit the inside of his cheek. "Yep."

Brown eyes, the same dark shade as Ben's mother's, turned wolf-amber in shock. "How come?"

"She didn't follow the rules."

Ben thought about it for a second, lines wrinkling up that baby-smooth forehead. "Is it like time-out for grown-ups?"

"Yep."

"Oh." A decisive nod. "I'll tell Marlee."

"Is Marlee sad?" The girl was Sienna's cousin and part of his pack—Hawke wouldn't allow her to be hurt.

Ben shook his head. "Her dad said that Sinna had been naughty and that's why she got put in jail, but Marlee said you wouldn't put Sinna in jail and that Sinna was probably just grumpy and didn't want to talk to anyone."

Having—somehow—followed all that, Hawke rose to his feet and tousled Ben's dark hair, the little boy's head warm under his touch. "She'll be out in a few days." And working in the nursery. The work itself, he knew, wouldn't be a chore for her. She was a natural protector, and like any protector, wolf or not, she enjoyed watching over the pups. They, in turn, felt utterly safe with her.

So no, it would be no hardship for her to work in the nursery. It was the fact that she'd been taken off the duties befitting and expected of her rank that was the punishment—a public indication that he didn't have trust in her ability to do the job. The blow would strike hard at the pride she wore like armor, but his wolf had no doubts about her steel spine, her iron will. Sienna wouldn't allow anything to crush her, *especially* not Hawke. On principle.

The thought made his wolf bare its canines in a feral grin. "Go on home, Benny."

The pup fell into step beside him instead, those short legs pumping as he ran to keep up. "Where're you going?"

"Out."

"Can I come?"

"No."

"How come?"

Leaning down, Hawke picked Ben up under one arm like a football. "Because you're too short."

Ben giggled and pretended to swim. "I'm taller than I was last week."

"Who says?"

"Mama."

Hawke's lips curved at the sheer love in that single word. "I guess it must be true, then. But you're still too short."

A huge sigh. "When am I going to be tall enough?"

"Before you know it." Placing Ben down in front of the door that led to the White Zone, the safe play area for the kids, Hawke nudged him forward. "Go kick a ball around. It'll make you grow."

"Really?"

"Uh-huh."

Ben ran over to a clearing in the left section of the White Zone, to join in a game already in progress, one being watched over by an off-duty dominant who'd come to hang with the little ones. Half the pups were in human form, the other half wolf. Clearly this was changeling-rules football, which included judicious nipping to make those in human form drop the ball.

Normally, the sight of a wolf streaking away with a football in his mouth as his friends tried to bite down on his tail would've made Hawke laugh, join in. Today, his skin was too tight over his body, his own wolf edgy. Turning away, he headed into the hush of the forest, intending to work off the tension with some hard physical exercise. He hadn't made it more than a hundred meters beyond the White Zone when he froze.

The damn cub had his hands on Sienna.

His claws were slicing out of his skin before he'd processed the thought.

As he watched, Kit angled his body to tuck Sienna even closer, his hands cupping her face to draw her in for an open-mouthed kiss that lasted long enough to have Hawke considering dismemberment. But the young leopard male broke the kiss before Hawke's wolf took control, clasping Sienna's hand to tug her deeper into the dark green firs that covered this area, the spaces between the tall, straight trunks shadowed by late afternoon sunlight.

Hawke didn't have to be a genius to figure out what the boy planned.

"Hawke!"

Retracting his claws, he attempted to wipe his expression clean as he turned to face a woman who was one of his most trusted friends.

And could be a royal pain in the ass.

Indigo frowned as she closed the distance between them. "Was Kit here?" A pause as she obviously caught a second scent. "Ah, Sienna's using her free hour."

"Did you need me for something?" He held his hand out for the datapad by her side. "Is there a problem with the extended patrols?" They'd set up the patrols deep in the forested interior and along the isolated mountain edges of den territory, after Councilor Henry Scott's games a couple of months back—games that had almost stolen the life of Indigo's mate, Drew.

Things had been quiet since then, but the pack wasn't about to drop its guard, especially when it appeared the Psy Councilors had their knives out for each other. Like it or not, the Psy were the most powerful race on the planet. If they imploded, the repercussions would make everyone bleed. "Indigo, I don't have all day." Sharp words.

The lieutenant's response was to fold her arms, her name-sake eyes bright with challenge. "The young males are start-ing to show signs of aggression. You know why."

"I'll take care of it." It was a statement brimming with dominance, one that would've made almost any other indi-vidual tuck tail and run.

Indigo gave him an easy, dangerous smile. "I know all you have to do is snap your fingers and women throw themselves into your bed—" She held up a hand when he growled. "I'm not saying you use your position, but the fact that you're alpha, the reason *why* you're alpha—your strength, your speed, your sheer dominance—that's potent stuff. Not to mention your pretty face."

It was a struggle to keep his focus when the back of his neck burned with the snarling awareness of what was going on not far into the forest. "Thanks for the pep talk." It came out wolf rough.

"Shut up." Indigo was one of only two people in the den who could say that to his face and not get herself in seriously deep shit, and she used that knowledge ruthlessly. "I know damn well you could go and scratch that itch right now if you wanted to, but why don't you think about whether scratching it with just any packmate—even one you like—will have any effect whatsoever."

KIT halted now that they were out of range of keen changeling hearing—even that of a wolf so close to his animal that his senses were more acute than normal. Because while Kit was happy to prod at Hawke, he also had a healthy respect for the SnowDancer alpha and wasn't about to push him beyond a certain point.

That fact might've annoyed his leopard had it been another dominant male closer to his own age, but just as Kit's leopard knew its own strength, man and leopard both also knew that Hawke was a predatory changeling male in the prime of his life. The wolf alpha would wipe the floor with Kit without so much as breaking a sweat.

Sienna tugged her hand out of his. "Why did you do that?" Curious, not angry.

"Don't say my kisses aren't nice?" He couldn't resist the tease.

Folding her arms, she pinned him with one of those looks she'd picked up from her mentor, Indigo. "That was the problem, as I seem to recall."

Kit's pride winced. Just a little—before his leopard shrugged it off with feline confidence. "Want to try again? It was only one kiss."

Shadows clouded her expression, turning her gaze to midnight. "Kit, I—" Eyes narrowing as she glimpsed the grin tugging at his lips, she mimed throwing something at his head. "Not funny."

Laughing, he pulled her body against his with one arm around her neck, deeply conscious that such informal skin privileges came hard for her, that he was one of the few people she trusted in this way—enough to have allowed him to spring a kiss on her. "How could I resist, Sin? You're so adorable and earnest."

She elbowed him. *Hard.* Wincing, he continued to hold her by his side. "So, still no chemistry, huh?" He nuzzled the top of her head with his chin. "Pity. Because you know you're smoking hot."

"Also not funny."

"Wasn't a lie." He knew from the slight shake of her head that she thought he was spouting a whole boatload of shit, but the fact was, Sienna was gorgeous—in a way every dominant changeling male in both packs had noticed.

Hers wasn't a delicate feminine beauty, for all that she was small and fine-boned. No, Sienna carried within her a deep, deep core of strength that had etched itself onto her face. This was a woman who would stand her ground, come what may. And to a predatory changeling male, that was both purest temptation and the most enticing challenge.

He got another intriguing glimpse of that internal strength when she pushed away to face him once more. "You didn't answer my question."

"I scented Hawke walking out," he said, eyes never moving off her . . . so he saw the immediate stiffening of her shoulders, the pinched tightness around the lush curves of her mouth.

When she spoke, her voice held a husky undertone that stroked over his senses like rough silk. "Did he see us?"

"Yes." Leaning against an old lodgepole pine, the trunk clear of branches high up into the canopy, he hooked his thumbs into the pockets of his jeans, thinking again that chemistry was a bitch. But disappointing as it was that there were no fireworks between him and Sienna—oh, there'd been sparks, sure, but not enough to satisfy either one of them—he had the rock-solid feeling that their friendship was here to stay. And Kit took care of his friends. "Don't look at me that way."

Arms crossed over her chest once more, she pinned him with an angry stare. "You know I don't like to play games."

Yes, he did. Sienna was smart on a whole different level than the majority of people, but she'd also spent most of her life in Silence. The conditioning designed to suppress her feelings, her very heart, had left her with huge gaps in her emotional education—which was why she needed friends to watch her back, especially now. "There are games, and then there are strategic moves." He shook his head when she would have spoken. "Predatory changelings are possessive; it's part of the package. Alphas take that to an entirely new level."

"That doesn't apply here." A hard angle to her jaw, those arms so defensively folded. But she didn't try to pretend she didn't know what he was talking about. "He doesn't see me as an adult female, not in that way."

"Hence my helping hand . . . or lips, as the case may be." Walking over, he tugged on her braid because not touching someone he cared about was incomprehensible to his leopard. "Trust me, kitten. I know when a man wants to rip my head off." Followed by various other parts of his anatomy. "Hawke was ready to make leopard mincemeat of my insides and feed it to those feral wolves who follow him around like he's their alpha, too."

"Even if you are correct"—tight words, tendons pulled taut along her jaw—"it won't matter. He's made up his mind."

That, Kit agreed, was a problem. Because if there was one thing he knew about the wolf alpha, it was that Hawke's will was as intractable and immoveable as granite.

*   *   *

HAWKE finished the last of the two hundred crunches he'd set for himself, and sat up. It was three a.m. and his body was still buzzed, in spite of the fact that he'd been in the small indoor gym for over an hour, doing everything he could to exhaust himself. "Hell," he grunted.

Getting up, he wiped off his face using a towel, then flicked on the entertainment screen on the wall, programming it to show financial reports. Cooper and Jem, in concert with a dedicated team, did the day-to-day caretaking of Snow-Dancer's investments, but Hawke made sure he stayed up to date as the two lieutenants often used him as a sounding board.

But today, all he saw was gibberish, his brain hazed by a sexual hunger so raw and wild, he knew he'd have to take care of it or his wolf would begin to fight him, inciting a dangerous level of aggression in all the unmated males in the pack. Right now, they were edgy but the level was still manageable. If Hawke's wolf slipped the leash . . . Shoving his hands through his hair, he was about to reach for the water bottle when he heard someone enter the training room next door.

Likely one of the night-shift soldiers, he thought. Taking a long drink, he put the bottle on a nearby bench as he pushed through the connecting door into the other room, intending to ask if they'd be up for a sparring session. Riley was the only one in the den who could take on Hawke at full strength and make him hurt, but Hawke often practiced with other packmates—just made sure to rein his strength back a fraction.

He halted three steps into the room, the scent of autumn fire, of some rich exotic spice twining around him, as the door closed with a quiet snick at his back. She hadn't seen him, the woman dressed in black *gi* pants and a deep green tank top who moved with such fluid grace in the center of the room. The precise, stylized movements spoke not of combat, but of an attempt to find peace.

She'd pulled her waist-length hair into a neat braid, and the dark rope gleamed with ruby red highlights. It made him feel like a cradle-robbing bastard, but he couldn't help but imagine those silken strands spread out all over his hands . . .

over his pillow. *Fuck*. He should turn around right this second and walk out. There was a reason he made sure never to be alone with her in this kind of a mood.

But it was too late.

She went motionless, the stance of prey scenting a predator. When she turned, it was with wary cautiousness. Not a word passed her lips, but he knew he was intruding on her allotted free hour for the day to come—because whatever else she did, Sienna never lied, never tried to get out of punishment once she'd broken the rules.

He should've left. Instead, he shoved aside the voice of reason and walked to her, aware of her spine going stiff, her shoulders squaring. But it was the sheen of perspiration across her collarbones that fascinated him. The wolf wanted to lick, see if she tasted of the spice so hot and sweet in her scent.

In spite of what might have gone on in the forest earlier, the leopard cub hadn't managed to imprint his scent into her skin. It was all Sienna. Swallowing his growl of satisfaction, he reined in the primal impulse to taste, to take. "Your arm," he murmured, moving to stand behind her and stroking his hand down that arm to raise it, "should be straight on that final turn. You're dropping it."

Her pulse thudded hard and fast against the delicate skin of her neck, and it was all he could do not to drop his head and bite down on it. Not to hurt. Just a nip. Just enough to leave a mark. "Like this." He moved his hand along the smooth warmth of her arm until it was straight. "Do you see?"

No sound as she angled her head to one side. He knew she hadn't meant it to be, but it was an invitation to his wolf, the offering of that vulnerable part of her. He could close his hand around her throat, close his teeth around her jugular, anything he wanted. He was so much stronger than her that he could do that no matter what, but conquering wasn't the same as surrender. "Do it again," he whispered. "I want to watch."

It took every ounce of will he had to drop her arm, to not accept the unintended invitation and take them both to the floor in a tangle of skin and heat. But he couldn't stop himself from running the knuckles of one hand down her throat as he stepped away, his gut tight, his body so damn hard he might as well have been made of steel. He moved until he was in prime position to watch her, and then he waited. She did nothing for a long, still moment, and he thought she would deny him this.

But then Sienna began to move.

And his wolf stopped pacing.

Chapter 5

HUNDREDS OF MILES away, in the barren heart of another continent, an Arrow named Aden scanned his gaze over a desert wasteland that was a rich rust red under sunlight, but now glimmered silver in the glow of the moon. "Why do you always come here?" he asked the fellow member of the squad who'd teleported him to the location.

"There's clarity here," Vasic said, looking out at the rolling vista of sand dunes, his eyes a piercing silver that echoed the brilliance of the moon.

"There's nothing here."

Vasic merely shook his head. "Pure Psy."

"A possible problem." Aden sometimes wondered if he and Vasic hadn't formed an inadvertent subconscious telepathic connection, they understood each other so effortlessly.

"Perhaps," Vasic said with unerring accuracy, "it was when we were placed in training as children. Bonds are more easily formed prior to complete Silence."

Aden preferred not to think about those days. A child was weak, simple to break. He was no longer that child. "Pure Psy," he said, returning to the reason for this meeting.

"Gutierrez and Suhana are already inside and reporting back. We may lose Abbot and Sione."

"That's not unexpected." The two Arrows both had unstable abilities.

"No."

Aden watched as a tiny insect crawled across the sand at his feet. "The adherents of Pure Psy say they seek to preserve the integrity of Silence." The insect stumbled, turned onto its back.

Vasic righted the creature with a delicate touch of Tk, and it hurried into its burrow. "What is said and what is done are often two different things."

"Yes." More than a century ago, Zaid Adelaja had formed the Arrow Squad to watch over Silence, to ensure it would never fall and shatter the PsyNet. But now . . . "We will have to make a choice soon."

Going down on his haunches, Vasic picked up a handful of sand, the silica catching the moonlight as it passed through his fingers. "Yes."

What neither of them said was that it was a choice that might well change the face of the PsyNet forever.

Chapter 6

THE INDULGENCE OF the previous night came back to bite Hawke the next morning. His wolf had had a taste of Sienna Lauren, and it was through with waiting. It wanted her, and it wanted her now. The scent of her—the maddening spice and steel of it—lingered in his skin until he drew it in with every breath.

He couldn't allow himself to surrender to the compulsion. Everything else aside, she was nineteen years old, for Christ's sake, nowhere near mature enough to handle either man or wolf, especially given the razor's edge he was walking right now. More than likely, he'd terrify her.

His jaw tightened.

Making a decision, he packed up some gear and strode down to the underground garage where SnowDancer stored its vehicles. "I'll be back in two weeks," he told Riley when the lieutenant met him beside the camo green all-wheel-drive. "I'm going to head up into the mountains, make sure we haven't missed any vulnerable spots along the perimeter."

It was a legitimate way to burn off his frustration, especially given the extra patrols they'd been running in that region. Riley would simply switch Hawke in for one of the other soldiers and reassign their packmate a task closer to the den—no one would complain since the mountain shifts tended to be quiet and lonely. "Hold the fort." His unflinching trust in his lieutenants was the only reason he could consider being out of the den for such an extended period.

"Don't I always?" Riley folded his arms, those dark brown eyes watching Hawke with a patient calm that did nothing to hide the incisive mind behind them. "You have your sat phone in case we need you?"

Hawke held it up. Nothing would keep him from returning to the den if called, whether through technology or through the music of a wolf's howl.

Riley pulled a small datapad out of his pocket. "I'm promoting Tai from senior novice status to full soldier."

"I had a feeling." The young male had gained a maturity this year that would hold him in good stead when it came to his new responsibilities. "I'll make sure to speak to him when I get back."

A nod. "As for Maria—she'll be on supervised shifts after she's out of confinement."

"Good."

"Sienna's going to be spoiling for a fight when her punishment is done."

Hawke dumped his gear in the truck with more force than necessary. "No more long leash for her, Riley. She steps out of line, slap her back into it."

His most senior lieutenant, his friend, raised an eyebrow. "You know what I said about taking you down if you so much as looked at her?" A reminder that both Riley and Drew considered Sienna family and thus theirs to protect. "Well, I'll still beat you bloody if you hurt her, but I won't stand in your way if you want to court her—she's no longer as vulnerable as she was back then."

Getting into the driver's seat, Hawke brought up the manual steering wheel and reached back to slide the door closed, his actions rough with the wolf's fury at being denied. "Doesn't matter." He couldn't let it matter. Not and live with himself.

"Yeah?" Riley braced his arms on the door's window frame, his expression as relaxed as if they were talking about the most mundane den matter . . . except for his eyes. Those eyes, they saw everything. "Then why the hell are you about to drive up into the most godforsaken corner of den territory and go lone wolf?"

He started the engine. "You know why. I need to run it off." Hawke knew full well that he could seduce Sienna, and not only that, that he could make her enjoy it—it wasn't arrogance but simple fact. The sexual attraction between them wasn't in question. Her skin had burned with the heat of it last night, her pulse a thudding erotic beat he'd hungered to trace across every intimate inch of her body. Add his experience to that, and he had not a single doubt in his mind that he could bring Sienna Lauren sweetly into his bed, take what both man and wolf craved until it was no longer a claw tearing at his gut.

His hands flexed on the wheel at the idea of it, his mind cascading with images of limbs intertwined on tangled sheets, her skin a smooth cream kissed by gold against his darker flesh. But that was where those images would remain—locked within his mind. Because he was no lover for an innocent who didn't understand the sheer depth of the demands he'd make on her . . . even knowing he could never give her the bond that would make up for the raw intensity of all he'd take.

SIENNA scrubbed the large pot used in the communal kitchen that fed most of the unmated adult wolves in the den, her energetic movements driven by aggravation. "We have high-tech abilities," she muttered. "Why do we need to blacken pots?" Three days into the third week of her punishment and she was building serious muscle from the hard labor.

"Because," Tai said from beside her, where he was stacking plates, "some things only taste right when cooked in a pot. So says Aisha and her word is law." Unlike her, Tai wasn't in trouble, simply doing his shift in the kitchens, which was why he was so annoyingly cheerful.

"Four more days and I'm free," she said under her breath, focusing on the manual task in an effort to fight the memory of Hawke's hands on her skin, his breath so hot against her temple, her neck.

She'd spent the day following their encounter in a knot of anticipation . . . only to find that he'd left the den. Her hands moved harder on the pot, the force of it turning the scourer black. She wasn't wolf, but she understood exactly what he was doing. That night in the training room would not be repeated—he'd have considered it a lapse of judgment on his part, conduct unbecoming an alpha. Sienna Lauren was not a suitable lover for the man who was the heart of SnowDancer.

Her knuckles scraped against the inside of the pot, but she hardly noticed, her chest ached from so deep within. Once, the intensity of her response would have set off a wave of dissonance, shards of agony designed to remind her of the need to maintain Silence, but Judd had helped her remove the final emotion triggers six months ago.

Sienna had resisted taking that step for almost a year— since Judd first worked out how to disable the pain protocols. The only reason she'd finally agreed to the removal had been because of the increasing strength of the dissonance. There had been a risk it could begin to cause permanent and irreversible brain injury. Now Sienna was free to feel everything . . . including the bone-deep terror that the X-marker might yet make her a mass murderer.

"Hey." A nudge from Tai.

"What?" she asked, rinsing off the pot.

"You shouldn't take it so hard, you know." His muscled body was warm against hers as he leaned into her for a second. "I got busted off my sentry duties one time after I did something stupid. It happens."

Touched by his attempt to make her feel better, she pushed past the knot of frustrated anger, which never seemed to go away. "I heard you went out with Evie again." Putting the pot on the drying board, she started on the next one.

Tai pushed himself up to perch on the counter, long legs almost touching the floor. His shoulders had filled out in the past year, and he had, she realized, become a big man, almost as big as Hawke—

No. She would not think about him. He certainly hadn't had any problem walking away from her. "So?"

"If you tell anyone I admitted this," Tai said, "I'll call you a liar without any compunction whatsoever." Throwing the dish towel over his shoulder, he pinned her with a scowl that did nothing to detract from the exotic lines of his face.

"I'm good at keeping secrets." It was a survival skill. No one, she'd realized at an early age, wanted to know a monster.

"I want to write goddamn poetry to her"—Tai's embarrassed voice, breaking into her thoughts—"fucking serenade her and steal a kiss under moonlight, cover her room in candlelight just to see her smile, hold her all night long so I can breathe in her scent as I wake."

Sienna's hands had stopped moving with his first startling statement. "That's beautiful." Her heart pulsed with a fragile need she hadn't even known she had until that moment.

Tai's slightly uptilted eyes were sheepish when he said, "Yeah?"

"Yeah." Swallowing the strange, incomprehensible softness inside of her, she added, "Maybe not all of it at once, though."

"If I survive Indigo," Tai muttered. "She's so freaking protective, it's like running a gauntlet each time I dare ask Evie out."

"Can you blame her? Evie's so gentle." Sienna had been certain Evie would be horrified by her when Indigo insisted on introducing Sienna to her sister—but in spite of her too-kind heart, Evie had a well-hidden streak of mischief. It had made them fast friends and, once upon a time, accomplices in some of the most spectacular stunts ever pulled in the den.

Tai nodded. "I think that pot's done."

Handing it over so he could dry and put it away, she wiped down the sink and made a quick getaway. It wasn't until she was outside in the dark green shadow of the forest giants that she realized how much she'd missed the crisp air of the Sierra during her hours in the kitchens. Before defecting to Snow-Dancer, she'd spent her days inside high-rise buildings, in the middle of a city, and known no different. Now she'd tasted not only the wild, rugged beauty of the mountains, but learned what it was to have friends, to have family in more than just blood.

"I've made my decision," she said to the man who'd come to stand beside her with an assassin's quiet grace. "No matter what, I won't return to the PsyNet, to Silence." It had been an option she'd been forced to consider when it appeared her abilities were spiraling out into chaos and destruction.

"How good," Judd said instead of responding to her statement, "is your control?"

"Strong as steel." Her time away from the den, in the care of other defectors, including one who was a genius at shield construction, had given her a second chance. She would never forget the death that lived within her, but—"I'm going to make it, Judd. I'm going to spit in the face of that bastard who sentenced us all to die."

Judd said nothing to strike at Sienna's confidence, aware she'd need every ounce of it if she was going to survive the coming darkness—because he knew something she didn't. It was a truth he'd carried in his heart for years, a truth he would never, ever share with her. To do so might well turn it into a self-fulfilling prophecy.

He'd hacked into secret Council archives when Sienna had been ten, helped by fellow Arrows who'd understood that his niece might one day end up in the squad. Only he had read the files that went back 150 years, and so only he knew the brutal facts: The longest any X-Psy had ever survived, *even under Silence*, was to age twenty-five.

That twenty-five-year-old X had registered as 3.4 on the Gradient.

Sienna was off the charts.

HAWKE had spent his first week in the mountains avoiding contact with even the sentries. He'd known he wasn't fit company for anyone. The feral wolves, too, had given him a wide berth after he snarled at them . . . though they still came to huddle around him at night, all of them sleeping in a big pile of fur. It was difficult to maintain a bad temper in the face of such fierce affection, but Hawke's wolf was riding him hard.

The dreams sure as hell didn't help.

Ruby red fire and smooth sun gold skin; autumn and that rare, wild spice. The echoes of her haunted him until he couldn't close his eyes without it whispering over his senses, a fleeting silken touch.

So vivid were the dreams that he woke hard as stone and furious with himself for his lack of control. As a result, he was leaner and feeling a hell of a lot meaner when he returned to the den. He'd run himself to exhaustion, and though his wolf was behaving, he knew it would take only the slightest provocation, the slightest touch, to send him over the edge. And still, he had to fight the compulsion to track her down, make sure she knew he was back. "Fuck."

Throwing his gear on the floor of his bedroom, he'd pulled off his T-shirt in preparation for a shower when he scented a familiar female. Snarling, he stalked to the door and wrenched it open. "Not a word," he snapped at Indigo.

Freshly showered and dressed in jeans teamed with a plain white T-shirt, her hair pulled back in a ponytail, Indigo favored him with a slow smile before running her eyes down his body, up again. "I guess that whole not-sleeping thing has its advantages."

Hawke bared his teeth. "Go gawk at your mate."

A snort. "If Drew was here, do you think you'd rate a glance?"

"Go away."

"I will—after I get what I want."

"What?"

"Hold on." Indigo shifted to glance down the corridor. "Here she is."

"Sorry," Yuki said, neat and pressed in a suit that told him she was heading to work. "Thought we were meeting in your office." Reaching into her satchel, she withdrew a printed form attached to a clipboard.

Indigo took it, shoved it at him. "I decided to beard the rabid wolf in his den."

Growling, Hawke grabbed the pen. "What is it?" he asked, signing without reading. That was a trust reserved for the lieutenants. If it got to a point where he didn't have total faith in them, then the pack was in serious trouble. That had happened only once in their history, and Hawke was determined to never let those painful events taint the relationship he had with his men and women. "Don't usually need a lawyer to witness things."

"Do for this," Indigo said, scrawling her name beside his, then handing Yuki the pen so she could follow suit. "It gives Riley power of attorney over your worldly goods in exigent circumstances."

He looked up. "Indigo."

"I'm serious. It also gives him the right to make life-or-death decisions on your behalf should events warrant it."

"Since when is that necessary in a pack?" Pack was one. Pack was family.

"Since Judd pointed out that if you get incapacitated," Yuki said with a frown, "it'd make things a lot less complicated if we had the legal papers. Otherwise, anyone who wanted to undermine the pack could use the opportunity to throw roadblocks in our path. I'm annoyed I didn't think of it myself."

Hawke had to agree it made sense. Especially since . . . *Oh.* "It's because I have no next of kin." No parents. No siblings. No mate.

Yuki shot him a sharp glance, an abrupt reminder that Elias's loyal mate and Sakura's loving mother was also a pit bull for her biggest and most demanding client—the Snow-Dancer pack. "I'd rather we never had to use these papers, so don't get hurt." Putting the clipboard and its contents back into her bag, she looked at her watch, her glossy black hair swinging to brush her jaw. "Have to run, got a meeting in Sacramento." The last words were called out over her shoulder as she left.

"I second everything Yuki said." Indigo leaned forward as if to embrace him. When he stepped back without meaning to, she narrowed her eyes. "You're in a shitload of trouble if you don't trust yourself to touch a packmate in whom you have no sexual interest whatsoever."

"I told you I'd take care of it."

Realization had her lips flattening into a thin line. "Damn it, Hawke." Arms folded, she shook her head. "I know what you're planning, that you think you're protecting her—but you do this and Sienna will never forgive you. You sure you want to end any chance the two of you might have?"

He caught her gaze, allowing the wolf's dominance out to play. She held it longer than anyone else aside from Riley could have.

"Damn it." Blinking as she looked away, she sighed. "You're a stubborn bastard, you know that?"

"I am who I am." And what he was, was a man who needed to satiate his sexual hunger before his wolf took the decision out of his hands. Because that wolf would track only one scent.

RECOVERED FROM COMPUTER 2(A)
TAGS: PERSONAL CORRESPONDENCE, FATHER, ACTION NOT REQUIRED

FROM: Alice <alice@scifac.edu>
TO: Dad <ellison@archsoc.edu>
DATE: March 16th, 1971 at 10:13pm
SUBJECT: re: Your Mother

Dear Dad,

Tell Mom the reason I never e-mail her is because she gets the phone calls. I must be fair or one of you will accuse me of favoritism.

Before I forget—thank you both for the gift. The sculpture is extraordinary and will look perfect in my study. You and Mom know me too well.

You were asking about my new project. I've barely begun and while my Psy colleagues have agreed to publicize my call for information on the PsyNet, I've already hit the first hurdle—the sheer rarity of X-Psy. I only have two signed up to participate so far, but I'm not giving up. That isn't the Eldridge way.

Say hello to the pharaohs for me.

Love,
Alice

Chapter 7

"I KNOW HE'D chew me up and spit me out, but God, it's all I can do not to strip myself naked and beg for him to bite me any way and anywhere he wants."

Overhearing that heartfelt feminine sentiment, Sienna dropped her fourth dish of the day. The chief cook, Aisha, raised a hand and pointed, banishing her to the sinks. She went without argument—scrubbing the hated pots was all she'd been good for since the moment she'd learned of Hawke's return, her brain scrambled like the eggs Marlee and Toby loved to eat on Sunday mornings.

As if she'd conjured him up by thinking of him, her brother appeared at her elbow. "Wow, that's a big pot, Sienna."

Deep warmth spread through her veins. For Toby, she'd do anything. Born with a slight empathic gift, he was goodness, was heart. He made her want to be good, too—even though she knew that to be an impossible goal. X-Psy were born for, and useful for, only one thing.

Destruction.

A hand on her forearm. "Sienna."

Dropping the pot, she bent to wrap her soapy arms around that gangly preteen body that was no longer that of the child she'd tickled into bed just last year. "How do you always know?" she whispered into his hair.

His arms locked around her neck. "I can see you in our Net," he said, speaking of the psychic network that tied all the members of the family to each other. It provided the bio-feedback needed by their Psy minds, was what had kept them alive when they'd defected from the sprawling vastness of the PsyNet. "Your mind goes all icy."

She heard the fear in his tone. Any time she got "icy," as he put it, Toby got afraid. Because he understood what she was on an instinctive level that meant she'd never been able to protect him from the harsh truth—Toby saw the monster within and still he loved her, still he needed her.

"Don't go back to the Net, Sienna." A plea. "Please."

"I won't, Toby. I won't." Her earlier intent solidified into stone. If, in spite of everything, she failed to contain her ability, then she would, as Councilor Ming LeBon had once put it, take herself "out of the equation." Her death would hurt Toby, but it wouldn't savage him—not like if he had to watch her turn cold, a Silent stranger who rejected his love as if it was a worthless token. *I love you, Toby.* A telepathic communication between siblings, as easy as a breath.

I'm so glad you're my sister, Sienna.

They held the embrace a long time. Though Aisha ran a tight ship, she didn't tell Sienna to get a move on. Aisha's eyes smiled when she glimpsed them—the wolves understood touch, understood affection. They couldn't know how much it meant to Sienna that she could openly hold the boy who was a living, breathing piece of her heart.

Since the moment of his birth, she'd had to hide, had to bury everything she felt when it came to Toby. If Ming had discovered the searing depth of a love that had defied Silence itself, the bastard wouldn't have done anything to her. She'd been too important. But he might well have ended Toby's life to "safeguard" Sienna's Silence.

She would've killed him for it, of course.

Hiding that dark thought in a secret corner of her mind where Toby would never sense it, she drew back and brushed his hair out of his eyes as she had a habit of doing. "Why aren't you in school?" Toby attended the small internal school for ages five to thirteen—the older teenagers generally went to a high school outside den territory, except for a few who'd chosen distance learning.

"We got the afternoon off today 'cause the teachers got a meeting."

"Toby, your grammar is atrocious." His enunciation and

grammar had been PsyNet perfect when they defected—she much preferred him this way.

"Aw, Sienna." Two kisses, one on each cheek. "Can you help me with my homework after you get out of the kitchen?"

"Sure." She rose back up to her full height. "What subject?"

"Science. I have to build a volcano." Cardinal eyes gleamed. "It's going to explode and everything."

Her hand clenched on the scourer she'd just picked up. "Wow." Forcing her fingers to relax, she nodded to the fruit bowl. "Eat an apple. It's good for you."

Toby made a face but obeyed. "Can't I have a cookie instead?"

"No."

"Abuse." But he was smiling as he bit into the shiny red fruit, the smile turning into a grin when Aisha slipped him a palm-sized oatmeal raisin cookie.

"Finish the apple first," the cook ordered, tousling his hair.

"Thanks, Aisha," Toby said before looking back at Sienna, his eyes sparkling in a way that would've startled her if she hadn't seen Sascha Duncan's eyes do the same thing. Because the stars were no longer white. Not quite. It was as if Toby's eyes shimmered with color . . . with life.

Sometimes, Sienna thought Toby had been sent into the world to balance the scales, an antidote to the sister who loved him to the depths of her soul, but who could create only pain, only suffering, only horror.

HAWKE blocked Elias's kick and put the senior soldier on his back. "Damn it, Eli. You're leaving yourself wide open."

Elias lay on the ground, chest heaving. "No, I'm not. You're just not pulling any punches." He winced. "I'm going to set Yuki on you—she doesn't like it when you beat me up."

Unamused, Hawke waited as the other man rolled to his feet. "You said you wanted to spar so you could figure out what you needed to work on."

"I take it back." Elias braced himself with his hands on his knees. "The single person who can spar with you in this kind of a mood is Riley." Rising fully, he shoved a hand through dark brown hair damp with sweat. "I need to give you my report anyway."

Hawke's wolf was tensed and ready for action, but he drew in a long, deep breath, brought the animal under control. "Problems in the city?" DarkRiver and SnowDancer had both kept a constant and visible presence in San Francisco ever since the attempted bombings the previous year.

"I dunno." Elias rubbed his jaw. "The leopards always get the best intel, so you should liaise with them, but my instincts are itching. I can't quite put a finger on it—the thing is, you know we've got more than the usual number of Psy coming into the area."

"Yeah. Side effect of Nikita deciding she no longer supports Silence." Not out of the goodness of her heart, but simply because it made the most political sense. Sascha's mother was one cold bitch. "They causing trouble?"

"No, quiet as church mice." Elias fell into step beside him as Hawke began to make his way to the training run. The obstacle course would give him a much-needed physical outlet before he headed inside to talk to Tomás about a couple of people Hawke wanted to send to the lieutenant for training.

"But with so many of them coming in," Elias continued, "it's hard to pinpoint the friendlies from the others."

Hawke had raised the same concern with Lucas not long ago. "The Rats," he said, referring to the small changeling group that ran a very effective spy network, "know to keep an eye out for any unusual Psy activity, but I'll have Luc talk to them, have them amp up their efforts." He trusted Elias's instincts. The soldier was one of his most capable men, not dominant enough to be a lieutenant, but smart and experienced—and more important, he had a head as stable as Riley's.

"Thanks." Elias looked at the training run, blew out a breath. "Jesus, Riaz is a sadist. What the hell are those spike things? They weren't there last time."

"Time me." Hawke's wolf bared its teeth in anticipation. Riaz had outdone himself this time. As Hawke ran up the first incline, he hoped like hell that Elias's gut was wrong for once, but given the events of the past few months—and the fact that every F-Psy on the planet was apparently forecasting war—he knew that to be a bleak hope.

WALKER went to retie the ribbon around his daughter's ponytail, playing a game with her on the LaurenNet as he did so. She was fascinated by the unusual twisting motion at the center of the mental star that was his mind, and kept getting distracted.

He'd been something of a puzzle to the staff at the Psy-Med hospital, too. No one had ever been able to explain the reason for the odd moving helix that had become apparent long after he was past childhood. There had been discussions about studying it further, but when it became clear the twist neither detracted from nor added any strength to his already strong telepathic range, the issue was put aside.

It had, however, proven an excellent gauge of a child's psychic development—to the extent that Walker had come to believe that to be the reason for it. Since his telepathic touch worked particularly well with the young and the helix had developed soon after he began teaching, it made sense. As it was, while Toby had matured to the point where he could ignore the distraction of the motion, Marlee hadn't.

Almost, he encouraged on the psychic plane as the ribbon slipped out of his grasp on the physical. Picking it up, he said, "You know I'm not good at this." His hands were too big, too clumsy for such a delicate task. "Why didn't you ask Sienna?"

Waiting until he finished and moved around to crouch in front of her, she wrapped an arm around his neck. "I like it when you do it." A wide smile.

In the three years since their family had defected from the PsyNet, Walker had learned many things—how to live in a world without Silence, how to manage the dominance challenges within a wolf pack, how to look after Marlee and Toby in a way for which he had no template. But the one thing he still hadn't learned was how to handle the overload of emotion caused by his daughter's smile.

When she threw both arms around his neck in a spontaneous embrace, it only caused the tightness in his chest to grow—until it filled every part of him. Wrapping his own

arms around her, he rose to his feet. She made a startled
sound. "I'm too big!"

"You'll always be my child." He wished he could say the
soft, sweet words he heard changeling parents say constantly
to their children, but he'd been an inmate of Silence for four
long decades. The words were hard to form, to get out. But
it was incredibly easy to lift his hand, to stroke away the
baby-fine strands of hair that had escaped Marlee's ponytail,
to press a kiss to her temple.

When she said, "Can we go see if Toby's volcano is
ready?" he could no more deny her than he could stop breathing.

It was another punch to the heart to walk into the large
rec room near the family quarters to see Toby and Sienna
with their heads bent together over a lopsided volcano. This,
he thought as Marlee wiggled out of his arms to join her
cousins, all of them frowning over the lack of symmetry, this
was why he'd survived defection from the PsyNet.

To watch over his daughter and the son of a sister he'd
never been allowed to love. And Sienna, too, for all that she'd
been forced to be an adult before she'd ever been a child. They
were his reason for being, for existing. As for the kiss that
had threatened to make him forget the rest of the world for
one blinding, pleasure-drunk moment . . . he'd made the right
decision.

Even if the sensations from that single searing contact
continued to haunt him two long months later.

HAWKE stared at Matthias's face on the comm screen the
next morning. "You're certain?"

"Yes," the lieutenant answered. "Definite indications of
weapons coming into the country on a large scale. They've
been doing it bit by bit—I'm guessing some of it has been
teleported in. But they've also been bringing in armaments
via ship."

"Any idea who?"

"No."

"I'll check with Nikita and Anthony." It was odd to say
that, odder yet to know that SnowDancer had any kind of a

working relationship with two members of the Psy Council. "Any reason why I shouldn't share this with the cats?" The SnowDancer-DarkRiver alliance was all but cemented in stone; however, they were still two predatory changeling packs. Total, unquestioning trust would take decades.

"No. They have good contacts, better than we do in the city." Matthias frowned. "I think you should also tell the falcons to keep an eye out—they see things from up high that we might not."

Hawke agreed. The alliance with WindHaven was new but very much functional. "Send me the details. I'll have a look and pass on the necessary info."

"You'll have it in the next couple of hours." Matthias went to sign off, then paused. "How're Indigo and the young pup?"

The "young pup," Drew, was Hawke's eyes and ears in the pack, as well as SnowDancer's tracker. "I caught them in a storage closet not long ago. They weren't exactly looking for supplies." His wolf bared its teeth in amusement.

Matthias howled with laughter. "Don't you fucking try to convince me you didn't scent what was going on?"

"I was very discreet." Hawke grinned. "I just opened the door a crack and asked them to keep it down."

"And got a mop thrown at your head, I bet."

"Actually, it was a giant roll of thread—mending supplies closet." Shaking his head, he answered the question more seriously. "Their mating, added to Riley and Mercy's, Cooper's with Grace, and Judd's with Brenna, is good, really good for the stability of the pack." Having his lieutenants in such strong pairings soothed his wolf's frustration at not being able to give SnowDancer the security of a mated alpha pair.

"Yeah, everyone's more settled." Matthias leaned back a little. "I might head down to the den sometime next month. That work?"

Hawke nodded—all his lieutenants passed through the den at least once every couple of months, to ensure the pack stayed connected in spite of the massive breadth of their territory. "Have you spoken to Alexei lately?"

"You caught that, did you? Told him you would." Matthias's expression was wry. "He's fine, just frustrated at the recent dominance challenges from out-of-towners."

Unfortunately for Alexei, he had the face of a young golden god. People who didn't know him had a tendency to focus on that face and ignore the fact that his dominance was a quiet, powerful pulse beneath the skin. "Anything I need to discuss with the other alphas?" Dominance challenges between packs happened every so often, mostly when a strong wolf was seeking to create a new pack or searching for a mate, but poor Alexei tended to bear the brunt of them.

"Naw." Matthias shook his head, dark hair catching the light. "Our Russian Bridegroom wipes the floor with the idiots—then ropes them in as senior soldiers."

"He know you call him that?"

"Do I look like a moron? Alexei might be pretty, but he's also a mean sucker."

Laughing, Hawke ended the call after a few more quick words. His wolf had been prowling beneath his skin the entire time, if not content, then at least not snarling. Now, it urged him to get outside, to shift and run through the wild heart of SnowDancer territory. Hawke growled low in his throat, fighting the instinct.

The wolf pushed. The human held firm. However, the strength of the urge made it plain he could no longer avoid taking this step—he had to do something about his sexual hunger before the primal part of him seized total control. Picking up the phone, he made a call.

"Hello." A husky female voice.

"Rosalie, it's Hawke."

Chapter 8

HAVING SERVED THE last hour of her punishment doing the evening shift in the kitchens, Sienna took ten minutes in the night air before walking back inside to the apartment she shared with Walker and the kids. Her uncle had just sent Toby to bed when she arrived, so she ducked in to say good night, peeking in at an already fast asleep Marlee as well, the younger girl's bedtime being earlier.

However, that took a bare few minutes, and she was alone in her room all too soon. The instant she was, the thoughts she'd been avoiding all day crashed down on her with the violence of a Sierra thunderstorm.

She'd tried not to listen, not to hear, but she knew Hawke had been seen in the company of the luscious, sexy, and experienced Rosalie both yesterday and today. The wolves' penchant for gossip being what it was, she also knew conflicting schedules meant he probably hadn't been to bed with her yet . . . but it wasn't likely to be long before he did. Perhaps even tonight.

Raw, dark power rippled through her body, gathering in her fingertips.

An instant's loss of control and she'd destroy this wall, collapse the ceiling. Gritting her teeth, she fought the fury that made her an X, a fury that whispered that Rosalie and her ilk were nothing, would crumble to dust in the face of the deadly strength that had once made Sienna so very, very valuable to Ming. It was a horrible thought, and it brought her back.

So did the pain.

Brutal and blinding.

She could still taste the shock that had rippled through Judd's telepathic touch when they'd first discovered the second intricate level of dissonance programming. But that hidden knife blade of pain had made perfect sense to Sienna—it wasn't tied to emotion and had nothing to do with Silence except in that the mechanism had been developed as a result of the Protocol. Instead, this level of dissonance only kicked in when her X abilities triggered without her conscious awareness, a blaring warning that she was about to go active.

Now, the spike of agony down her spine had her close to blanking out, white dots floating in her vision. She rode the razor's edge, allowing the dissonance to dig in its vicious claws until she staggered and brought herself back to her room in the family quarters . . . a room she'd hung with Toby's graphic art and Marlee's watercolor paintings.

Nausea curdled her stomach, bile burning the back of her throat. She was moving to throw clothes and personal items into a duffel even as her body continued to tremble with the aftereffects of the dissonance—she had faith in her ability to control her "gift," but she was still an X. Mistakes happened.

Walker was sitting at the dining table, making notes on a datapad when she came out. "Going somewhere?" Cool green eyes held her to the spot.

"I'm moving to my quarters in the soldiers section on a permanent basis." Her fingers clenched on the canvas handles of the bag. "I'll talk to Toby and Marlee tomorrow, explain." The words hurt coming out, emotion a rock in her throat.

Walker rose to his feet. "They'll be fine. They understand your position in the pack." He didn't ask the question, but she felt compelled to answer anyway. That was the thing with Walker—he wasn't her father, had never tried to take that role, but he was, for all intents and purposes, the patriarch of the Lauren family.

"I'm emotionally unstable and it's affecting my psychic control," she admitted, a cold sweat breaking out along her spine. "If I suffer a shield breach, I don't want to be anywhere near where I could hurt them."

"Do you need to return to DarkRiver?"

"No." Distance wasn't going to do it any longer—not when

she'd be thinking about Hawke the entire time anyway. At least here, she'd know as soon as he took Rosalie to his bed, not spend her days with the possibility eating away at her insides as she waited for it to be confirmed. "I'll take care of it."

"Sienna," Walker said when she was almost to the door, "you're not alone. Never forget that."

She nodded, but as she headed down the corridors toward the area of the den set aside for unmated soldiers, she knew the words for a lie. She was alone in a way none of her family could understand.

Sienna Lauren.

Designation: X.

Rating on the Gradient: Cardinal.

She was, in fact, the only cardinal X ever to survive to adulthood according to the records in the PsyNet. Perhaps the only cardinal X ever to have been born. The mutation was rare—so rare that she hadn't been properly classified until she was five.

She'd almost killed her mother that day.

Dropping the duffel on the bed when she reached her quarters, she shoved the unbearable memory to the darkest recesses of her mind and sat cross-legged on the floor to do mental exercises designed to wrench her abilities back under the strictest control. An hour later, her T-shirt was plastered to her body, her hair sticking to her face, but she'd safely corralled the raging ferocity of her power.

It was as she was stepping out of the shower that she got the call and invite. "I'm in," she said, because staying here with the gnawing cruelty of her own thoughts was not an option.

Hanging up, she pulled on some panties before beginning to rummage through her clothes—both what she'd carried over in the duffel and the things she'd stored in the closet here, most of them items she rarely wore. First, skintight jeans. They were all but painted onto her body by the time she managed to twist, shimmy, and curse her way into them— she'd never have bought them on her own, but one of the leopards near her own age, Nicki, had dragged her along on a shopping expedition not long ago.

Sienna had glanced down at the plain jeans and gray sweatshirt she'd been wearing at the time. "What's wrong with the way I dress?"

The petite honey blonde's response had been a despairing shake of the head. "It says you're two hundred and counting."

Sometimes, Sienna felt exactly that, but that day, she'd given in to Nicki and gone wild. Kit had whistled the first time he'd seen her in the jeans, while Cory had fallen to his knees, hand over his heart. Sienna hadn't yet worn them around the wolves . . . around Hawke, but her pride wouldn't allow her to sit in her room while he put those strong hands all over another woman.

Her own hands fisted. *No. No. No.*

He wasn't hers, had made it clear in a hundred different ways that he didn't want to be hers. *Fine.*

Jeans on, she clipped on a red satin bra edged with white lace—one that plumped up her chest in a way that had had her arguing with Nicki in the dressing room. "I can't wear this. It's like I'm advertising!"

"Sweetie, if I had ta-tas like that, I'd advertise, too." Nicki had looked down at her own smaller breasts with a mournful sigh.

"Jase seems to like yours fine."

A peach-colored blush. "Now, tops. Come on."

Sienna pulled out one of the resulting purchases and slipped it on. A black shirt with long sleeves, it fit snug to her body and made it unmistakable that she had curves. The buttons were snaps of pounded metal, the only other decoration two tiny black pockets with the same type of buttons above her breasts. While she didn't usually wear things that followed her shape with such caressing closeness, she had to admit she liked the way the shirt made her feel.

Sexy.

Then there were the boots. Slick and black, they encased her legs to the knees, the heels wickedly spiked.

Her cell phone beeped as she was zipping up the second boot. "Hello."

"Sin, it's Evie. You ready?"

"Almost." She paused. "We are getting dressed up, right?"

"Of course! I'm wearing my silver dress."

Evie's enthusiasm had Sienna setting her jaw, determination arcing through her veins. "That dress will get you arrested."

Her best friend laughed. "You know you'd bail me out. See you in ten!"

Hanging up, Sienna quickly put in her special contacts, hiding the night-sky gaze that betrayed her identity, then pulled her hair back into a tight ponytail. She'd spoken to Indigo and her own family about her hair, and everyone had agreed the unusual color was no longer an issue, it had changed so much since she'd joined the den. Added to the fact that her friends had taken to calling her "Sin," plus the contacts, it turned her into someone Ming LeBon wouldn't even consider worthy of his attention.

That done, she pulled out the cosmetics case Judd's mate, Brenna, had given her, making up her eyes in a "smoky" way she'd learned from Indigo. Nicki had liked the effect so much, she'd asked Sienna to teach her. That had felt good—being able to share such an innocent thing with a friend. It had made her feel young, not the old woman she'd been since the day she first understood why Ming LeBon wanted her by his side, his own personal monster on a psychic leash.

"Stop," she ordered the brown-eyed woman in the mirror. "Not tonight. Be young and carefree tonight. Dance, drink, and laugh." With that, she slicked on poppy red lip color, grabbed a small purse, and stepped out.

"Oh, Jesus Christ, thank you God."

Startled by the masculine exclamation, she looked up to find herself facing Riordan, a novice soldier a year older than her. "Are you coming out with us?" she asked, closing her door.

"If I wasn't, I damn well would be now." He offered her his arm, bare below the short sleeves of a stone gray shirt that looked good on his muscular frame. "Paint yourself to my side, Sin. Real close. I think I feel a chill coming on."

Shaking her head, she began to walk down the hall, her heels clicking on the floor. A few seconds later, she realized he was trailing behind her. "What's the holdup?" Glancing back, she caught him red-handed. "Are you staring at my butt?"

Riordan didn't bother to pretend innocence, his deep brown eyes full of wicked appreciation. "Hey, it's a nice butt. And those jeans, oh, mama."

It was exactly the confidence boost she needed. If Hawke refused to acknowledge the pulse of attraction between them—though she'd waited years to grow old enough for him, years where she'd blocked her ears to the gossip about who he was with and when—then she wasn't going to take it lying down. "Pick your tongue up off the floor, and let's go. Evie, Tai, and Cadence are probably already in the garage."

She was proven right. But they weren't the only ones. Maria was there, too, along with her boyfriend, Lake.

"Hey," the other woman said, a tentative smile on her face. "I wanted to say sorry. It sucks that you got a worse punishment than me."

Sienna shrugged. "My own fault." It would be the last time she let her near-painful response to Hawke get in the way of how she lived her life. "No hard feelings."

"Could we just . . ." Maria angled her head.

Nodding, Sienna stepped a little distance away from the others so she and Maria could talk in private. "I understand," she said once they were out of hearing range. "We fought because your wolf wanted to establish dominance."

"Yeah, well, that didn't go so great." A self-deprecating grin. "But what I said about you being cold-blooded—"

"It's fine." On edge and angry with herself for being unable to forget Hawke, she'd been feeling raw, vulnerable, had struck out at Maria's jibe without stopping to consider the fact that the very state of her emotions made the accusation patently untrue.

"No." Maria put a hand on her arm. "It's not fine and we both know it's not true. I was talking any bullshit I could to goad you into a fight. My only excuse is that wolves my age tend to be dickheads."

Sienna's lips twitched. "Difficult since you don't possess that particular body part, either on your head or elsewhere."

Maria snorted. "I dunno—I did a pretty good job of acting it." Tucking her hands into the back pockets of her jeans, she rocked back on her heels. "I was meant to be your partner and I fucked with you." No smile now, dark eyes solemn.

"It'll never happen again. I want you to know I'd have you at my back anytime."

"Same," Sienna said without hesitation. In the PsyNet, she'd have looked for the betrayal hidden behind the contrition, but she'd been in SnowDancer long enough to see Maria's words for what they were—a declaration of both loyalty and friendship. "And it wasn't all you, you know. I was looking for a fight." Maria had just provided a handy excuse.

"You sure have a mean kick," the other soldier said as they headed back.

"Judd makes me train with him."

"I don't know whether to be jealous or offer commiseration."

They were both laughing when they reached the rest of the group.

"Now that that's sorted"—Evie wrapped her arms around their waists, her personality evident in the radiance of her smile—"are we ready to dance?"

Not only was Sienna ready to dance, but if a man made a move on her tonight . . . well, she might just let him. She was through with waiting.

ALONE in the apartment but for the sleeping children, Walker found himself looking at the sat phone he'd recently been issued courtesy of his position as "Head Wrangler" for the ten-to-thirteen-year-olds.

The phone came preloaded with contact information for the other senior members of SnowDancer. Flicking through the directory, he stopped at Lara's name. The healer would be a good sounding board when it came to his concerns about Sienna's emotional state—Lara was one of the most sensitive people in the pack.

His thumb hesitated over the Call button, the sensual echo of that kiss the night of the party causing every one of his muscles to go taut in a waiting kind of expectation. Unlike the changelings, he wasn't a man driven by the desire to touch, but Lara made him react in unexpected and uncomfortable ways. He wasn't used to having his body respond in such an undisciplined manner, but more, he wasn't

used to having the reins slip from his grasp when it came
to his mental reaction.

So many weeks later and he could still feel the softness
of her skin beneath his fingertips, the warm seduction of her
body under his palm, the sweetness of her lips parting as they
met his own. She was small but curvy in a way that had made
him want to stroke his hands over her at his leisure, to explore
the intriguing shadows and arcs of her body. He'd kept his
hands from roaming that night . . . but not his mind.

He glanced at the phone again.

If he called her, she would come. He hadn't been an Arrow
like Judd, but he'd had his own reasons for learning to read
people—he knew that in spite of the fact that their friendship
appeared irreparably damaged, Lara had the softest of hearts.
The second he mentioned his concern about Sienna, he'd have
her immediate attention. And the instant she was in his quarters . . . images of kiss-wet lips, of a warm feminine form
under his hands.

His body grew hard.

It was an unwelcome reminder of how she impacted him,
how she skewed the rules on which he'd rebuilt his life. He
took his finger off the Call button . . . and got up. There was
a chance he could catch her at the infirmary.

BY midnight, fighting the constant compulsion to track down
Sienna had gnawed Hawke's temper to a fine edge. It wasn't
the best of times for him to receive a call from the manager
of Wild, the changeling-owned bar and dance club that sat in
a small but popular nightlife area just beyond the edge of den
territory.

"Hawke, I need you to come pick up your pups."

Hawke rubbed his forehead. The only time José ever called
him was when things had progressed to breaking point. "How
much?"

"No bill for damages," José said to his surprise. "But if
you don't get here soon, you'll probably be bailing a few of
them out of jail." The deer changeling—a dominant bull who
could bash heads with the best of them, for all that he was
non-predatory—hung up.

"Shit." Already dressed in jeans and a T-shirt since he'd been wide awake, he pulled on well-worn work boots, then buzzed Riley.

His lieutenant was not impressed. "Do you know what time it is?"

"Yeah, yeah. How many of them went down to Wild tonight?" Riley would know. Riley knew everything.

"Seven, but Ebony and Amos were in San Francisco for a security run"—a small pause—"and the system's not showing them logging back into the den, so they probably took a detour."

"Thanks."

"You'll need a second driver."

"Stay snuggled up to Mercy," Hawke said, already halfway to the garage. "I'll get one of the night-shift people."

"Don't be too hard on them."

Hawke paused. "What?"

"You're in a mean mood, Hawke. Don't take it out on them."

Growling, Hawke snapped the phone shut. He was alpha for a reason—and part of it was that he knew how to handle his people. Of course, Riley was also his most senior lieutenant for a reason. "Shit." Jogging the rest of the way to the garage, he volunteered Elias as the second driver. "Were they driving when they went down?"

Elias checked the computronic log. "Yep. Two vehicles. GPS says they're both parked a five-minute walk from the club."

"Good. We'll drive one down—you can bring up the second. One of the soldiers on city security tomorrow can swing by and pick up the other."

The drive took more than an hour, and Hawke hoped like hell the young group hadn't gotten into worse trouble in the meantime. Since José's radar was finely tuned, chances were good he'd alerted Hawke in plenty of time.

Parking the vehicle a block away, he and Elias made it to Wild around one thirty in the morning. The bouncer, one of José's big, strapping cousins, raised his hand in a wave when he saw them. "That pretty little one with the cherry-tinted hair"—he whistled—"where you been hiding her?"

Hawke went motionless.

Chapter 9

"WHAT'S THE TROUBLE?" he asked, the wolf in his voice.

The other male avoided his eyes, as if aware Hawke was too much on edge to accept even the slightest challenge. "Go in and see."

Entering the bar, he stayed to the shadows as he took in the lay of the land. The place was full of humans and changelings—leopard, wolf, deer, swan, even a Rat. Their scents were clear threads to him, even entangled as they were in the confined space. Most of the non-predatories stuck together, while the predatories did the same. But wolf and leopard were mingling. *Plenty.*

Ebony was currently happily pasted up against a cat, while Riordan was all but devouring a leopard girl with his eyes as the two of them stood talking a small distance from the dance floor. Evie—oh, dear God, but Indigo was going to blow a gasket—was dressed in a tiny strapless dress made from some sparkly fabric that only just covered everything that should be covered. She was also giggling and drunk, a frothy pink cocktail in hand. Tai sat holding her against his chest, looking sober. Maybe there was hope for them yet.

Maria, Cadie, and the rest were out front, cheering.

At Sienna.

Who was dancing on the bar.

In fuck-you boots and a shirt that barely contained her breasts.

Eyes going wolf, Hawke began to stride through the crowd. A few aggressive young males turned to give him a talking-to . . . and froze, their gazes jerking away when they met the dominance in his own. Even the humans understood, going pale as they moved out of his path as fast as possible.

He realized part of the reason for José's call when he saw the human men lined up along the bar, all of them with a look in their eye that said they'd spill blood to possess the woman who danced with such wild, sensual grace. The SnowDancer males would, of course, have defended her with fists and claws the instant anyone tried to touch her.

And José's bar would've been trashed in minutes.

Then there were the leopard and wolf males giving each other dirty looks as interpack flirting took place. Riordan was being watched by at least three cats with violence on their minds, while Lake and Amos were currently glaring with intent at Ebony's dance partner.

The entire thing had the makings of a clusterfuck.

Shoving away the humans at the bar with rough hands, he reached out and gripped one leather-covered ankle.

Sienna stopped moving.

"Down," he growled, meeting brown eyes so much less extraordinary than the truth of her cardinal gaze. *"Now."*

Music still pumped but the bar had gone silent.

Sienna didn't immediately obey, and that just infuriated the wolf. "Last warning, baby."

Holding his gaze, Sienna said, "I'm not breaking any of the pack rules."

Every single person in the bar sucked in a breath.

Hawke didn't pay them any attention. He'd had enough. A single, precisely timed tug and he tilted her off balance. As she fell, he caught her, throwing her over his shoulder. "Out!" he ordered the other wolves as he left.

Sienna, having apparently recovered from the loss of breath caused by his sudden move, began to wiggle and twist. "Let me go!"

He tapped her behind, a short, sharp shock that had her freezing. "Don't make me any more pissed than I am right now."

"Bully." It was muttered under her breath, but he heard it. "You've got no right to punish me. None."

He tightened his hold on her as they hit the cold night air. "You want to talk punishment, fine. What the fuck did you think you were doing on that bar? Were you *trying* to cause a riot?"

"I was having fun." Heaving breaths. "Put me down. I can't breathe with your shoulder in my stomach."

"Tough." He didn't take his hands off her until he dumped her in the front passenger seat of the vehicle he'd driven down. "In," he ordered her friends, all of whom had obeyed his order to leave.

Tai raised his hand, one arm around a suddenly sober-appearing Evie's waist as he tucked her into the heat of his body. "I haven't had a single drink. I can drive the other truck."

Hawke's nose told him the young soldier was telling the truth. "Fine." He looked over the others. "You're lucky José called me before a punch was thrown."

Guilt on several male faces, while the women frowned. The men knew damn well what had been building in that bar.

"Next time I get a call like this, I'm instituting a curfew. Understood?"

"Yes, sir."

As everyone dispersed, splitting themselves between Elias's truck and the one Tai was going to be driving, Hawke realized he was about to spend over an hour alone in a confined space with a female he'd made every effort to avoid ever since she hit eighteen. A female who was almost spilling out of her shirt, allowing him glimpses of red satin against creamy gold skin.

Great, just fucking great.

SIENNA glared out the window as her friends scattered. "Traitor," she mouthed to Evie when the other woman glanced back.

Evie winked at her. "Give him hell . . . baby," Evie mouthed back.

Sienna's cheeks flamed as she remembered Hawke using the endearment in that taut, angry tone, which had raised every hair on her body. It probably meant nothing, except that he saw her as exactly that. A child. It didn't matter what she did, how mature she acted, he only seemed to pay attention to her at her worst moments.

Like tonight.

No, she thought, furious with him—and with herself for continuing to let him affect her this way, that hadn't been a bad moment. She'd been having fun. Enjoying herself as she had every right to do. He was probably fuming because he'd been pulled out of Rosalie's bed. Her nails dug into her palms. If she'd had claws, they'd have been out right then, slicing savagely through the seats.

"Not a word," he snapped as he got into the driver's seat. "Did you know what you were doing up on that bar?" Not giving her a chance to answer, he continued, "Most of those men were ready to grab you and strip you naked right there."

Her simmering temper ignited. "I know how to defend myself, thanks to Indigo. And dancing wasn't a crime last time I checked."

"I said, *not a damn word*." His hands tightened on the steering wheel as he drove them out of the popular nightlife area.

She snorted, too mad to be thinking about the sanity of challenging a predatory changeling male in the grip of pure raging fury. "How about instead of orders, Mr. Alpha Wolf, you actually stop hiding and talk to me?"

"Don't push me, little girl." Quiet, quiet words.

The tone made every muscle in her body go tense, but she'd been trained by a cold-blooded Councilor. Fear was something with which she had intimate familiarity—and it wasn't hot, not like the emotion that burned through her veins at this moment. "You think I should just keep doing as I'm told?" she asked. "Is that what gets you off?"

"One," he said with such calm, she knew she was in the vehicle with a predator barely on the leash. "I'll give you one free pass because you're drunk—"

"I didn't have a single alcoholic beverage." Alcohol had unpredictable effects on Psy abilities, and she couldn't afford to lose even an ounce of mental control. "I'm angry at you because you get to win all the arguments by using your alpha status to shut me down."

A dangerous pause. So dangerous that Sienna snapped her mouth closed, swallowing the words that wanted to escape.

Until he brought the truck to a halt deep in an unfamiliar part of den territory. The night was pitch-black, starless, and moonless, the trees murky shadows that seemed to form an impenetrable wall around them. "Why are we stopping?"

"You wanted to talk. We'll talk."

Her palms went damp at that smooth, silky tone.

"I'm putting aside my 'alpha status.' "

Oh, he was furious.

"So let's see if you can win this argument." Turning in his seat, he leaned his arm along the back of hers. "Now explain to me how you would've stopped a massive fistfight in the bar tonight."

"That's not on me," she said, trying to breathe past the sheer *power* of him. "The women were an excuse—the males were itching to go at each other since the minute we walked in. They're always playing dominance games."

"So you knew that, and still you amped up the sexual energy in the room?"

The truck was suddenly too small, too confined, Hawke's hotly masculine scent seeping into her very pores, touching parts of her no man had ever stroked. "It wasn't my responsibility."

"Oh?"

"No." A sudden crash of anger. "I'm not accountable for everyone! Maybe I wanted to have fun for a change. Maybe I wanted to not be in control for a few short minutes! Maybe I just wanted to dance."

Hawke's lashes came down. When they lifted back up, his gaze was night-glow, a brilliant ice blue shot with light. She sucked in a breath, realizing she was talking to the wolf now.

"You want to dance?" Husky words that stroked along her skin like the softest fur.

She nodded.

"Then we dance." Reaching out, he switched on the vehicle's sound system and input a selection before stepping out.

Her door opened as a slow, smoky ballad began to play. "Come." An invitation—but mostly a demand.

"My shoes," she blurted out, anger buried under a wave of nervous anticipation.

"The ground's dry. They won't sink in."

Not sure this wasn't all a dream, she placed her hand in his and, fighting the wild rush of sensation engendered by his touch and his scent, allowed him to tug her around to the front of the vehicle. Breaking the hold, he put his hands on her hips and pulled her forward, his breath a heated caress across her cheek as he bent to speak against her ear. "Arms around my neck."

The command released her voice. "I thought you weren't being alpha here."

"I'm not."

Oh.

As she raised her arms, she realized her boots gave her enough height to cup his nape with one hand, while she placed the other on the muscled warmth of his shoulder. When he shifted position so that his jaw rubbed against her temple, her heart began to thud fast as a jackhammer.

This close, he was all hot, hard heat. Pure muscle and strength . . . and temptation. Always, he'd been her temptation. He was the reason her Silence had shattered into innumerable shards the instant she'd walked into SnowDancer territory. She should've kept her distance, but she couldn't. Just once—just for a little while—she wanted him to be hers.

Teeth nipped at her ear.

She jumped.

"Pay attention." A rumbling growl.

Her nipples tightened to stiff points she hoped he couldn't feel. It was beyond tempting to spread the hand on his nape upward, into the thick, silver-gold silk of his hair, but she didn't dare break the moment. He had such beautiful hair, the same color as his pelt in wolf form. That told her more about how close his wolf was to the surface than anything else.

"Sienna." A deep murmur against her skin, his lips brushing her temple. "This can't be. You know that."

Her blood was thunder in her ears, her skin stretching taut over a body hypersensitized by a raw, near-painful craving. "Is it because I'm Psy?" she forced herself to ask. Hawke hated the Psy—that much she knew, though she didn't know the reason behind the depth of his animosity. The fact that he'd accepted the Lauren family as deeply into the pack as he had was nothing short of miraculous.

A low growl that had her going motionless. "It's because you're barely grown." He stroked his hand down her back, as if in reassurance.

But she wasn't ready to be soothed. "I haven't been a child since the day they came for me when I was five." A cardinal X could not be allowed to live outside of Council control. "Ming LeBon sure didn't sing me any lullabies."

Hawke's hand pressed against her lower back, big and warm and shockingly intimate through the thin fabric of her shirt. "Five?" The wolf was so apparent in his voice, she had to focus to understand him. "You were a baby."

She laughed and knew it held no humor. "Cardinals are trained from before we gain the ability to speak." The years she'd spent with her mother, the commands had been gentle, given by a woman who had wanted her child to learn to protect herself on the psychic plane. Aware she'd have drowned under the deluge of voices otherwise, Sienna had never resented the instruction; she missed her mother's touch to this day. "The first conscious thought I remember having was about the need to shield."

But when they'd discovered she was an X, the shields they'd put around her had been brutal prison walls, unlike anything she'd known. She'd been so small, so scared. Even her brave, strong mother, with her gentle telepathic touch, was gone, unable to reach Sienna through the hard carapace of Ming's creation. It had probably been for the best—Kristine had stood no chance against a daughter who'd put her in intensive care with a simple childish display of temper.

"Did you ever play?" Hawke's voice so rough, his body so muscular and overwhelming.

She had never felt more feminine, never felt more like a sexual creature. "No."

A pause. "Sienna—"

"No," she said. "No more questions. Not tonight." She wanted to dance with him, be a woman in the arms of a man who made every part of her awaken in a hunger she'd never expected to feel and who, for this magical moment, was hers.

His jaw, heavy with stubble, rubbed against her temple again as he shifted his hold to press her closer. Then, as the music played, as the night grew softer and quieter, they danced.

FROM: Alice <alice@scifac.edu>
TO: Dad <ellison@archsoc.edu>
DATE: November 5th, 1971 at 11:14pm
SUBJECT: re: re: JA Article

I protest! I did very much enjoy your paper in the *Journal of Archaeology*, and it has nothing to do with being your daughter—I totally agree with you about your interpretation of the newly discovered glyphs. Cho is wrong. I know it and you know it.

Dad, I wanted to talk to you about something else, too, something that's troubling me. I now have four Xs enrolled in my study (Gradients 3 through to 4.2), and from everything the Psy academics tell me, it means I've done astonishingly well. The designation is so rare that if there were ten living X-Psy at any given time, it would be considered a miracle.

That isn't what worries me. Of the four I've located, none are over the age of sixteen. There was a fifth known X, one of the boys tells me, a girl he met on the PsyNet. I got the impression he had a crush on her. The heartbreaking thing is, she died just short of her nineteenth birthday when her power consumed her.

I don't want to see my Xs die.

Alice

Chapter 10

HAWKE'S WOLF WASN'T riding him as hard as it had been doing for the past week when he drove down to DarkRiver territory the next morning—to talk to Lucas about the weapons coming into the area, to see if DarkRiver had any news on possible Pure Psy operatives in the city. It didn't take much thought to figure out that the wildness in him had been temporarily sated by the contact he'd allowed himself with Sienna.

He'd been so angry at her—always pushing his buttons, that girl. But then he'd taken her into his arms, and all that anger had blazed into a darker, hotly possessive need that had urged him to bend his head, bite down on the throbbing pulse in her neck, leave a mark.

God, that shirt. One tug and those snaps would've come apart, revealing the gold-kissed cream of her skin. He'd wanted to taste her, stroke her, pet her. Simply holding her, simply dancing with her, had driven his wolf half to madness . . . but he would have shredded anyone who'd dared interrupt that slow dance stolen in the silken shadows of night.

"Your pelt," a lazy voice drawled as he walked into the clearing around Lucas's home, "would make a nice coat for my mate."

Giving Vaughn a desultory finger where the amber-haired sentinel stood in the shade of a large juniper tree, its trunk a rich reddish brown, Hawke said, "I can scent Luc—he inside?" He nodded at the cabin below another large tree, an unoccupied aerie perched in its branches.

"Yep. Don't even think about going in."

"Do I look like I've had a lobotomy?" Lucas's mate, Sascha, was heavily pregnant. As a result, the leopard alpha's protective tendencies had moved into the lethal range. "I'll wait here. He'll scent me soon enough."

Lucas exited the cabin on the heels of that statement. "Sascha's sleeping," he said, angling his head toward the forest. "Vaughn."

"I won't take my eye off the place."

"How is she?" Hawke asked as they stepped deeper into the dappled sunshine filtering through the canopy.

"Ready to give birth." A chuckle. "Unfortunately, the baby is comfortable right where he or she is."

"You still don't know the gender?" Hawke wouldn't have had the self-control to hold out—and yeah, it hurt like a bitch to know he'd never have the chance to test that theory, but that didn't dim his joy for the leopard alpha. "If I ask Sascha, will she tell me?"

"Try it." A feral grin that was all teeth. "So, fill me in on these weapons shipments your people have detected."

Hawke gave him a quick rundown. "My gut says the Scotts—everything points to them—are going to mount an assault this time. Full-out, open."

"Not surprising, given that they and the others have tried covert ops a number of times and failed." Lucas halted on the moss-covered verge beside a small, clear stream. "Sascha spoke to her mother—there's definite Pure Psy activity in the city, but they're being very careful. They're well aware that not only are they not welcome, but that the last operative ended up with his brains leaking out his ears after Nikita found him out."

Hawke didn't like Nikita Duncan, but he could appreciate the woman's efficiency in taking care of a threat. "That'll make them harder to pinpoint."

"Rats are spread out across the city. Smallest sign of a Pure Psy base and we'll know." The leopard alpha glanced at Hawke. "Are you planning on moving your vulnerable out?"

"Not at this stage." Hawke had already discussed it with his lieutenants. "There's no overt threat yet, and we're wolves, Luc." Evacuating their home on such flimsy grounds would demoralize any predatory changeling, dominant or not. "If and when there is a credible threat, that's when we'll evacuate the noncombatants." The escape plans had been drafted long ago, could be put into motion within an hour, and the entire den cleared of their vulnerable within four. It would take far longer than that for any invader to break through SnowDancer's first line of defense.

Lucas's eyes gleamed cat-green in the muted light of the forest. "We made the same decision. I want Mercy to liaise with Riley to coordinate our evacuation plans. Work for you?"

"Do it. I think we should give WindHaven a heads-up, too." The falcons could provide air support if necessary. "I'll have Drew talk to them," he said when Luc nodded.

"I hear your boy's been out to the Canyon."

"Falcons love Drew—I think he even had an indecent proposal or three."

Lucas's head turned toward the cabin. "Indigo know?"

"I didn't want bloodshed." Hawke fell in step with the other alpha as he began to head back. "Sascha awake?"

"Yeah."

A pang of envy uncurled in Hawke's gut. He wondered what it would be like to be connected to a person with such intimacy. Yes, he was alpha, linked to his lieutenants and, to a lesser extent, to the rest of his pack. But it wasn't the same. None of them were *his*.

A rush of memory, a sleek feminine body pressed against his own, the scent of wild spice in his every breath as the rapid tattoo of her pulse sang a siren-song to his dominant nature. The wolf whispered that she could be his, only his, until possessive hunger pulsed through him, turning his muscles rigid.

He parted with Lucas at the clearing, digging his claws into his palms to cut through the compulsion. The scent of blood licked into the air, and he let it overwhelm the burn of sexual need for the moment. It wouldn't last, he was fully aware of that. If he knew what was good for him, for his pack, he'd finish what he'd started a couple of days ago and take a lover. A lover who knew the score, who wouldn't look at him in the morning with eyes bruised with the knowledge that he'd given her all he could.

There was nothing else left in him.

*   *   *

HAVING done a half-day shift on perimeter security, Sienna was home in plenty of time to work on an academic project and have dinner with Marlee and Toby. "They're both in bed," she told Walker when her uncle walked in the door after a later shift.

Walker shrugged off his jacket to reveal solid shoulders covered in a rough denim shirt. "I've got it now."

Instead of leaving, she heated up a meal, put it on the table. Walker, having ducked into his bedroom to kick off his shoes and wash up, came in as she was placing a glass of water beside his plate. Putting his hand on the back of her head, he leaned down to press his lips to her forehead, much as she'd done with Toby and Marlee. "You're troubled."

It almost broke her, the tender way he held her. "It's nothing." She couldn't bear to discuss last night with anyone, to share the painful magic of a dance, a touch that might never be repeated and yet that had branded her. She could still feel the rough kiss of Hawke's jaw against her temple, his hand so big and warm on her lower back, his chest a hard, muscled wall that flexed against her breasts.

Drawing back, Walker looked at her with pale green eyes that saw too much, but he didn't push. Relief a crashing wave inside of her, she said a quick good-bye and shrugged into her own jacket, deciding to go for a walk under the starlit sky. That same sky had been pure midnight when Hawke took her into his arms, as if the universe itself was conspiring to allow them to steal a single hidden moment.

"Sienna!"

Startled, she turned to see Maria running her way. "Are you off to do your shift?"

A bounce of loose, silky curls as the other novice nodded. "So, you going to tell me what happened with you and Hawke last night?"

"Nothing." Nothing but a slow, heartbreaking dance that had destroyed her illusions about her ability to get over a man who refused to even consider the idea that maybe, just maybe, there weren't as many years between them as he believed.

Thankfully, Maria took her words at face value. "You had

the early shift, right? Must've been hard getting up after staying up so late."

"It was fine." There had been no need to get up—she hadn't slept since returning to the den. "Actually, do you mind if I run down with you? I'm not tired enough to sleep yet." If she slept, she'd dream, the scent of Hawke haunting her in the soft dark.

"Company's always welcome." It was the answer of a wolf.

They ran down in companionable silence to the perimeter section where Maria was taking over from Lake. Breathing hard but not winded, Sienna gave the two of them privacy as they touched each other in that affectionate wolf way—nose to nose, body to body, the kiss an extension of the full-body contact.

Sienna had done her own shift in a different area of den territory, so there were new things to explore here. But still she almost missed it: a pen, gleaming and dark. Guessing it had fallen out of a packmate's pocket, she picked it up—the pack was scrupulous about ensuring no garbage littered their land. It wasn't until it was in her hand that she realized the sleek metallic cylinder wasn't a pen at all but a high-powered torch, an expensive item.

The SnowDancers had a small number of them. Used almost exclusively by non-changeling members of the pack—the wolves' night vision was better than any illumination the torches could provide—they were logged in and out with meticulous precision. Someone was probably in trouble for losing this. Sliding it into a pocket, she walked over to join Lake as he got ready to return to the den.

Body exhausted enough that there was a chance of a dreamless sleep, she parted with him at the entrance and went to log in the torch . . . to discover each and every one of the pack's set sitting in the box where they were stored. Hairs rising on the back of her neck, she made a call to Maria. "Can you do me a favor?" she asked when the other woman answered.

"What do you need?"

"Go about a hundred meters east of where Lake was standing when we arrived, tell me what you scent."

No sounds except for rustling as Maria jogged over. Then, "Psy. I smell Psy."

*   *   *

HAWKE finished checking out the section where Sienna had found the torch. Like Maria, he immediately caught the harsh metallic scent exuded by some Psy—as if they'd gone so deep into Silence, they'd lost their humanity. Nothing but the most brittle cold remained.

Sienna hadn't been cold.

Warm and curvy and muscled in a supple feminine way, she'd surprised him with the softness of her. They'd always been antagonists, always fought. To have her so sweet and lush against him had been a gift, walking away pure torture. His wolf didn't understand why he'd done so—to the animal, she smelled like a mature female. It didn't comprehend that she was a young girl barely become a woman.

I haven't been a child since the day they came for me when I was five.

The memory incited a killing rage within him. He'd always known she'd been conditioned into Silence as a child, but until she'd said that, he hadn't understood the painful depth of what her gift had demanded from her.

She'd never played.

How was that possible? Play was as necessary for a wolf as breathing.

She played with us.

It was the wolf's voice. Scowling, he went to reject the assertion. Sienna had driven him crazy with her tricks since moving into the den. The party she'd thrown to celebrate her eighteenth birthday had ended up with a lot of naked wolves freezing their asses off in the lake, their clothes scattered over so many acres, he didn't ever want to know that the hell they'd been doing.

If her intent had been to drive him to the asylum—

"You confirm it?"

He'd scented Riley nearing, didn't startle. "Yeah. Definitely Psy."

"Damn." A harsh exhalation. "They're really going to do this."

"Any word from our sources?"

"Lucas spoke to Nikita. She says tensions are increasing in

the Council, and it's out in the open now. Henry and Shoshanna Scott are making it clear they think the two of them should lead. Anyone who argues differently is in their sights."

"We don't need to be in the middle of a Psy war." His duty was to protect his people—the Psy could destroy themselves for all he cared . . . as they'd once almost destroyed Snow-Dancer.

Riley said, "No," but his tone brought up another question.

Hawke stared at the pine needle–strewn land in front of him, the ground otherwise clear because of the heavy canopy. "You're thinking the same thing I am—no way is this going to be contained to the Psy."

"Like Max pointed out," he said, naming Nikita's human security chief, "this region's already seen as interlinked. No matter what, they won't leave us be." A shrug. "And fact is, we've bitten back and bitten hard. I think at least part of the Council has decided we have too much power to be allowed to continue as we are."

Hawke knew that. He also understood that Nikita and Anthony were the lesser of two evils, but it still pissed him off that the pack had been forced to work with a couple of Councilors. "Let's increase the security patrols around the boundary. Don't worry too much about the border with Dark-River, but we need to let them know the Psy might be sniffing around even though it looks like they're focused on us."

Riley nodded, his gaze thoughtful. Hawke waited for the lieutenant to speak. Riley and Indigo were the solid foundation on which he stood—Riley had been there since before Hawke became alpha at fifteen. At the time, Hawke had had the strength of the remaining lieutenants around him, but he'd gone most often to the levelheaded teenager who was his best friend. Indigo, a little younger, had entered the picture a few years later but had become Hawke's left arm as Riley was his right. They'd pulled Hawke back from the edge more than once, pushed him when necessary, and offered support without question. It was a gift, one he never took for granted.

"I'm going to ask Kenji and Alexei to fine-tune our strategic plan," Riley said. "The fact it appears they're running physical reconnaissance in our territory argues for a rapid escalation. We need to be ready."

Hawke nodded. The two lieutenants had the best tactical minds in the pack. "Use Drew as well. He might be able to pinpoint areas of vulnerability we might otherwise miss." The SnowDancer tracker wasn't only Hawke's eyes and ears among the most vulnerable in the pack; he'd also become a clearinghouse for all kinds of information.

"I'll grab him for the comm-conference with Kenji and Alexei tomorrow," Riley said, then glanced at Hawke. "I hear you went dancing last night."

The words made every muscle in his body go tight, but he kept his tone even. "I've had a talk with the young males and so has Lucas. That kind of bullshit won't be tolerated." A little posturing between young dominants was expected and accepted. Hard physical violence? No.

"Alliance?"

"Rock solid. This isn't about that—it's because of you and Mercy." Everyone was still trying to work out the rules for the whole interpack dating thing, juveniles and older adults included. Add in testosterone and you got last night. "Not that I don't appreciate you stealing us a leopard sentinel."

Riley didn't smile at the familiar joke, perceptive eyes trained on Hawke. "Why did José call you and not Lucas if both groups were making trouble?"

"José switches between us. Luc gets the next postmidnight call."

A silence filled only with the rustle of the trees as a stiff wind blew through the canopy.

"You need to talk about it?" Riley asked after the forest had gone quiet again.

"Nothing to talk about."

Riley's nickname wasn't The Wall for nothing. "You've never been one to ignore a problem."

"Not a problem."

"Then why does the gym log show you there half the night, every night?"

Hawke growled low in his throat. "Keeping tabs on me?"

"It's my job." Riley's temper remained even. "I let you go lone wolf up in the mountains, but if you think I'll watch you self-destruct, you don't know me."

Hawke's wolf snarled, but he and Riley had too much

history between them for him to shrug off the concern—and what it meant. "Can you cover for me tomorrow afternoon?"

"You don't have to ask." That the other man didn't question Hawke about what it was he was planning to do, told him exactly how well his lieutenant knew him.

Chapter 11

SASCHA RUBBED THE hard mound of her pregnant belly and stared at the jar of Moreno cherry jam. "No. Absolutely not," she said to the child in her womb.

The baby wiggled, its emotions sparking of hunger.

Groaning, she picked up the jar, unscrewed it, and spooned up the jam. It should've tasted far too sweet, far too rich. Instead, it was ambrosia on her tongue. Unable to stifle a moan of greedy pleasure, she leaned against the counter in the staff kitchen at DarkRiver HQ and licked the spoon. It was tempting to eat a second spoonful, but in spite of the baby's ravenous urgings, she closed the lid and put the jam away. *It's not good for you,* she told her child. *We already had chocolate-cherry ice cream.*

"You missed a spot." Lucas crooked a finger from the doorway.

Leaving the spoon in the dishwasher, she walked over. "Did I?"

"Hmm." He leaned over to lick up the jam with a quick, catlike flick of his tongue, his hand stroking with gentle possessiveness over her abdomen. "Mmm, cherries."

Laughter in her mind, pure delight. Their baby knew its daddy.

"You look more beautiful every day," he murmured in her ear, his breath warm, his body so sensually familiar.

Sascha ran her hand up over his shoulder to close around his nape. "Charm me some more."

A chuckle, wicked words that made her toes curl. "Dorian's

ready to drive you home," he finally said. "But maybe I should come instead."

"I'll never get any work done then." Unable to resist that look in his panther-green eyes, she pulled him forward to claim a single deep kiss. "Now, behave."

Laughing, he put one hand on her lower back and walked her down to the elevator. "I want to have a sentinel meeting tonight to discuss the security issues. You up for it?"

"I'll order the pizza." Nuzzling her face against his neck when he stopped to press the down arrow, she heard a couple of wolf whistles at her back.

Lucas grinned. "How's our little princess?"

He'd asked her not to tell him the sex of their child, but he was convinced it was a girl. "The baby—which may or may not be a girl," she teased, "is quite active and interested in the world this morning." Their child had an inquisitive mind. "High level of psychic activity."

Lucas waited until they were inside the elevator to say, "Any idea what type?"

"Strong telepathy," Sascha said, "but hard to know other than that. I'll have a chat with the Shine medic, see if he has any ideas about how best to measure the baby's psychic abilities." The Psy race, focused as it was on "purebred" Psy, didn't have the protocols in place to deal with a child who would carry its father's wild changeling blood intermingled with Sascha's own.

Shine, on the other hand, was made up of the descendants of Psy who'd defected from the Net at the inception of Silence and intermarried/mated with the human and changeling populations. "I'll need to make certain I teach our child the correct shielding procedures." Her heart ached with a sudden, potent rush of emotion. She'd never expected to be a mother, having decided long ago that she wouldn't sentence a child to the same half life she'd lived in the Net. Then Lucas had appeared in her life. *You are my heart.*

He wasn't a telepath, but their mating bond had grown even deeper during the pregnancy, and she knew he heard her. Turning, he took her into his arms. The words he whispered were raw, rough, the love words of an alpha to his mate.

Lucas could charm, but this was who he was at the core, and she adored him. "Come home early tonight," she said against his mouth when they parted.

Kisses on her closed eyelids, her nose, the corners of her lips. "Anything you want."

A couple of hours later, her body and soul were still humming in bone-deep contentment when someone knocked on the cabin door. The sole reason Sascha didn't send out an immediate alert was that she recognized the mental signature of the man on the other side. Opening it, she smiled. "Why do you live to aggravate my security?"

Judd Lauren glanced over his shoulder to where a scowling DarkRiver soldier had materialized out of the trees. "It's good to keep them on their toes. Can you talk?" he asked after she waved the sentry away.

Knowing the reason for the unexpected visit, she nodded at the outdoor furniture situated neatly under the eaves of the cabin. "Let's sit outside." Another man's scent inside the house would infuriate Lucas's panther right now. While Sascha had no problem confronting her mate when he got too overprotective, she also understood he was a predatory changeling male driven by the most primal instincts— expecting him to act human would be to ask him to deny an integral part of himself. "So," she said after bringing out a pot of vanilla-scented tea and taking a seat, "the Eldridge book."

Expressionless brown eyes met her own, but Sascha had felt Judd Lauren's heart, knew the former Arrow had the capacity to feel, to *love* with violent intensity. "Are you any closer to locating it?" he asked now.

"No." The second Eldridge manuscript, meant to be the result of a research project on X-Psy, was half myth, half legend. Both DarkRiver and SnowDancer were working every single Psy contact they had to discover the truth of it, because if it existed, it might contain clues that would help Sienna learn how to handle her abilities—as Alice Eldridge's first book had done for Sascha.

But, Sascha thought, cupping her hands around the porcelain teacup, though she hadn't known it at the time, she'd never been as alone as Sienna. Dormant they might be, but there were thousands of E-Psy in the Net. There were no other cardinal X-Psy. "How is she?"

Judd took a sip of his tea, made a startlingly *male* face—somehow, she didn't expect that kind of thing from a former assassin—and put it right back down. "She's maintaining," he said. "The issue right now isn't with her psychic control, it's with her emotional stability."

Sascha read between the lines. "Maybe I should have a talk with her." Sienna had become very much a part of Sascha's family in the time she'd spent in DarkRiver, and Sascha wanted to see for herself how the other cardinal was handling things with a man as dominant and as strong as Sascha's own mate. A man whose heart carried so many scars that Sascha would've warned Sienna away . . . except that Sienna bore her own.

Judd's fingers curled into a fist on the table, and for a moment, Sascha thought he might betray the emotions that had to be tearing at his heart, but all he said was, "I'll bring her down tonight."

Reassured by the knowledge that he'd confide in Brenna even if he spoke to no one else, she put down her own cup. "I'm hardly an invalid." He was as bad as a leopard. "I'll drive up with Lucas."

"He isn't liable to permit you that far from the heart of DarkRiver territory. Give the man some peace."

"Judd! No wonder you fit in so well with the wolves." Laughing, she decided it might actually be better for Sienna to have a break from the den. "Fine, we'll do it your way."

As the former Arrow melted into the forest, on his way to see a small boy who'd been born with the same gift that made Judd so lethal, Sascha poured another cup of tea and considered the mysterious Eldridge manuscript. She, Faith, and Ashaya had all exhausted their sources, to no avail. She'd even chanced trusting the director of Shine with the question—but Dev's people hadn't had an X in the original group of defectors and knew close to nothing about them.

As far as the mainstream world was concerned, there was no such thing as an X-Psy.

* * *

MID-AFTERNOON the day after Sienna had alerted them to
the Psy incursion, Hawke crouched in a sun-drenched corner
of a small clearing ringed by ancient sequoias with roots the
thickness of a grown man's body and dotted with a myriad
wild blooms adapted to the cold mountain climate. "Hey,
Rissa."

The only reply was silence. But it was a peaceful silence.
As this place was peaceful, a haven whenever he needed one.
And today, he needed it desperately.

"They all think," he said, clearing away a few stray leaves
to uncover a delicate patch of wildflowers the shade of the sky
at noon, "that I'm being stubborn without reason. They don't
understand I'm protecting her." He was brutally attracted to
Sienna. That much, he'd admitted to himself if no one else. But
the cruel fact was, he could give her little beyond a physical
relationship. "I gave my heart to you a long time ago."

Theresa had been five years old when she died in an avalanche. He'd been ten. Too young to love her the way a man
loves a woman, or even the way a boy loves a girl. But the
wolf had understood from the moment they met who she was
to him, who she would become—his mate.

They'd been best friends since that instant, the connection
between them a bright, shining thread, their relationship full
of laughter and a delight that was beyond innocent. It had
been nothing like the tumultuous nature of the craving that
raked him with blade-sharp claws anytime he was in Sienna's
vicinity. The scent of her alone could send his wolf insane,
the taste of her a lingering, maddening spice on his tongue.

"Wolves only mate once, Rissa," he said, using the old
childhood pet name he'd been responsible for coining. "Everyone knows that."

But we never mated.

The voice he heard in his mind when he thought of Theresa was never that of the child she'd been, but of the woman
she would've become. A woman full of warmth and gentleness, a woman who wouldn't have been a soldier but a maternal female, part of the beating heart of the pack.

"Doesn't matter," he murmured, refusing to give up a truth
that had shaped so much of his life. "You were my mate. We
would've mated when we grew old enough."

The wind whispered through the trees, through his hair. It was a touch he'd felt a thousand times over the years, and always, it had left him centered and calm. Today, however, as he rose to his feet and walked away from the final resting place of the girl who would've owned his heart as a woman, he felt strangely dissatisfied, off-kilter.

It wasn't a sensation either man or wolf enjoyed.

SIENNA was ready to head down to DarkRiver territory with Judd around eight that evening. Seeing Riordan as she left her quarters, she lifted a hand. "Hi."

"Hey." He stopped a few feet away, shifting from foot to foot and avoiding her gaze. "You okay? Hawke was pretty pissed when he came down to Wild the other night."

"You know he wouldn't hurt any of us." She made no attempt to hide her shock that he'd even asked the question, it was so incomprehensible.

Riordan colored, looked up. "Uh, yeah. That's not what I was talking about."

Sienna stared.

"Jeez, Sin, he made it clear you were his."

A punch of memory—a hard male body holding her close enough to kiss, his voice an intimate roughness against her senses, his hands so big and hot on her skin. "No," she forced out, "there's nothing there." He wouldn't permit there to be.

"You sure?" Riordan's eyes crinkled at the corners. "Thing is, no one else is going to come near you now."

"You're joking."

A shrug, a hand thrust through chocolate-dark curls. "He's the alpha, babe. Only an idiot would try to poach on his territory."

She gritted her teeth. "I. Am. Not. His. Territory."

"Hey, look, isn't that Marlee?"

Sienna turned automatically. Riordan was nowhere to be seen when she realized she'd been had and swiveled back to face him. "Chicken!" she called out before continuing on her way.

She ran into Evie not far from the exit, flat out asked her if the other novice had been spouting bullshit.

Her friend winced. "Um, no. Hawke definitely had the alpha-possessive vibe going on."

"He doesn't want me." Not enough to see past his preconceptions. Her jaw tightened, her muscles tensing as if in readiness for a fight. Stubborn, arrogant, infuriating man!

"Hey." Evie put her hand on Sienna's arm. "Maybe that's good news—seriously, any woman who takes him on is going to need brass balls. Big ones."

"Are you saying mine are too small?" It was easier to be flip, to stoke the heat of her frustrated anger than to acknowledge the hurt inside of her, the bruise that kept growing ever bigger in spite of all her vows to not allow this pull toward Hawke to savage her.

"Smart-ass." Laughing, Evie shook her head. "Look, if there really is nothing going on, he has to make sure the pack males know that. Otherwise, not only will your dating life go into a death spiral inside the pack, the boys will scare off any other male, changeling or human, who dares look in your direction."

"No?" Sienna had no interest in dating anyone else, but she would not be humiliated by being claimed by Hawke and then left unwanted.

"You've been around the XY component of SnowDancer for several years." Evie raised her eyebrows. "What do you think?"

"Pack males stick together."

With that thought circling in her mind, she wasn't in any mood to see Hawke walking out of the trees near the White Zone, where she'd gone to wait for Judd. His wolf-pale eyes spotted her at once, and he changed direction to block out the night in front of her. "Where are you going?" he asked, as if he had every right to know.

"None of your business." A dangerous silence greeted her words . . . and she couldn't help herself. "Unless you're pulling rank?"

A silence that had her skin stretching tight over her bones, her heartbeat hammering in her ears.

"Had to push, didn't you, Sienna?" Stepping close, close enough that she had to tip her head back to meet his gaze, he took a long, deep breath. "You changed your shampoo."

A sudden, melting warmth invaded her body at the sound of his voice—as if he was savoring the scent. "Lara had some samples she gave out to the women in the break room this morning." The SnowDancer healer had been in an edgy kind of mood, so Sienna had kept her mouth shut and taken the sample when it was shoved into her hand. "It's wild apples." She had no idea why she'd said that, why she continued to speak to him.

"I like it." He lifted his hand to run a strand of her hair through his fingers.

Fighting every cell in her body, she stepped back. "Stop it. No touching. No acting possessive."

Hawke's wolf prowled to the surface, a primal presence behind the human skin. "Oh?"

"All or nothing." She held her ground though she was shaking inside, her blood going alternately hot and cold. "If you want me, take me. Or let me go."

A slow blink, the force of his personality a pulse against her skin, a near physical push. If she'd been smart, she would've backed down, but this was her emotional life on the line, and she'd fought too hard to surrender it to anyone. Even an alpha wolf used to dominance. "I just found out," she said through a throat that was suddenly bone dry, "that none of the boys are going to ask me out after the scene you pulled at Wild."

"Take out an ad if you need to," she continued when the wolf just watched her without blinking, "but make sure they know I'm not yours." Her need for him was a claw ripping at her insides. When he finally slept with Rosalie or another packmate, it would savage her—she couldn't control that, but she damn well could ensure she didn't have to suffer the humiliation of being publicly discarded.

A low growl that made the hairs on the back of her neck rise. Staying in place was hard, so hard, when all she wanted to do was back down and crawl all over him. *No. No more. He plans to take a lover.* The mental reminder of what he intended to do to sate his wolf's touch-hunger was the last straw. "I mean it, Hawke." She was done with throwing herself at a man who didn't want her.

"So decisive," he murmured in that calm tone that had

adrenaline flooding her body, the primitive part of her brain conscious she was in the presence of a predator. "Got your eye on someone?"

She didn't know what made her say it. "No. But I have no plans to die a virgin."

Chapter 12

HAWKE WENT PREDATOR-STILL. "Kit's been a good boy, has he?"

"Again, none of your business." Refusing to be intimidated, she glanced over his shoulder. "Excuse me, my ride's here."

Hawke stepped sideways to block her. "No."

Her body threatened to lock her into place, so strong was the impact of him. Only her fury kept her going. *"Move."*

Ignoring her command, he continued to hold her gaze with that wild wolf one even as he directed his next words to Judd, who'd just hopped out of the SUV. "Where are you taking her?"

"We were heading down to see Sascha, but I've just had a contact I need to chase up fast." Judd looked at Sienna. "Okay if we delay this till tomorrow?"

"Sure."

"No need." Hawke smiled and held his hand back for the keys. "I can drive her to the cats."

Sienna stared at Judd, sending him telepathic messages that seemed to go unheard. "No, that's fine," she said out loud. "I can wai—"

But Judd was already handing Hawke the keys. "Better you go down tonight," he said. "Since the visit's been cleared with Sascha's security."

"I can drive," she pointed out through gritted teeth to the wolf blocking her way. "Judd was only coming with me because he wanted to take part in the discussion." She held out a hand. "I don't need a babysitter."

To her shock, it was Judd who stopped her escape attempt. "It's late. You've never driven this route in the dark—and it'll be darker still by the time you head back."

What is wrong *with you?!* she telepathed. *I cannot be in a car alone with him.* Especially when those ice blue eyes had gone slightly aglow.

Deal with it. It was a pitiless response. *If you need that to be an order from a lieutenant, then consider it done.*

She clenched her jaw, but no way in hell was she about to disobey an order and bring her maturity into question yet again. So either she allowed Hawke to drive, or she stayed put. It was tempting to seize the latter option, but not only did she want to see Sascha, she would not give Hawke the satisfaction of knowing he'd derailed her plans. "I'll wait in the car."

She was ensconced in the passenger seat, her wireless speaker buds in her ears, by the time Hawke finished talking with Judd and got into the driver's seat. He didn't say anything until he'd turned the SUV around and they were on their way. Then he leaned over and pulled out the bud on his side.

"Hey!"

But he'd managed to grab the tiny music player from her lap, too, throwing it over his shoulder into the backseat. "I don't like being ignored."

She set her jaw and twisted in her seat, reaching for the player. He let her find it . . . to take it off her an instant later with changeling speed. It landed on the backseat again, along with the bud still in his hand. "Next time, I throw it out the window."

"I could—" She let out an aggravated breath and removed the remaining bud, placing it on a tray on the dash. "Now who's being childish?"

He shrugged, relaxing into the seat when she made no further effort to retrieve the music player. "Country and western?" he said as he navigated the forest track SnowDancer kept deliberately crude, with plenty of low-hanging foliage to deter the use of hover facilities—to make sure no one could sneak up on the den by ground vehicle. "I would've picked you as a rock 'n' roll kind of girl."

She ignored him in favor of staring out the window.

Except it was hard to ignore over two hundred pounds of muscled male wolf when he didn't want to be ignored. Reaching out, he tugged on a strand of her hair. "Tell me about Kit."

She pushed away his hand, well aware she succeeded only because he let her. "Kit is smart, sexy, and gorgeous. A total package." He was also wickedly funny and could be charming in a way only a feline could be. Too bad she had the terrible taste to hunger for a wolf instead.

Hawke's hands tightened on the manual steering wheel. "A real prince."

"You could learn something from him."

"Careful." A quiet warning. "You only get to push so far."

She was too mad and sad and hurting to care. "Wow," she said with a wide-eyed look of mock amazement, "you lasted an entire *two* minutes before pulling rank."

To her shock, he laughed. It was an open, uninhibited sound, and it held her absolute and utter attention. Hawke rarely laughed like that, and never with her. With such open joy, his wolf in his voice, in his face. "You can be a real brat."

It was difficult to maintain a tough front when his laugh had wrapped around her like a rough caress, eroding her defenses to nothing, but she couldn't let him see that, see how very vulnerable she was when it came to him. "Doesn't make me wrong."

"Fine," he said. "When it's just us, there's no rank, no alpha, no soldier. Only Hawke and Sienna."

She'd never, in a million years, expected to succeed in getting him to put aside the hierarchy. Her breath stuck in her throat, her palms suddenly damp.

"Lost for words?" A glance of ice blue before he returned his attention to the forest track.

Since Hawke's eyes never changed color, no matter his form, most people found it impossible to tell whether they were talking to the man or the wolf. Sienna always knew. *Always.* The power inside of her recognized the same wild energy in the wolf who was Hawke's other half. "No," she said at last, "just wondering how long you'll be able to hack it before you fall back on those rules."

"Keep pushing, baby," he murmured in that low, deep

voice that touched places in her body it had no business touching. "We'll see what it gets you."

"Frustration!" she said, throwing caution to the winds on an adrenaline-fueled rush of courage. "That's all it's ever gotten me. If sexual attraction followed any kind of a logical rule, I'd be in bed with Kit right now instead of sitting next to a man too scared to take a chance."

A charged silence.

Sienna couldn't believe she'd said that. It was going too far, even for her. Hawke was alpha—whether or not the rules were currently in operation between them—which meant he was dominant beyond any Psy or human man, and most changeling males, too. Men like that did not like having their strength questioned on any level.

"After your meeting with Sascha," he said, his tone silky with menace, "that's when we'll talk about fear."

Sienna leaned back in her seat, trying to control her racing heartbeat. He could hear it, of that she had no doubt. But she was Psy, had been Ming LeBon's protégée. She wasn't about to let anyone scare her off—not even a predatory changeling wolf so lethal, the feral wolves treated him as their leader.

Brass balls. Big ones.

The memory of Evie's words gave her a slightly hysterical confidence, but it was confidence nonetheless. Using every ounce of the will that had allowed her to retain a personality even in Ming's tender care, she wrenched her heartbeat and breathing under control. It had nothing to do with what she felt and everything to do with playing a very dangerous game with a predator who had much bigger teeth.

A growl filled the vehicle, filled her senses, just as they entered the lane that led to a small clearing not far from Lucas and Sascha's home. "You taste of ice."

"It's necessary," she said with manufactured calm. "You know it is." He'd caught her in an active state not long before she left the den to spend several months with the cats, seen firsthand what she could do. She'd chosen an isolated section to attempt her experiments at harnessing the fury of the X-marker, but an hour into it, she'd turned around and there he was, a huge wolf, proud and beautiful.

Now, he didn't answer as he brought the vehicle to a halt.

Getting out, she took a deep breath, feeling as if she'd escaped the lair of the very big, very bad wolf. Then she met Hawke's eyes across the hood of the SUV. Oh, God. All eyes of ice blue and hair of silver-gold, he was her every fantasy come to life.

And he was focused on her to the exclusion of all else.

She wet dry lips, saw his eyes follow the movement. "Stop it."

A faint smile that made every tiny hair on her body rise in quivering attention. "How fast can you run?" A wolf's question.

"I'm not running from you." She held her ground.

"We'll see." Pushing off the SUV, he led the way to the cabin.

"You need to go away while I'm talking with Sascha," she said after she was certain the wolf wasn't about to make good on its threat.

To her surprise, he made no argument. "I'll go for a run. Luc doesn't like me close to Sascha at the moment."

"Really?" Startled, she looked toward where the Dark-River alpha was waiting with his mate, a small light illuminating the outdoor seating area. "I thought you two had trust."

"His mate is pregnant. It changes the balance." Raising his hand in hello to the alpha couple, he glanced at her. "I'll be back in an hour. Enough time?"

She didn't trust his sudden cooperation but tried to keep her own tone just as businesslike. "Twenty more minutes?"

"Fine." Then he was gone, a sleek shadow in the dark.

Her heart slipped the vise of her rigid mental control to slam against her chest at witnessing his incredible speed. If Hawke ever did chase her, she'd better hope she had one hell of a head start. Then again, it might be more fun to get caught.

"Sienna." Lucas's voice broke through her stunned realization that she wasn't as averse to the idea of playing prey to Hawke's wolf as she'd thought.

Closing the distance to the cabin, she smiled, hoping her distraction didn't show. "Hi."

"Grab a seat." The leopard rose from his own chair. "I'll stay out of earshot and make sure the sentinels are, too."

Sienna knew the reason for the courtesy was because his

mating bond with Sascha meant he'd know the instant she felt in any way threatened. "Thanks."

Lucas left with silent feline grace. Getting to her feet at the same instant, Sascha motioned for Sienna to follow her inside. "Warmer there. Plus, I have your favorite chocolate-caramel slice."

A spark of childish joy. "Really?" It was hard for her to resist sweets—in the Net, she'd been disallowed anything sensual, including food. Since getting out, she wanted to gorge. On food, on feeling . . . but mostly on Hawke.

Heat bloomed low in her body, and she had to focus to catch Sascha's next words.

"I had Lucas hide it in the aerie before the sentinels got here for a meeting tonight. Otherwise"—a warm laugh—"you'd have been lucky to scrape up a crumb. Sit. I'll get the tea."

Sienna nudged Sascha down instead. "I'll do it—I know where everything is." Bringing the pot to the table, she put it aside to steep while Sascha cut the slice.

"So," the empath said, putting the rich chocolaty treat on her plate, "Hawke wants to chase you."

Sienna froze. "Lucas heard that from all the way over here?"

"Uh-huh. And Hawke knew he would."

It took Sienna several seconds to process the implications of that statement. "He told me flat out that there couldn't be anything between us." Yet he'd just come perilously close to staking another claim.

"Hmm."

"What?" It was a relief to be able to talk this over with Sascha. While Indigo had become her friend and guide in many ways, Hawke was the one subject Sienna hesitated to discuss with her, not wanting to put the lieutenant in an awkward position.

"I heard what happened at Wild."

"I could still kick him for that." Pouring the tea, she pushed one of the quirky tulip-shaped cups toward Sascha. "He treated me as if I was ten years old." Except for when he'd tapped her butt, kept his hand there. Her thighs clenched at the memory.

"There is that, isn't there?" Sascha's tone was gentle. "The age issue."

"Nothing I can do about that. I'm always going to be younger." Afraid she'd break the teacup with the force of her grip, she put it down. "But," she added, voice vibrating with feeling, "I've not only survived and gained control of my abilities, I've done so outside the PsyNet. Hardly the act of a child." She'd earned the right to live her life as she pleased. "I'm not about to let His Wolf Highness disregard all that because it makes it easier for him to not recognize—"

Sienna bit off her words, but Sascha didn't need them. From the moment she'd seen the young X with Hawke, she'd felt it, that tug between them. It had had no name at the start, no definition. Even now, it remained a raw, nameless thing, but it was *powerful*. Powerful enough to have Hawke overriding his own decisions about keeping Sienna at a distance, powerful enough to have dragged him out of the shadows.

The first time Sascha had touched Hawke with her empathic senses, she'd felt such blood rage she'd been staggered by it. This man, she'd thought, would never love, not so long as that anger was a red haze across his vision. But then she'd seen him with Sienna. Month by month, year by year, the strange alchemy of their adversarial relationship had removed the poison of that anger until what remained was a gleaming, honed blade, still lethal, but far healthier.

However, Sascha had sensed something else that night when Hawke asked her to prove her claim to the E designation. It was a truth she'd never say aloud, an empathic secret she'd never share, but there was a deep loneliness within the wolf alpha, a part of himself he kept separate even from his beloved pack. If Sienna could reach that wild, broken heart . . .

"An alpha," Sascha began, wanting to give the other cardinal all the help she could, "needs his woman to come to him stripped bare of all pretense. No barriers. No emotional shields. I am the one person Lucas knows is his without question, the one person who will stand by him no matter what, who'll tell him the truth even if it's harsh."

Sienna, to her credit, didn't shy from the frank discussion. Instead, those starlit eyes turned midnight in intense concentration. "What about the sentinels?"

"That, too, is a rare kind of trust, but . . ." The bond was near impossible to explain to someone else, but Sienna needed to understand, so Sascha found the words. "With me, he's never, ever my alpha. He's simply Lucas, the man who holds my heart."

"Isn't that . . . Doesn't that depth of vulnerability put you in a weaker position, given an alpha's natural dominance?"

"No, because he gives the same back." Loved her with all the untamed power and fierce devotion of the panther's heart. "He gives more."

"I don't know if I can have that kind of a relationship with Hawke," Sienna murmured, "even if I manage to make him listen, make him *see*." Not discouragement, more a contemplative statement. "He's not like Lucas."

Sascha waited.

"I understand Lucas could and would kill me with a single blow if he considered me a threat to you or the rest of the pack," Sienna said, "but he smiles and laughs and plays."

"Hawke's done more than his share of teasing." Sascha couldn't count the number of times the wolf had flirted with her in order to annoy Lucas.

Sienna pushed the chocolate slice around her plate. "He never plays with me."

"Wolves have a strange sense of play according to my mate." Sascha shook her head. "He lets you drive him crazy, doesn't he?"

"He punished me."

Sascha laughed at the disgruntled statement. "You probably deserved it."

"Yes, I did." A scowl that Sascha guessed was self-directed. "But he's given me the green light to ignore the hierarchy while we're alone together."

Sascha sat up, her amazement so huge that the baby kicked, wanting in on the secret. Smoothing her hand over her belly at the same time that she soothed their child's active mind, she used her other hand to touch Sienna's. "In that case," she said, hope a brilliant spark inside of her, "ambush him if you have to, but *get him alone*."

Chapter 13

ALMOST READY FOR her date, Lara smoothed the dress over her hips. It was a bright sunshine yellow, an impulse buy she'd been certain would spend a short life languishing in her closet before she gave it away. But Drew of all people had convinced her to give it a go, and what do you know, it looked stunning against the natural dark tan of her skin.

The design itself wasn't fancy. The dress had a simple square neck and thick straps, the bodice fitted down to her waist, where it flared out in a gentle swirl. A feminine dress reminiscent of the 1950s, she thought, putting on earrings she'd bought from a street stall during a trip to New York. The tiny fall of sunflowers glinted cheerfully through the corkscrew curls of her black hair.

After slipping on a thin gold bracelet, she pulled on the strappy sandals she'd bought on the same frustration-and-nervous-anticipation-fueled shopping trip that had resulted in the yellow dress. A wrap to ward off the evening air and a sweet little vintage purse beaded with vibrant color finished off the look. Maybe she'd never win any modeling awards, she thought with determined confidence, but she looked pretty.

The knock came a second later.

Opening the door, she said, "You're right on time," to the man on the other side.

Kieran flashed that trademark playful smile of his, a deep dimple creasing one cheek. "Wouldn't want to be late when I finally got the prettiest woman in the den to agree to go on a date."

With his skin a lighter shade of brown than her own and hypnotic gray-green eyes courtesy of his Tajik father, Kieran was an unashamed flirt. He was also several years younger than her and had broken more hearts in the den than most of the other men combined . . . but Kieran also knew how to make a woman feel beautiful, desired.

Tonight, after not having been out with a man for six months—since the first night Walker had stopped by for a late-night coffee—Lara needed to feel exactly that. "Where are you taking me?"

"I thought that Italian restaurant by Wild. I know you love their gelato."

"You did your homework." She slid her arm into his, appreciating him though he didn't make her wolf freeze in quiet, panicked anticipation when he was near, didn't make her heart skip a beat.

Kieran responded as they rounded the corner, but his words were lost in the crash of white noise inside her head. She saw Walker coming down the corridor, the faded blue of his jeans a contrast to the deep navy of his shirt. Masculine and confident, he walked with the stride of a man at ease with his body . . . a body that was all lean muscle and strength.

She hadn't seen him since their conversation in the forest, though she knew he'd come looking for her the other night. It was pure luck she hadn't been in—but even if she had been, she would've handled it. The time for avoiding Walker was over, and while she couldn't see them resuming their friendship, there was no reason they couldn't maintain a cordial relationship. "Hi," she said when he stopped.

Those light green eyes skimmed over her and to Kieran, before returning to her. "The temperature's dropped," he said. "You should take a coat."

Kieran laughed, slid his arm around her. "Hey, man, if she has a coat, how am I supposed to use the cold to get her to cuddle close?"

Walker left with a curt nod.

It was only after he was gone that Lara realized she'd stopped breathing.

* * *

HAWKE had meant to stay the hell away from Sienna after he returned from visiting Theresa. So he had no idea why he was waiting for her at the car ninety minutes after having dropped her off, anticipation a slow burn in every cell of his body.

It was no surprise to see Lucas walking toward him. "Did you get my message?" the leopard alpha asked as he got closer.

"Yeah. Revised evac plan looks good to me." On one point he and Lucas were in glorious agreement—it was damn fine to have a sentinel-lieutenant mating. Not that Riley and Mercy particularly enjoyed their glee. "It'll get everyone out faster."

Lucas shoved a hand through his shoulder-length hair. "We shouldn't need to consider an evacuation from our own land, but the bastards have been getting smarter and more focused with each attempt. Learning more about us."

"So have we. If it does come down to war, it's going to be a level playing field." That wasn't false confidence—Hawke had made certain SnowDancer would never again be a defenseless target. He'd been fifteen when he'd taken control of the pack, but he'd understood the grim reality of Psy power better than anyone, his childhood having ended in a spray of blood and betrayal caused by the cold psychic race.

Then, he'd hated them all. Now he knew it was only the Council and its flunkies that were the enemy. "I was thinking I should go say hello to Sascha darling." In truth, his mind was on another woman, one with hair of ruby red and a mouth that had a way of saying things that both amused and incensed his wolf.

"Go for it." Unruffled words, eyes gleaming cat-green.

Hawke smiled, his wolf finding the idea of poking at the leopard alpha an amusing distraction from his compulsion to run a certain Psy to ground. "What if she invites me? I should call out, let her know I'd like to see her."

A languid shrug. "If you want your teeth in your gullet, go ahead."

"You sure you want to make Sascha mad?" The wolf laughed husky and low at Lucas's battle-ready stance. "I am one of her favorite people, after all."

Instead of snarling, the other alpha started to smile a very feline kind of a smile. "You know, I think maybe I should invite Kit over. He'd love to see Sienna again."

Hawke growled before he could stop himself. The damn leopard grinned.

"Funny," Hawke muttered.

"From my perspective, it was hilarious." Lucas unfolded his arms, sliding his hands into the pockets of the black cargo pants he wore with a T-shirt of a shade that matched his eyes. Hawke knew without asking that Sascha had bought that T-shirt.

"They're not dating, but he's very protective of her," Lucas said as Hawke was about to rib him on his sartorial elegance in retaliation for the other man's quip, "just so you know."

Hawke didn't bother to respond to that—he'd eat the baby cat alpha for breakfast. "What did José say when you talked to him?"

"Guess." Lucas shook his head. "Come over for a beer tomorrow afternoon. Sascha will be at Tammy's. We'll talk."

It was strange, that he'd become almost-friends with this alpha who'd once been an adversary. "I'll see if I can swing it. Might have a comm-meeting."

Lucas nodded the instant before Hawke caught the first hint of an exquisitely familiar scent on the breeze. Autumn leaves and spice and strength. His wolf stretched out at the intoxication of it. Maybe she wasn't his mate, but the animal wasn't bothered. It still wanted the man to take her, to claim her. To bite her.

Jesus.

"Did you two have a good visit?" Lucas asked, walking over to touch the back of his hand to Sienna's cheek in a gentle caress.

The only reason Hawke's wolf didn't eviscerate the other male was because Lucas's mate was walking with Sienna. And Sascha could get even a demon to behave. Mostly. "Hello, Sascha darling," he murmured, dropping his voice into bedroom territory. "Miss me?"

"Terrible man," Sascha said, trying to get around her mate. Lucas refused to let her pass. "Both of you." But she allowed Luc to wrap her in his arms, press his lips to her temple.

"Did I ever tell you I knew another empath once?" Hawke

said, buying himself time to temper his response to Sienna. "She was part of SnowDancer when I was a child, mated to a wolf long before Silence." Zia had been near to a hundred and thirty, a low-Gradient E, but one of the first to notice that something was wrong in the pack. If only people had listened.

Sascha's eyes went huge. "No, you didn't! Why don't—"

Lucas squeezed her. "He's trying to lure you with his stories. Go away, wolf."

"Lucas!"

Sienna was smiling as she looked at the couple, but that smile faded when she met his gaze.

It made him wonder what she saw. "Let's go."

She got into the SUV without a word, and they headed off after waving good-bye to Lucas and Sascha. Uncomfortable as his relationship was with Sienna, Hawke liked being around her—a fact he was positive would surprise her. But when she wasn't fighting with him, she was smart, with a wit the wolf found endlessly amusing. "Want to go for a run?" he asked as they hit the edge of den territory. "I promise not to chase you."

A lush burst of feminine arousal had him gritting his teeth to fight his body's instinctive response. "I'm nowhere near as fast as you," she said at last. "Not like Judd."

"Don't have to go fast." He shrugged, the wolf happy because she hadn't said no. "Sometimes, it's just about feeling the wind against your face, the earth under your feet."

She tugged the sleeves of her checked shirt to her fingertips. "Okay."

"It's cold out." The Sierra Nevada had slipped into the quiet beauty of night, the heat of the sun's rays long gone. "There should be a sweatshirt in the back you can wear."

Twisting in her seat, she reached for the sweatshirt . . . and her music player. Shooting him a dirty look, she put the little device in the space on the dash and undid her safety belt long enough to pull on the large gray sweatshirt.

That quickly, she was covered in his scent.

Watching her roll up the sleeves to her wrists, he hid his possessive satisfaction behind a lazy comment. "You're kinda small, Sienna." She never seemed that way, her personality that of someone much larger and stronger—he bet if he asked people in the den to describe her, most would give her at least half a foot of extra height, more muscle.

"Maybe you're too big." She continued to fold up the sleeves with methodical precision.

Grinning at being so politely insulted, he didn't say anything until he'd parked the vehicle a little ways from the den. Sienna was more than strong enough to cover the remaining distance on foot. "Ready?"

She was already opening her door. "I don't recognize this area."

He wasn't surprised. Den territory was a vast, sprawling wilderness, most of it inaccessible to vehicles—and unlike the wolves, Sienna couldn't explore as much area on foot. "I want to show you something."

She clambered over a fallen tree on the path, and he had to stop himself from reaching over and picking her up, caressing her waist with his hands as he slid her oh-so-slowly to her feet. Her movements were smooth and lithe—Indigo had done a good job with her training, but it was Sienna's will that had led to her becoming as good as she was. Hawke knew the offensive capability of each and every soldier in the pack, and—putting aside her psychic abilities—Sienna was exceptional for someone who wasn't changeling.

"A little farther," he said when they reached a stand of conifers intertwined with a delicate dark green vine.

Picking up a small pinecone off the forest floor, Sienna rubbed her thumb over the rough edges. "Are you doing anything tomorrow night?"

He caught the nervous bite in her scent, caught, too, the determination. His gut clenched. *"Sienna."* Hurting her was the last thing he wanted to do, but he wouldn't lead her on. "I have plans."

Cardinal eyes slammed into his. "Rosalie?" A single frigid word.

His wolf peeled back its lips. "She's an adult wolf, who happens to be a friend."

"As opposed to an immature girl you can't stand." A challenge, the gauntlet thrown.

He picked it up. "I need something she can give me." Rosalie was wolf enough to accept and offer the physical intimacy his own wolf craved without expecting a depth of commitment he simply couldn't give . . . and much as he valued her friendship, Rosalie didn't tempt him to brand her with his claim, even knowing it would destroy her in the end.

THE pinecone dug into Sienna's palm, but she hardly felt it against the pain of the body blow Hawke had just delivered. Why had she asked the question when she'd known the answer? It was nothing a Psy—a true Psy—would've ever done. But when it came to this man, she had as little control as the child he called her. "Is it enough?" she asked with a fury that sought to draw blood. "Just the physical act."

"Don't try and bring it down to that." Cold, cold words. "You've been in the den long enough to know we don't use each other."

No, they didn't. That made it so much harder to bear. With wolves, sexual contact was warm and joyful and treasured. Rosalie would lie with Hawke with a packmate's genuine affection, luxuriating in having a partner who could ease her own physical needs so very well—because while Sienna might be inexperienced, she understood that Hawke would never leave a woman unsatisfied. He was too much the dominant male to accept anything but total erotic surrender in bed.

And when he and Rosalie parted, whether it was after a day or after a month, it would be with smiles and laughter. She'd seen the same with other members of the pack, knew that several of her friends were involved in affectionate, sensual relationships that wouldn't be permanent—but would be respected and cherished.

"I'm sorry," she forced herself to say, nausea curdling her stomach. "That was uncalled for." Chest so tight it ached, she said, "Is this the way to the den?" glad that her voice came out calm, betraying none of the hurt that had her curling into a fetal ball inside her mind. Because it didn't matter how much time alone she had with him if she had to spend her nights knowing those strong hands were stroking over another woman's skin, another woman's breasts.

"No"—his voice a slow caress, an unintended taunt—"it's a small detour."

"I'd like to go back." At that moment, the last thing she wanted was to be here, with him, not when she could almost hate him for what he was able to do to her.

"Throwing a tantrum, Sienna?" Ruthless words, that caressing tone suddenly a blade. "I thought you'd retired the spoiled brat act."

How would you feel if the woman you wanted beyond all others planned to take another man into her bed? She didn't yell the words, holding on to her tattered pride. *Enough.* Just . . . enough. Some things, a woman could not accept and live with herself. "Why are we here?" she asked in a voice touched with ice. "Why are we walking under the stars, late at night?"

Wolf-pale eyes gleaming at her in the dark, the gaze of a man used to getting exactly what he wanted. "We're packmates. It's a beautiful night. Simple as that."

"Bullshit." A harsh renunciation that scraped her throat raw. "You're giving me just enough to make sure I can't forget you and not enough to go against your all-important principles. Well, fuck you." Quiet, quiet words, because she would not scream and yell, would not allow him to see her break. "I don't want the crumbs from your table." Turning on her heel, she started heading through the trees in the direction she thought would lead home.

"Sienna."

She could not, would not, stop. If she did, he'd see the tears burning at the backs of her eyes, see what he did to her, and her humiliation would be complete.

"Stop right now."

The words were right against her ear, the wolf having moved with preternatural speed. It was too much. She snapped.

HAWKE was about to close his hand around Sienna's nape when she twisted to face him, her eyes devoid of stars. Knowing what she could do, he expected an attack, but she took a deep breath, dropped her head . . . and went up in flames.

A violent red licked with streamers of amber, the inferno gave off no heat, and yet he knew without a doubt that it was lethal beyond anything known to man. Fighting the wolf's frenzied attempts to reach out, to protect, he forced himself to stand in place and look, really look. She was fine inside the blaze. No, not fine. Every muscle in her body was rigid, her hair blowing off her face in a savage psychic breeze, but whatever the fire demanded from her, her skin remained untouched.

Even being able to see her safe, the ten seconds he spent in the heart of flame were the longest of his life. "Do that again," he growled the instant the fire blinked out, "and I swear I'll throw you into the lake."

She raised her head, embers continuing to flicker in her eyes. "I'd like to see you try."

The wolf wasn't used to being so flatly challenged. "What the fuck was that?" He'd seen her exercising her ability before, but never like this, until she was consumed by it.

"A simple energy release." She began to walk away from him again.

His wolf saw red. "Baby, if—"

"Don't. Call. Me. Baby." Turning on her heel, she stared at him, her gaze potent with such destructive power, lesser men might've trembled.

But he was an alpha wolf, and if Sienna thought she was going to make him back off, she had another thing coming. "I'll call you anything I damn well please." He stepped into her personal space, until she had to either step back or have her breasts brush against his chest with every breath.

She held her ground, paradoxically pleasing the wolf. "The only man," she said, her words wrapped in that cold darkness he hadn't seen in her since the first few days after her defection, "I'll allow to use that particular endearment will be my lover. You are no longer in the running for the position."

The rage that tore through him was a ravaging beast full of claws and teeth. But he bit back the primal demands that wanted to escape. And said the words that would keep her with him a while longer. Yeah, he was a selfish prick, but he'd never argued otherwise. Not when it came to Sienna Lauren. "I've never shown anyone else this spot."

The cold dark retreated to reveal the stars in her eyes. "You're playing me." A stark vulnerability in her face, her soul stripped bare.

It didn't rock him how much he wanted what he saw in her—the need had become an unrelenting ache by now. "Doesn't make it any less true." His wolf waited, tense.

When she fell into step beside him again, he clenched his hand to keep from reaching out to fist it in the jewel-dark silk of her hair, to tug her close, close enough that he could rub his face against it . . . close enough that he could pet and cajole her into melting into him. "Do all Xs have hair like yours?" he asked, needing to hear the sound of her voice if he couldn't have the touch of her skin.

A genuinely startled glance. "I don't know. But it's funny how my hair fits, isn't it?"

Fire hidden in darkness. Yes, her hair fit. "Tell me about your abilities."

"You already know."

"Not from you." Judd had given him the lowdown, instructed him on what to do if Sienna ever went critical and the others in the LaurenNet were incapacitated. His wolf snarled. Hawke had made some ruthless decisions in his time, but he didn't know if he had it in him to cause her that kind of hurt, the kind that would slam her into immediate unconsciousness.

There was a long silence from the woman by his side. As the minutes passed, he began to hear faint rustling in the undergrowth, nocturnal creatures starting to go about their business again after the brutal blast of Sienna's power. "They call it cold fire . . . X-fire," she said at last. "It can burn things to ash . . . bodies to ash, within microseconds."

He heard old pain in her words. "Were you a child?"

A rough nod, but she jerked away from his touch, refusing comfort. Her voice, when it came, told him they wouldn't be talking about her childhood pain. It was coated in frost, but he heard the tremor beneath. "The cold fire is the first wave. The power has the capacity to build until it reaches—"

Another silence, his heartbeat synchronizing with her own.

"Synergy, it's called synergy. If I ever reach synergy—" A sharp inhalation. "There's a reason they call us living, breathing weapons." Turning to him for the first time since she'd begun to speak, she shot him a piercing look. "You don't

have to worry about the pack being in danger. It does sometimes scare me that I'll lose control," she said with raw honesty, "but that means I spend even more time strengthening
my shields. We also have a failsafe set in place just in case."

Understanding that that failsafe might well be a lethal one,
he said, "Do you really think I'd let you go that easily?"

An implacable glance from eyes that were suddenly decades older than him. "I'm not yours to let go."

RECOVERED FROM COMPUTER 2(A)
TAGS: PERSONAL CORRESPONDENCE, FATHER, ACTION NOT REQUIRED

FROM: Alice <alice@scifac.edu>
TO: Dad <ellison@archsoc.edu>
DATE: November 18th, 1971 at 10:32am
SUBJECT: re: re: re: JA Article

Dear Dad,

Thank you for your last e-mail. Yes, you're right. What I'm doing, it
may one day help the Xs. That's what I must cling to as things get
harder.

This is just a quick note as I'm in Paris, about to head out to
meet one of my volunteers. He's a fascinating boy—intelligent,
witty, and far too calm for his age. I've noticed that with all the Xs
I've met in person. I hate to write this, to recognize the reason
behind it, but it's as if they live their lives in fast-forward, growing
old before they've ever been young.

I'll write again after the meeting.

Love,
Alice

Chapter 14

IT WAS LATE afternoon, with both Toby and Marlee involved in after-school activities, when Walker cornered Lara in the break room of the infirmary, shutting the door behind himself.

Having obviously scented him as he neared, she leaned against the counter, arms folded. "Yes?" Her eyes, a tawny shade of brown that reminded him of a fox's bright gaze, held nothing but professional interest. "Is someone hurt?"

He echoed her position against the door, making an unexpected discovery—he'd gotten used to the way Lara had looked at him until the day on the cliff. It caused a strange, sharp sensation in his chest to no longer see that indefinable something in her gaze. "How was your date?" he asked, not certain why he felt compelled to ask.

Lara's smile was a sultry curve of her lips. "Kieran knows how to make a woman feel good."

An icy calm came over Walker's mind, cold intent spearing through his veins. He was a telepath trained to work with children, his touch subtle, but he measured at 7.8 on the Gradient. It meant he had the capacity to kill without leaving a mark. "He's younger than you." Too weak and green to ensure Lara came to no harm, regardless of where her vocation might take her.

Lara shrugged, her full breasts pushing against the rust-colored fabric of the V-neck sweater that shaped itself to the curves of her body. "Not by much."

"That's not what I meant."

Turning, she began to prepare coffee with swift, sure

movements of those capable hands he'd seen care for so many in the den. "I won't argue he's a little immature, but aren't most men in their early twenties?"

Walker knew she'd given him her back very much deliberately, the rebuff no less pointed for all it was silent. However, the only orders Walker had ever followed were the ones that meant his family would be safe. "He has no idea who you are." Even at thirty, Lara was young, very young, to be the healer assigned to the den.

Unlike most packs, SnowDancer had more than one healer spread throughout its vast territory, each blood-bonded to a SnowDancer lieutenant to permit a type of power transference unique to changelings. Though several had decades on Lara, who was blood-bonded directly to Hawke, she held their unqualified trust and respect. Her healing abilities were unparalleled, but more, she had the will and the heart to handle the most dominant members of the pack without flinching. That woman deserved a man as strong, not a callow youth.

"Really, Walker," Lara said, facing him with coffee cup in hand, several of her curls having escaped the bun at the base of her neck to kiss her face. "You'd think I was going to mate with Kieran." Blowing a breath across the hot surface of her drink, she stepped forward, her smile so shallow, it cut like a scalpel. "I need to check on a patient."

He had the feeling she was lying to him, but he couldn't be certain, so he permitted her to pass, the warm elegance of her scent stroking over him as she left. She was halfway to the patient rooms when she glanced back and caught him with that fox-brown gaze. "Sometimes," she said, "it's just about sex."

SIENNA had the afternoon free, but after completing the coursework for an advanced physics class she was taking through the online branch of a major university, she decided to head out to the White Zone and volunteer to assist with the after-school activities. As she walked, she tried to keep her mind on dry academic facts, but it was impossible not to think of the emotional storm and dark beauty of the previous night.

The moss-laden grotto Hawke had led her to after the cold

burn of her ability had encased her in violent flame had been alive with night-blooming wildflowers, the small pond at the center so tranquil and clear as to be a mirror. Her soul had filled with wonder as she touched her fingertips to a delicate bloom, her heart aching with the realization that he was giving her a gift, giving her a piece of himself he'd never shown to another.

It had threatened to break her. Because no matter how drawn he was to her, no matter how potent the tug between them, Hawke had a will of iron. That will would have him shredding her to bloody pieces tonight as he put his hands on another woman. As he kissed her. More.

"Sinna!" Ben skidded to a halt at her feet not far into the White Zone, breaking the agonizing loop of thought. "Hi!" He threw his arms wide.

Going down on her haunches, she cuddled him tight, whispering, "Do you want me to do up your shoelace?" in his ear.

A furtive nod.

Smiling at the male pride that wouldn't let Ben admit the need for help to the other kids, she did up the dangling lace, then rose to her feet to find herself being called upon to referee a game of hide-and-seek. Drew tracked her down there ten minutes later. "Hello, sugarpie." Wrapping an arm around her shoulders, he tugged her into the warmth of his body even as she scowled at the ridiculous pet name he'd given her after discovering—and feeding—her addiction to sweets.

"Temper, temper." A finger tapping her nose. "Play nice or I won't give you the pecan-and-nougat candy bar *somebody* really loves."

In spite of the pain wracking her insides, it was impossible not to smile at this man who'd claimed her as a sister, who'd laughed, tricked, and teased his way into her life. "I thought you were in Arizona with the falcons."

"Got back a couple of hours ago." He slid the candy bar into her pocket.

Leaning into him, she sniffed, loud and obvious. "Hmm, freshly showered. What did you do when you got back?"

Drew gave her a wicked, wicked smile that creased his cheeks with lean male dimples. "Well now, I'll just leave that to your imagination, Ms. Sienna Lauren."

Laughter bubbled out of her, pumping through the giant bruise that was her heart. "You like being mated." He'd always been one of the most easygoing people in the den, but there was a fierce happiness to him now, his adoration of Indigo open.

"Yep." He lifted a finger to his lips when a little girl poked her head around the bush where she was hiding. She ducked back. "I've come to give you some sage advice, being as I'm so much older and wiser."

"Says the man who once stole Indigo's phone and recorded himself howling her name as the ringtone."

His responding words were unexpectedly serious. "I had the same problem as you."

Sienna went to snap back a reply but closed her mouth partway. "Yes . . . you did." Drew was only four years younger than Indigo, but he didn't occupy the same place in the hierarchy. It had made his courtship of the lieutenant difficult.

"I didn't give up."

Stung, she pulled away. "I'm not giving up." She'd *asked* Hawke to be with her, been rejected with such finality she was still bleeding inside.

"I dunno, sweetheart." Drew rubbed his jaw, his gaze astute for all that his comment was a lazy drawl. "From where I'm standing, it sure as hell looks like you're giving Rosalie and Hawke the green light."

Cold fire licked at her fingertips. Smothering it in her palm, she checked to make sure the kids were happy in their game before hissing a response under her breath. "I'd like to point out that you had a more powerful platform." Drew might not be a lieutenant, but Sienna had seen the way Hawke and the others listened to him.

"Yeah, that does kinda suck for you."

"You make me want to throw things at you."

He hugged her again, before she could put some distance between them. Then the most sneaky wolf in the den lowered his voice and whispered, "But you've got an advantage, sweetheart. You're already in his head. And you know how to mess with it."

*   *   *

HAVING spent the day buried in strategy and preparation sessions for a war that seemed inevitable, Hawke didn't get outside until after night had fallen in a lush black blanket. He was at the lake nearest the den, staring at the gentle lap of water when Rosalie appeared out of the trees to make her way across the pebbled shore. Her walk was that of a woman confident in her sensuality—the complete opposite of the cardinal Psy who watched him with an unstudied hunger that had almost broken his resolve last night.

A single touch and he would've had her naked in the silver kiss of the moonlight, her back cushioned by the softness of the lush green grass, her hair a ruby red flame over the wild-flowers. So vivid was the image that the wolf growled, wanting to take control, to go hunting its favorite prey.

"That is not," Rosalie said, fitting her tall, voluptuous body to his side, "the look of a man who can't wait to get me into bed."

He played his fingers through her hair, and though the thick, mahogany waves were beautiful, his mind kept circling back to the dark fall of silk he'd seen under the moon last night. "You're too good for me, Rosa."

A husky laugh. "Of course I am." She pressed a kiss to his jaw, her breasts brushing his chest as she shifted to face him. "I can feel your wolf tugging at the reins."

Hawke hated that he was being pushed into this by the physical needs of his changeling nature. But that had nothing to do with Rosalie. "I'm a bastard."

"That you are," she agreed, linking her arms around his neck.

He raised an eyebrow.

"Wow, talk about alpha. Makes me want to say 'yes, please and again.'" Tracing his lips with her fingertip, she gave him a solemn look from those thickly lashed eyes of deepest green. "You know this, us, it's freely given? No strings."

Instead of lunging at the invitation as he'd half expected, Hawke's wolf sat sullen, though it was being torn apart by the most savage sexual need. "I know."

She tipped her head to the side, her hair cascading over her shoulder. "Then why aren't you ripping my clothes off?" There was no judgment in the words, only the concern of a friend.

Reaching up, he brushed his fingers over her cheekbone. The wolf found her sensual, beautiful, intelligent. The man agreed. There was just one problem. "Indigo was right"—a realization that tilted his world on its axis—"it won't satisfy my hunger." The need that ravaged him was hotly specific, targeted to only one woman.

"You mean," Rosalie said, hands on her hips, "you're blowing me off after getting me all hot and bothered?"

"You mad?" He nuzzled at her, because the wolf didn't want to hurt her.

Rosalie laughed, and it was a big, sensual sound from a woman who lived her life with a generosity of spirit that didn't allow her to hold grudges. "It's not exactly a surprise, sweetie." Still smiling, she kissed him full on the mouth. "I came to you because we're friends—you needed touch, and I figured you were too stubborn to go after her. I didn't realize it had gotten to this point between you two."

Hawke growled at the implied conclusion in her statement. "Just because I realize the need, doesn't mean I'm going to act on it."

"Let me make sure I have this right." Rosalie poked him in the chest. "You want her so bad I can all but taste your arousal—and damn, but it's sexy—but you're not hunting her down?"

Hawke thought of how young Sienna was, how untried. *I have no plans to die a virgin.*

He was no lover for a virgin, especially now, with his control so ragged it was in fucking shreds. Hell, he'd probably scare her so bad she'd never want to have sex again. "It's complicated."

"Huh." Rosalie didn't sound convinced, but his sat phone rang before she could grill him any further.

Answering it, he was surprised to hear José's voice. "It's Luc's turn," he said curtly, in no mood to babysit packmates who should know better. If they got into shit tonight, he'd let them cool their heels in jail.

The bar owner blew out a breath. "I'm thinking you don't want another man handling your girl."

Hawke's claws sliced out. "Anyone touches her, they're dead."

"She's fine—if you don't count the amount of alcohol she's slugging back . . . or the cat keeping her warm."

Hawke's growl rolled up out of his chest to color the air. "Make damn sure she doesn't leave with him." Stabbing the End button, he looked up to find Rosalie grinning from ear to ear. "Quiet."

"Hey, I'm just an innocent bystander." She raised her hands. "Though you might want to take off your mean face before you go get her."

"She can bloody well deal with it." It was a snarl.

SIENNA surreptitiously passed "her" sixth shot to Kit.

He made a face. "Did you have to order this girly shit?"

"I am a girl, in case you failed to notice." The vodkas she'd ordered earlier had been easier to get rid of—the colorless liquid blended in with the empty or ice cube–filled glasses the waitstaff cleared away on a regular basis. The shots, on the other hand, would stick out.

Shuddering, Kit made quick work of the butterscotch liqueur and slid the glass over before anyone was the wiser as to who had taken the actual shot.

"Dear God that was foul." He gulped his beer. "That's the last one I'm doing for you."

"I think that should do the trick. José's giving me the eye." Sienna smiled goofily at the bartender, playing drunk.

The big deer changeling gave her a stare as flat as any wolf's.

Deciding not to push her luck, she dipped her head toward Kit—to find him looking unexpectedly serious. "What is it?"

"I know you've got strong feelings for Hawke," he said, angling his shoulders to face her, "but are you ready for where this, tonight, might lead?"

Sienna had asked herself the same question and found only one answer. "I'll never know unless he gives us a chance." She closed her hand over Kit's. "Maybe I'll discover I've taken on more than I can handle," she admitted, because Hawke was never going to be an easy lover—if she even got him to consider the idea of a relationship. "But I know, I *know*, that I can't sit by and watch him go to another woman."

An intent gaze. "You've really thought about it."

"Yes." Whatever happened, continuing on as they had—with the relentless beat of unresolved tension between them—was no longer an option. "Doesn't mean I'm not nervous."

Kit turned up his hand to squeeze hers, a feline smile in his eyes. "My money's on you."

Leaning forward to press her lips to his cheek, she said, "When should I climb on the bar again?"

"Given the time José made the call, and how fast Hawke is probably driving, I'd say in about two minutes."

"Good." Picking up her cell phone from where it sat on the bar, she tucked it into a back pocket, having not brought a purse. "That gives you two minutes to get out."

"I'm not running." Pure affront.

Sienna had been in a pack long enough to understand male pride—even stupid male pride. "It's not running. You'll mess up my whole plan if Hawke's focused on you instead of me."

"Huh." Finishing off his beer, he rose off the bar stool.

Then he did something completely, totally unexpected. Hauling her against his body, he took her mouth in a hot, wild tangle of a kiss that spoke of the man he would one day become. Her heart was pumping double-time by the time he finished. "Um, well, that was . . ." Okay, she thought, okay. Maybe they didn't have the combustible chemistry she had with Hawke, but Kit could get her into bed if he put his mind to it. And that was a surprise. "Not nice," she finally managed to get out. "A very 'not nice' kiss."

Smiling in masculine satisfaction, Kit rocked back on his heels. "Fair warning—now you smell like me in an intimate way. He's not going to like that."

Cunning cat. Good thing he was on her side. "Showtime."

Kit leaned in to speak with his lips brushing her ear. "I won't be far. If he's too out of control, I'll get you out."

"He won't hurt me." Of that she was more certain than she was of anything else in her life. "Haul me up."

Kit lifted her onto the bar beside another girl, a slender leopard female who blew Sienna a kiss. Whistles sounded from around the bar as Kit melted away, leaving the two of them silhouetted against the electric blue lights of the glass wall behind the bar, the bottles of alcohol so many glittering jewels against the glow. Well aware Nicki was only flirting with her to tease Jason, Sienna blew back a kiss, and the bar exploded.

The crowd was chanting "kiss, kiss, kiss" when Hawke walked inside.

That was when Sienna learned the meaning of the term *alpha*.

Chapter 15

HE DIDN'T SAY a word, didn't so much as make a sound, but as soon as one person saw him, they nudged another. It took less than thirty seconds for the club to go deadly silent, José turning off the music at the same instant.

Nicki slid down the bar into Jason's arms, mouthing, "Good luck," at Sienna before she disappeared into the group of DarkRiver youths in one corner.

Reaching the bar, Hawke looked up. It was the wolf who watched her, the wolf who said, "Shoulder or feet?"

She swallowed. "Feet."

"Good choice." He didn't step back as she sat down and slipped off the bar, his body heat slapping against her bare skin with masculine aggressiveness.

Suddenly, the corset-style top she'd bought on her own after that shopping trip with Nicki didn't seem such a great idea. It left her feeling all but naked, her shoulders bare, her breasts plumped up above the bodice, her abdomen exposed from just below her belly button to the top of her low-slung jeans. With her breath coming in jagged bursts, it felt as if she was offering her breasts to him with each inhale.

Hawke didn't say a single word, gave no indication that he'd noticed her state of dress as he put his hand on her lower back and herded her to the door.

She almost went.

Halfway there, she dug in her heels, determined to make him admit he wasn't just here to pick up a pack member who'd had too much to drink. But one look at his face and she knew it'd be a *very* bad idea to confront him here. She could see

Nicki and Evie over his shoulder, frantically shaking their heads. Jason was wincing, but edging forward while Kit and Tai had begun to shoulder their way through the crowd—as if to protect her.

Their loyalty ignited a deep warmth with her.

But this was a private war.

Sliding her arm through Hawke's, she pressed her breast against the part of his arm bared by the short sleeves of his white T-shirt. "Where's the car?" She didn't bother to slur her voice. His senses were too acute to have missed the fact that she was stone-cold sober.

In response, he untangled his arm from hers, put his hand on her lower back again—the touch a hot, rough shock that made things low in her body clench—and walked her out.

"Good luck," the bouncer muttered as she passed, not even making a token attempt at pretending he was going to stand in Hawke's way.

If she'd been him, she wouldn't have either.

Because unlike the other night, Hawke didn't look pissed. This was an anger that went deeper, ran far colder. Why the difference, she didn't know . . . until they got to beside the SUV, and he leaned down to growl, "You smell of another man."

Her body flared with sensation at the heat of him so close, but she wasn't about to surrender and lose the ground she'd gained. "Yeah, well, I'm not a wolf, but I'm guessing you smell of another woman."

He bit her. No warning, no nothing. His teeth just sank into the curve where her neck flowed into her shoulder. She jumped, felt his hands lock onto her hips. Her spine was melting, her skin taut in expectation—but if she gave in now, it was all over. *Think, Sienna, think.* Close to impossible when he was surrounding her, when he was taking her over. Damp heat bloomed between her legs, and his nostrils flared. *Oh, God.*

Acting more in self-defense than as a result of rational thought, she raised a fine line of X-fire where he gripped her.

He wrenched away with a snarl. "You burned me." The wolf. Very much the wolf.

Raising her hand to her shoulder, she touched the lingering heat of his bite. "Just a warning." She'd been careful not to burn, only to threaten. "I don't like having your teeth in me."

His eyes gleamed. "Liar."

She couldn't hold back her gasp as he was suddenly in her face again, but found the will to say, "Did you take out that ad?"

He traced the bite mark with his thumb. "Why are you half-naked?" An almost careless question . . . except that his free hand was on her lower back again, and this time, he was using the rough pads of his fingers to stroke the strip of skin bared by her top. Slow and easy. And again.

She shivered.

"You're cold."

He'd thrown her into the SUV and come around to take his seat before she knew it. They were already halfway down the block by the time her heart stopped racing enough that she could speak. "I don't want to go home." Part of her was terrified because she had no idea what to do with him in this kind of a mood, but retreat was not an option. Not when she was playing for keeps. "Hawke? Are you listening to me?"

Picking up a bottle of water from the holder between the seats, he said, "Wash off his scent."

Her thighs clenched at the possessive demand in that tone, but she folded her arms. "No."

A low growl filled the SUV, tightening her nipples to pain-ful points. Unsettled—though not shocked—by the visceral depth of her response, she was attempting to find some kind of solid ground when he wrenched the car to a stop on the side of the road and turned. "Then I'll do it." Pale, pale eyes gone night-glow, a voice so calm as to make it patently clear the predator was well and truly off the leash.

Difficult as it was to withstand the impact of his domi-nance, she reminded herself his wasn't the only power in the vehicle. "Touch me and I'll singe your eyebrows off."

A shrug. "They'll grow back." Tugging off the scarf she'd used to tie up her hair, he dampened it in the water.

"Hey!" She pushed back at him as he crowded her into the corner.

"You wanted to play, baby." Soft words that had her freez-ing in place. "So we'll play."

Her mouth went dry as he ran the damp cloth over her lips with piercing focus. She knew she should protest his actions, but her voice seemed to have deserted her with him so close—so big and gorgeous and furious that he took over every inch of space, every breath of air. "There," he murmured, running the cloth down her neck and over her shoulder before leaning down to press his lips to the bite mark.

Arousal twisted through her body, until she had to sink her teeth into her lower lip to still her moan. That wasn't an erogenous zone. She knew that. And yet she didn't dare move for fear he'd stop the delicious torture. Another kiss, wet and hot. His hair brushing against her skin as he licked the mark, each strand a searing brand.

"Next time that cub puts his hands on you," he said, raising his head after another lingering taste of her skin, "I'll tear out his throat and feed it to him." The words were said in such a reasonable tone that it took her a minute to process their meaning.

Lurching up, she grabbed the front of his T-shirt. "You will not touch any of my friends."

Patient wolf eyes. Deadly wolf eyes.

"Hawke."

He leaned forward and licked the bite mark again.

Her entire body shuddered, her breasts protesting the stiff confines of the corset. "No touching Kit," she whispered, barely able to speak past the dark pressure of a desire so long denied, it threatened to devour her.

His hand closed around her throat. Not a threat. Just the most possessive way a predatory changeling male had of touching a woman outside of sex. "Don't say his name." He brushed his thumb across her pulse.

Closing her hand over his wrist, she said, "You're being unreasonable." The instant the words left her mouth, she realized she wasn't going to get "human" behavior from him tonight. Hawke's wolf had always been close to the surface, and right now, it was in charge. Or perhaps it was more accurate to say that both man and wolf had shrugged off any pretensions to civilized behavior.

"I still don't want to go home." It wasn't quite the truth—she'd be delighted to be alone with him. But if she was going to win him, and keep him, he had to understand that he wasn't going to be able to walk all over her. Because he damn well would if he thought he could.

His gaze went watchful, waiting.

"I want to go dancing again."

A slow smile.

"In a club," she added, quite certain rational thought would become a distant memory if he took her into his arms when they were alone, if he put his mouth on her skin, his hands on her body. "There." Breasts flushing at the hot pulse of need in the most intimate part of her, she pointed to a random club. "That one looks popular."

The growl was so low and deep that she felt it with her body first, her skin shimmering in reaction, the stiff points of her nipples rubbing against the corset. Only the discipline she'd learned in the Net kept her from giving in. "Stop trying to intimidate me."

Instead of answering, he returned his attention to the road and began driving. It didn't take her long to realize they were most definitely heading back to den territory. Recognizing she'd lost that round, she forced herself to regroup, to remember that she wasn't dealing with the cool, calculating alpha of SnowDancer at this moment, but with the wildness that lived in his heart.

That didn't mean she was about to surrender. Even if she had no idea what she'd do if he decided to stop stalking her and pounced. "Do you like my top?"

"Is that what it is?"

"Latest style," she assured him, ignoring the silky menace of his response. "Laces up the side, so it's easier to take off."

His hands clenched on the steering wheel as he headed up into the mountains.

"And the boots." She lifted one leg up to the dash, stroked her hand over her thigh. "They make me—"

The car shuddered to a halt near the perimeter of den territory. Hawke was turning to her when he went motionless in a way she recognized. Predatory. Listening. Snapping to alertness, she brought down her leg and swept out with her telepathic senses . . . to find more than a few Psy minds in the vicinity.

"Psy," Hawke said under his breath at the same instant. "Stay in the car." He was gone before she could argue.

Tempting as it was to disobey him, her damn boots would make her a liability. So she gave him a different kind of backup. Keeping him on the periphery of her psychic senses, she expanded her telepathic reach once more. Unsurprisingly, the intruders were shielded. Hawke's mind was even more impenetrable, his natural shields a solid wall. She'd never know if he was hurt or in trouble.

Frustrated, she slid back her door with utmost care.

The night air raised goose bumps over her body, but she brushed aside that minor concern and focused every one of her senses on *listening*. With all of her senses—psychic and otherwise. The instant she heard even the slightest indication of a fight, she'd blow out every Psy mind in the vicinity.

This was her home. Her man. No one was allowed to fuck with either of them.

IT took Hawke's wolf a bare minute to realize that Sienna was too smart, too dangerous, not to have come up with a plan in case things went balls-up. *Shit*. Pulling out the sat phone from his pocket, he typed in a short, terse message.

Do not act unless I give the signal. A howl from the wolf could carry for miles in the right conditions. *Don't give yourself away.* If anyone on the Council learned that she was alive, they'd come after her, no holds barred. Since Hawke had no intention of letting them take her, things would turn brutal fast.

Then don't get hurt.

The return message made him grin despite the tense circumstances. Slipping the phone back into his pocket, he made his way with wolf-stealth to the area where he'd scented the intruders. His wolf was angry at the trespass, but its anger was a silent, focused thing, both parts of him conscious of the need to uncover the enemy's agenda. SnowDancer stood in danger of becoming arrogant after their recent successes at foiling the covert operations, but the fact was, the psychic race posed a powerful threat.

Shifting from shadow to shadow without a sound, he brought himself to within five feet of the intruders.

". . . too many trees."

"He's correct. We need a more—" The speaker paused for a few seconds. "We'll have to continue this later. I'm needed at the base."

The third Psy put one of his hands on each of the other two men's shoulders and teleported them out. Hawke could've taken down at least one, maybe two, before the teleport, but he let them go. The first order of business was to figure out their game plan, something that'd be far easier to do if whoever was leading this wasn't tipped off to the fact that Snow-Dancer was aware of any planned assault.

Checking to confirm the area was secure, he was about to head back to the SUV when he paused. Sienna had been Ming's protégée, had spent most of her life studying military tactics and strategies utilized by the Council. While the protective side of him wanted to cocoon her in safety, he was also the alpha of SnowDancer—cool, calculated, and willing to use any advantage to protect his pack.

Bringing out his phone, he called her. "Can you get to me?" he asked, stepping a small distance away from the actual site to avoid being seen or heard by any concealed technology—it paid to be extra paranoid after what Henry Scott had almost pulled off last year.

"Yes. I can see you with my telepathic eye."

He frowned but didn't say anything until she appeared out of the night, her skin silver in the moonlight where it was bared by that ridiculous strip of fabric she called a top. "Can I be tracked that way by all Psy?" he asked, figuring it'd take a single, precise claw swipe to cut the ties that held the corset so snug to her body.

Sienna shook her head, hair once more tied up with that scarf. "Not you, specifically. I meant I did a telepathic sweep and found a single changeling mind."

Satisfied, he pointed out the compromised area, told her what he'd overheard. "Anything strike you?"

Scanning the lightly wooded section, Sienna rubbed her hands up and down her upper arms in an absent manner. "Nothing you haven't already considered, I'm sure—if they need a more open space, I'm thinking staging post."

"Yeah." Walking over, he wrapped his arms around her

from behind. "You're frozen." Not surprising. But his wolf wasn't irritated at her choice of clothing anymore, not now that he'd claimed skin privileges. "Come on," he said, breathing in the wild spice of her scent, "we won't learn anything more here tonight." He'd get the techs to come out tomorrow and do a sweep, check the area was clean.

Sienna was uncharacteristically subdued as they walked to the car and got in. Though the cold didn't bother him in the slightest, he turned on the heater to high as he pulled away. "What's going on in that head of yours?"

"My race attacks your people again." Quiet words. "Is that why you hate the Psy? Because they never stop?"

Echoes of blood and pain, of watching people he loved fall under claws and teeth as packmates turned on one another. "No." The scars left by the violence over two decades ago would never disappear, but he'd learned to move past the feral anger that had driven him those first few years. "I don't hate all Psy. Just those who follow the Council."

Sienna squeezed her arms tight around herself, though the car was plenty warm now. This was the one thing, the *one thing* she'd never factored into the equation. Yes, the attraction between them was the rawest of cravings, strong enough that it had finally brought Hawke to her. But, how could she possibly expect him to feel anything deeper for her, for a woman born of a race that had caused him so much pain that his voice went wolf when he spoke of it even now, his expression grim with old shadows.

The den had become home, the SnowDancers her friends and family, but she remembered how it had been when they'd first arrived. Coping with the dual shock of being severed from the Net and of her inexplicable, violent reaction to the alpha with ice-cold eyes, Sienna had focused on simple survival those first few months. Still, she'd trained under a Councilor, was the niece of an Arrow. She'd filed away the whispers, the overheard snippets of conversation. All to do with the pack's stunned amazement that Hawke, "of all people," would give a Psy family sanctuary "after what they'd done to his own."

Her throat was suddenly lined with razors.

"Were the Psy," she said, forcing herself to ask the hardest question, "responsible for the deaths of your parents?" She knew he'd lost them as a child, but no one ever spoke of the circumstances of that loss.

Hawke didn't react for almost a minute. When he did, it was only to say, "There are some things you don't need to know." A slap down. Cool. Unvarnished. Absolute.

It was in her nature to rebel against him, deepest instinct telling her that he would only ever respect a woman with the strength to stand up to him, but she had no right to ask him to return to a nightmare. "I apologize." Turning her attention to the passing darkness of the forest, her trembling fingers hidden in her fists, she stared unseeing into the night.

RECOVERED FROM COMPUTER 2(A)
TAGS: PERSONAL CORRESPONDENCE, FATHER, ACTION NOT REQUIRED

FROM: Alice <alice@scifac.edu>
TO: Dad <ellison@archsoc.edu>
DATE: February 12th, 1972 at 10:00pm
SUBJECT: Published at Last!!

Dear Dad,

I've just received the first copies of my book. I know you didn't care for the non-scholarly title but I do think *The Mysterious E Designation: Empathic Gifts & Shadows* sounds snazzy.

To answer the question in your last e-mail—yes, I am still single, but I have time yet before you're consigned to retirement without grandchildren (especially since you plan to never retire). Tell Mom I went over to the house and the flowers are blooming beautifully—one of my empathic friends has been helping me with the gardens. E-Psy have such green fingers. Maybe I should study that next time.

As for the X Project, it's been almost a year since I began and I've realized I can't rely solely on my tiny live sample. I've asked for and received archival assistance from a Psy librarian who will mine the PsyNet for data about past Xs, while I do the same in the libraries I can access.

My premise is that this mutation would not exist unless it had a purpose, but George pointed out how many rare diseases are caused by mutations. If I were to follow that line of thought, I'd have to conclude that the Xs are so uncommon because they have no function and that their deaths are an attempt by nature to control a dangerous disease. That's not a thought I'm comfortable having, but as a scientist, I know it's as viable a theory as any.

I so wish you were home so we could have these discussions in person.

Love,
Alice

Chapter 16

LARA SAT AT her desk in the infirmary, having stayed late to keep an eye on an elderly wolf who'd had a fall, but her mind wasn't on the papers in front of her. She'd enjoyed tormenting Walker about her date with Kieran, but her amusement had faded the instant he'd left, to be replaced by a throbbing ache that mocked her attempt at getting over him.

The fact was, the attraction she felt toward Walker Lauren was no simple thing—it had been growing slowly ever since he entered the den, layer by layer, word by word. The more she learned about the man behind the reserved mask, the harder she fell. His rebuff had bruised those emotions, bruised them badly, but she'd been stupid to think they'd disappear just because she wanted them gone.

It didn't surprise her how tempting it was to cling to the apparent jealousy that had driven him to seek her out. But even if she had read him right, she was certain the emotion wouldn't make him change his mind—Walker wasn't the kind of man who vacillated, and he'd been damn unequivocal that their single kiss had been a mistake.

However Lara, too, wasn't a woman who made decisions lightly, and she'd made one to move on. And as her friend Ava had pointed out in her frank, no-nonsense way earlier today, Kieran might not have been a good fit for her, but he was the first man she'd gone out with in the past six months.

"You haven't," Ava had continued, "given any other man a chance to impact your feelings toward Walker."

With that truth in mind, she called up a senior tech who'd asked her out three months ago, and set up a lunch date for the following day. Feeling good about his instant agreement, she was just hanging up when she saw Walker in the doorway. Once, she'd have assumed he'd come to see her. Tonight, her immediate thought was that someone was hurt. "Who?" she asked, rising to her feet. "What do—"

He halted her with a hand on her wrist, his skin rough against her own, his grip unbreakable. Startled, she froze. Her shock was the only thing that muted her instinctive response to his touch. Because she loved Walker's hands, loved the calluses that came from what he did in his spare time, the beautiful things he created—including tiny pieces of furniture for his daughter's cherished dollhouse.

Now, that strong, warm hand held her in place as he leaned forward to put a tray of food on her desk, the dark water and snow-dusted fir of his scent enclosing her in a sensual prison that allowed no escape. "You missed dinner. Again."

Her wolf's entire body quivered at what from a male wolf would signal the start of a serious courtship, but Lara squelched that reaction. She wasn't about to set herself up for more hurt. "I was busy." In spite of her calm words, when he nudged her back into her chair, she went without argument.

However, when he leaned that tall, strong body back against her desk—so close that she could've stroked her hand over his jean-clad thigh, the worn denim stretched taut over firm muscle—picked up the plate, and went to feed her a forkful, she jerked herself free of the lingering tendrils of shock. "Here," she said, taking the plate. "You don't want to do that."

"Why?"

Sliding her chair a little farther from him, she forced herself to answer. "It's an intimacy . . . like skin privileges."

Walker didn't ask any further questions, but neither did he leave—as Lara's body language indicated he should. He knew he was pushing uninvited into her space, but he also knew he didn't like it when she didn't take care of herself and he'd had enough of watching that happen. And though it might've been smarter to keep his distance, given her disconcerting effect on him . . . he'd missed her.

"Did you hear," he asked, because Lara was the one person with whom he'd always found words, "that Marlee joined the children's choir?" It was the first time he'd made a deliberate effort to initiate—rebuild—any kind of a bond with a woman.

A genuine smile broke through the shadows on Lara's face. "I heard Ben and her practicing. She's got a beautiful voice."

So, Walker thought, did Lara.

SIENNA jerked upright in bed, her plain black tank top stuck to her skin. The nightmare hadn't raised its ugly head for months, but it had made up for lost time tonight. Shoving off the blankets, she swung her legs over the side of the bed and pushed back strands of hair that had escaped her braid to stick to sweat-damp skin.

"Perfect." Ming, looking at her as a human might a high-performance vehicle. "You really are the most perfect genetic specimen."

Perfect—if you wanted a cold-blooded mass murderer. Except of course, her blood no longer ran cold. "Still a potential murderer," she whispered, trembling so hard her vision wavered.

"We are who we make ourselves." Judd's voice, compelling in its very quietness. "Don't ever give up your will to some idea of genetic predestination."

She clung to his words. Judd had made it. He'd changed the nature of his gift from death to life, become a healer. That wasn't a path Sienna could follow, her ability too much of violence, but she'd forge her own path—and not as the butcher Ming had intended her to be, the butcher he'd spent so many years grooming in the expectation of owning her body and soul. Until she'd proven too dangerous even for him. "You didn't break me, you bastard." Not then, and not now.

Rising to her feet, she stripped and walked into the shower, setting the temperature close to boiling point. Only when her skin was pulsing with heat almost painful in its intensity did she step out and rub herself down. A glance at the clock showed her it was five a.m. Dressing and plaiting her damp hair, she logged in to the roster to double-check her schedule and saw a reminder that she was meant to attend a training session from noon until late in the afternoon.

Checking the rest of the roster, she coded in a call to

Riordan. It went through with visuals. A rumpled-sounding wolf said, "I'm getting up, Mom. I promise," from under a blanket. "Gimme just a minute."

Her lips twitched. "You mind if I take your shift this morning?" He was rostered on from six to eleven.

Riordan raised his head to meet her gaze, his hair sticking up in a mess that was mysteriously attractive. "Dear God, you're showered. Crazy woman."

"Since I am . . ."

"You sure?"

"Wouldn't ask if I wasn't." If she kept moving, then maybe she'd forget the bleak insight she'd had in the SUV last night, forget that the past stood as an opaque barrier between her and the only man who'd ever broken through her own shields. "You can pay me back later in the week."

"Sounds good. Thanks, Sin."

Logging off, she grabbed a small daypack and walked out to the communal kitchen/dining area in this sector of the den. It was empty, the lighting dim. But someone had started the coffee, and there was a still-warm tray of muffins on the counter. The sight made her heart lift.

Forcing herself to wait, she stashed a water bottle in her pack, along with a sandwich she put together using the fresh ingredients in the cooler. That done, she poured herself a glass of milk—a habit for which both Evie and Riordan teased her unmercifully—chose the biggest muffin on the tray and sat down to indulge. Her eyes almost rolled back into her head at the first bite.

Cream cheese and peaches—her favorite.

Licking her fingers after finishing it, she glanced at the tray, bit her lower lip. Food was the most innocent of sensual pleasures but one she never took for granted, remembering all too well the nutrition bars that had been the mainstay of her diet for so many years. It was Hawke, she remembered with a stab of pain deep within, who had given her her first bite of something that had set her senses humming.

She'd been shaky, on her knees on the grass, her arms around the kids as they'd blacked out after Walker cut their connection to the PsyNet. Judd had stood in front, Walker at the back, both of them giving her time to make certain Toby and Marlee wouldn't break away from the newly created familial net into which Sienna had pulled them, wouldn't seek to rejoin the Net.

So blue, she remembered thinking as she raised her head and met the gaze of the man who stood opposite Judd's protective form, his hair brilliant even in the dull sunlight that fateful morning. *So lethal*, had been her next thought. They'd done their research, and so she'd known who he was, what he might yet do to the adults, herself included.

But Toby and Marlee, they were children, and wolves loved children. Judd, Walker, and Sienna had bet the kids' lives on that bit of knowledge, hoping against hope that the two youngest members of the family would find some way to gain the necessary biofeedback from the wolf pack once the adults were gone. Because though—once he'd realized they'd fetch no ransom—the wolf alpha had ordered them to cut their PsyNet links if they were to have any chance of gaining sanctuary, none of the adults expected to live through the day.

It was only later, with the children secured in the Lauren-Net, that Sienna realized the wolf alpha was biting out clipped orders to his men and women. Blankets had already appeared for the children in the time she'd spent on the psychic plane. Sienna stood with Marlee in her arms, while Walker took Toby, and Judd stayed as their shield. Her body swayed.

The wolf alpha's eyes snapped to her. "Give her to me."

She should've let Judd answer, but she was a cardinal who'd effectively been on her own since she was five—she knew a challenge when she heard it. "No."

A single raised eyebrow. "You've defected, sweetheart. No use worrying about the big, bad wolf now."

She was aware of Judd speaking, but her attention never shifted off the man who was a predator, for all that he wore a human skin. When he peeled open and held out a bar of some kind, she took it, aware low energy levels could be dangerous when it came to her ability to keep a handle on the cold fire. "Thank you."

A faint smile, a strange amusement in those icy eyes. "You're welcome."

It was the most polite interaction they'd ever had.

* * *

HAWKE spent the morning in a business negotiation—the other party was attempting to get SnowDancer to increase its offer by dangling a bullshit competing bid in front of them, an underhanded tactic, but one Hawke understood. What he had a problem with was the fact the Psy conglomerate thought SnowDancer too stupid to know the difference between a fair if tough price and a scalping.

"I'm sorry," the Psy negotiator said from the comm screen, her face pristine in its lack of expression. "I'm afraid we can't accept anything less than a fifteen percent increase."

"In that case," Hawke said, having had enough, "I guess this negotiation is over." Ending the call before she could respond, he glanced over at Jem, who'd sat in on the session from L.A. "Find us another supplier."

"I'll have a short list by tonight." The lieutenant's eyes narrowed. "They really think we got to where we are by being dumb shits? You'd think they'd know better by now."

Hawke shrugged, ignoring the flashing message that said the negotiator was trying to reinitiate contact. "They will, when their shares take a nosedive." SnowDancer was the largest pack in the country and had the attendant economic power. While Hawke had a preference for dealing with changeling or human companies—for the simple reason that the Councilors had interests in, and control over, so many Psy businesses—Psy were the only option in certain sectors. Except—"That small human start-up, what was it called . . ."

"Aquarius?"

"Yeah, that's the one. Can they supply us?"

Jem took a moment to check her files. "They have the intellectual know-how, but it'll stretch their capacity." A pause. "Of course, with a contract this big, they'll be able to afford to expand."

"You want to talk to them?"

"I'll set up a face-to-face today."

Leaving Jem to handle that, Hawke headed out for a hunt in wolf form with some of his senior soldiers. It was something he did on a regular basis, having no desire to be an alpha who didn't know the wants and needs of his people.

More, it was a need within his wolf, to run side by side with those who were his own.

As a result of the hunt, and the ensuing conversation, he didn't get back to the den until after four. At which point, he showered, dressed in clean clothes, and took one of the SUVs for a drive down to the city.

TIRED from the physical day and devastatingly conscious that Hawke hadn't sought her out since walking her to her quarters the night before . . . when he'd been reminded once again of what the Psy had taken from him, Sienna sat cross-legged in bed, planning to work on a physics problem. It would keep her mind busy until exhaustion kicked her into dreamless sleep. That was the hope, anyway.

She'd picked up the datapad and was about to bring up the file when there was a knock on her door. Expecting it to be Evie or one of her other friends, she put aside the device and jumped up to open it without bothering about the fact that she was wearing her favorite soft black pajama pants and a faded gray T-shirt.

But it wasn't Evie at the door.

"What are you doing here?" It came out husky, near soundless.

Ice blue eyes traced the contours of her face. "I had unfinished business." He brought out a small wrapped box from behind his back. "Here."

She took the box without a conscious decision to act, stared.

Hawke leaned his arm against the doorjamb. "Aren't you going to open it?"

It was hard to think with him so close, his voice a deep murmur that turned her doorway into a private alcove, the moment into a slow, potent seduction. "What's inside?" Her fingers closed around the box, possessive as any predatory changeling.

"If I told you, what would be the surprise?" The heat of him caressed her as he took over her world. She couldn't see around him, his shoulders too wide, his presence too compelling. "I am, however"—his voice dropping, that wolf-blue gaze focused on her mouth—"willing to trade kisses for the secret."

The languid comment had her toes curling. Determined not to let him disconcert her any further, she undid the gauzy white ribbon with care and put it on top of the little shelf that stood against the wall beside the door, before beginning to unwrap the silver paper.

Hawke chuckled. "So neat."

"It's the way we were taught in the Net." Such habits were more necessary for her than most, a reminder to ensure mental discipline. But that was the last thing on her mind at that instant, because she'd finished unwrapping her gift.

Lifting off the top part of the metallic cardboard box, she set it beside the paper and picked out the item wrapped in several layers of tissue. Hawke took the other half of the box and put it on the shelf as she pulled away the tissue to reveal—"Oh." Wonder unfurled within her at the sight of the tiny penguin formed of shining metal, complete with black tuxedo and gold saxophone.

"Here." Reaching out as she stood the painstakingly crafted object on her palm, Hawke turned the key at the back.

The penguin began to "play" the sax with its fin, dipping and raising its head in time to the tinny saxophone music that appeared to emanate from the instrument at its mouth. The song was hauntingly familiar. Frowning, she turned the key when it wound down, listened again . . . and lost any hope of holding out against the wolf at her door even if she'd wanted to. "We danced to this." Under the moonlight, deep in the forest.

"If you'd forgotten," Hawke said, his head close to hers, though she couldn't remember seeing him move, "I'd have had to bite you again."

Her hand went to her shoulder. "The mark's gone."

Reaching out, he tugged at her T-shirt to bare the vulnerable skin, rubbed his thumb over the spot. Wolf-blue gleamed between slitted lids. "Come here."

The shiver that rocked through her at that low demand almost unseated the whimsical toy on her palm. Shaking her head at the wolf who very definitely wanted to use his teeth on her, she said, "Where did you find this?"

"There's a little shop in the city—I'll take you there some-day." His hand slid to the back of her nape. "I asked the owner to use that song."

It was tempting, so tempting, to lean her head against that wide chest, to stay in this perfect moment and ignore the words spoken in the car last night, but she'd never been a woman to hide from the facts—once, it had been because she'd had no choice, but now it had become part of her very character.

Raising her head, she looked into that wild gaze, that of a human with the heart of a wolf. "Why are you giving this to me?" It was a silent apology, she understood that—but the reason behind his harsh words last night couldn't remain un-said. Not when it cast a dark shadow over any future relation-ship.

It was the wolf who answered her. "I just am."

"Do you have any others?" she asked, changing tack.

"Maybe."

It was the most peculiar feeling, having this conversation with Hawke, neither of them trying to draw blood. "May I see them?"

A shrug. "If you're good."

Her skin was suddenly too tight over her breasts, even the softness of the T-shirt too abrasive. "How many do you have?" she asked as he stepped impossibly closer, until the muscled strength of his thighs bracketed her own.

"All these questions." His hand tightening on her nape, his body hard and demanding against the sensitive tips of her breasts. "Maybe I want something in return."

"I—" she began, not knowing if she was going to sur-render or push for the answers she needed when Hawke's phone beeped.

"Hold on," he murmured without breaking the searing eye contact, without removing the rough heat of his hand from her nape. "That's Riley's code." He placed the phone to his ear.

And everything changed.

Chapter 17

"KEEP THEM CONTAINED. I'll find Judd and head down." Hawke saw Sienna's eyes sharpen, realized she'd put the pieces together. "No. No communication. If they talk in spite of the order, shoot the men in the legs."

The woman across from him didn't appear the least shocked by his instructions. "More intruders," she said when he ended the call.

Rubbing his thumb over her lips in lieu of the slow, deep kiss he'd intended to coax from her, he dropped his hand and said, "Can you telepath Judd, get him to meet me at the garage?"

"Yes. I'm doing it now."

Hawke had turned and was on his way before he stopped to think that maybe he should've said some sweet words instead of making such an abrupt departure, especially after last night. Even the most mature of women tended to get miffed about things like that. Pulling out his phone as he ran to the garage, he coded in a call.

Sienna picked up at once. "Is there a problem?" No anger, only an incisive intelligence.

That was when he remembered that this woman had been raised in a military context, understood about the need for a rapid response. "How far away is Judd?" he asked instead of the pretty words he'd much rather save to whisper in her ear when she was naked and well pleasured under him. *Very* well pleasured.

"Almost there." A pause. "Be careful." It held the distinct edge of a command.

Surprised but not opposed to the idea of that particular command from this specific woman, his wolf pricked up its ears. "Yes, ma'am." Hanging up, he entered the garage just as Judd appeared from the opposite corridor.

JUDD stopped in the heavy dark of the trees surrounding the clearing where the SnowDancer unit held four men and a pregnant woman at gunpoint. "Confirmed, Psy," he said in a subvocal murmur to the man who stood beside him. It had taken him time to learn to speak that low, so low that he couldn't hear his own voice—but that changelings could discern with unerring accuracy.

"Anything else?" Hawke asked, his attention focused on the intruders.

"No symbols on their shoulders," he said. "That's on purpose—those are military uniforms, should have emblems."

"The woman?"

"She's not touching her abdomen." A pregnant woman who cared about her unborn child would have made some protective move that betrayed the disintegration of her conditioning—rather than standing with military stiffness. Still . . . "I can't say with certainty that her state is meant to manipulate your emotions. Her Silence could simply be too strong." He melted farther back into the dark as Hawke stepped out to stand beside Riley.

"Gentlemen—and woman," the wolf alpha said with deceptive calm. "Would you care to explain the reason for this territorial breach?"

The man who replied was tall, with features that placed his ancestry as originating in the Indian subcontinent, most probably on the border with China. "We have defected." A frigid statement, but that meant nothing. Judd had sounded as cold once upon a time. "We seek sanctuary."

"What makes you think SnowDancer would offer sanctuary to a bunch of Psy?"

"There are rumors you have done so on at least one previous occasion."

Judd's blood chilled in his veins. His entire family had

disappeared off the grid, was meant to be listed as dead in the Net. "He's fishing," he said into the microphone clipped to the collar of his leather-synth jacket, though he knew Hawke was well aware of that fact.

Now, the SnowDancer alpha curved his lips into a grin that was all teeth. "We may have run across the occasional stray," he said, reaching down to pet one of the wild wolves that had streamed out of the forest in response to his presence.

"Then you indeed offered them sanctuary?"

Hawke stroked the wolf at his side, a beautiful creature of deepest black . . . the same shade as the much larger changeling wolf who prowled out to join the circle of watchers. *Riaz*. The SnowDancer lieutenant stared unblinking at the trespassers with eyes a startling shade akin to ancient gold.

"Depends what you define as sanctuary." Hawke's tone was easy, as if this was an everyday conversation. "I'm sure they no longer feel any pain . . . no longer feel anything."

"Are you saying they're dead?"

A faint smile. "Now, if I said that, I'd be admitting to murder." He angled his head toward the woman, and Judd knew the wolf was assessing the truth of her. "Our legal team would frown on that." Then he did something Judd would have never expected.

Throwing back his head, he howled—the sound eerily beautiful, seeming to come from a wolf's throat, not a human's. The wolves around him, wild and changeling, reacted in a split second, forelegs bunching as they launched themselves at the intruders. Only someone who'd been watching with utmost care would've seen that their lunge would have them streaming around the woman.

The Psy weren't paying that kind of close attention. But the woman didn't clamp her hand around her belly, didn't try to shield her womb, didn't attempt to protect her body in any way. Instead, she, like the others, slammed out a hand in a telekinetic thrust that shoved the wolves back . . . and teleported out.

At a speed that meant each had done their own personal teleport.

Judd hissed out a breath. There was no chance of four teleport-capable Tk-Psy—all of whom would've been pulled into the Council superstructure as youths—deciding to defect at the same time. *No* chance. It would provoke too much attention, incite too massive a search. No Council operative would make that mistake—and all four of the intruders had been standing in a battle-ready stance that revealed their training.

"Clear!" one of the SnowDancers called out, holding up a gadget Brenna and the other techs had put together to detect any surveillance devices in their territory.

Only then did Judd step out of concealment. "Somebody suspects we're still alive."

Hawke, having crouched down to stroke, touch, and play with the wild wolves that swarmed over him, now rose. "Our demonstration should put that rumor to rest."

"Especially when it happens to be so close to the truth."

Hawke's grin was that of the wolf, amused and dangerous. "You're lucky I was feeling mellow the day the five of you turned up in our territory."

Judd knew now that Marlee and Toby had *never* been in any danger—the wolves balked at harming any child, even one who might be a threat. It was their Achilles' heel, one the Council could not be allowed to discover, because they were fully capable of breeding and sending in child operatives. "Let me talk to my contacts, see if I can get an idea of who might've been behind the fishing expedition."

"A Councilor has a hand in it somewhere with all those Tks."

"There is a second option."

When Hawke turned to him in question, he said, "I didn't recognize them, but it's possible they were recruited into the squad after I left." Arrows didn't turn against their own, but Judd had defected and, in so doing, broken the covenant. "They might be hunting me." Feeling a wolf brush against him as he finished speaking, he glanced down at Riaz, who'd wandered over from the other side of the clearing. "Yes?"

But the lieutenant was only interested in Hawke, walking over to sniff at the alpha. Judd was certain he saw the black wolf grin before Hawke warned him off with a low growl. Judd didn't have changeling senses but he had a brain. Still, he made no comment. Not yet.

* * *

IT was late when Hawke returned to the den. He should've gone to bed, but instead he tracked a certain scent through the corridors until he located Sienna in the same training room where he'd watched her once before. This, the thing between him and Sienna, he didn't know where it was going, and yeah, his guilt at claiming her when he had so little to offer continued to be a claw raking his gut—but as proven by his inability to keep his distance, ignoring it was no longer an option.

As for the guilt? Turned out it stood no chance against the piercing pleasure he derived from being in her presence. Locking the door behind himself now, he sat down on a bench to savor the sight of her moving with such lithe grace. "Couldn't sleep?" he asked when she saw him and halted.

She pushed a flyaway tendril out of her eyes. "I was worried." A statement without sophistication, stark in its honesty. "I wanted to telepath Judd, but I knew he wouldn't tell me anything without authorization."

Protecting his own was instinct, but this was her life—a life she'd fought for from the start. He wasn't about to handicap her by leaving her blind to a possible threat.

She sucked in a breath as he started giving her the rundown, her face going pale under those intriguing freckles she'd gained during the summer months. "Me," she whispered. "I've given us away."

He was already rising to cup her jaw, run his finger over the softness of her skin. "No one would have recognized you," he said, thinking she was worried about her visits to Wild, the city. "Hell, I hardly recognized you."

"No." A violent shake of her head, her eyes gone midnight. "When I 'earth' the X-fire, it causes a psychic shockwave. They'd have to be close to feel it—"

"But," he said, seeing the lethal point she was trying to make, "Henry Scott's men have been lurking on the fringes and maybe even in interior sections of den territory for months."

She gave a jagged nod. "I'm sorry. I should've realized—"

He stopped her with a finger on her lips. "Even if they did catch something, it must've only been the barest hint, or they'd have been a lot more certain tonight."

"They'll come back." She spoke against his touch, and it was instinct to trace those full lips, to indulge himself that much though he knew he couldn't allow himself to go any further. Not tonight. Not when she was so shocked and vulnerable.

"Then," he said, drawing in her scent, "we'll take care of them." He rubbed the rough pad of his thumb over her lower lip, deeply satisfied to hear her breath catch. "Can you mute the release of your power in any way?"

"Yes." Hot breath against his skin, the thudding beat of her pulse a caress that had his body going rigid in want. "I'll go deep into SnowDancer territory, places I know are under heavy guard and highly unlikely to be compromised."

"Good." It was beyond tempting to bite the flushed curves of her mouth, but he resisted and said, "What were you reading when I came in earlier? I saw the reader on the bed."

Sienna had been sick to her stomach when she'd realized her actions might've brought danger to her whole family, but now, a wholly different sensation skittered within her abdomen. "Shouldn't we," she said against that thumb that continued to tease her until it felt as if her lips were connected in a direct line to the damp heat between her legs, "discuss the security issue?"

"Nothing more to discuss yet." Wolf eyes looking out of a human face, his body so close her own brushed against the implacable strength of him with every breath.

When he moved that tormenting touch away from her lips to close his hand over the sensitive column of her throat, she shuddered. "A physics text." Part of her said she was letting him have too much control of the situation, but the rest of her waited in strained anticipation to see what he would do next.

"Hmm." Reaching back, he undid her braid, sliding the dark mass over one shoulder so it tumbled over her breast. "You're getting straight A's."

Surprise cut through the desire so heavy in her limbs, in her blood. "How did you know?"

A slow smile. "Because I know your brain never stops working."

She didn't know how to take that. "Are you making fun of me?"

Sliding both hands down to her waist, he said, "No," and stroked his hands up, back down again. "I like how smart you are."

It was an unexpected compliment, one that meant far more to her than the most flowery of words. "I like your mind, too," she whispered as her arms rose of their own volition to wrap around his neck. He was too tall for that, so she curved her hand around the side of his neck, the shift of muscle and tendon a stark intimacy under her palm. "Your thought processes fascinate me." He could be so icily rational, and yet the wolf was always there, primal and untamed.

"Then we're equal." Cupping her nape with one hand, he moved the other to her lower back. And somehow, they were dancing, though the only music was the thudding pulse of her heart, the rough caress of his breath.

JUDD managed to get in touch with the Ghost around three that morning, the other man agreeing to meet him an hour later in the murky confines of an abandoned building project. Black plastic fluttered in the night winds, the solid skeleton of the house providing an illusion of permanence. "You've been hard to track down of late," Judd said to the rebel who was so close to the Net, Judd worried its madness was starting to seep into the Ghost's brain.

Face hidden in the gloom, the Ghost leaned back against one of the supporting beams. "You asked me once what my reason was for doing this."

"This" being their combined efforts to topple the Council . . . though no longer Silence. The question had become more complex than that. As evidenced by the second level of dissonance in Sienna's brain, some Psy *needed* Silence, or some aspect of it, on a basic level. "Are you ready to share?"

The only thing the Ghost had admitted to date was that there was at least one individual in the Net who had some value to him, one person he did not want dead. That was the solitary thing that kept him from annihilating the entire Council, an act that would cause a psychic shockwave and destabilize the Net, killing millions.

"No," the rebel said in response to his question. "But I have one, that much you should know."

Judd understood without further explanation that that unnamed reason lay behind the Ghost's recent lack of availability. "I need to know if my cover is blown."

"No. Your entire family is presumed dead."

"Any rumors?"

"There is a myth of a cardinal X, but you and I both know that to be impossible."

Judd wondered just how much the Ghost knew and how far the rebel's allegiance went. But he also knew that while Sienna had gained control of her ability with the sheer, stubborn refusal to surrender, there would come a time when the X-marker would demand more from her than she could give. He had to take a chance on the Ghost's loyalty, to roll the dice. Because if he didn't and Sienna's power did spiral out of control . . . "Have you heard of Alice Eldridge's second manuscript?"

"The dissertation on designation X?" The Ghost straightened. "Yes. It's one of the most hidden, yet persistent rumors in the Net."

"Any indication the rumor might hold a grain of truth?"

A long, quiet pause. "I'll do a search."

"I'll owe you one."

"No, Judd. Don't ever say that to me—I may very well collect." There was a chill darkness to that statement, as if Judd would not like the payment demanded.

"Then I withdraw it." Hair blowing back in a sudden gust that sent the black plastic flapping, he glanced at the man of whose identity he was ninety-nine point nine percent certain. "Have you ever considered taking the rebellion into the open?"

"It would never succeed. First the foundations must be set. Only then can the wave crest."

Judd thought of everything they'd done together, everything they'd accomplished, considered the cost. "How is your mental status?" It was a question he'd never asked with such bluntness, but times had changed.

"Sane." A short answer. "Though sanity is a question of interpretation."

Chapter 18

ALTERNATING BETWEEN CONTENTMENT and frustration at the remembered feel of Sienna in his arms, Hawke was drinking his first cup of coffee the next morning when he got a call from Kenji, the SnowDancer lieutenant based near the San Gabriel Mountains. With his high cheekbones, startling green eyes, and violent magenta hair, he looked like an escapee from a desert rave—or maybe some avant garde catwalk show.

"What the fuck did you do to your hair?" Hawke asked, almost choking on his coffee. Because while he might be channeling a Japanese rock star, the fact was, Kenji was about as avant garde as your average elementary-school teacher.

"It annoys Garnet. Reason enough." He tapped a rolled-up chart on the comm screen. "I've had an interesting contact from the BlackSea Coalition."

Hawke put down his coffee. BlackSea was a changeling pack—in a sense. It was a coalition of all the water-based changelings. As single entities, their population numbers were miniscule, with only one or two recorded instances of some changeling types. However, rather than being powerless, they'd grouped together to form a close-knit network that gave them considerable negotiating and territorial power.

"Business?"

Kenji shook his head. "They want in on an alliance."

"Send me the data." It would go to the top of his list, because unlike any other pack on the face of the planet, BlackSea had members worldwide. "Copy Riley on everything."

"Will do." Kenji signed off.

Seeing a scrawled message on his desk, Hawke headed out to speak to Indigo about some of the younger pack members she'd had under supervision.

"You're more balanced," she said after they'd finished the discussion, long legs crossed on top of her desk while he stood with his back against the closed door of her office.

"Yep." The contact he'd allowed himself with Sienna had satisfied both parts of him to the extent that his need was no longer bleeding out to everyone around him. More to the point, the wolf was willing to be patient now that he'd decided to go after her—it understood the hunt, understood that sometimes you had to stalk your prey. "I hear Tai's dating Evie," he said in an effort to distract Indigo because he wasn't ready to discuss his decision.

Indigo's expression said she was onto him, but she let it slide. "I've promised to break both his arms if he makes her unhappy in any way, shape, or form." A pause. "I should promise to do the same to you."

Hawke narrowed his eyes. "Don't go there."

"Of course I'll go there—that's why I'm a lieutenant." Swinging her legs off her desk, she picked up a small datapad. "But not today. I'm late for a session with the novices." Rising, she waited for him to open the door. "On second thought . . ." She pushed her free hand into his hair and pulled down his head.

"I almost let the best thing that ever happened to me slip away because I was hung up on ideas of what I 'should' want. Sometimes there is no 'should,' there's only a single chance to grab on to happiness." Pressing her lips to his in a fast, affectionate kiss, she let go and strode off.

Her parting statement, however, didn't disappear as easily.

SOMEHOW fighting the distraction of last night's memories, Sienna had just sent in a completed physics project using the computronic resources in the den library when she ran into an elderly changeling. "I've got it," she said, catching the book she'd knocked from his grasp. "I'm so sorry, sir."

Dalton chuckled as he accepted the book, his white eyebrows bushy over dark, dark brown skin marked with a thousand laugh lines. "Makes me sound about a hundred years old."

Sienna wasn't sure Dalton wasn't exactly that age. The man the kids in the den affectionately called a whitebeard wasn't a librarian, he was *the* Librarian, the repository of Pack knowledge. "Were you undertaking research?"

"It's all up here." He tapped his temple, his sparkling eyes the same warm tawny brown as his granddaughter's. "I came to get some light reading." Holding up the heavy tome she'd caught, he beamed. "In the original French!"

Sienna nodded as if she knew what he was talking about. "I hope you enjoy it."

"I'm sure I will." Tucking the book under his arm, he touched her on the shoulder as he passed.

Sienna blurted out, "Wait," before her courage deserted her.

"Yes, dear?"

"The Pack archives—are they accessible to anyone?"

Dalton's eyes were piercing when he looked at her, leaving no doubt that whitebeard or not, his brain was as acute as it had always been. "Yes. But certain truths, while written, are kept out of reach—because there are some wounds that don't need to be reopened."

Sienna felt her fingers curl into fists. "I understand."

"Do you, young one?" Dalton shook his head. "The histories I write give the facts, but for the heart of it, you must ask those who were there."

Sienna didn't move for several minutes after Dalton left, remembering the way Hawke had shut her down the one time she'd brought up the past. He'd held her last night, danced with her until the entire den seemed to go quiet, as if they were the only two awake in the hushed time between midnight and dawn. She'd never felt more alive, more a woman. However, Dalton's words made her confront a stark truth: that despite the escalating physical contact, Hawke hadn't yet—might never—trust her with his secrets.

Sienna. Judd's telepathic voice, slicing through the bleakness of her thoughts. *Hawke's office. We need to discuss what you told him about the cold fire.*

The reminder of the danger stalking them was an icy trickle down her spine. *I'm on my way.*

* * *

HAWKE noted Sienna's expressionless face, the flat ebony of her gaze, and scowled. "You release the X-fire to keep from reaching synergy, correct?" he asked, figuring he'd get to the bottom of the emotional change in her as soon as he had her alone.

A crisp nod, her stance that of a SnowDancer soldier in front of her alpha. "Earthing helps me maintain a stable psychic balance."

"How often do you earth?" Judd had told him to ask the question, though the Psy male had refused, "until he had more answers," to say why. It was a measure of Hawke's trust in the lieutenant that he'd left it at that—for now.

"Several times over the past few months," Sienna admitted. "Before that, I was only doing it once or twice every half year. My theory is that the change is linked to my increasing control—I'm no longer releasing power inadvertently, so it builds up faster."

Judd spoke for the first time. "Do you foresee doing it again soon?"

"No, I don't think so." However, there was a hesitation in her words, a crack in her confidence. "The pattern's become less predictable of late, but that could be due to a simple fluctuation in my abilities. That's happened once or twice before, and it's always subsided without any discernible aftereffects."

Hawke pinned her with his gaze. "You'll tell me the next time you need to earth." He wasn't letting her head out alone, not when the Psy might have her in their sights.

"Yes, sir."

He'd never been called "sir" with such insulting politeness. Wolf settling at the return of the acerbic edge in her voice because he didn't like seeing her lost and unsure, he turned to Judd. "Anything else I should know?"

"No, I'm still working my contacts." Turning toward the door, he said, "Sienna?"

Hawke held up a hand. "We have something to discuss."

Judd looked up, met his eyes, but spoke to Sienna instead. "Wait outside." There was a command in his voice, that of a lieutenant speaking to a lower-ranking soldier.

Hawke had the feeling that while Sienna might have argued with her uncle, she obeyed the lieutenant—albeit with a tight set to her jaw—sliding past Judd and into the corridor. Only when she was gone, the door shut, did Hawke raise an eyebrow at the Psy male who'd returned to stand opposite him.

"You have my loyalty," Judd said in the quietest of tones, "but she has a piece of my heart."

Hawke had known this was coming, was ready for it. "I won't hurt her."

"Sienna is strong," Judd continued, as if he hadn't heard Hawke's vow, "older than she should be. But in many ways, she's far more vulnerable than any other female in this den. She broke Silence at a critical age, and it altered her emotional psyche."

Hawke's wolf wasn't pleased at being taken to task, but he listened. "From what I see," he said, thinking of her empty eyes when she'd walked into the office, "she seems damn good at reining in emotions."

It should've made him happy that she had the capacity to maintain that distance—he always chose lovers who wouldn't be hurt by his inability to give them everything. But last night, as he indulged himself by claiming the first level of intimate skin privileges, he'd discovered something—when it came to Sienna, he was beyond selfish, beyond possessive. She was his. And he wanted all of her.

"That's not what I'm worried about." Judd's eyes were arctic blue with intent when they met Hawke's. "She has no off switch when it comes to those she loves. She will do anything to protect them, even murder. Do you understand what I'm telling you?"

Hawke curved his lips in a faint smile. "Sounds like a predatory changeling."

"Yes. Except unlike a changeling, she didn't grow up around simple kindness, much less touch and affection." A harsh reminder that Sienna hadn't even had the cold childhood of most Psy. "On an intellectual level, she might understand that intimate physical contact doesn't mean a commitment, but when it comes to you, that isn't going to matter a damn." Cool words no less forceful for being delivered in a tempered voice. "Once you turn that key, be sure you're ready." It was a warning.

Hawke's wolf heard it loud and clear—but it also heard what Judd didn't say. "Why aren't you telling me to stay the fuck away from her?" he asked, because while it was too late for that, it angered him that her family hadn't thought to protect her.

Judd's own anger was an icy whip. "You insist on seeing her as a child when the truth is, she was forced to make adult decisions long ago. She's earned the right to live her life as she pleases."

"Doesn't that piss you off? That she was never allowed to be a child?" It sure as hell pissed him off.

"Yes—but she survived." Not even by the flicker of an eyelash did Judd betray the depth of emotion that had to be riding him, but the chair next to him turned into a pile of splinters between one breath and the next.

Hawke's wolf saw, understood. "You'd kill them all if you could."

"Sienna could do that herself."

SIENNA knew they were talking about her in there, and though it frustrated her to be shut out, she'd been part of the pack long enough to understand hierarchy. The truth was, annoyance at situations like today's aside, she appreciated it.

SnowDancer, at its core, operated very much like a military unit—albeit one with a warm emotional center, and that was a pattern of behavior her mind understood and accepted, the strict nature of it acting as an outside restraint on her abilities. Sienna was deathly certain she wouldn't have survived in a more laissez-faire environment.

However, that didn't mean she wouldn't be letting both Hawke and Judd know what she thought of their arrogance in excluding her from a conversation that had her as its focus. The irritated thought had just passed through her mind when a brilliant spark of joy burst onto her psychic senses. *Toby.* Her brother had phenomenal shields, but he tended to broadcast when in high spirits. *What's got you so happy?*

Sascha's here.

Sienna frowned. *Really?* It didn't fit with what she'd witnessed of Lucas's protective nature.

Lucas is with her. And like a hundred other soldiers.

That made more sense. *Be good.*

Drew says I should be bad sometimes.

He's a terrible influence. But she let Toby feel her laughter, hear that she was joking. *Just don't be too bad.*

A starburst of love from a brother who'd had this aspect of his abilities buried in the Net. Then Toby was gone from her mind and the door to Hawke's office was being pulled open. "Sascha and Lucas are here," she said to Hawke when he followed Judd out into the corridor.

"I know." He held up a sleek black phone. "Riley will handle anything they need. We"—his eyes locked to Sienna's—"are heading out for a while."

Per their agreement, she didn't question the order until Judd left them at the junction. "You were talking about me," she began. "I—"

"Uncles," Hawke interrupted, "brothers, fathers have always had and will always have private 'discussions' with males who want to touch their women. You're never going to win that argument"—a playful tug on her braid—"so give it up."

Glaring at him, she pulled her hair from his grasp. "That is the most sexist statement I have ever heard."

"Doesn't mean it's not true." He shrugged. "Ask Riley sometime about the nice little chat Mercy's brothers and father had with him."

Irritation derailed by curiosity, she said, "What about Indigo?" The lieutenant was the third-highest-ranking individual in the pack, needed no one's protection.

"You know Abel," he said, referring to Indigo's father. "What do you think?"

Sienna knew right then that the arrogant wolf had won, because Abel adored his girls, had probably threatened to rip out key parts of Drew's anatomy. "Where are we going?" she asked, foul-tempered and not bothering to hide it.

"In a bit." Nodding his head toward one of the conference rooms, he said, "Toby's in there." An unasked question, silent consent if she needed to go to her brother.

"He's fine," she said, wondering how the wolf-eyed male could be so infuriating and so very wonderful at the same time. "He loves his lessons with Sascha."

"She gets something out of it, too, you know."

"She's a cardinal empath. Toby's E abilities are barely 3 on the Gradient." Her brother's cardinal status came from his telepathy.

"But he *is* an E in some part," Hawke pointed out. "He exists."

Yes, she thought, Hawke was right. It explained the hereto inexplicable depth of Sascha's joy whenever she was with Toby. "I've never met another X." She didn't know why she told him that.

Hawke didn't respond until they'd exited the den and were heading out on a path that would lead eventually to the training run that had gotten ever more fiendish since Riaz's return from a stint abroad. "How about a weak X?" he asked, his face lifted up to the clean, bright Sierra sunshine.

Beautiful man. "It's such a rare designation," she said when he shot her a questioning glance, "that there's probably less than ten of us at any given time." Even that was a generous estimate, considering what she'd gleaned about their life expectancy. "The theory is that Xs below 2 on the Gradient don't manifest, so no one ever realizes. As for the others . . . I know of one who died during my teen years. I heard of another two who died before I was brought in."

So much sadness, so much death.

"Of the two other living Xs I knew of in the Net," she continued, "one was psychotic and the other hypersensitive." It felt strange to talk of the X designation without feeling the vicious spear of pain down her spine that was the first level of dissonance, a warning not to speak of things the Council would prefer to keep secret. "It was possible I'd set him off if we came into close contact."

"Didn't that volatility make him a danger?" Hawke pushed silver-gold strands off his face, catching her eye.

"Yes," she murmured, "but he must've been useful in some capacity because they permitted him to live." Hawke had, she thought, the most fascinating hair, unusual and beautiful as his pelt in wolf form. "Why don't you grow out your hair?"

"You mean like Luc?" He shrugged. "Not me, I guess."

She had to admit she loved the way the strands brushed his nape, just long enough to be rebellious . . . to invite the caress of a woman's fingers. Unsure where they were in terms of a relationship, what he'd accept, she tucked her hands under her armpits. "Why are you so like your wolf in human form?"

"There was a time when I needed it to be the dominant aspect even when I was in human form—the wolf was more mature than the boy." He led her past the training run and into the trees. "My wolf was always near the surface. The experience heightened the effect."

Startled at getting a straight answer, she scrambled to gather her thoughts. "I've heard changelings say it can be dangerous to spend too long with the animal in control."

"It couldn't be helped. I was fifteen when I became alpha."

"So young?"

"Our alpha was dead, and so were most of the lieutenants and senior soldiers."

"That's why SnowDancer has such a young population." Nowhere near the level of older people you'd expect. She went to ask another question when she realized they'd stopped in the shadow of a slender tree, its branches hung with elegant leaves that shimmered in the wind.

"I'll give you," he said, "a twenty-minute head start." A pale-eyed wolf watched her out of a human face.

Chapter 19

THE FINE HAIRS on her arms rose. "To do what?"

"You have to get to the lake before I catch you." A slow, provoking smile that kicked her straight in the gut. "Let's see if you're smart enough to fool the wolf."

"Why would I want to do that?" Sienna had paid her dues, earned her status. "Is this a test?"

"Nope."

Folding her arms, she spread her feet in a defensive stance. "Then I don't have to do it."

"I'm asking you to." He angled his head to the side, the motion nothing human. "Afraid you'll lose?"

She set her jaw. "I can beat you with my eyes closed."

"I'm scared." The wolf was laughing at her.

If she'd been able to growl, she'd have done it right then. "Are you allowed to circle to the lake and wait for me?" He was faster, would win even with the head start.

But he shook his head, strands of that gorgeous hair sliding over his forehead. "What would be the fun in that?"

She knew he'd manipulated her into accepting the challenge, but her competitive streak had kicked in, wouldn't allow her to back down. "Fine. Start the clock."

"Done." He closed his eyes. "Before you go, I should tell you what you get if you win."

"What?"

"A surprise."

Oh, she very much wanted the ability to growl. "What if I lose?"

"I might throw you in the lake. Maybe."

Not trusting him an inch when he had that smile flirting with his lips, she took off. He was far, far faster—she'd seen him run, and the sight had brought her heart into her throat. Built like the most beautiful living machine, all fluid sinew and tendon, muscle and strength, he so outclassed her when it came to speed that she didn't stand a chance.

But there were other ways to tangle with a wolf.

MAN and wolf were both a little disappointed in Sienna. She'd gone in a straight line to the lake, hadn't even tried to use the nearby waterways to mask her scent. The shining thread of wild spice and autumn leaves spilled out ahead of him, an unmistakable lure to his wolf. He'd have to have a—"Fuck!"

He was upside down, watching the pine-needle-strewn earth pass this way and that several feet below him, his right ankle caught securely in a rope. Twisting to stare up at his ankle, he shook his head. Stared again. Started to laugh. *Smart, smart girl.* It wasn't a rope at all, but a thick vine that grew everywhere around here. Sienna had to have spent most of her twenty-minute head start laying this trap. A trap he would've normally avoided—except that he'd written off her skills on this playing field. That'd teach him to be an arrogant ass.

Contorting his body, he went to slice the vine with a claw.

Only to fall short just shy of his goal.

Swearing, he tried again, and again. By the time he got the damn thing off, he'd painted the air blue, and it didn't exactly help when he landed hard on his tailbone. The wolf was not amused . . . except that it was because *this* was a game. Getting rid of the remnants of the vine around his ankle, he stretched to reset his muscles, then restarted following her scent—being far more careful this time.

He saw the vine she'd strung across the path and lifted his feet over it without tripping the snare. Only to find his damn ankle—the same one—stuck in a hole. Growling, he brushed away the leaves to discover the brat had dug three holes on the other side. He'd managed to find the center one.

Clever, his wolf thought, delighted with her, *very clever.*

Digging out his abused ankle, he spent several minutes

undoing the trap so others wouldn't be caught unawares—as he had a feeling she'd known he would—then changed tack. Instead of moving directly toward her scent, he took a longer route, coming in at an angle. He saw where she'd rested, glimpsed another smart, sneaky trap. It cost him precious minutes to undo it but far fewer than if he'd been caught up in it.

Five minutes later, a long strand of ruby red hair glinted at him from a bush, the area thick with her scent. Certain he'd run her to ground, he went to part the bush . . . and only just snapped his hand back in time. His curvy little brand of trouble had almost led him into a thicket of poison ivy. Oh, now he was mad.

Grinning, he looked down and saw her sweatshirt hidden under the bush, likely pushed there by a stick. "Crafty Psy." Aware now of the caliber of opponent he had on his hands, he began to track her in earnest, flying over the earth at inhuman speed, every one of his senses on alert.

There.

She was a mere kilometer from the lake, hair tied back, her arms bared by her T-shirt as she knelt on the ground laying another trap for him. Instead of pouncing on her, he moved silently around to watch. Such a quick mind she had, he thought, seeing how she used the springy branch of a tree and another one of the vines to create her latest snare.

Every other opponent he'd had in this game had tried to mask his or her scent, to confuse and disorient. She was the single one who'd thought to use her time to set traps—and the wolf appreciated her cunning. It was only her lack of speed that had allowed him to catch her. But caught her he had . . . and he had a few tricks of his own.

SIENNA went motionless as her nape prickled in warning. Nothing. No sound, definitely no shout like the one that had gone up when Hawke had walked into the first trap. She'd been less than ten meters away, having had barely enough time to pull it together. Oh, he'd been pissed.

But then he'd laughed.

She'd never expected that, and it had made her understand.

A game. They were playing a game. Except for with Toby and Marlee, she'd never played a game before that wasn't connected to learning military tactics. Even with her brother and cousin, she was focused on their enjoyment, more a co-ordinator than a participant.

This—it was play for play's sake.

The efficient X-Psy inside of her said she was wasting time, but she shushed that voice. Because she'd never felt as light, as young as she did at this moment, sneaking through an ancient forest, trying to outwit a wolf with pale blue eyes and hair of silver-go— "?!#"

The sound that erupted from her throat was unintelligible as she found herself dangling by one ankle at least five feet off the ground. "No," she muttered, staring around in disbelief. But of course the answer was right there in her current predicament. "You win!" she finally called out in a fit of temper.

He appeared out of the forest, looking at her with quizzical eyes. "What are you doing up there, baby?"

"Rrrr." She slapped her hands over her mouth to still the feral sound.

Hawke's cheeks creased into a delighted smile. "Do that again."

Never. "Get me down."

He rocked back on his heels. "What do I get in exchange?"

"I won't fry you to a crisp."

"You wouldn't anyway," he said with such insouciant confidence it was pure provocation.

She shot a bolt of fire past his hair, but he'd already shifted sideways. "Tut, tut. That's cheating."

"Urgh!" Twisting her body with serious effort from her abdominal muscles, she went to aim her hand at the vine, sure she could sever it with her abilities.

"It'll hurt like hell when you fall."

She paused. He'd set his trap so she dangled higher than he had. It *would* hurt. Dropping back down, she blew out a breath. "What do you want?" It was a snarl; she'd never snarled before.

Walking close enough that he could put one hand under her nape, the other on her lower back, tilting her head up into a more comfortable position, he leaned in so close that all she could see was translucent ice blue. "A kiss for the big, bad wolf."

Her throat locked, the words stuck in her throat.

But he didn't close the distance between them. "Yes?"

Swallowing, she nodded.

"You have to say it."

"Yes," she managed to force out, gripping his shoulder with one hand.

"Yes what?"

Some of her frustration reignited, returning her voice. "You know what? I don't think I care how far I fall!"

Laughing lips descended on hers, one big hand cupping her cheek as his other held up her neck.

It was—

It was . . . She had no words for it, this shock of sensation that speared through her, raw and primal, swelling her breasts, melting the place between her thighs. All because those firm lips were tasting hers with a playful gentleness interspersed with more than a few nips and licks. She moaned into his mouth, got a nip on her lower lip as her reward.

Then he licked his tongue across her own.

Oh, God.

Wanting more, she dared reach out with her own tongue. He made a low, deep sound in his throat and returned the caress with interest, his fingers massaging her nape. The merest pause for breath before her upper lip was being sucked, her lower lip captured between strong masculine teeth for a teasing bite.

When it felt as if he'd lift his head, she arched toward him. He opened his mouth over her own, danced his tongue against hers, before breaking the kiss with a nuzzling slowness. "I'd have given you another kiss," he murmured, nipping at her pulse with his teeth, "but you made me mad."

Dazed, she said, "I did?"

"Did you really think I'd let you fall?" A bite lower down on her neck. Harder this time.

She jerked, hand clenching on that shoulder heavy with muscle. "You can't go around biting me whenever you feel like it." It was very alpha male behavior, and he hardly needed any more encouragement.

He licked his tongue over the mark. "Cut the vine."

This time, she didn't question him, using a targeted laser of cold fire to sever the trap. He caught her so fast she didn't even experience the sensation of falling for an instant. Lowering her to her feet, he held her against him as she got her balance back, one of his hands on her lower back, the other playing with strands of her hair.

When she looked up, he was watching her with an absolute focus that stole the air from her lungs. "You're a good playmate," he said, dipping his head to speak against her lips. "You get to pick the next game."

Stealing tiny kisses as she stood with her chest pressed to his, she felt the vibration of his growl in every inch of her. "When?" she managed to get out, her nipples hard little points, her breasts so sensitized she wasn't sure she'd be able to take it if he touched her.

"Tomorrow." Leaning down, he nuzzled at her, only taking a small bite before rubbing his lips over the spot. "Time to go back."

"Just a minute more." Scared this was a dream, she dared to wrap her arms around his neck, stroke her fingers over his nape. He was much taller, but he stayed in position so she could hold him, his breath hot against her skin. Just for a minute.

LARA wasn't surprised to see Walker in her office that night. He'd come to her the previous evening, too. The part of her that was still bruised had her keeping a wary emotional distance, but that same part held her complex, painful feelings for the quiet Psy male, and they left her unable to ask him to leave—especially when she sensed a subtle difference in him, a lessening in that wall of reserve.

However, not wanting to set herself up for another fall, she'd brought up something she was sure would have him making a fast exit last night. "You never talk about Marlee's mother."

To her shock, she'd gotten an answer.

"Her name was Yelene," he'd said, his expression telling her nothing of his emotions toward the woman who had borne him a child. "We lived together in a family unit, both of us of the opinion that psychologically speaking, it was the most secure way to bring up Marlee and, later, Toby."

Such a cold rationale on the surface, and yet beneath it was a love that had led him to walk into near-certain death on the slim chance that the children would find sanctuary. "I'm sorry about your sister." She knew Walker was the eldest of the three siblings, Judd the youngest. Sienna and Toby's mother had fallen in the middle . . . and died far too soon.

"Kristine was gifted but troubled."

"I'm glad Toby had you to turn to." Because Walker, he would've understood a child's pain at the loss, even in Silence.

"I couldn't protect Sienna"—dark, edgy words—"but I wouldn't have allowed anyone to seize Toby from us."

Devastatingly conscious of what it must've cost him to see Sienna taken by Ming, she hadn't asked the question on the tip of her tongue yesterday. Tonight, however, as they sat at the small table in the break room, his long legs encroaching on her space, she couldn't contain it any longer. "Yelene," she said. "What was she like?"

"Our genes were a good match." His big body betrayed nothing of his inner thoughts as he gave her that nonanswer. "It was predicted that we'd create high-Gradient offspring, and Marlee is living proof of the veracity of the geneticists' predictions."

Lack of overt body language or not, Lara knew he wanted her to back off. But she had no intention of turning back the clock, of returning their relationship to what it had been before the kiss—when she'd allowed him to dictate the boundaries in that subtle way of his. "You felt something for her, didn't you?" Every instinct she had urged her to touch him, to connect with him on the most basic level, but Walker hadn't acceded her those skin privileges, and even if they had had more between them than this strange friendship, he wasn't the kind of man with whom a woman could demand.

"I was Silent," he said, his jean-clad leg brushing her own in a rough caress that made her breath catch in spite of her warning not to let herself read too much into his visits, his words. "I felt nothing."

"Walker."

He put down the coffee she'd made him. "There was no love or affection—not as you feel it. But there was, I believed, a true commitment and loyalty to the family unit. I was wrong." So cold and final, the statement told her the subject was now off-limits.

It wasn't Lara's determination that had her fighting his dominance to say what she did next, but the deepest instincts of her healer's heart. "She hurt you."

A tendon pulled taut on his jaw. "She made the most logical choice when the entire family was slated for rehabilitation." Walker would never forget the day, the *minute*, he was served the edict and told he had three days to put his affairs, and those of the minors under his care, in order; three days to prepare his daughter and the boy he considered a son to undergo a psychic brainwipe that would turn them into vegetables suitable only for the most menial tasks.

"According to the rehabilitation order, the Lauren line had been judged 'unstable' and 'undesirable.' " Kristine's suicide had been listed as one of the pieces of evidence, but Judd and Walker had always known that to be nothing but a convenient excuse. "Yelene's name wasn't on the notice."

He'd gone home to discuss the situation with her, to lay out the plans he and Judd had put in place, both of them having seen the writing on the wall when the extent of Sienna's powers became clear. Add in Judd's telekinetic strength and Walker's telepathy, as well as Marlee's and Toby's nascent abilities, and the Lauren family had become a threat that needed to be neutralized.

"She was packing her bags when I walked in." At first, he'd believed she was preparing for a defection attempt. To this day, he didn't know what had stopped him from sharing their plans—perhaps some part of him had always understood that though Yelene had carried Marlee in her womb, their child was only a collection of cells to her . . . a replaceable entity. "When she saw me, she said point-blank that she didn't intend for her genes to die out alongside mine."

Lara's pupils dilated, taking over those tawny irises. "I

can't understand." Disbelieving bewilderment. "I never will. All I can do is . . ." She put her hand on the table, palm up.

A silent offer of surcease.

Walker had learned to touch since his defection, learned to hug, to give pats on the back or a squeeze on the shoulder. But he'd never touched a woman for no reason except that it would soothe something jagged in him to do so. Lara's fingers began to curl when he didn't move, her hand starting to slide away.

His fingers closed around her wrist before he was aware of moving his hand, his thumb on the fluttering beat of her pulse. Her skin was so soft, stirring fantasies of what it would be like to explore the skin of her breasts, her inner thighs. Softer still, he thought, she'd be softer still in those places.

"I'm not Yelene," she said, a quiet strength to her that had compelled him from the first. "I won't ever walk away from those who are mine."

No, that wasn't the way she was built. But—"Yelene has nothing to do with this."

"Liar." A whisper that put him on notice that she wasn't about to back off. "What she did hurt you on a level you won't accept, and that hurt continues to drive the decisions you make about women, about relationships."

"The old bonds," he said, holding that tawny gaze so she would know he told her the utter truth, "the love for the children, they survived Yelene, survived the defection. But the rest of me is damaged." In spite of his need for her, he wouldn't lie . . . even though he knew his words would push her into the arms of one of the other men drawn to the warm glow of her spirit.

His mind went cold with anger, but he wrenched it back, knowing he had no right to the emotion. "I was too long in Silence."

Lara shook her head, something in her expression he couldn't read, fine lines around her mouth, fanning out from the corners of her eyes. "You've formed new bonds of loyalty, of trust, with packmates. We're . . . friends."

"Yes." He rubbed his thumb over her pulse, wanted to touch his lips to the spot. Physical hunger wasn't the problem, but Lara wasn't a woman for whom that would ever be

enough. She was a healer, built for family, for laughing children, and a mate who knew how to love with the same fierce
depth of heart as she'd love him. "I don't appear to have the
capacity to feel anything deeper." Maybe the scar tissue was
too thick, or maybe a critical aspect of his emotional psyche
had been broken beyond repair, but there was a wall inside
him that nothing could penetrate.

   Not even Lara.

RECOVERED FROM COMPUTER 2(A)
TAGS: PERSONAL CORRESPONDENCE, FATHER, ACTION REQUIRED*

FROM: Alice <alice@scifac.edu>
TO: Dad <ellison@archsoc.edu>
DATE: April 10th, 1973 at 11:44pm
SUBJECT: re: hello

Dad,

I'm so excited! Perhaps I shouldn't be, but I may have found the most extraordinary correlation. It began when I was able to track down the descendants of a woman named Jena Akim, an X-Psy who lived in the sixteenth century and was part of a high-Gradient family. The information on her and her family is more legend than fact, but if true, it might be the answer.

What is crucial is that unlike most Xs, who are put into specialized training as soon as they begin to show their X tendencies, Jena was never separated from her family unit. That of course is the key and why this has been missed so far. Perhaps it might even be that it is hidden or less visible in weaker Gradient minds—but I can't draw any conclusions until I'm able to confirm if my theory is correct.

If so, it *cannot* be coincidence—my studies show that the rules of the psychic plane are multi-layered and textured, so complex that even the Psy don't have a handle on them, but, and this is critical, there *are* rules.

Love,
Alice

File note: Action unable to be satisfactorily completed. Parents' minds show evidence of a subtle telepathic wipe in relation to the X Project—neither has any problematic or useful knowledge. Akim descendants unaware of any discovery relating to their genetic line.

Chapter 20

SIENNA OPENED THE door the night after the kiss to find Hawke waiting, his hand braced on the doorjamb.

"Ready to play?" the wolf asked.

Her heart kicked against her ribs, the memory of the wild bite of his taste entangling with the blatant masculinity of his scent—but just like with his previous visit, his phone beeped before she could respond to the invitation.

"This better be important," he barked into the receiver, clearly as frustrated.

A pause and then he snapped upright. Reading his expression, she went for her work boots, tugging them on with hard, fast motions. He glanced over but didn't say anything.

"Where?" he asked, his tone so calm and controlled she knew something bad had happened. "No, you're right. Do what you can. I'm on my way with Lara."

Sienna jerked up her head at the name of the SnowDancer healer. Pulling her unbound hair into a rough ponytail, she pushed past him into the corridor. "I'll alert Lara," she mouthed as he asked the person on the other end for further details.

Eyes very much that of the alpha, not the sensual predatory changeling male who'd come to her door, he broke from the phone conversation to say, "Bring her to the lower garage. She'll need extra supplies—more than one injured. Don't bother Judd. He needs to recover from some teleportation he did earlier."

Leaving the instant he gave another nod, she ran to the healer's apartment, which happened to be right next to the infirmary. No answer. But when she looked in the infirmary itself, she found Lara at her desk, reading some kind of medical journal. Giving the healer a concise summary of everything she knew, she helped gather the supplies.

"You did level-two medic training, yes?" Lara asked, moving fast and efficient.

Sienna acted the pack mule as Lara loaded her up with gear. "I completed the level-three class while I was with the leopards." All soldiers were required to have a secondary proficiency—a tech course would've been far less demanding for Sienna, given the way her mind worked, but being able to help people on any level was a gift beyond price for her, a tiny way to balance the violence of the X-marker.

"That's right. I got the competency notice." The healer nodded, as if making a decision. "Lucy did a double shift, so I'm not waking her up," she said, naming the young Snow-Dancer who'd just finished nursing school to take up a full-time position as Lara's assistant. "You're drafted." Her phone beeped at that moment. A quick conversation later, she said, "That was Hawke. We're going to need more help."

"Judd isn't wiped out." Sienna didn't know where her uncle had been teleporting, but she'd seen him at dinner with the children, was able to gauge his energy levels. "I don't think he'll be able to teleport us down," she said, aware Lara had been briefed on his Tk, including his ability to heal using telekinesis on the cell level, "but he can help with the injured."

"Get him," Lara said, then rubbed her forehead. "I'm going to have to wake poor Lucy up after all."

Five frantic minutes later, Lara and Sienna reached the garage with a couple of packmates who'd pitched in to carry the gear, to discover that Judd had beaten them there. "Hawke's already gone," he told them, strapping the supplies onto the bed of the truck. "I'll drive you two down. Another team will follow in a bigger truck with stretchers to help ferry the wounded back to the den."

"Lucy's coming as well." Lara turned to look over her shoulder at the entrance to the garage. "She should be—There she is."

A rumpled, red-eyed Lucy scrambled into the backseat beside Sienna. "What're we dealing with?"

"Multiple gunshot wounds," Lara said, "laser burns."

"Any critical injuries?" Judd pulled out and onto a narrow forest track. "I may be able to get you down there faster, but it'll wipe me out."

"It'll be better if you're able to help with the healing. Hawke will hold everyone until we get there."

Judd glanced at the healer, verbalizing the question Sienna had been about to ask. "I realize Hawke can push his strength into those with whom he has a blood bond, but is he able to reach others in the pack as well?"

"Yes." Lara was checking her phone for updates as she spoke, in touch with the person who had made the original call for help. "It's not as easy or as effective as the blood bond with the lieutenants, or the bond he has with me, but he can hold them there with the power of his presence."

"Hierarchy," Sienna said, realizing the true depth of the foundation that underpinned the pack for the first time. "Wolves will obey their alpha, even in that extremity."

"Exactly."

Sienna turned to Lucy when the nurse reached back to plait her sleep-mussed hair. "I can do that if you like."

"Thanks."

"Are you going to be okay with so little sleep?" Lucy reminded Sienna of Riley, though they had no physical similarities. It was, she thought, the calm stability of their natures. From everything she'd heard so far, that solid calm would be much needed tonight.

Lucy nodded. "Got used to it when I did some work for CTX during my breaks from nursing school—the news sleeps for no one." Her stomach growled on the heels of that statement. "Damn, forgot to grab something to eat. Crashed without dinner."

"Here." Judd threw a granola bar over the seat. "Had it in my jacket pocket."

"I avow my love for you here and now," Lucy said as she tore open the wrapper.

Sienna wondered if Judd had really had the bar, or if he'd executed a deft telekinetic "fetch." Having witnessed the price it demanded from him, she knew telekinesis wasn't an easy ability in any sense of the word, but it was one she wouldn't have minded in place of the fire and pain that was the X designation.

It was that kind of violence, however, that awaited them on a border section of den territory that backed onto DarkRiver land, an area thick with firs that pierced the glittering beauty of the night sky. Two of the cats were there, one of them performing first aid. The other, she realized, as her vision adapted to the glow of the field lamps stuck into the ground, had been shot through the arm—and yet he was attempting to do what he could for the others, all of whom were more badly injured.

"Oh, God," Lucy whispered, grabbing a medical kit from the truck. "Riordan must've come down early for the shift change."

Sienna followed the nurse's gaze to see that the big, playful wolf was bleeding heavily from a wound in his abdomen as he sat propped up against a tree. "He's hurt bad." So was Elias. The senior soldier appeared to have been hit with a laser along one side, his burned flesh no doubt causing him horrible pain, though he'd gritted his teeth against the screams. "Where's Hawke?"

They both realized the answer at the same instant. Simran, Elias's partner on watch and the woman whose place on the border Riordan would've taken, was down, blood seeping from a wound in her neck. Sienna knew it was a fatal injury—or should've been. Hawke knelt beside Simran, his hand clamped over the bloody gash, such intense focus in those wolf-pale eyes that she knew he was holding the sentry to life with his will alone.

It was only when she saw the light gleam over his naked back that she understood he'd run here, his speed outstripping any vehicle when it came to this place of mountain and forest, rivers and lakes. But to have reached Simran before the sentry slipped away . . . It was unimaginable, the sheer fury of his speed.

"Judd's got Riordan," she said to Lucy, compartmentalizing because if she allowed herself to think about the people who lay bleeding on the cold earth, it would paralyze her. "You take Eli and I'll check out the leopards."

Barker didn't protest when she sat him down against the

rough bark of an ancient pine, having lost enough blood that he'd started to waver on his feet. "Through and through," she said after inspecting the wound. "I don't think the bullet caused any major damage, but it needs to be looked at by someone better qualified." Slotting an antibiotic magazine into the pressure injector, she placed it against his skin.

The medicine punched through to his system an instant later. She followed it up with a painkiller before he could tell her he didn't need it. "I'm guessing you want Tamsyn to look at this?" she said, referring to the DarkRiver healer.

It was Barker's partner, Rina, who answered, having returned to his side. "As long as you think he can wait another hour or so? Tammy's on her way."

Sienna checked Barker's vital signs using a scanner. "He's stable for now." Glancing up at a slight sound, she realized the clearing was ringed by wild wolves, their bodies sleek shadows in the dark.

"They arrived with Hawke," Rina said, shaking her head in disbelief. "I think they're standing guard."

"Yes." Sienna began to disinfect the mangled flesh—to Barker's withheld hiss. "How did you end up in the middle of this?" As to what this was, that would come later, after the injured were safe.

"Our watch overlaps with Elias and Simran's," Rina said as Sienna nodded for the voluptuous blonde soldier to press sterile pads over both sides of the wound so she could bandage it up for the time being. "We sometimes stop for a couple of minutes, shoot the breeze. We'd barely gotten here tonight when those Psy bastards came out of nowhere." A pause, a wince. "No offense."

"None taken." Sienna knew who she was, knew too that had things been different, she might have ended up one of the Council's pet killers. "They teleported in?"

Rina brushed Barker's rich brown hair back from his sweat-soaked forehead, tucking her body even closer to his in that changeling way. "Rappelled down from a stealthcraft."

That made sense, because teleport-capable Tks were a limited commodity—though you wouldn't know it from the way Henry Scott had sacrificed several of his in recent months. "How did they get you all so fast?"

"Overwhelmed us with sheer force. It was obvious they meant to leave no survivors."

"The craft was close to silent," Barker said, leaning into Rina's tender touch, "but we caught a hint of it the second before they began to rappel." He clenched his jaw as Sienna fixed the bandage, the painkiller obviously not strong enough for the bone-deep pain of the wound.

Calculating his body mass and concluding it was safe, Sienna upped the dosage.

That he didn't object told her how bad he was hurting. "That," he continued after she put down the pressure injector, "and the fact Reen, Riordan, and I were here tipped the balance—they weren't expecting the three of us."

Sienna's gut went cold with the slowly dawning realization that the attempted murder of five people was only the tip of the iceberg. "If you start to feel worse," she said to Barker as she finished up, "I want to know right away."

"I'm fine." White grooves bracketed his mouth.

"How bad," she said, "would it suck to have 'stupid moron died of shock' on your gravestone?"

A roll of bright hazel eyes. "Definitely trained by Indigo," he muttered, skin sheened by cold sweat. "If I don't tell, Rina'll tattle."

"That's my job, doofus." Rina pretend thumped him on the forehead.

Satisfied, Sienna got up and walked to where Lucy sat beside Eli, doing what she could for the now-unconscious soldier. Burns charred the entire left-hand side of his body, glimpses of raw pink flesh beneath. "You sedated him?" Sienna thought of little Sakura, what it would do to her to see her father so hurt. And Eli's mate, Yuki . . .

"He was in a lot of pain." Tight words, anger contained. "He needs Lara, but Simran and Riordan were more critical."

"Will Lara be able to heal him?" Nausea churned within her as she knelt, helpless, beside the soldier . . . because she could burn a living being, too. Worse than any laser.

"Yes, but it'll take her some time."

Thank God. "Anything I can do?"

"Help me shove these sticks into the ground so the thermal blanket doesn't touch his skin when I unfold it over him."

That task done, Sienna rose to see that Lara had moved from Simran to join Judd at Riordan's side—the young male had also lost consciousness, his face leached of color. Not far away, Hawke had Simran curled up in his lap, her head tucked under his chin, her sleek black hair cascading over his arm. Noticing the woman was shivering, Sienna ran back to the truck and pulled out two more of the silvery thermal blankets. "Here," she said, giving one to Rina for Barker, before heading over to cover Simran.

Hawke tugged it around the fallen sentry, careful not to jostle her. "They're all okay." The wolf in his eyes, in his voice.

Never had she been more aware of the fierce strength of his love for his pack. "Yes," she answered, though it hadn't been a question. "I think Elias is going to end up the worst off—at least, until Lara can get to him." Sienna wasn't sure if Judd could heal burns using his Tk-Cell abilities, even if he had the strength after helping Riordan. "We can keep him sedated till then."

Tucking in the edge of the blanket under Simran's feet, she looked around, thought back to the supplies she'd hauled for Lara. "I think there are energy drinks in one of the boxes. I'll get some into everyone who's conscious." Healers and injured both needed to keep up their strength, especially given the chill night air.

SO calm, so efficient, Hawke thought, watching Sienna move with grace and speed across the clearing as she bullied and cajoled the drinks into the others. His wolf felt more than a lick of pride, but it was focused on far more painful matters. "Lara?" he asked when the healer drew back from Riordan.

The answer was instant. "Yes, more."

A single instinctive thought and the strength of his men and women flowed into him through the alpha-lieutenant blood bonds. Indigo's incredible heart, Riley's solid loyalty, Matthias's quiet determination, Riaz's intensity, Alexei's barely tempered power, Cooper's stubborn tenacity, Jem's wildfire, Kenji's calm will, Tomás's energetic wildness. The only thing missing tonight was Judd's cool touch—the Psy male was focused on healing the last of Riordan's injury as Lara staggered over to Elias.

Funneling that power to Lara's form through the bond that every alpha had with his healer, he watched color spill into her cheeks . . . then drain away as she ran her hands over Eli's ravaged flesh. She cried no tears. Never did Lara cry—not until her people were safe. Only then would she collapse.

Dark rubies glimmered in the light of the field lamps as Sienna ran to meet the truck that had just arrived, helping to snap out the field stretchers. She, too, he thought, wouldn't break down here, on this bloody spread of ground. Not Sienna. Not the woman who'd survived a Councilor, survived the brutal demands of her own savage gift . . . and almost won a game played against an alpha wolf.

HAVING taken a bare few minutes to shower to wash off Simran's blood after Lara pronounced that there was no more healing to be done, Hawke returned to the infirmary. "Tell me," he said to Lara, aware of Sienna moving between patient rooms, keeping an eye on things—the healer had ordered both Lucy and Judd to bed as soon as everyone was stable.

"Riordan and Simran should pull through okay," Lara said, raising a hand to the wild energy of her curls. Her fingers trembled for a second before she fisted her hand, dropped it to her side. "I heard from Tammy—Barker will be fine, too."

"Eli," he asked, conscious she hadn't mentioned the senior soldier. "I know you have to heal burns in small steps. How bad is it?"

Lara's eyes drifted to the room where Elias lay under a curved panel that covered his body from neck to toe. "I've taken care of the life-threatening damage, but he had to wait so long his body went into shock. I won't be sure of anything until he wakes."

"You did everything you could," Hawke said, knowing the words wouldn't be enough, not for a healer. About to ask her to go into the office so they could talk privately—so she could drop her stoic front for a therapeutic minute—he saw someone unexpected walk out of Elias's room.

Yuki flew into the infirmary at the same instant, stopping only long enough to whisper, "Thank you, Walker," and brush her hand over the Psy male's, before she entered the room where Elias lay unconscious.

Hawke knew Yuki had left to check that Sakura was fine with her grandparents, hadn't realized Walker had stepped in to sit with the fallen soldier, though now that he thought about it, it wasn't a surprise. He'd seen Elias and Walker talking more than once, noticed their girls playing together, realized that the two must have formed a friendship.

"Eli's got Yuki watching over him," Walker said to Lara, his intent gaze taking in the shadows under her eyes, the lines around her mouth. "The other injured are in a medicated sleep. You can't do anything until they wake. Rest."

Lara's lips thinned. "I'm fine." Folding her arms, she turned back to Hawke. "I'll monitor them through the rest of the night—I need to make sure we didn't miss any hidden damage."

Hawke waited to see what Walker would do.

The other man folded his own arms and said, "Hawke, notice how she's wavering on her feet?" in the most reasonable of tones.

Lara's eyes flashed fire, but Hawke had to agree. "Take an hour—I'll keep an eye on everyone," he ordered, tugging her into an embrace and nuzzling a kiss into her hair. "Don't be ornery just to piss Walker off." His wolf didn't know what was going on between the two, but there was no mistaking the tension.

A scowl marred those fine features. "Ornery?" But she softened in his embrace. "A rest does sound good. Wake me the instant anything changes."

Hawke didn't miss the way Walker watched them. Neither did he miss the fact that the tall Psy male followed Lara to her office, where she kept a sofa. Moving out of hearing range, he checked in on the injured, found Sienna sitting at Riordan's bedside, her hand on his. "His mom started to cry so his dad took her out for a few minutes," she said in a subvocal murmur, her eyes devoid of stars. "They didn't want him to hear it in his sleep."

He waited with her until Riordan's parents returned. The couple allowed his wolf to give comfort to theirs, but he knew nothing would truly soothe them until their child woke. Leaving them with their hands touching Riordan's skin in silent support, he intertwined his own fingers with Sienna's.

Chapter 21

LARA FELT THE back of her neck prickle with awareness as the door shut with a quiet snick. Conscious her tiredness could undermine her resolve where Walker was concerned, she bought time by shrugging off the sweatshirt she'd pulled on over a faded pair of jeans after a two-minute shower to wash off the blood. Her wolf had been unhappy to leave the injured for even that long, but the doctor in her knew the value of cleanliness in a medical surrounding.

"Look," she said at last. "I know we're friends"—it physically hurt to say that in spite of the fact that she'd made the decision to accept the friendship, continue on with her life in every other way—"but I really would prefer to be alone." A painful lie. She was a healer, a wolf. She loved being around her pack. But more, she needed to be around *her* man. Unfortunately, the man both woman and wolf had chosen was unable to give her what she needed—Silence and a stranger named Yelene had ruined the finest man Lara had ever known . . . and it appeared the damage was irreversible.

Sinking down on the sofa with that truth weighing down her already heavy heart, she bent to unlace her boots.

Dark blond hair threaded with the barest glimmer of silver filled her vision as Walker knelt to do the task. "Don't," she whispered, her defenses shattered by the events of the night, until she could no longer hide the ache in her soul, the empty space where he should've been.

He ignored her to undo the laces and remove her boots with quick, steady hands before tugging off her socks. She gave up trying to stop him, gave up trying to fight the need tearing her apart, and simply indulged in the sight of those strong shoulders below her, the fabric stretched taut over solid muscle.

A teacher, that's what everyone said he'd been in the PsyNet. But Lara had always wondered if there was more to it—there was something about Walker that spoke of shadows, of hidden truths. Things she knew he'd never share. Not Walker.

"Sleep." A single deep word as he rose and picked up the blanket from where it had fallen off the couch.

Surrendering both to exhaustion and to his indomitable will, she laid down her head and closed her eyes. She felt the blanket being unfurled over her, felt his fingers push rebellious curls off her face with a tenderness that made her throat lock, but she didn't open her eyes. For this single, shimmering moment, she'd indulge in a fantasy in which Walker wasn't broken. Tomorrow would come soon enough.

ONCE in the break room, Hawke grabbed a seat at the small table and pulled Sienna into his lap. She turned stiff. "What are you doing? Anyone could walk in."

His wolf peeled back its lips, a low growl rumbling in his chest. "Do you think I'm planning to hide this, hide us?"

"No." Yet the edgy distance remained.

Neither part of him liked it. "You've seen me holding packmates."

"Never me." The absolute lack of emotion in that simple statement killed him.

"No," he agreed, stroking his hand over the dark beauty of hair. "Let me hold you tonight."

It took time for her to soften, to curve her hand over his shoulder, settle her head against him. And he knew—because he *knew* her—that that would be all she'd give him unless he pushed. Sienna was used not only to keeping secrets, but to fighting her battles alone. No more.

One arm around her shoulders, the hand of the other on the sleek muscle of her thigh, he said, "Eli's injuries got to you." He'd been focused on Simran, but his wolf had sensed Sienna arrive, had him glancing up to see her eyes turn to midnight when they landed on the injured soldier.

There were no words from her, not for a long time. When they did come, they were brittle shards. "I could do that. I have done that . . . and worse," Sienna said, not knowing why she was admitting to the true horror of her nature. "No one knows."

Hawke's hand stilled on her thigh for a fraction of an instant before he began to pet her again with those small, slow movements. "Talk to me."

She'd kept the secret for so long, not wanting anyone to see her as a monster, but tonight, she knew that to be a false hope. She *was* a monster. That could not be changed. "When I was five years old," she said, her mind acrid with memory— the lash of cold fire, the agonizing sound of a high-pitched scream, the nauseating scent of burned flesh and melted plas as the datapad fused into the soft flesh of a hand that had only ever touched her in gentleness, "I set my mother on fire."

"Ah, baby." The tenderness in his voice almost broke her.

"That's how it happens with the lucky ones," she said, the piercing echo of her mother's screams something she would never forget. "The unlucky ones immolate themselves the first time the X-marker kicks in." Unlike with the majority of other designations, it was near impossible to identify an X while the ability lay dormant.

"I know your mother survived."

"Yes, she was a powerful telepath." Sienna's shields had been basic at that stage, with her mother providing the necessary psychic protections. As a result, Kristine had had full access to her mind. "After the first shock, she did the only thing she could and knocked me unconscious." The medics had been able to repair all but the damage done by the datapad. Kristine had carried a fused patch of skin and plas on her palm until the day she died—and never once had she blamed Sienna for it.

Hawke settled her deeper against him, the hand that had been on her thigh moving up to cup her face. The guilt inside of her made her want to avoid his gaze, duck her head, but she'd never before done that with him, recognizing instinctively that to bow down in such a way was to signal something to his wolf that she did not want. "That was when Ming came," she said, meeting those wolf-blue eyes though shame curdled her stomach. "He wanted to cut me off from my family at once, except that my mother had been unconsciously subduing my urges since birth."

No judgment on his face, nothing but an intense concentration. "Is that normal?"

"In a way. Psy children often don't know what they're doing with their abilities, so most parents keep a psychic eye on them."

"The same way adult changelings make sure pups don't claw each other by accident."

His words, the attempt to find common ground between them, thawed a little of the frozen lump in her chest. "Yes. But my mother, she was a cardinal telepath, very, very strong—she didn't realize just how much power she'd been utilizing to block me. If she'd been weaker . . ." She shook her head, the chill returning to infuse her very bones. "I would've killed either myself or another child much earlier."

Hawke sensed the gut-deep pain behind the calm, almost flat words. *Five years old.* A baby, and she'd been in Ming's care. "Your mother went with you?"

A nod. "I didn't know then, I didn't realize, but my mother was different. Most women would've handed me over to Ming and released themselves of all liability, but even after he was able to take over what she'd been doing to help me on the psychic plane, she refused to sign away her rights as my mother." Gleaming pride melded with a furious depth of tenderness.

"However," Sienna continued, "she couldn't teach me control. She was a communications specialist, not gifted in mental combat like Ming. It took him four months to safely isolate and contain me behind his own telepathic shields. Then he taught me. It was hard."

Such a simple statement. Such a terrible statement. "I hate Ming for what he did"—because that isolation, that containment, Hawke understood it had been a prison cell around the mind of a scared child—"but he helped you stay alive."

"No," Sienna disagreed, "he helped me become Silent. Most Psy graduate the Protocol at sixteen. I was Silent by age nine. Sometimes, I think that's why my mother decided to have Toby—because she knew I was gone from the instant Ming walked into our home."

And yet, Hawke thought, Sienna had never lost her soul. She'd retained the capacity to love Toby with a fierceness that was wolf in its strength, retained the loyalty to family that had seen her defect to save the children's lives. It staggered him to realize the incredible will she must've had even as a child that she'd been able to hide and protect that part of her psyche from a Councilor.

About to speak of the depth of his pride in her, to tell her she had no reason to carry any shame, he heard a slight sound. "I think Simran is up."

Sienna flowed off his lap, concern replacing the heavy darkness that had fallen over her face as she spoke of her mockery of a childhood. "Should I fetch Lara?"

"No, let me check first. But why don't you look in on the others?"

When he walked into Simran's room, it was to find the injured sentry smiling weakly at the woman who sat by her side, a lanky soldier so fleet of foot that Hawke often used her as a messenger across den territory. "Inés," he said, running the back of his hand over her cheek. "When did you get back?"

"Ten minutes ago." Her body trembled as she leaned in to rest her head against his side. "Simran won't tell me how badly she was hurt."

Simran said, "No need," her throat husky.

Making a hushing sound, Inés reached for the bottle of water on the bedside table. "I'm talking to my alpha, if you don't mind." The words were chiding, the tone affectionate as she put a straw into the bottle so the wounded sentry could take a sip.

Hawke pressed his lips to Inés's temple when she put down the bottle. "It was bad," he said, ignoring Simran's scowl, "but I had her and I wasn't letting go."

"I'm so glad you're a stubborn bastard." Inés's thin arms hugged him tight before she leaned over to brush the hair off Simran's face with fingers that were exquisitely tender.

Riordan, when Hawke glanced into the novice soldier's room, remained in a sedated sleep, but Elias had regained consciousness, his hand on his mate's head as she pressed it to his uninjured side. *Thank God.* Figuring Lara would forgive him for not waking her up since it was good news, he was about to leave the couple in privacy when Sienna brushed past him and into the room. "Here," she said, putting a warmed-up cup of soup in Yuki's hand. "Drink it or you know he'll keep fussing."

"I don't fuss." Rasped-out words. "Now drink it."

Deep shadows lingered beneath the liquid dark of Yuki's expressive eyes, the lids swollen and red, as was the tip of her nose, but there was no lack of energy in the face she made at her mate. "Bossy man."

"You're stuck with me."

"Yeah." A smile so intimate, it felt wrong to witness it. "For the next century, at least."

Lara appeared in the doorway beside Hawke right then, her cheek bearing marks of sleep. "What's the ruckus?" she asked with a beaming smile before shooing both Hawke and Sienna away. "Get rested in case I need you tomorrow."

Seeing that Walker had returned to the infirmary, Hawke acquiesced. "I want to grab some fresh air," he said to Sienna.

"Good idea."

It wasn't until they were outside, with her leaning up against a gentle knoll in the White Zone, that she said, "It must be nice, don't you think?"

He braced one arm on the grassy surface beside her head, his wolf strangely content in spite of the skin hunger that continued to be a constant ache at the back of his mind. "What?" Twining a strand of her hair around his finger, he rubbed it between fingertip and thumb.

"To have a hundred years with someone." Her voice held such haunted need it shook him. "I never imagined that was possible before I came here."

"Most folks live at least three decades beyond a hundred," Hawke said, stepping close enough that one of his thighs brushed hers, "so it's not unusual."

Sienna didn't pull away, the scent of her an unintended caress across his senses. "But together . . . imagine how deeply you'd know someone after all that time, how very complex the love would be between the two of you."

It was time, he thought, to lay things out into the open. "No hypotheticals, Sienna. Me and you. Is that what you want?"

"I've made that pretty clear." An acerbic reply accompanied by arms folded across her chest.

His wolf liked the bite of her, but he had to be certain she understood the implications of being with him. All of them. Fisting a hand in her hair, he pressed in close until she had to unfold her arms, her hands landing on his waist. "Do you know what it would mean for you if I take you as mine?"

Though her pulse was a frantic beat he wanted to lick, she stood her ground.

"No matter what, I can't give you the mati—" he began, because he would not lie to her.

"I know," she interrupted. "I heard . . . I put things together."

Of course she had, his smart Psy. But that wasn't the only thing he had to say. "No more flirtations with boys your own age," he said, gripping that stubborn jaw with his fingers. "No more dancing with any male but me. No more time to learn who you are before you have to hold that personality against mine. No more freedom to explore your sensuality before I own it."

Right at that moment, face-to-face with the dominant force of his personality, Sienna realized exactly how much Hawke had been holding back, and part of her hesitated. The fact was, while she was intelligent and off the charts when it came to psychic strength, she had no true knowledge of how to deal with males . . . no, with *this* male. He was the only one who'd sliced through her every shield to impact the very core of her, the part she'd protected with single-minded determination even as the rest of her turned Silent.

"Scared?" Hawke's smile held no humor. "You should be, baby." Then he kissed her, and it was no tender exploration, no playful tease. This was the kiss of a man who knew precisely what he wanted and had no compunctions about getting it. Using his grip on her jaw to angle her how he wanted, he nipped at her lower lip hard enough that she gasped, opened her mouth.

Making a deep sound low in his throat, he swept in, tasting her with a proprietary thoroughness that caused a tremor to shiver through her frame. Instead of easing up on the kiss, he pressed deeper into her, letting her feel every hard inch of him as he licked and tasted and demanded. Never had she realized how soft her body was in comparison to his, how much hotter he burned.

It was a lesson, and when it was over, she had kiss-swollen lips, a body so sensitized to his touch that it burned a craving across every inch of her . . . and a sudden awareness that maybe, just maybe, she hadn't thought this out as well as she'd believed.

Chapter 22

THE GHOST THOUGHT of the uses he could make of a cardinal X, fully cognizant that he was more than capable of double-crossing Judd. Except for one thing—his reason for building the fires of rebellion, for not executing the entire Council in a bloody burst of violence, it held him back, acting as the conscience he didn't have.

As a result, instead of spending his time strategizing about how to gain control of the rogue X, he dove into the slipstream of the Net, the psychic network created by the minds of millions of Psy across the world, each mind an icy white star on an endless spread of black. The Net existed in every place on the earth, a vast sprawl that had no limits.

In this infinite system ran rivers of data, millions and trillions of pieces of information uploaded each and every day by the minds hooked into the network. It was the biggest data archive on the planet, the storehouse of knowledge for their entire race. The unwary could get buried under the weight of it, but the Ghost was a shark gliding through the slipstream in lethal silence, filtering data with a speed and specificity that was almost preternatural.

Rumors, whispers, conspiracy theories centered around the time and manner of Alice Eldridge's death, all of it floated to the top of his consciousness as the Net gave up its secrets. None held anything of substance. Either the Arrows had done an immaculate job of wiping Eldridge from the Net, or the data had degraded in the years since her death.

That left him with the Obsidian archive. Created by the NetMind, the neosentience that was the guardian and librarian of the Net, the Obsidian archive was a backup in case the PsyNet ever suffered a catastrophic failure. The Ghost had named it Obsidian because the complexity of data within it made it all but a wall of black. Only a rare few individuals had ever realized the Obsidian archive existed.

Even fewer knew how to access it.

If there was anything to find on Alice Eldridge's second manuscript, it would be buried in that immense hoard of information. Otherwise, Sienna Lauren was on her own.

Chapter 23

SIENNA CAUGHT HAWKE as he was heading out of the den early the next afternoon. "Wait." The tense line of her spine told him she'd forgotten nothing from the previous night.

Neither had he. "Talk fast, baby." It came out curt. Yes, he'd meant to scare her, but to be honest, he hadn't expected it to work. That it had irritated his wolf. "I've got a meeting."

"If it's to do with the attack, you need to hear this." She walked at a rapid clip beside him as he continued on outside, where he'd left a vehicle.

"I'm listening."

"What they did, it's a tactic Ming used to talk about."

"A quick hit designed to hurt the pack's morale." The death of five changelings would've been considered a bonus. "I guessed that." His fury was a cold thing, his wolf thinking with clear-eyed precision.

"No, it's more." She almost ran as he lengthened his stride. "It's the beginning of a war of attrition. They're not going to come at you full force until they've whittled down your numbers through surgical strikes. Because you don't have an obvious target against which to retaliate, you'll splinter your forces in an effort to keep up, further fragmenting your strength."

Catching the assurance in her voice, he came to a stop. "You sound certain."

"I am." There was nothing of reserve in her now, only steely-eyed conviction. "The fact that whoever was behind this used a stealthcraft rather than telekinetics, when they know changelings have superior senses and might well detect a physical intrusion, tells me their Tks were doing something else."

"You're assuming they have telekinetics."

"Anyone with enough power to mount that kind of op has the pull to have a unit of Tks under his or her command." She put her hands on her hips. "I want to borrow Brenna for a couple of hours, have her bring up satellite images of certain areas."

She was a novice soldier, didn't have the rank to make such a bold demand—but she'd also been the protégée of a Psy most considered the Council's military mastermind. "How do you plan to figure out where to look?" he asked instead of dismissing the request outright.

She tapped her temple. "Ming was, and probably still is, the best of the best when it comes to martial strategy. No matter who's running this, I can outthink them if I think like him."

He took an instant to weigh the variables, almost able to see the impatience flashing in her eyes. That was his girl, he thought, hiding his grin. "You can have Brenna—for half an hour," he said. "She's got too many other things on her plate."

Lines formed between her eyebrows but she nodded. "I'll narrow things down as much as possible before I go to her— that'll make it more efficient."

An hour and a half later, he could still see the white-hot rays of the Sierra sun glinting off the red in her hair as she turned to jog back to the den. The woman in front of him was an altogether different creature, had no fire in her soul. Nikita Duncan had given birth to an empath, then thrown her away. She was as cold as her daughter was full of heart. Even in looks alone, they were poles apart.

Nikita had cool white skin, eyes from Japan, and cutting cheekbones that complemented the razor-straight jet of her hair. Sascha's skin was colored a warm brown, her hair a curling tumble of soft black, her face softer, more rounded. Both unquestionably beautiful women. Except one had the blood of a reptile, while the other would spill her own to save a stranger.

"How are you, Sascha darling?" he murmured under his breath as Nikita turned to say something to the other Councilor at the table, the enigmatic Anthony Kyriakus—tall, patrician, his black hair silvered at the temples.

Sascha made a rueful face from his left. "About to give birth. That's what it feels like, anyway."

Her muttered words made him grin, but he could see that Lucas wasn't amused. He wondered how big of a fight the two had had today about Sascha's attendance at this meeting— not that Lucas would've taken any chances with really riling her up now that she was so close to her due date. If Hawke had to guess, he'd say the leopard alpha had bitten his tongue even as his animal went insane at the idea of his pregnant mate so close to those who might cause her harm. And for once, Sascha, the empath, seemed clueless.

Moving his lips to her ear, he murmured, "Sweetheart, you know I love you, but you need to get Luc away from here before he loses his mind."

Sascha froze, stared. Her eyes turned midnight within one blink and the next. "Oh dear," she whispered. "How did I miss that?"

"Probably because you're nine and a half months pregnant."

Rolling her eyes at him, she leaned over and pecked him on the cheek.

Lucas's growl was audible.

"Lucas," Sascha said at the same moment, "I don't feel that great."

The DarkRiver alpha shoved back his chair and bundled Sascha out of the room so fast that Anthony and Nikita were left staring. Vaughn, having been holding up the wall at their backs, slid into Lucas's seat with smooth feline grace, while Nathan took the one Sascha had vacated. Across from them, Nikita continued to stare out the door.

"She's not about to give birth," the Councilor said into the silence a second later, and Hawke realized she'd been tele-pathing her daughter.

Interesting.

"How close is she?" Max Shannon asked as he walked in. "Sorry I'm late—got caught up in traffic."

"Where's your J, cop?" Vaughn asked instead of answer-ing the question.

"On her way," Max said, referring to his wife, a former Justice Psy who remained uplinked to the Net in spite of her broken Silence. "She might have some info for us."

Hawke didn't trust anyone hooked into the PsyNet given how deep the Psy Councilors' tentacles were on the psychic plane, but he had nothing against Max's J in particular. In fact, he kinda liked her—Sophia carried shadows in her eyes. Shadows meant a life lived, a personality beyond the ice.

Riley stirred beside him. "Did you both read the report we sent through?"

"Yes," Nikita and Anthony answered simultaneously.

Again, interesting. It made Hawke wonder what other machinations the two were getting up to behind everyone else's backs.

"Neither one of us orchestrated the attack on your people," Nikita said. "Whether you believe that or not is up to you, but it makes no logical sense for us to weaken this region at present."

Meaning that if the other Councilors hadn't been a threat, Nikita might well have spilled changeling blood. Then again, Hawke thought, considering everything they knew about her, Nikita followed the money—war would be bad for her bottom line. There was also the fact that her security chief was a man with an impeccable code of honor, a man who'd laid his life on the line to protect the innocent.

As for Anthony, quite aside from the fact that the cats had vouched for him on previous occasions, the man controlled an empire of F-Psy worth billions. No one and nothing could shake him from that position. More to the point, the NightStar Group had always been willing to deal with anyone who could pay the fees demanded for a forecast: human, Psy, or changeling.

Max tapped the table now. "Plus, neither Nikita nor Anthony have the manpower. Simple as that." It was an admission of weakness, an opening gambit.

"Who else can you rule out?" Nathan, the most senior of Lucas's sentinels and a man with a head as calm and clear as Riley's, leaned forward.

"It's not Kaleb," Nikita said at once. "He's distracted by another matter at present." ·

"Our information," Riley inserted, "is that Kaleb has either gained, or is close to gaining, control over the Arrow Squad."

A long, careful pause. "You have excellent sources," Anthony replied at last. "Yes, it does appear the Arrows have shifted their allegiance from Ming to Kaleb—and their priority has always been Silence and the integrity of the Net. The squad disassociated from Ming because he lost sight of that priority. Kaleb is unlikely to repeat the mistake."

That tracked with the information Judd had been able to get from his contacts.

"It's possible Tatiana is backing the Scotts," Nikita added, "but she'll have kept enough distance that nothing rebounds back on her. As for Ming, he has spoken against the Scotts in Council and appears to be more focused on internal matters."

Hawke entered the conversation. "You seem certain the Scotts are behind this." Their own intelligence supported the same conclusion, but he wanted to hear Nikita's and Anthony's reasons.

"It's patent they want total, unopposed control of the Net," Anthony said, the aristocratic lines of his face without expression but holding a charisma that would've made the man a force even without his command. "Aside from Kaleb, who is too formidable an adversary to challenge at this stage, Nikita and I are the only ones standing in their way—because we're acting together and in a region that can defend itself."

"We won't be able to pin it on them," Nikita said with a frigid bluntness Hawke was coming to associate with her. "They'll have made certain of it."

SEVENTY minutes later, Hawke had another discussion, this time with a much tighter group. Him, Riley, Judd, the two DarkRiver sentinels who'd attended the meeting, plus Lucas and Sascha. They met outside the alpha pair's cabin. Hawke didn't tease the leopard male today, knowing how on edge he had to be, having his mate so close to those who weren't Pack. It didn't matter that the wolves were allies—it was about the animal's need to protect.

Frankly, Hawke was surprised Lucas had agreed to the meeting . . . but no, perhaps he wasn't. Sascha and Lucas had the kind of relationship that every alpha craved, Hawke included. Sascha wasn't just a lover, wasn't simply a playmate in the best sense of the word; she was a partner, Lucas's first port of call when he needed advice.

It was instinctive to think of Sienna. So young . . . too young.

Ming was, and probably still is, the best of the best when it comes to martial strategy. No matter who's running this, I can outthink them if I think like him.

Frowning at the reminder of exactly how she'd gained that depth of knowledge, he turned to Luc. "What's your gut say?" He knew the alpha had sat in on the meeting via the subtle comm system Vaughn had been wearing.

"Nikita's right—no way to pin the violence on the Scotts, though everything points to them." Lucas rubbed at his stubbled jaw. "But who says we have to?"

"If we strike back and hit the wrong target," Hawke responded, "we lose the element of surprise."

"I know it's not my mother," Sascha said from the cushioned wicker chair positioned against the cabin wall. "Not because she's my mother, but because I know how she works. If someone was trying to mount a hostile takeover of Snow-Dancer's assets, cut you off at the knees in financial terms, I'd be the first to point the finger at her."

"It's not Anthony," Vaughn said without clarifying. The fact that he was mated to Anthony's daughter, however, did give the jaguar changeling a high level of credibility. It also made Hawke wonder, not for the first time, about Anthony Kyriakus's loyalties.

"I agree with Nikita about Ming and Kaleb Krychek," Judd said. "Ming's taken a hit with the loss of the Arrows and will still be consolidating his remaining troops. I can say with categorical certainty that the squad won't have mobilized on this big an operation for Kaleb yet."

Riley, pragmatic as always, asked the critical question. "Does Krychek have access to other operatives?"

"Yes. But fact is, he's a powerful enough telekinetic that he doesn't need anyone when it comes down to it. This is a man who could cause an earthquake, collapse the entire city."

"Jesus," Vaughn said as Lucas whistled. "Seriously?"

"His abilities are so far off the scale that the Gradient is meaningless." Judd's tone was matter-of-fact. "He's a master game player, so I won't discount him totally, but Kaleb's got two powerful packs in his region, and he's exhibited no aggression toward either."

"BlackEdge and StoneWater." Riley nodded. "We've got a line of communication with them, and from what they've shared, it looks like Krychek leaves them alone as long as they do the same with him. Doesn't make sense that he'd come out here to pick a fight with us."

"If we take Krychek off the table," Hawke said, "it leaves us with the same three Anthony and Nikita fingered."

"We go after all three." Lucas's tone was hard. "Surgical strikes, same as their hit."

Hawke, his mind awash in the blood scent and pain of his fallen, growled in agreement. "It has to be hard, and it has to be fast." The enemy had to understand the packs had teeth and no hesitancy about using them.

"The Scotts and Tatiana," Judd said, "are all protected behind walls of near-impregnable security. It's going to be difficult to get close to them."

"Not them," Sascha said, then yawned. "Sorry."

Everyone laughed, and the moment provided some much-needed levity.

"Okay, what I was saying before I fell asleep"—she leaned against her mate's thigh, where he stood with his back to the wall by her side—"is that you don't go after them. You go after something that represents them. Something big and shiny."

Judd's eyes landed on Sascha. "Are you sure you're an empath?"

"I grew up with Nikita for a mother."

It was relatively easy to choose a target for Henry Scott—

his London residence was in an eminent location and worth millions. The bonus was that Judd had been in and around the place as an Arrow, knew how their people could evade security. Shoshanna Scott also presented little problem. She'd bought a huge office building in Dubai a month ago—currently untenanted, it had minimal security.

"No casualties—security guards have to be clear before we strike," Hawke said, because killing innocents would make them no better than the Councilors. "We don't compromise on this."

"Agreed." Lucas closed his hand over Sascha's shoulder. "Do you have anyone in London? I know Jamie's roaming in that area, so we can pull him in."

Hawke gave a crisp nod. Wolves didn't go roaming as often as the cats, but given the Council's increasing aggression, SnowDancer had made a deliberate policy of stationing people in and around the world's major cities. Riley rotated their more lone-wolf types until the men and women wanted to come home. The latest to return had been Riaz.

The bulk of their time was spent handling SnowDancer's international business interests, but they also kept an eye on certain more covert matters, feeding information back to the den. However, every one of those lone wolves was a high-level soldier, more than capable of handling this type of task. "Dubai won't be an issue either." There was a SnowDancer within easy flight distance.

Lucas nodded. "That leaves Tatiana."

"That's a problem," Judd said. "She's bought interests in human companies—we hit any of those, we affect a large number of blameless people."

Hawke's cell phone rang at that moment, the code making his wolf come to wild attention. "Hold on," he said to the others and walked a small distance away. "Talk to me, pretty baby." Yeah, he was having trouble with the boundaries when it came to Sienna, even when he was the one who'd put them into place.

Brenna's voice came over the line. "You sweet talker." The words were tart.

His wolf grinned. "Put her on."

"Here—she was just double-checking something."

"Brenna and I were able to pinpoint three incursions made by the Tk team," Sienna said without any prelude. "Far as we can figure, they were laying charges. Indigo took people to check out the locations, and from the data she sent back, they're getting smarter. No metal components, hidden deeper to beat your senses, difficult to detect unless you're right on top of the devices."

Hawke's wolf bared its teeth, but his thought process remained icily rational. "Good work, both of you." Certain Indigo would have the situation under control, he moved to another matter. "Sienna, while you were with Ming, did you ever learn about a property or holding on which Tatiana Rika-Smythe places particular importance?"

"She has a tendency to buy into other companies," Sienna said, "rather than building herself. But . . . wait a second."

Brenna came on the line. "Your pretty baby is running a search."

"Smart-ass."

"I'm casually walking over to where she can't hear us."

"Why?"

"To ask you if you're courting her properly. Really, Hawke, a girl deserves flowers at least."

"I don't do flowers." And right now, the whole courtship thing was in the air. As last night had shown with inescapable clarity, she was nowhere near ready to handle the truth of him. The thought had his hand clenching on the phone.

"It's not hard," Brenna muttered. "Call up a florist, buy a bouquet."

Hawke's wolf liked her too much to be annoyed. "Let me talk to her, brat. I have to get back to my meeting."

"In a second. First—how's *my* pretty baby?"

Hawke glanced over to see Judd listening to something Vaughn was saying, his head angled toward the ground, a frown on his face. Unusual for the former assassin. "Flirting with a jaguar."

"You're not funny, mister," Brenna said before the phone passed hands and Sienna came back on the line.

"You'll have to confirm this," she said, "but it looks like Tatiana is still the sole owner of a sculpture that stands in the middle of a small park in Cambridge, England."

"A sculpture?"

"Yes, Ming found that odd, too, so he had me research it as part of my training. It was commissioned by a Smythe a hundred years ago, after the deal that led to their fortune. I don't know if it's the kind of thing you're looking for . . ."

"I might even kiss you for it. All over." Hanging up to her sucked-in breath, he walked back to the others. "I have a target for Tatiana." As for Sienna, he'd give her a bit more time, but . . . he was a wolf. Who the hell said he had to play it civilized? She was his. She *would* learn to deal with him.

RECOVERED FROM COMPUTER 2(A)
TAGS: PERSONAL CORRESPONDENCE, FATHER, ACTION REQUIRED AND COMPLETED*

FROM: Alice <alice@scifac.edu>
TO: Dad <ellison@archsoc.edu>
DATE: April 14th, 1973 at 10:32pm
SUBJECT: re: re: re: hello

Hi Dad,

Yes, my last e-mail did make no sense. I'm afraid I was giddy from the possible discovery. However, as you know from my phone call to Mom, my theory will be difficult to prove without bringing others into the equation, people who may not have the best interests of the Xs at heart. If only I was in the PsyNet, I could see for myself.

Love,
Alice

File note: See note on e-mail dated: April 10th, 1973. Parents have no useful or problematic knowledge. Terminal action not required.

Chapter 24

WALKER WALKED INTO the infirmary the night after the attack to find Lara coming out of Elias's room. "How is he?"

The deep purple shadows under her eyes when she met his gaze betrayed how little she'd rested since waking from her nap the previous night. "Good. Healing. I have to wait for his body to recover from this session before I can carry on. He'll be here for a while yet."

Seeing Lucy examining the readout on the panel in Riordan's room, he held out his hand. "Come with me, Lara. You need to have a break."

"No, I can't—"

He took her hand, halting her words midstream. "Either you walk out with me," he said, keeping his tone calm though his words were nothing reasonable, "or I'll take a leaf out of Hawke's book and carry you out." That situation, too, was something he had his eye on, but it wasn't time for him to say his piece. Not yet.

Lara's mouth fell open. "You wouldn't."

He waited, let her eyes scan his face, see the truth.

Cheeks flushing a dull red beneath that deep tan skin, she said, "You would." A small tug as she tried to free her hand, failed. "I need to tell Lucy."

"She's seen." Then he began walking, pulling Lara along.

She made a small growling sound he'd never before heard from her. "I'm a wolf, not a dog."

"You'd treat a pet better than you treat yourself."

Neither of them said another word until they were some

distance from the den, beside a waterfall that froze in the winter months but was at present a roaring spray.

Releasing his grip on her, he pointed to a rocky ledge. "Sit before you fall down."

"Argh!" She slammed fisted hands against his chest. "Would you like me to shift and wag my tail while I'm at it?" Anger turned her tawny eyes dark, thinned the soft invitation of her mouth.

"No," he said, grabbing her wrists, her bones delicate under his touch. "I'd like you to permit me to take care of you." It was a raw craving, this need he had to ensure she wasn't hurting herself. He didn't understand it, had never felt its like.

Lara shook her head. "I can't do this." Breath hitching, she pushed against him. "You can be my friend, Walker. But you don't have any other rights—you didn't want them."

"Lara," he began, continuing to maintain his grip, but she shook her head again.

"You were honest with me, so I'll be honest with you. The kind of rights you want, the kind you're trying to claim? They're intimate rights." Wet shimmered in the expressive depths of her eyes. "I can't give them to you. They belong to the man with whom I'll build a life, have children."

This time, when she pulled, he released her wrists, watched her leave.

The spray of the waterfall was cold on his skin.

THE day after running the surveillance search, Sienna found herself with time on her hands. Aware Hawke was busy organizing something with DarkRiver, she decided that rather than give in to her frustration at being shut out because of her rank, she'd make productive use of her time to go speak with Sascha.

When she moved out of the woods near the cabin, it was to see the empath walking back and forth in front of the home she shared with Lucas. "Thanks for agreeing to talk to me."

"Hush." A hand cupping her cheek for a warm moment. "You know you're always welcome."

"Where's Lucas?" It was a given that he wouldn't be far with Sascha now only days from her due date.

Sascha lifted a finger to her lips, then pointed up. Following the cardinal's gaze, Sienna found a black panther draped in graceful sleep over one of the thick branches that supported the aerie the couple planned to move back into after Sascha recovered from the birth.

"Wow," Sienna whispered, having never before seen Lucas in animal form. "He's beautiful."

The cat's tail waved lazily.

Sascha laughed. "He heard you—he's just dozing. Stayed up rubbing my back most of the night."

"Shouldn't you be sitting down?"

A black scowl. "Sienna, don't make me deck you."

"I don't know much about pregnancy aside from the facts, or what I've learned from being around you," she admitted. "I wasn't there while my mother was pregnant with Toby." No, she'd been trapped in a telepathic prison created by a master of mental combat. Awful as that had been, she wouldn't change it—because Ming had trained her in his own image, taught her the skills to fight those who would hurt her brother, her family, her pack . . . her man.

"Then we're in the same boat." One hand bracing her back, Sascha reached over to tuck Sienna's hair behind her ear. "You wanted to talk, kitten?"

Sienna looked up at Lucas, dropped her voice. "Can he hear us if we keep the volume low?"

"I'm afraid so. He's got bat hearing these days."

The panther made a low grumbling sound but didn't leave his branch.

Much as she respected the leopard alpha, Sienna wasn't sure she was comfortable discussing this particular topic with him in hearing range. "It's okay. You need to relax anyway."

"Talking to you is hardly a strain." A chiding look. "Luc will be a Sphinx, won't you, pussycat?" Her mate's responding rumble made Sascha smile. "He's feeling very grumpy this afternoon."

Needing answers, Sienna decided to ask her questions and trust in Lucas's discretion. "With Hawke," she said, walking with Sascha as the empath continued her easy pacing, "I . . .

something happened." Though it was in her nature to be private, she shared the gist of what had taken place between them the night of the attack. "He's been busy since then, but even when we've run into each other, he hasn't made a single move—it's like his wolf is watching, but for what, I'm not certain."

"Hmm." Sascha rubbed at her belly, her head cocked at a listening angle. "Oh, well, yes."

Sienna looked from the empath to her mate. "You have a telepathic bond?" *Extraordinary.*

"It's grown exponentially during the pregnancy." Digging the heel of one hand into her back while cradling her abdomen with the other, she blew out a breath. "I think Lucas is right—he says Hawke is waiting for you to go to him."

"He's not the kind of man who waits." If Sienna knew one thing, it was that immutable fact, which was why his sudden watchful distance had left her so at sea. "Sascha," she said, noticing the wince on the empath's face, "your back's hurting you."

"It'll be worse if I sit." Waving off Sienna's gesture toward the wicker outdoor furniture, Sascha continued to walk. "The thing is, Hawke needs to know you're making a conscious choice to be with him, even understanding that it's not going to be an easy road—though I have no doubt his patience will be shoved aside by his arrogance very soon and you'll find yourself hunted."

The black panther jumped down from his branch to stand against Sascha's side as she completed that dry statement. Smile curving her lips, the empath stroked her hand over that proud head. "There's also—" A startled cry, liquid gushing down her legs.

And Lucas was shifting in wild sparks of color. "Sascha, did your water just break?" Stunned leopard-green eyes.

"I've been having small contractions since the middle of last night," Sascha admitted, chest heaving. "I didn't want to call Tamsyn too early."

Rising without another word, Lucas gathered his mate into his arms, carrying her with no evidence of strain. "Sienna."

"I'm on it." Grateful she had the DarkRiver healer's code on her cell phone, she stabbed at the touch pad of her phone, missed. Tried again.

Tamsyn's calm response settled her own frantic heart. "I want you to go in," the healer said, "time her contractions, keep me updated. Can you do that?"

Sienna nodded, then realized Tamsyn couldn't see her. "Yes, yes, of course." She was a cardinal X and a SnowDancer soldier. She could time contractions. *Sascha was having her baby!*

"I'll be there in less than ten minutes."

Heading inside, Sienna knocked on the bedroom door before entering. Lucas had pulled on a pair of sweatpants and sat behind Sascha on the bed, one hand tangled with hers, the other petting her abdomen with soothing strokes. "How long till Tammy arrives?"

"Under ten minutes."

Sascha blinked. "So soon?"

"You think I'm an idiot?" Lucas's voice was a growl, his touch unbearably tender. "I knew you were having contractions, stubborn woman."

Sascha laughed, then winced. "Oh, here we go again."

Sienna started timing.

SASCHA felt another contraction building as Tammy walked in through the door, a competent, unruffled presence. "I'm so glad to see you." She'd been so sure she'd timed it right, except her own body had decided to reschedule things.

"I was never far away," the healer said with a smile as she checked the progress of the labor, her touch gentle and capable. "Sienna's in the kitchen with Nate. She's putting together food for the people she knows are going to start dropping by any minute—that girl is terrifyingly efficient."

"I thought," Sascha said, clutching at the topic to keep her mind off the rippling waves of pain, "she was going to pass out when my water broke."

"No, that was me," Lucas growled next to her ear. "Now, remember, don't try any more shit—do it like we practiced. Funnel the pain through the mating bond and into me."

It went against everything in Sascha's nature to cause him pain, but she knew he'd never forgive her if she didn't allow him to help her through this. "You have a terrible bedside manner."

A nip on her ear. "This is my first time."

Her heart bloomed. "Me, too." Gripping his hand as her abdomen rippled, she diverted the pain along the mating bond to the panther who held her so tight, so close.

His body jerked before he hissed out a breath. "Jesus H. Christ. I have new respect for the female of the species suddenly."

Tamsyn snorted. "You ain't seen nothing yet, buckaroo." Glancing at Sascha, she added, "I think it'll help if you walk around for a while. Nate will keep everyone from the back of the house if you want to go out there."

"Yes, okay." The next several hours were the most scary— and most wonderful—of Sascha's life. Exhausted, her hair sticking to the side of her face, she clung to Lucas's hand and rode out the contractions as they got progressively longer and closer together, until she couldn't stay on her feet. He took most of the pain, her panther, but her muscles ached, so many strands of jelly in her body. "Oh dear," she said toward the end of the third hour.

"What?" Tammy and Lucas asked at once, acute concern in their voices.

"The baby's decided it wants to stay right where it is." Sascha could feel its anger at the current circumstances clear as day. "It is not impressed by all this squeezing and jostling about and could we *please* stop."

Tamsyn's eyes widened. "Wow, everyone knows babies must feel like that, but you actually *know*. Since you do— you're going to have to convince the little darling to come on out. Your body is ready."

Sascha touched her babe's mind. *It's warm in my arms, too,* she cajoled. *Your papa's waiting to kiss you, pet you. Don't you want that?*

A vocal negative, for all that their child had no words yet.

"Come on, princess," Lucas murmured in his deep voice, stroking Sascha's abdomen with strong, loving hands as she lay with her back to his chest, "you know I've been waiting a long time for you. How am I ever going to hold you if you stay in there?"

The baby wasn't convinced, but Sascha felt a slight hesitation. "Keep talking," she said, continuing to reassure their child with her own loving murmurs until another contraction bowed her back.

The baby was shocked, scared.

You're safe. You're safe. She wrapped it in a warm blanket of love. *I've got you, my baby.*

"This time," Tamsyn ordered, *"push."*

"Hear that, princess?" Lucas whispered, pressing his lips to Sascha's temple. "Help your mama out."

Their child still wasn't sure they knew what they were talking about, but it was ready.

Just in the nick of time.

The next contraction almost lifted Sascha off the bed. She forgot all about funneling pain, all about doing anything but pushing, her grip on Lucas's hand a steel trap.

"One more time." Tammy's encouraging voice. "Come on, sweetheart."

As Sascha shuddered, tried to breathe, Lucas tangled his fingers with those of her other hand, too, bent to press his lips to her ear. "I've got you, Sascha darling."

Those were the last words she heard before she pushed one final time, and suddenly, her child was no longer inside of her, its angry screams filling the air. *Our baby.* Her heart clenched, and she felt Lucas stop breathing. "Go cut the cord," she urged him, knowing he was torn between the need to hold her and cradling their baby. "Go."

Sliding out from behind her with care, he followed Tammy's directions to cut the cord. The wonder on his face as he took their squalling child into his arms was a gift for Sascha's heart, a moment she would never, ever forget. "Hush, sweet darling." A deep murmur that washed over mother and child both. "Papa's got you." When he looked up, those wild green eyes shimmered with such protective love that she knew their child would never, for one single minute, feel unwanted, unloved.

Fingers shaking, she opened the top buttons of her maternity smock. Lucas moved to lay their baby skin to skin against her without a word. Tears rolling down her face, Sascha held their baby's fragile body while her mate cupped her cheek and touched his forehead to hers. "God, I love you."

Her laughter was tear-wet. "Even now you've gotten your little princess?"

Lucas's smile creased his cheeks, brought the cat into his eyes. "I told you it was a girl."

Chapter 25

SIENNA FELT AS if she'd burst out of her skin when she heard the baby's first cry.

The bedroom door opened what seemed like years later to reveal Lucas holding a tiny—so *tiny*—bundle wrapped in a soft white blanket. The sentinels and their mates, all of whom had arrived over the past two hours, crowded into the cabin.

"I'd like you," Lucas said, his smile touched with a fierce tenderness, "to meet Miss Nadiya Shayla Hunter."

Dorian peered at the baby. "Can I hold her?"

"Don't flirt," Lucas said as he handed the baby to the blond sentinel, who was immediately surrounded by his mate as well as the mates of the other men. Stealing the newborn for a cuddle, the women finally handed her back to a scowling Dorian before slipping in to see Sascha. Laughter drifted out of the bedroom soon afterward.

Deciding to take advantage of the lower number of people between her and the baby, Sienna made strategic moves around the room until she ended up next to Mercy—who'd stolen Nadiya from Nate, who'd stolen her from Clay, who'd stolen her from Dorian.

"Here," Mercy said, "you want to hold her?"

"I'm terrified." It was the first time in her life she'd ever said that aloud.

Laughing, Mercy showed Sienna how to support the baby's head, and then Nadiya was in her arms. "She's so small." Brushing aside the blanket, she looked at that miniature face, those fisted hands with their tiny fingers and miniscule nails. Lucas and Sascha's baby had slept through the adoration, but she waved her fists now before settling back down. Sienna was fascinated, could've watched her for hours.

Aware, however, that everyone in the room wanted to hold the newborn, she reluctantly relinquished her to Vaughn. The jaguar sentinel touched a gentle finger to the sleeping child's nose. "Hello, little Naya," he said. "Aren't you a pretty darling?"

Lucas smiled. "That's what Sascha thought for a pet name, too." Reaching out, he took the baby from Vaughn's careful hands. "Come on, princess. Mama's missing you already—you can break hearts later."

Everyone laughed. And that was the sound Sienna remembered most as she described the events to fellow SnowDancers later that night.

"We got a message both mother and child were doing well," Hawke said, leaning against the counter of the common room where they'd gathered, "but I figured I'd better not go down just yet."

Sienna, sitting at a table opposite him, had to fight the urge to get up, cross the distance between them, and reinitiate the contact that had been missing for over twenty-four hours. Now that she'd touched him, kissed him, she couldn't imagine how she'd survived before. "I think that's a good idea," she said. "Lucas is very close to his cat right now." The alpha's eyes had been those of the panther—a happy panther, but still a wild thing.

"What does the baby look like?" Brenna asked from beside her, jumpy with excitement.

"Tiny with her eyes scrunched shut."

"Marlee looked like that, too," Walker said when the laughter faded. "She cried as if she'd had her favorite toy stolen from her—on both the physical and psychic plane."

Judd glanced at his brother. "She *was* loud."

Sienna hadn't known her uncles had both been around at the time of Marlee's birth. Before she could ask about that, Brenna touched Judd's thigh, where he sat beside her. "How do they handle childbirth in the Net, honeypie?" The last word was clearly a private joke, because Judd reached out to tap his mate's lips, saying, "Remember the rules."

It was Walker who answered Brenna's question. "A strong telepath," he said from where he sat on Sienna's left-hand side, "will ease the mother into a near-unconscious state as he or she takes over the fetus's mind for the duration of the labor."

A long silence.

Sienna hadn't known that, found herself asking, "Doesn't it hurt the baby?"

Walker shook his head. "It's something our race used to do before Silence—the telepaths are trained to handle developing minds. We had to come up with something since women in childbirth are unable to neutralize their pain on any level."

Sienna believed him about the birthing process not harming the fetus—Psy cared too much about the mind to risk damaging one. "I think I heard Tammy say that Sascha was talking to her baby to convince her to come out. Wouldn't that kind of connection be worth the pain?" Her eye caught Hawke's at that moment, glimpsed the dark, unnamable emotion in the wolf-blue.

She knew without asking that he was thinking of his mate, of the children he would never have with her. But for the first time, Sienna didn't turn away, didn't yield to a ghost—she'd listened, she'd learned, so she knew that while it was harder than in a mating, changelings could and did have children in long-term, committed relationships.

Hawke's eyes narrowed at the challenge in hers. Later, after everyone else had left the room, he snapped his fingers around her wrist, tugged her close, and whispered, "You sure you want to play with the wolf, baby?"

Her stomach somersaulted, but she was ready. "Sure you're ready to handle an X, wolf?"

Chapter 26

FOUR HOURS LATER, in a fortified compound in southern Australia, Tatiana Rika-Smythe looked at images of the wreckage that had once been a solid marble sculpture. The cost of the piece—miniscule—was of no relevance. The destruction was a message, and as that, it hit the mark. She used the comm panel to input a call to Henry.

It wouldn't go through to his London residence, so she traced him via the PsyNet. "You—" she began when he answered her psychic hail.

"I can't have this conversation now, Tatiana," he interrupted without any attempt at courtesy and disappeared back into his mind.

Tatiana wasn't used to being brushed off, but she was also not stupid. Dropping out of the PsyNet, she brought up the feed from the spy satellite she used to get information on Henry, having increased her surveillance of him after he'd begun to act in a way that suggested he had become the driving force in the Scott partnership.

A two-second delay and the visuals came into crisp focus. Henry's London residence was collapsing. Slowly enough that she could see it had been evacuated, but there was no way to rescue it. The charges had been laid with careful precision—which begged the question of how anyone could've skirted Henry's security to get that close to the building.

Certain now that there would be a third target site, she began switching through the news channels. It took her only seconds to find it. Shoshanna's new office tower looked spectacular as glass fell in rippling blue sheets from its windows. The building was a skeleton in under a minute, its metal bones gleaming under the unforgiving desert sun.

The conclusion was clear—the Scotts had underestimated the changelings. Again.

Picking up her cell phone, she sent Henry a text message, the method of communication an indication of precisely how much she valued his mind at present. *Leave me out of it.*

HENRY received a call three minutes after Tatiana's curt message.

"A miscalculation," the male voice said. "But better now than later."

"So," Henry said, "you don't plan to pull out?"

"No."

Chapter 27

"WE MIGHT HAVE given them pause," Hawke said to Riley, Riaz, and Indigo as they stood on a cliff overlooking Snow-Dancer territory four days after the retaliation, "but they've succeeded in one respect. We're running at high alert—how long can we keep that up before our people begin to get exhausted?"

"I have an idea about that." Riley's eyes swept over the clearing below, and Hawke knew he was looking out for the sentry on duty. "A soldier can maintain this pace for a week without starting to slip—we run each for five days, swap him out with a soldier from one of the other sectors."

Right then, a wolf loped across the verdant land below and into the thick stand of firs that seemed to sprawl to the horizon. Tai, Hawke thought, identifying the large tan-colored wolf. "Can that be done without flicking up warning flags?" They could betray no hint of weakness.

"We do it in stages," Indigo said, namesake eyes even more intense in the mountain sunlight. "Set it up so the ones closest to den territory are moved in first, those who are farther out rolling in to take their places. We do it right, no one knows any different—Psy sure as hell can't tell one wolf from another when we're in animal form."

"Except for you," Riaz muttered to Hawke. "Because you have the bad taste to be a color that yells 'Here I am, shoot me now.'"

"Let's see who's a target when the snow falls, shall we?" Hawke turned a fraction to welcome the feral wolves loping up the rise. They wiggled between Indigo and Riley—on either side of him—to press against his legs.

"Spoiled," Indigo said, shaking her head. "They think you're theirs."

Hawke let his lips curve a little. "Do the rotation. But shorten the shifts to four days spread out over a week—I want everyone rested up if we have to kick into full defensive mode. Can we work that?"

Riley and Indigo both nodded, though Indigo was the one to speak. "I think it might actually work better that way." She growled when one of the feral wolves pushed too hard.

The wolf retreated.

"What about the cats?" Riaz asked, hunkering down to mock fight with another wolf. "Are they going to need extra manpower in the city?"

"I've talked to Mercy about it," Riley said, "and we're splitting duties unless any of you disagree. Leopards are going to focus on San Francisco while we handle the rest. We're also aligning our sentries so rather than doubling up in some spots, we're going to start working DarkRiver and Snow-Dancer land as one big territory."

No one disagreed, and for a moment, they simply stood there, looking out over the flourishing green of the valley, the slender spires of the pines, the jagged snow-kissed peaks of the mountains. It was a beautiful piece of the earth, but more, it was their heartland, singing a song of welcome to any lost or wounded wolf.

"We fight," Hawke said quietly. "All the way."

SURE you're ready to handle an X, wolf?

The operation against the Councilors and the ensuing time he'd spent helping maintain security, along with his other responsibilities as alpha—in combination with Sienna's duty schedule—had kept him from following up on her brazen challenge, but Hawke was ready to hunt today. Unfortunately, Judd had other ideas.

The Psy male walked into his office just as he was about to head out. "We need to discuss the Pure Psy camp in South America." Using the comm panel on the wall, he brought up surveillance footage on one side, a map on the other.

"How recent is this?" Hawke asked from beside him.

"Early this morning. I've kept a constant eye on any and all movements since I first became aware of its purpose."

Hidden deep in the mountains, Hawke knew the small "village" was a training facility for Henry Scott's increasing army of fanatics.

"As we discussed when I first located it," Judd continued, "it didn't make sense to eliminate or disable them at the time."

"Better to know where the bastards are hiding," Hawke muttered, zooming in on an aerial photograph taken by a falcon in animal form.

Judd wondered if Hawke had thought that far ahead when negotiating the alliance with WindHaven. Knowing the way the alpha's mind worked, Judd wouldn't be surprised. "However," he added, pulling up an overlay that showed the population inside the camp, "there's been a significant increase in their numbers in the past three weeks. They've also begun to bring in a large number of weapons. Intel about their target remains the same." The city, den territory.

"Will they be able to teleport out that many people and weapons at a speed that could prove dangerous to our defenses?"

Judd took a moment to do the mental calculations. "If they had an Arrow named Vasic, it would be a problem." Vasic was a Tk-V, the only true teleporter in the Net. He was also one of the extremely rare Tks who could go to *people* as well as places. As such, he'd have discovered the Laurens two seconds after they dropped out of the PsyNet if Walker hadn't used his considerable telepathic skill to create and then teach both Sienna and Judd how to weave a deflective shield around their minds prior to defection.

His brother had handled the children, though Toby, Marlee, and, in all probability, Sienna, no longer needed that shield, their appearance having changed enough to deny Vasic a "lock." "I've seen no sign of him in the surveillance footage, however," he continued, "and there's no indication that Henry has Arrow support." Though Judd's gut said at least some of the squad would find themselves compelled by the idea of Purity, of unadulterated Silence, of the promise of peace from the raging violence of their abilities.

Hawke brought up an older report. "Henry lost several telekinetics in the last skirmish with us."

"Yes, so even a generous estimate of the number remaining in his unit doesn't give him anywhere near the capacity to move the camp using Tk. Logic says he'll want to save their energy for the assault, so the camp will mobilize using more standard means." Increasing the image size, he pointed out the half-complete runway. "We need to start thinking about how we're going to disable them when the time comes."

"Ideas?"

"It's not subtle, but I could work at rigging the entire place to blow, focusing on the sections where they've stockpiled weapons." He could teleport in under cover of night, place the charges, and be gone with security unaware of a breach. "If I link the charges to a remote signal, we can detonate when necessary."

Hawke shifted the images around, bringing up more detailed terrain and aerial maps, the population overlay. "The area is too large for you to handle alone—the teleporting will wipe you out," the alpha said at last, displaying an understanding of Judd's abilities that, at one time, would've surprised him. That was before he'd learned that Hawke knew the capabilities of each of his lieutenants down to the wire. "Aside from the delay while you recover, a second incursion increases the chances of discovery."

Judd had to agree. "Alexei and Drew would both be suitable for this kind of an op, but it's a risk to go in with anyone who can't teleport out, though I can handle a second individual if the circumstances demand a quick exit." It was the other issue that was more problematic. "The guards will be on constant alert for non-Psy minds. Even a hint of an intruder, and floodlights will blaze over the entire compound." Not to mention the number of Pure Psy units who'd respond to mount a search.

Hawke cleared the maps and brought up a list of names. "Psy in the packs. Who has the training to do what you need?"

When the Lauren family had first joined SnowDancer, Hawke would've never trusted two Psy with such a critical operation. It humbled Judd, how the changelings had the capacity to accept with such depth and honesty. Once Pack, you had to betray their trust at the basest level to be booted out. It was, he thought, strangely akin to the blood-loyalty that tied the Arrows to one another. An odd correlation.

"Walker is an exceptionally strong telepath," he said, "but he's had no training in handling explosives." No, his brother had been trained in something far more subtle. "Ashaya isn't military. Neither are Faith or Sascha—quite aside from Sascha's current physical status."

He brought up a separate screen. The woman on it wasn't Pack, but she was linked to a group that had proven friendly. "Katya Haas has had some military instruction, from what I've been able to discover, but not enough to make her suitable."

"I don't think Santos would go for the idea anyway." Hawke rubbed his jaw as he named Katya's husband—the head of the Shine Foundation. "You trust any of your other contacts?"

Judd thought of the Ghost and his enigmatic priorities. "No." Then he added another name to the list of Psy who were Pack. "She has both the training and the psychic skill to escape detection."

"No." Flat. No room for compromise. "I can't believe you'd even suggest it."

"Ignoring who and what she is," Judd said, fighting his own instinctive need to protect the girl who looked so much like his lost sister, "is more dangerous than taking her into an operation." Sienna wasn't only powerful, she was disciplined and knew how to obey orders in a tactical situation. "There's a reason Maria felt compelled to challenge her. You know it and so do I."

Hawke had been called a coldhearted bastard more than once. But never when it came to those who were his—he valued the life of each and every member of his pack, would lay down his own for them without blinking. "I don't send novices into situations that could be lethal."

"That's not what this is about."

Hawke's wolf bristled at the quiet challenge. "I wouldn't send Maria or Riordan, even Tai, into that situation."

"None of those three spent ten years living with Ming LeBon." Judd kept speaking as Hawke's vision went wolf-bright. "She was taught to handle explosives when she was nine years old."

Hawke snapped his head around to face the former Arrow. "Not even in the Net would they do that to a child."

"Yes, they would." Judd stared at the stone walls with piercing intensity. "What better way to teach a child control than to put her in a room designed to blow up with her inside if she got something wrong."

Hawke's wolf wanted to savage the bastards who'd tortured Sienna, its rage turning his voice almost unintelligible as he growled, "Damn it, Judd. You were an Arrow!"

Judd flinched. It was such a slight reaction Hawke only caught it because his wolf was watching the other man with a predator's gaze. "We couldn't risk defection when Marlee and Toby were babies." Words so precise, they were coated in frost. "There was a high probability the severance of the PsyNet link—and we always knew we'd have to do that to truly escape—would've killed them outright."

A metal letter opener flew off Hawke's desk and slammed *into* the stone wall, the handle quivering from the force of the impact. Judd closed his eyes, fisted his hands. It took him over two minutes to speak again. "We had to wait." The bleakness in those words betrayed the cost paid for that wait.

With a wolf, Hawke would've clamped him on the shoulder, dragged him into a hug. But Judd wasn't wolf. Grabbing the handle of the letter opener, he pulled it out with a grunt and handed it to the Psy male. "Get it out."

The letter opener began to twist methodically into a complicated shape before being crushed into an unrecognizable ball of metal, which Judd began to slam into the wall again and again using his telekinesis. Stone chips flew to the floor.

"Did Sienna know she was going to be getting out?" Hawke asked when he judged the Psy male was able to speak again. Know she hadn't been abandoned?

"No. Not for a long time." Judd caught the distorted ball, held it in his hand. "She was too young, and she spent the majority of her time with Ming. We could only trust her with the plan once her shields were strong enough to hide her thoughts from him."

Hawke imagined Sienna as a small girl with eyes of cardinal starlight and hair of darkest red; thought, too, of the fear that must've stolen her breath, squeezed her chest as she was locked inside rooms full of explosives. "One slip of her gift . . ."

"It was a lie at first," Judd said. "Ming wouldn't have risked a cardinal X in such an accident. When she did make a mistake, they triggered explosions calibrated to knock her unconscious and injure her enough that she'd remember to be more careful next time."

Hawke's claws sliced out. "And later?"

"She asked to be put in those rooms." The metal ball spun at rapid speed in the air. "She had to know she'd be safe enough to defect with us."

Hawke didn't know whether he wanted to strangle Sienna for playing with her life that way or hold her tight, shield her from the world. Except, of course, that was an impossibility—she was an X, her mind meant to be a weapon. "Will she obey your orders?" His wolf raked him with its claws, but even it knew the decision was the right one.

"Yes." A pause as the ball of metal came to a gentle rest on Hawke's desk. "Yours are the only ones she's ever had trouble with."

No fear, Hawke thought. Even after all she'd been through, Sienna had never been afraid to stand up to him. Good. "I want this planned down to the last minute—in and out as fast as possible."

Judd gave a swift nod, his eyes holding an icy determination, an echo of the memories. "I'll do the prep work today. I'd rather reserve my psychic energies, so we'll fly out tomorrow morning into one of the larger cities. I can teleport us the rest of the distance after nightfall. Do you want in on the planning?"

"No." Hawke knew his instincts when it came to Sienna would get in the way. "Keep me updated."

"I'll get Sienna now."

"Judd." When the lieutenant halted, Hawke walked over and dragged him into a rough embrace. Psy or not, he was a SnowDancer. "Thank you for getting her out." For protecting her when Hawke hadn't known she was out there, hurting.

Judd's eyes were midnight when he pulled back. "She's stronger than all of us."

The words circled in Hawke's mind long after Judd left, but they didn't make his decision any easier to swallow. He was about to send a young woman, *his* woman, into a hot zone.

JUDD needed his mate with a ferocity bordering on insanity. All but dragging her from her workspace in the tech core of the den, he pulled her into their bedroom and pinned her to the wall. She gasped into his kiss but cooperated when he tore off her clothes, when he opened the front of his jeans and lifted her up by the thighs.

Too fast, too fast, his mind warned. Gritting his teeth, he tried to slow down.

The whisper was a soft, hot breath against his ear. "It's okay, it's okay. Come inside me."

"Brenna." Thrusting into the tight, wet heat of her in a single hard push, he shuddered.

Her nails dug into his back, her legs wrapped around his waist, and her mouth, it took his, holding him safe as he surrendered to the searing depth of his need for her.

Afterward, as they lay on the futon, he told her everything. "I wish I could protect her from this, but if we don't give her an outlet, it'll lead to a dangerous level of frustration."

Brenna drew patterns on his chest with a fingertip. "We women are tougher than you men realize." Propping herself up on one elbow beside him, she braced her cheek on her hand. "She doesn't need that kind of protection anymore—you're giving her what she needs; support to live her life."

"I haven't interfered, but this thing with Hawke . . . I don't know if she's ready."

"Sweetheart, no woman's ever going to be ready for Hawke." It was the driest of statements as she leaned in to press an affectionate kiss to his jaw. "But from what I can see, she's holding her own."

Her words, her touch, it anchored him, settled him. "I need you," he said to her, this woman who'd fought for her own right to live her life free of limits, "to build me some remote detonation devices."

Amazing brown eyes shot with blue peering into his as

she pressed her nose to his. "You always say the most romantic things."

His laughter came from deep within, tangled with her own, as his mate cupped his cheek and took him with a tenderness that made him her slave.

RECOVERED FROM COMPUTER 2(A)
TAGS: PERSONAL CORRESPONDENCE, FATHER, E-PSY, ACTION
REQUIRED BUT NOT COMPLETED*

FROM: Alice <alice@scifac.edu>
TO: Dad <ellison@archsoc.edu>
DATE: December 11th, 1973 at 11:23pm
SUBJECT: re: Silence

Dear Dad,

Yes, this idea of Silence disturbs me, too. It's why I've been so leery
of trusting the Psy archivist with my conclusions—there are certain
worrisome undercurrents in the Psy population at the moment. But
the good news is that one of my Es has agreed to do some
"undercover" scouting for me, and you know I would trust an
empath with anything. He says that what I posit should be easy to
see. If he finds what I expect him to find, then I'll have to figure out
how to test the theory.

Going back to Silence—George is a telepath, as you know, and a
more emotional man I have yet to meet. But even he says that
sometimes he wishes the voices would be silent. My Xs are all in
favor of it, and I can't say I'm surprised.

Have you spoken of it with your Psy colleagues?

Love,
Alice

P.S. Don't think I've forgotten your birthday. I have a surprise up my
sleeve.

*File note: The E in question has disappeared from the Net—all attempts
to find him alive or locate his body have failed. An active alert has been
placed with Enforcement and all hospital facilities.*

Chapter 28

SIENNA SAT ON a quiet spot overlooking the lake several hours after nightfall. It had shocked her when Judd told her about the upcoming op—but not because she couldn't do it. The exercise would be relatively free from danger given the strength of her shields and the fact that she could debilitate anyone who threatened her. Of course, contact was to be avoided at all costs, their objective being to get in and out without being detected.

Soft warmth covered her shoulders.

Startled, she turned to see Hawke. It was his jacket he'd put over her shoulders. "We didn't get to play our game." The part of her that had never had a chance to be a child was bitterly disappointed.

He sat down with one hand braced on the ground behind her, their bodies close enough that they touched hip to thigh . . . more. "It'll keep."

Unwilling to let it go at that, she held out a fist. "Ready?"

"You're going to attempt to beat me up with that puny hand?" Complete disbelief. "Okay, I'll pretend it hurts."

She *would not* laugh. To do so would only feed his arrogance. "Try again."

Frowning, he held out his own larger fist, smiled. "One, two, three!"

"Rock beats scissors." It was impossible to restrain her smirk.

A very wolfish look. "Best of three."

She held out a hand, called the countdown. Found her

paper being cut by the scissors. Laughing at the playful way he pretended to chop at her, she made a fist again. "Last one."

They moved their hands in unison.

Hawke grinned at the result. "Well, there are people who say we both have rocks in our heads, so I guess that's apropos."

"Speak for yourself." But she curled her hand back inside his jacket, luxuriating in the dark masculinity of his scent. "Judd told me about South America." A silent question hidden behind the statement.

"We need to discuss that." No longer any humor in his voice. "I need to be certain you're not only on board with this, but capable of doing it."

The words pricked her pride. Once, she might've snapped at him, but she was no longer that impetuous girl, hiding her mental fragmentation behind a mask of rebellion. Instead, she considered things from his point of view: a young, untried soldier going into an operation that required the utmost subtlety. If she'd been in charge, she'd have asked the same questions. "Yes, to both," she said. "Judd didn't know until I told him this afternoon, but I did an op very similar to this in a training situation."

He stroked his hand up her back to curve around her nape, hot and strong, a shock to her system. "How old were you?"

"Fifteen," she said over the wild rush of sensation. "Ming gave me a very simple brief—to get in and out of one of his installations. To pass, I had to set a number of charges in different locations and escape undetected." When Hawke remained silent, she asked, "Don't you want to know if I succeeded?"

He moved his thumb on her skin. "You wouldn't have remained Ming's protégée if you hadn't."

"Yes." Goose bumps on her flesh that had nothing to do with the temperature. "But I did make one error—I escaped even Ming's detection."

Rising without warning, Hawke took a seat behind her, pulling her into the circle of his arms, the bracket of his thighs. "Okay?" An intimate question against the sensitive curve of her ear.

"Yes." Except for the fact her heart was about to beat right out of her chest.

"The student showed up the teacher," he said, returning to their discussion of Ming. "That's when you knew you didn't have much time left."

Unable to resist, she curled one of her hands around the corded strength of his forearm, playing her fingers over the vein that ran so strong under the heat of his skin. "The rehab order came only a few months later. All orders are officially from the entire Council, but the Councilors act as individuals most of the time. Ming's signature was on ours. If he ever finds out I'm alive, he'll do everything he can to get rid of me."

"I don't know." Muscle and tendon flexed under her touch as he tugged her closer. "According to our intel, Ming has taken a couple of hits in the past few months. He might decide he's better off with you by his side."

"I'd kill him," Sienna said with cold precision. "The instant I had him in my sights, I'd burn him up and watch him die. And I'd make it slow, so he'd hurt for a long time."

Hawke didn't tell her that wasn't a good thought, that revenge would eat her alive. Instead, he nuzzled at her neck, and said, "I'd rather you focus your energy on helping the pack."

She angled her head to the side in shameless invitation, her hand moving up to close over his bicep. "I'd do anything for SnowDancer." *For you.*

"Tell me about your designation." Kisses along the line of her throat.

Her toes curled. "What do you want to know?"

"Why X?" The kiss of teeth.

Instead of pulling away, she gripped his arm tight. "Some people say it's from the Latin word *exardesco*, which means 'to blaze up.'" The words came out husky. "I think 'rage' is also another way it can be defined."

He raised his head, and it was then that she realized what it was she was saying, what it betrayed. No wonder he didn't want to touch her. Ice in her veins, she straightened and finished the story, because that was the only thing she could do. "It's said we were once called the burning ones, so the Latin roots would make sense. But I've always thought it was because of what we leave behind when we go supernova: nothing."

Hawke snarled at the self-condemnation in that last word. "Would you call me a monster, Sienna?"

She tried to jerk up and out of his hold. "Of course not."

He wouldn't release her. "Yet I've killed."

"In defense of your pack," she said, her hand gripping his forearm again, her touch satisfying a bone-deep need. "That's different."

He regretted none of the blood he'd spilled in defense of those who were his own, but— "It leaves a mark on the soul nonetheless."

"When I was younger," she said in a voice so quiet it was near soundless, "my hold on the cold fire erratic at best, Ming would put those he wanted executed in a room with me, and then he'd use every psychic method he had to push me over the edge. It was his way of teaching me control." A jagged breath. "He made sure they were conscious. The screams . . . I hear them in my sleep, over and over, and over again."

Hawke clenched his jaw to keep his claws inside his body, knowing that wasn't what she needed. "That's on him, baby. Not you. *Never you.*"

Sienna dipped her head, her hair sliding forward to obscure her face. "People think that after the first kill, it becomes easier. It never does."

"No." It struck him then that this wasn't a conversation he should have been able to have with a nineteen-year-old woman. Yet that made it no less real, made her scars no less deep.

Dipping his head to push back her hair and kiss the throbbing pulse in her neck, he said, "Turn around," his voice rough with the raw fury of his emotions.

A shiver as she twisted around to face him on her knees. His jacket slipped off, but he put it back around her shoulders, finding a primal satisfaction both in keeping her warm and in having her covered in his scent. "Enough talk of death," he murmured, sliding his hand under the cool silk of her hair to cup her nape—driven by the wild need to do everything he could to wipe the sadness from her. "Let's live." He dropped his eyes to her mouth.

Her lips flushed under his regard, her pulse thudding in a

rapid tattoo that drove his wolf insane. "Scared?" He traced the full curves with one fingertip.

"You *do* bite."

Smile creasing his cheeks, he gripped her chin, pressing down with his thumb to part her lips, and then he kissed her. No sweet, playful thing this, but a hot, wet demand that had a moan escaping her throat, her body arching against the hard wall of his chest.

He half expected her to shy as she had that night outside the den, but her fingers clenched on his shoulders, her lips generous and sweet under his voracious mouth. "You shouldn't give me everything I want," he chided.

"Why?"

"Because it makes me greedy." Stroking his hand down over her throat to her chest as he claimed her lips again, he curved his hand over the lush swell of one breast.

She froze.

Nipping at her lips, he flicked his thumb across the taut peak he could feel through her thin black sweater, had the satisfaction of shocking a gasp out of her. "Now imagine," he murmured in her ear before kissing that beautiful throat once more, drinking in the quivering intoxication of her arousal, "what it'll feel like when I rub your nipples after I've stripped you bare."

Sienna shuddered. "Don't stop."

Petting her down from the edge, he took his hand off her body, his lips off her skin, and nudged her until she lay on her back on the earth, his jacket protecting her from the cold. "Is this hurting you?" He'd caught no indication of it, but he had to be sure.

A quick shake of her head. "We disabled that layer of dissonance."

That layer.

Which meant there were more, but they wouldn't talk about the subject tonight, because tonight, he wanted to pleasure her, tease her, indulge her. "Pretty, troublesome Sienna," he whispered, bracing himself beside her on one elbow and stroking his hand under the bottom of her V-neck sweater to lie over the taut smoothness of her abdomen.

Her muscles tensed under his touch, her eyes dark as the night.

"That feels . . ." A trembling breath. "May I touch you?"

His cock, already rock hard, turned excruciating at the polite question. That was when he realized he didn't have the patience to play with her, to ease her into the storm of his sexuality. Not today, when his wolf had been pushed to the edge by what she'd shared, the decision he'd made.

More, Sienna needed to rest, to preserve her strength for the op.

Groaning, he kissed her hard and wild, then rolled up to his feet, dragging a bewildered Sienna up with him. Unable to stop himself, he cupped her face, took her mouth again with possessive heat. "We'll finish this"—another kiss—"later." A bite on her lower lip. "After you get back." With that, he bent, grabbed his jacket, and put it around her.

He wasn't ready for the kiss she laid on him.

Son of a bitch.

His hands clenched on her hips, one step away from pulling her up and against the hard ridge of his cock. From there, it'd be about two seconds before he had her sweater shoved up to her neck, her bra ripped off so he could feast on her breasts. Another five—maybe ten because he had a feeling he'd be greedy about her breasts—before she was pinned naked to the nearest tree.

Wrenching away from the enticement of her, he stalked to the edge of the rise, but he was still too close, the autumn and spice of her lingering in his mouth, in the air, on his skin. Teeth gritted, he scrambled down the slope to the lake and walked to the water's edge to throw the frigid liquid on his face. *Christ!*

His wolf, though not normally bothered by the cold, didn't care for the shock, but it was in control by the time Sienna joined him. He pointed a finger toward her. "Behave—unless you want to be naked and under me in about five seconds flat." Or maybe the wolf wasn't in control.

She blinked, swallowed, shook her head. "I don't think I'm quite ready."

Neither did he. Which was why he had trickles of icy water rolling down his neck as he got to his feet. "Do you like the lake?" Not the most subtle change in the direction of the conversation, but he wasn't exactly Mr. Smooth right then.

"Yes." She fell into step beside him. "It's peaceful."

"I used to play down here with my friends all the time as a child." Rissa had loved jumping in the water in wolf form.

"Did you love her very much?" Quiet, quiet words.

Though she'd voiced the question, he could tell from the way she held herself, her face wiped of expression, that she expected him to tell her it was none of her business. It was what he'd have done, had it been any other person of her rank. Except it wasn't any other person asking this. It was the woman he'd kissed senseless a minute ago, the woman he was sending into a potentially lethal situation tomorrow, the woman who'd had a hold on him since the instant their eyes collided in that dark green glade the day of her defection.

"We were children," he began, voice husky with memory. "I only knew her for three years." They'd spent those three years in each other's constant company. "We were two of the lucky ones—we found each other early."

"How did you know?" There was a deep, haunting curiosity in her face, in her words. "That she was your mate."

"I knew." It was a resonance of the soul, a hunger of the heart, a sweet welcome home he'd missed every day since her death. "I was five years old when she was born and seven when we met. I remember walking along the corridors with my mother the first time I saw her.

"Later, my mother told me that all of a sudden, I just turned down a hallway and began running." She'd always laughed as she told that story, his gifted, fey mother with her sea green eyes and wild tumble of hair. "She was so startled that she decided to let me be, see what was so interesting. Until I ran into the nursery."

"Was Tarah the nursery supervisor then?" she asked, naming Indigo's mother.

"No, and Evie hadn't even been born." He couldn't believe that so many years had passed . . . that Rissa had been gone all that time. "My mother was sure I'd gotten myself in big trouble for interrupting nap time, especially when she found me laughing with a toddler with thick black curls and brown eyes."

He would never forget the wonder that had bloomed inside him when Rissa smiled at him. *Mine.* A crystal-clear thought. As a child, he'd had no understanding of the depth to which that feeling would one day grow—back then, it had been a simple, primal possessiveness. "The healer at the time told me that that was the earliest she'd ever known for a changeling to find his mate." Some people took years to awaken to each other; Drew and Indigo were the perfect example.

"That's so beautiful." Sienna's words sang with wonder. "She lived the majority of her life knowing she would never be alone, that someone would catch her whenever she fell."

Hawke hadn't ever considered it in that light, so that Rissa's short life was touched only with joy, not sorrow. "Thank you." Feeling the most furious tenderness in his heart for this woman who bore so many scars on her soul, he stroked his hand over the heavy silk of her hair. "Stay safe. We have something important to finish when you get back."

LARA tracked Walker down the morning after Sienna and Judd left the den with such stealth, she'd never have known they were gone if she hadn't gotten up before dawn to check up on Elias and glimpsed them slipping out. When she'd confronted Hawke, pointing out that she ranked as high as a lieutenant, he'd told her what was going on.

Now, she pushed open the door to the small workspace she knew Walker had commandeered in an isolated section of the den. His tools lay neatly along a bench he'd built with his hands, while the man himself stood at another bench, sanding the edges of a rocking chair so delicate and graceful, she knew it was meant for a young girl. "Did you build that for Marlee?"

He looked up, taking off and placing his safety glasses aside. "No. It's a gift for Sakura."

It was a kind thing to do for the little girl whose father was not yet totally recovered, the type of thing Walker did so often without fanfare or any expectation of kindness in return. "I brought you something." Steeling her shoulders, she crossed the space between them to place a mug of coffee and a plate of buttered toast on the bench. It was what he preferred for breakfast. She knew that because she noticed everything about Walker Lauren.

Putting aside the sander, he dusted off his hands and picked up a piece of toast. Neither of them spoke until he'd finished. "They're both skilled individuals," he said at last. "There's no reason for anything to go wrong."

The knot in her stomach unfurled at the realization that he wasn't going to make this hard. She was the one who'd walked away . . . but she'd regretted her decision every hour since. She'd *missed* him. No other man came close to creating the depth of feeling in her that Walker did with a simple look, a simple word.

Faced with that indisputable conclusion, she'd canceled all future dates. It wasn't fair. Not to her and not to the males.

Instead, she'd looked hard at her relationship with Walker—not just what he'd said to her, but what he'd *done*. Quiet, reserved Walker Lauren, who rarely spoke to anyone, had come to her night after night, trusted her with things she was becoming certain no one else knew. Not only that, but he'd cared for her in that same quiet way. Maybe the words were the truth and his actions an inadvertent lie, but Lara had made the decision to see this through to the end.

Never did she want to look back and wonder. Because he mattered. *So much.* Enough that she was willing to take the biggest risk of her life and continue this friendship that was nothing so simple. "You'll worry all the same though," she said. "He's your baby brother, and she might as well be your daughter."

Pale green eyes widened the tiniest fraction. "Judd would be startled to hear himself described in such a way."

Laughing at the unusual show of emotion, she stole a sip of his coffee before passing it over. "I won't tell if you won't."

"Agreed." He took a long drink before placing the mug beside the plate and reaching to cup her jaw. "You're more rested."

Her skin burned where he touched it. "Yes."

"I'm glad." Running his thumb over her chin, he dropped his hand. "Talk to me."

As he worked, she did exactly that, keeping his mind from

dwelling on the truth that two people he loved were in danger. When he touched her now and then, whether it was an accidental brush or a deliberate act as he helped her perch up on the bench, she quelled the urge to demand more.

This man, he was worth waiting for.

RECOVERED FROM COMPUTER 2(A)
TAGS: PERSONAL CORRESPONDENCE, FATHER, ACTION NOT
REQUIRED*

FROM: Alice <alice@scifac.edu>
TO: Dad <ellison@archsoc.edu>
DATE: March 2nd, 1974 at 10:18pm
SUBJECT: <no subject>

Dear Dad,

My empathic connection came through. He confirmed my
hypothesis, though he tells me that in all four cases, it was near
impossible to spot and he did so only because he knew what to
search for—and even then, he had to spend considerable time
studying the target minds on the PsyNet.

My tentative conclusion from this is that it must relate in some
way to the Xs' rating on the Gradient. Unfortunately, I have no Xs
beyond 4.2 on the Gradient in my project, so there is no way to
prove that.

However, I've decided to continue on—see if I can design a test
to prove or disprove the second part of my theory. Of course, the
Ethics Committee will take forever giving their approval since it'll
involve live volunteers. In the meantime, I plan to continue with my
historical research.

I loved visiting the dig. I miss you both already.

Love,
Alice

*File note: No request filed with Ethics Committee. No indication of
any unauthorized experimentation.*

Chapter 29

WE HAVE SOMETHING important to finish when you get back.

Lying flat on the earth on a moonless, starless night far from home, the air thin, the mountains unfamiliar, Sienna kept Hawke's final words close. He'd kissed her. Held her. Shared an important part of his past. Not only that, but he'd sent her on this mission, accepting that she wasn't just another young soldier, but an X-Psy honed in the coldest fire.

Finally, he *saw* her.

We were two of the lucky ones—we found each other early.

Wolves who lost their mates never mated again. It was once, and it was for life. Did it matter? *Yes*. Maybe it was selfish, but she wanted Hawke to be hers, to see home in her eyes as she saw it in his.

Time.

Thoughts switching to martial mode at the psychic alarm, she rose up out of the grass after ensuring the area was clear and made her way on silent feet to the first target. She'd been good at this as Ming's trainee, but she'd become even better in the years since. With Ming, she'd relied as much as possible on her psychic abilities, while in Snow-Dancer, she'd had to maintain iron control over those same abilities.

That discipline came in use tonight.

She was invisible to the psychic senses of the guards. She knew that because Judd had tested her shields—and been surprised enough by their efficacy to ask her how she'd done it. When she'd shown him, he'd remodulated his own shields to match hers.

It wasn't simply because of your X status that Ming took you as his protégée.

Corralling the whisper of memory, she completed her task and crossed over to the shadow of the second warehouse to duck into a small recess. A second later, she froze as the sentry turned the corner to head toward her, right on schedule. At least here, she didn't have to worry about being betrayed by her scent; changelings had a real advantage there.

It struck her that that might be why Ming was trying to track her. Because though she hadn't said so to anyone yet, gut instinct kept circling around to the suspicion that it was *Ming* who'd been behind the four Tks on SnowDancer land, not Henry. Henry had no reason to recognize the distinctive psychic signature of an X. Ming, however, would only need to take a single look at any report to know. He'd consider her a treasure trove of information about the SnowDancers. Which she was.

Go.

Moving at the internal command, she slipped out as the sentry disappeared from sight once more, laid the second charge, and was hidden behind another building before he returned. She wanted to telepath Judd, check he was safe, but they'd decided on telepathic silence except in an emergency.

Being able to detect telepathic communications in progress was so close to impossible that most people accepted it as such. But there were a rare few Psy who could pick up the faint psychic energy exuded during the act. Oddly enough, she'd had her first experience of it with a non-Psy. Lucas apparently had Psy DNA in his ancestry and could always detect psychic activity in his vicinity, telepathic and otherwise.

Sector 7 complete.

With that mental note, she shifted to sector 8. Judd had sectors 1 through 6, all more heavily trafficked than the sectors he'd assigned her. It made sense, since he could teleport in and out—plus, he'd been an Arrow. Sienna knew her own strengths. She also knew that Judd could snap her neck and she'd never see it coming.

Time.

*   *   *

HAWKE decided to get the hell out of the surveillance room
when even-tempered Brenna almost snarled, "They're maintaining radio silence. We won't hear anything unless they're
in trouble."

Realizing he was agitating her wolf, he touched the back
of his hand to her cheek and got out of her way, knowing she'd
contact him the instant she had something to report. But there
was no way he could sit and wait—shifting into wolf form,
he headed out into the cold, clear night. As he ran, greeting
his packmates in passing, he considered the information Cooper had sent through earlier that day.

"I've got rumors of weapons moving down into the wider
Bay Area." The lieutenant's jaw had been a brutal line.
"They've learned, Hawke. They're dodging our regular
traps—it fucking frustrates me that we haven't been able to
find or halt a shipment."

It frustrated Hawke, too, but part of him had always known
this day would come. It wasn't just the people the Council
had lost to the changelings, it was what those defections had
done to the perceived power of the Council *and* of the packs.
SnowDancer and DarkRiver were no longer seen as dumb
animals but as serious threats.

Switching direction after passing through Sing-Liu's
patch, the human soldier calling out a hello, Hawke crossed
the border into DarkRiver territory. The two packs had free
passage over each other's land, but still, it felt different being
away from his own. He was spotted at once since he'd made
no attempt to conceal his presence.

To his surprise, the leopard male who saw him signaled
for him to stop. Sides heaving from the run though he could
go for miles yet without pausing, Hawke walked to stand a
couple of feet from the man. The wolf recognized this male's
scent, identified it as that of Sentinel Clay Bennett.

"I tried to call you earlier," Clay said in lieu of a greeting.
"The Rats found something."

Hawke cocked his head.

"Weapons components in the city's storm water system,
so no way to know their exact origin. But," he added, "Rats

were able to use a map of the system to figure out that the pieces must've come from somewhere around SoMa. Maybe one of the old converted warehouses that have been shut up for maintenance."

Hawke's wolf considered that, permitting the human part of him to come to the forefront. Unlike other changelings who'd let the wolf have control for extended periods, Hawke had never been in danger of losing his humanity. His wolf had taken charge when he'd needed it to as a youth, helping him make decisions the boy had been too young to make, but it had withdrawn as soon as Hawke found his feet.

The animal had a very black-and-white view of life, didn't understand the games played in the human world. It understood face-to-face combat, understood killing to survive, to defend. It did not understand killing for political gain. The human, however, had lived through a massacre, comprehended the darkest of motivations all too well.

"I've got the Rats doing some more sneaking tonight," Clay continued. "No one ever notices them. Tomorrow, I figured we'd meet up, work out a plan for the rest. I'm thinking we should utilize the youngsters—the novices who look like teenagers."

Clever, Hawke thought. Teens were universally ignored, they were such a ubiquitous sight in their noisy groups. Giving a crisp nod, he stepped back, leaving the sentinel to his post and allowing his wolf to rise to the surface once more. He saw several more leopards as he went deeper into DarkRiver land. A couple of the youths even ran with him, trying to outpace an alpha. The wolf laughed husky and deep as it let them play before continuing on his way, leaving them winded and tired.

He covered miles and miles and miles.

But not for one instant did he forget that Sienna was on the most lethal of playing fields.

SIENNA tripped. *No, no, no!*

Twisting her body with an awkwardness that went against Indigo's teachings, she fell hard. Something snapped, and she was pretty certain it was a rib. The pain was a stabbing shock, but she'd evaded the searchlight sweeping over the area.

Sucking in a quiet, pained breath, she rose and did a quick physical check to confirm she hadn't injured anything vital. Everything was functional—except that breathing had become difficult. Taking an extra minute and reworking her mental countdown to compensate for it, she divorced the pain from her conscious mind.

It was a military trick and could prove dangerous if utilized with a severe injury, as the mind would ignore the cues sent by the body—however, it was the perfect solution to a broken rib. That done, she inspected the explosive components in her pack to verify their undamaged state, then continued on her way, silent as a wolf in the forest. She was two steps from the edge of a building that should've been empty according to their recon, when everything went wrong.

The door swung open.

She froze behind it, unable to see through the metal to the individual on the other side. But she could hear him . . . them.

"How many tonight?"

"Fifteen."

"It's happening slower than I'd like."

"We can't move too fast or they'll detect us."

"Yes." A pause. "It's reached this point because of the weak ones on the Council."

"We won't have to worry about them much longer."

One of the speakers—a tall, black woman—stepped out and began to close the door. Sienna held her breath, so motionless as to be a statue as the door was pulled shut from the inside. The woman checked something on a small organizer, began to turn.

Another second and she'd see Sienna.

Throat dry, she flexed her telepathic fingers in anticipation of a strike.

HAWKE looked over Brenna's shoulder the next morning. "Talk to me, sweetheart." He'd kept his distance after returning from the run, busying himself drafting a list of novices who could work the warehouse district, and briefing them on the task, but it was way past time for Judd and Sienna to have checked in.

Walker had already confirmed a lack of telepathic communication. "They're alive," he'd said ten minutes ago, fine lines flaring at the corners of his eyes. "I can sense them on the LaurenNet."

"Can you chance contacting them through your network?" He didn't want either Judd or Sienna distracted, but he needed to know if something had gone wrong so the pack could mount a rescue.

Walker had shaken his head. "The LaurenNet has limitations because of its size. It can compensate for one of the adults being in a distant location, but with two of them gone, the network is stretched. It'll hold, but I can't risk a loss of focus."

A breach, Hawke knew, would have catastrophic consequences. "Take care of Toby and Marlee." That had to be the priority. Neither Sienna nor Judd would want it any different.

"I'll let you know the instant I hear anything. And Hawke?" Pale green eyes holding his. "We need to talk after they return."

Now, in the communications hub of the den, Brenna shook her head in response to his words. "I gave them both untraceable cells, but they might've decided not to chance a call anyway."

Hawke clenched his hand on the back of her chair. "Can you track them on the airjet?" The two were meant to board a flight home in a few hours.

"No." Brenna pushed her bangs out of her eyes. "We infected the airport computers with a subtle virus. It erased them from the systems, so it'll be no use hacking into the visual imaging files." Releasing a steady breath, she reached back to put her hand over his. "They'll be fine."

Startled by the confidence in her voice, he looked down into her face as she tipped it up. "So sure?"

"I'm worried. Of course I'm worried," she admitted, the darkness in her eyes a silent echo of her words. "But Judd's sending me 'I'm safe' vibes through the mating bond."

Hawke's wolf scowled, because it couldn't keep tabs on Sienna that way.

"Plus," Brenna continued, "my mate is a complete badass. Seriously, your girl couldn't be in better hands."

In spite of the wolf pacing within his mind, he felt his lips tug up at the corners. "I'll have you know, Sienna is a trainee badass." Accepting that the only thing to do was wait, though such inaction grated, he said, "I'm heading down to talk to the cats about another issue—the instant you hear anything, you call me. Understood?"

"Absolutely." Rising to her feet, she said, "I could do with a hug."

He enfolded her in his arms without a word. She was Pack. It soothed something in him to hold her, too. But he knew the wolf would continue to prowl half-mad inside his mind until Sienna was back safe in his territory. "Better?"

"Yes."

He left with a caress to her cheek. Picking up Riley from the cabin the lieutenant shared with Mercy, he drove them both down to the meeting spot, which happened to be the home of the DarkRiver healer.

"It's a huge indication of trust, isn't it?" Riley said as they came to a stop in front of the graceful split-level home. "To allow us so close to their healer. We've come a long way."

Hawke had to agree. "Honestly? I never expected an alliance of any kind with the cats when they first began to make their presence felt." He'd wanted only that they stay out of his way while he rebuilt his shattered pack.

"No."

Neither of them made a move to exit the vehicle.

"Hawke," Riley said into the tense silence, "I can handle this. You don't want to be here."

"I need to be doing something. Might as well be this." He got out, slamming the door.

Riley glanced at him when they met at the front of the vehicle. "Word of advice. Strong women don't take well to being snarled at."

"Tough." She'd be lucky if all he did was snarl at her, he thought as he headed into the meeting, his mind on the phone in his pocket.

When a message did come in, it only said, "Still no contact."

Chapter 30

ADEN LOOKED OVER at the Arrow who stood beside him on the sandy beach along the Amalfi Coast. Abbot was a telekinetic, 9.1 on the Gradient, incredibly powerful, incredibly skilled, incredibly cursed. It had come as no surprise to discover that the twenty-six-year-old was drawn to the idea of Purity.

"Have you come to stop me, Aden?" the other Arrow asked. "Ask me not to join Pure Psy?"

Aden shook his head. "I'm not Ming, to force you to follow my own political agenda. But you must know—you cannot be both an Arrow and a member of Pure Psy."

"So you would exile me."

"No, Abbot. That isn't who we are." The water held an edge of luminescence in the dark of the night that had fallen on this side of the world, and he made a note to do some research, find out what sea organism caused the effect. "But the squad works on unconditional trust." On the knowledge that the Arrow at his back would never use the position to knife him. "Once you give your allegiance to Pure Psy, you must follow their goals."

Abbot took his time replying, his ink black hair blowing back in the salt-laced wind coming off the Gulf of Salerno. "You're not a Tk."

"No."

"What does Vasic say?"

Aden thought of the Tk-V who could lift blood out of walls and bodies from within graves. "You should ask him."

"No games, Aden. You know his mind—he speaks to you."

Aden looked down at the glowing foam before the sea sucked it back in. "Vasic believes it doesn't matter the Councilor at the helm, or whether the machinery is called Council or Purity—in the end, we're nothing but warm bodies to bleed for them." So many Arrows had died to protect Silence. Their only reward had been more death.

"Yet we give our allegiance to Kaleb Krychek."

"There are reasons."

Abbot looked out toward the lingering golden light in the windows of some of the homes that hugged the cliffs, and Aden saw bleak longing in those eyes as blue as the deepest part of the Aegean. A breach of Silence, but an Arrow never betrayed one of his own.

"We are Arrows for a reason," the other man said at last. "We cannot survive without Silence."

"Perhaps." Aden thought of Vasic again, of the price the Tk-V had paid to retain his sanity. "But perhaps the price of survival has become too high."

Chapter 31

TEN HOURS AFTER the meeting on DarkRiver land, Hawke had to fight the urge to simultaneously pull Sienna to his chest and strangle Judd. The two of them walked into the den after having finally checked in by phone when they landed in San Francisco—six hours behind schedule. He did neither.

"Why the hell," he said the instant the office door was shut, "did you not tag Walker with a telepathic report?"

"We had a situation," Judd said, making Hawke's blood run cold. "I had to do a fast teleport to get Sienna out of a tight spot. Combined with the teleport in and out of the village for both of us, as well as what was necessary to complete the op, it brought me close to flaming out."

Eyes on Sienna, Hawke said, "Explain."

She drew up her spine. "Since Judd was effectively drained, we made the decision to conserve my psychic energy. A long-distance telepathic report would've only utilized a small amount of power, but that may have counted in a confrontation."

Heart an ice-cold block in his chest as he read between the lines, Hawke nodded at Judd to continue.

"We missed our scheduled flight because I needed time to recover enough that there was no chance of a collapse." Judd carried on when Hawke didn't interrupt. "The charges have been placed. Brenna can activate any or all of them from here."

"Have her build two remotes as well—I'll carry one, you take the spare," Hawke ordered. "We need to be prepared in case we have to abandon the den."

Judd's eyebrows rose. "Has that ever happened?"

Hawke gave a curt nod. "Once. The location had been leaked." As a lieutenant, Hawke's father had known too much when he'd been compromised.

The only reason SnowDancer had managed to reclaim the den was that the men and women who'd been left after the blood and death had gone out and quietly executed the small group behind the psychic rapes. No one had ever connected the deaths to SnowDancer, a deliberate choice on the pack's part. They'd been too weak to chance a Psy reprisal. But they were no longer weak, no longer broken. "Tell Brenna the remotes are a priority."

Judd nodded. "We also captured detailed images of the camp with the cameras hooked into our collars."

"Mariska can clean up and summarize the footage." The twenty-eight-year-old senior tech was so shy she appeared standoffish, but had a mind like a scalpel.

"I'll drop it off to her. If you haven't got any more questions, we should get changed and try to rest."

"From the way Brenna kissed you at the entrance, I don't think you'll be doing much resting," Hawke said, and saw Sienna's lips tug upward a tiny fraction.

Judd, on the other hand, showed no physical reaction. "Good night, Hawke." Cool, very Psy, very Judd. "Sienna, you should get to bed, too."

Sienna glanced up, expecting Hawke to stop her, but he'd already turned away to look at something else on his desk. Deflated, she exited with Judd.

"Sienna," he said, halting her when they would've split two corridors later, "you did very well."

Her shoulders went tight at the memory of that instant before the guard had been distracted by a call. It had given Judd the time to answer her telepathic hail and 'port her out. "I could've gotten us both caught."

"Things happen in the field—the mark of a good operative is how you respond to the challenge. You stayed composed and silent, the right course of action given the circumstances."

It felt good to hear that. "Thanks."

"How's your rib?"

"Fine." Judd hadn't mentioned it to Hawke, but the work

he'd done to knit the bone was the real reason he'd been so wiped out. She'd been hurt worse than she'd thought. "Doesn't even feel bruised."

"Good." Leaning over, he pressed his lips to her temple. "Go shower. I'm sure you'll be having a visitor in another ten minutes, at the absolute maximum." His tone was so even, it took an instant for the words to penetrate.

"I'll attempt," he added, "not to 'port in and break his legs for having the gall to be in your room."

She stared, stunned, after he stalked off.

Ten minutes, at the absolute maximum.

Jolted to action by the mental echo, she ran to her room, dodging any attempts by packmates to stop her. The instant she closed the door behind herself, she stripped and jumped into the shower.

She was rubbing the towel over her wet body when there was a hard knock on the door.

Definitely not ten minutes.

More like four and a half.

"Just a second!" Grabbing her dirty clothes—scattered all over the floor—she threw them into the bathroom, then raced to pull on underwear.

The knock came again, more impatient.

"I'm coming!"

Her jeans hooked on her ankles. Cursing, she managed to get them on and struggled into a forest green T-shirt, pulling her damp hair out from under the back as, breathless, she opened the door partway through the third knock. "Wha—"

The door was closed, and she was pressed up against the solid mass of it before she knew what was happening. "Hawke, I—"

His hands cupped her face, the wolf looking out of his eyes. Her words faded away, her heartbeat accelerated, and still he continued to watch her with that complete and unwavering focus. When his thumb moved over her cheekbone, she jumped.

"I," he said in a quiet, quiet tone, "will not send you into a hot zone again."

So easy, it would be so easy to let the overwhelming power of him take her over. "You must." Her voice came out husky. "I was born for war."

One hand stroked down, over her jaw, to collar her throat. "No." A single word spoken in a warm rush of air against her skin, his body aligned to hers.

"I am what I am." It was hard to continue speaking when he was so very hot and beautiful against her, the maleness of him a living caress. "Fire contained in a small box die—"

Hawke's mouth stole her words, the taste of him a blast to the senses. This kiss was unlike any of the others. Moving the hand on her throat to cup her jaw, he angled her head just the way he liked, pressed his free hand to the door beside her head, kicked her legs farther apart . . . and then he took her.

Hot and wet and open-mouthed, it was a devouring kind of kiss, the kind of kiss that made it plain he considered her *his*.

Sienna shuddered. He was so big, so gorgeous, so *close* that her hands didn't know where to land. Gripping at the back of his black shirt, she tried to make herself taller, to offer up more of her mouth, taste more of his.

A growl rumbled out of his chest as she moved her body, and she realized that somehow, she was riding his thigh. Another time, it might have embarrassed or shocked her, but tonight . . .

More, she thought, *give me everything*. She might never hold all of him, but this she would claim. His lost mate had never touched this wild, hungry part of him, never caressed the powerful body that pinned her against the door, never tasted the dark heat of that demanding mouth. This fire between them, it was for her and her alone.

"Why aren't you wearing a bra?"

Shocked by the rough question against her lips, she sucked in a gasping breath. "You didn't give me time."

A wolfish smile. Kisses over her jaw, along her neck. She braced herself for a bite, but it didn't come. Instead, he slid his hand down to her lower back and nudged her more firmly onto his thigh. She couldn't help the whimper that escaped her throat.

Yes, she knew about sex—quite aside from her clinical lessons in health studies, the women's magazines in the novices' common room had proven *extremely* instructive. But no amount of research could've prepared her for this. Never had she understood what it would be to be so very, very close to him, the muscled strength of him rubbing against her most intimate place.

"Such big eyes." That was when she felt teeth.

On her lower lip. A slow, sexy bite that dared her to retaliate. Shifting her hold to around his neck, she clenched her fingers in the thick silk of his hair and arched up to claim his mouth. She was Psy, her mind her greatest asset—she'd made note of what he liked without realizing it, used the data, and was gratified at the growl that rolled into her mouth . . . vibrated against the stiff peaks of her nipples.

Jerking back, she looked down at the soft cotton of her T-shirt. And wondered what it would feel like if they were skin to skin.

But Hawke hadn't had enough of the kiss. Tugging her back with a grip in her hair, he reclaimed her mouth. Darkly intense, a searing brand. His free hand stroked down to grip her thigh as he urged her to move on him. "That's it, beautiful." Husky words against her lips as her body began rubbing against his without her conscious control, a tight kind of need unfurling in her abdomen.

More kisses, strokes along her thigh. "Open your mouth." She obeyed because she didn't want him to pull away, to leave her bereft when she could almost taste—

The seam of her jeans pressed onto her clitoris and everything fractured. Even the agonizing pain of the second level of dissonance wasn't enough to blunt the impact.

HAWKE saw the flickers of dangerous red and lethal yellow out of the corner of his eye, plastered his body to hers. "Baby, you hurt?"

"Wh—what?" A dazed-sounding question. "Hurt?"

"Did the fire touch you?" Reaching down, he stroked her hair off her face.

Huge obsidian eyes looked up at him, devoid of the stars that denoted a cardinal. "Only inside."

"What?"

"The fire only touched me inside."

Figuring out what she was talking about, he grinned, then

took mental inventory of his own body. No burns. "Interesting," he murmured.

Something in his voice—likely the smug arrogance—had her blinking, trying to come back. He didn't want her thinking coherently yet. She was all loose and sated right now, and he wanted nothing more than to hold her, to pet her as he wished. Shifting before she could stop him, he sat down on her bed with her cuddled into him. "You sure got a quick trigger, Sienna," he teased, in control for the simple reason that she was in his arms, under his protection again.

A solemn look. "Is that bad?"

He couldn't help it. He kissed her, indulging himself in the vibrant life of her. She wasn't dead in some Pure Psy camp, hadn't come back bloody and broken. "No," he answered. "I like making you come. I plan to do it often and well."

Color swept up on a red tide over her face, and she pressed it down against his chest. So young, he thought, feeling the raking claw of conscience. But he was no hypocrite. He'd sent her into an enemy camp, sent her into a situation that could've resulted in death. If she was old enough to die for the pack, she was old enough to choose who she wanted as a lover. "Tell me," he said, weaving his fingers through her damp hair, "about the operation."

Instead of pointing out that Judd had already done so, she gave him a step-by-step debrief. "I know I shouldn't tell you the next fact because it puts me in a lesser bargaining position," she said, "but I was scared."

He squeezed her thigh. "I'd be more worried if you hadn't been—fear keeps us alive, keeps us alert." Now if he'd just listen to himself instead of feeling a feral anger at the idea of her afraid and alone in the dark.

Sienna sat up, one hand braced on his chest. "That's not true. Arrows feel no fear, and that makes them strong."

"Yes," he agreed. "But an Arrow won't have a kiss waiting for him at the end of a hunt, no warm body next to him when a nightmare strikes."

A steady look—no longer that of the girl who'd blushed, but of the woman who had taken him on more than once. "Hawke?"

"Yes?"

"What does this mean?"

He curled a strand of ruby red around his finger. "It means you have to learn to deal with me." There was no going back. Not from this.

Furrows on her brow. "Perhaps you should learn to deal with me instead."

His wolf bared its teeth in a feral grin. "Baby, I've been trying to master that trick since the day I met you."

"Liar," she said. "Your wolf thinks it can control me." A shift of her lower body as she got more comfortable.

He hissed out a breath. "Easy."

"You're aroused." Such a cool statement, but he could scent the earthy warmth of the damp heat between her legs, hear the rising pulse of her heartbeat.

Leaning forward, he nuzzled at her throat, licking up the salt and spice of her. "I can handle it." His wolf had had a taste, was starving for more, but it understood that to claim her to the deepest level, man and wolf both would have to move carefully. Neither part of him ever wanted to see fear in her eyes when she looked at him, especially in bed.

SHIVERING against the impact of those slow, wolfish licks, Sienna clenched her hand in Hawke's hair. "Your hair is beautiful. You know it, don't you?"

She felt his lips curve against the sensitive skin of her neck before he nipped at her. Jerking, she curled her other arm tighter around him, her cheek pressed against the abrasive stubble of his. Then she did what she'd wanted to do for so long. She petted him, stroking her fingers through the heavy strands of silver-gold until he relaxed . . . and switched their positions so she found herself flat on her back with him stretched out on top of her, his weight braced on his forearms.

For a second, she halted in her caresses, overwhelmed by the sheer, wild masculinity of the wolf in her bed. He growled low in his throat . . . and her skin stretched tight over her body. Sucking in a breath, she began to pet him again, this gorgeous, powerful man who wore his wolf so very close to the surface. One of his own hands settled on her hip, heavy and warm and possessive.

"What was it like?" she dared ask. "To have the wolf in charge while you were in your human skin as a teenager?"

Nudging her legs apart, he settled more heavily against her. "It just was." A very wolflike answer. "The wolf sees in black or white, no shades of gray. At that time, that was what was needed.

"And," he continued, surprising her with his willingness to talk, "I was always present. The wolf didn't truly take over, so much as allow the boy to borrow its strength for a while."

Sienna parted her lips to ask about the Psy, what they'd done to SnowDancer, closed them before the words could escape. That darkness had no place here, no place in this room, in this bed. Instead, she continued to stroke him, not realizing until several minutes later that her own body had relaxed under his, one leg raised at the knee to press against his side.

Smart wolf.

He began to kiss the sensitive slope of her neck again, slow and wet and a little rough.

Sexy wolf.

Chapter 32

HAWKE'S WOLF WAS drunk on the taste of Sienna, on the scent of her, but it halted, clawed at the human half until it paid attention. Raising his head from her neck, he shook it, trying to find a glimmer of rational thought.

"Hawke?" Sienna's hands stroked up his nape and into his hair, the spot so sensitive that had he been a cat, he would've purred. "Why did you stop?"

It was the answer to his own confusion, putting the wolf's hesitation into words. "Because," he murmured, pressing an open-mouthed kiss to the hollow of her throat, "you're tired on both the physical and psychic levels." His need for her was a wild thing, but for her first time, she deserved better than a frantic coupling.

Scowling, she tugged at his hair. "I don't need you to make that decision for me."

He settled his lower body flush against her, growled in satisfaction when she made a hot little sound in the back of her throat. "I need to make this decision for me." No regrets, that's what he wanted to see in her passion-flushed face after their first time together.

Fingers going motionless, she searched his eyes. "All right." It was a solemn whisper, as if she'd read his thoughts. "Kiss me before you leave."

"Baby"—a nip of that lush lower lip—"I have plans to do a lot more than that." He wouldn't take her, not tonight, but neither was he noble enough to walk away without indulging himself with a long, deep taste.

Her nails dug into his nape. "How far?"

So serious. It turned his wolf playful. "I intend to get to second base."

When her chest rose up in a jagged breath, he knew full well she understood the sexual reference. "What's second base on a man?"

Blinking, he raised his head, having never had cause to consider that question. "The same, I guess."

"Then take off your shirt." She undid the first button, went for the second.

A hundred images flashed into his mind, all of them involving the sweet heat of her breasts rubbing against his bare chest. Gritting his teeth, he grabbed her hands in one of his and pinned them above her head. "No touching."

"Hawke—"

Kissing the complaint off her lips, he slipped his hand under her T-shirt to spread his fingers over the taut silk of her abdomen. Her skin quivered as he moved that hand up to settle over her ribs, her heartbeat jagged under his touch. "Yes?" he whispered, nuzzling a kiss to the tender spot beneath her ear. "It'll feel so good." For both of them.

Her wrists flexed in his grip, but she didn't attempt to pull away. "Yes." Husky acquiescence.

Lifting his head from the intoxication of her skin, he held her gaze as he moved his hand up just enough to brush his thumb along the underside of her breast. She came up off the bed, pushing her soft flesh into his touch. Shuddering, he cupped her, squeezed her, rolled her nipple between his fingertips to her restless movements, her erotic cries. His mouth watered to push up her T-shirt, taste the hard little nub.

It took every ounce of will he had not to reach down, undo the damn zipper on his jeans and put her fingers on him. *Patience. Patience.* He chanted the word at the back of his mind as he moved his hand to her neglected breast, as he petted her to piercing need . . . and found he was rocking his cock against the feminine arousal he could taste so earthy and rich on his tongue.

Shit.

Sienna stared up in disbelief as he jerked up and out of the bed. Her nipples peaked against the soft cotton of her T-shirt, taunting him. "You can't just—"

"Leave you hot and frustrated?" Leaning down with his hands braced on either side of her, he closed his teeth over one provocative nub, wetting the cloth with his tongue. Her cry was sharp, her arousal a lash against his senses. "I damn well can," he said, raising his head, "when my cock is about to break in half."

Chest rising and falling as she gulped in air, she shook her head. "Not my fault."

"All your fault." Not daring another kiss, he cupped her jaw, stroked his thumb over her lower lip. "Damn, but I like making out with you, Sienna. Let's do it again tomorrow."

He left to the sound of a feminine snarl. It made his lips curve into a feral smile.

SASCHA was in the large, comfortable chair in the living room, Nadiya in her arms when Lucas stepped out for a second. He walked back in with an envelope in his hand. "Kit said this was delivered to the office by courier earlier today. Addressed to both of us."

Smiling at the thought of the youth who was growing into a strong, wonderful man in front of her eyes, she said, "Has he gone?"

A nod. "He had a perimeter shift, but he's going to drop by in the morning before he heads home. Not to see either of us, of course."

Laughing, she watched Lucas tear open the letter, scan it. His own grin faded. "According to this," he said, "an anonymous benefactor has opened a trust fund worth five million dollars in Naya's name for her education, the balance to be paid out when she's twenty-five."

Sascha let Naya grip her finger as their little cat yawned, settled back down to nap some more. "Mother."

Placing the letter on the coffee table, Lucas said, "What do you want to do?"

She loved him so much, but it was at moments like this that it struck her how very lucky she was. So many men would've rejected the trust fund out of hand, never asking the why of it all. "I've come to realize that I don't know my mother as well as I thought I did." It had changed her perception of her childhood, forced her to view everything through a different lens. "Let me talk to her."

"Do you want me to put Naya down?"

"You just want to go cuddle with her."

He didn't deny the charge as he took the drowsy newborn from Sascha, his lips curving in the most tender of smiles. Fatherhood suited her panther—though she knew she'd have to watch out for his overprotective tendencies or poor Naya would never go on a single date. A quiet laugh bubbled out of her. It delighted her to think of the future, of all they'd experience together as a family.

Following her mate into the bedroom, she watched as he settled down on the bed with Naya skin to skin on his chest. His hand all but covered her tiny body as he stroked her in that changeling way, bonding with her on the most elemental level. Then he purred, and Naya made a happy little sound of delight, very much a cat in her love of touch.

Sascha laughed at the sight of the two of them so contented and lazy. "Room enough for three?"

Lucas held out his arm, eyes panther-green. "Always and forever."

He stopped her heart sometimes, this man. "Don't make me cry. I'm still hormonal." Cuddling next to him when he smiled, she reached for the cell phone on the bedside table. It took a bare few seconds to send the text message. Nikita answered using Tp an instant later, her reach long enough that she'd hear Sascha's far weaker telepathic voice.

Sascha.

Mother, we've received the letter advising us of the trust fund.

What does that have to do with me?

Her mother lied, Sascha thought, with such effortless ease. Instead of forcing the issue, she said, *You know I've given birth?*

Your child carries a Russian first name. I expected you to sever all ties with your past.

Sascha had considered that, but she carried the past within her. The echo of it would resonate to her child, if only in the fierceness of the love Sascha felt for her. *Lucas and I decided it was important for Nadiya to know both parts of her heri-*

tage. The line of Slavic monikers went back to Sascha's grandfather, while Naya's middle name had been that of Lucas's healer mother. *Would you like me to e-mail you an image of her?*

We cut our familial ties, Sascha. A statement so cold, it was beyond cruel. *She means nothing to me.*

Once, the words would've made her bleed. Now, Sascha saw the truth buried beneath the lie. *No, of course not.* Because if Nikita acknowledged Nadiya as her grandchild, the baby became a target. *Mother, the trust fund—*

Is a private matter in which I bear no interest.

A single tear trickled down Sascha's cheek. *All right.*

The telepathic connection ended in silence.

"Sascha." Lucas's arm curled around her chest to hold her against his side, the tension in him communicating itself through the mating bond. "What did she say?"

"Nothing hurtful." Turning, she rubbed her face against his chest as she watched Naya's fragile body rise and fall in innocent sleep. "I'm a mother now, Lucas. I would do *anything* to keep Naya safe, even if it meant she would hate me for the rest of her life." Swallowing, she touched a finger to their baby's plump cheek. "It makes me wonder if that isn't exactly what Nikita did."

STILL able to feel the canvas of Sienna's body against his own the next afternoon, and wondering why the hell he'd given in to his good side and stopped, Hawke finished clearing the decks. He and Kenji had had an interesting conversation with the BlackSea Coalition this morning, and the lieutenant was following up on the details.

In Los Angeles, Jem was doing the same with Aquarius. Shooting back a reply to an e-mail she'd sent, he checked the other things on his mental list. The novice teams were scoping out the warehouse district, Brenna was building the remotes, while Mariska and Judd were going over video footage. Riley had the rotation of soldiers in hand, Indigo and Riaz the newly revised training schedule.

Finding Lara, he got an update on everyone who'd been injured in the attack. Simran was almost recovered and resting at home, as was Riordan. Elias, however, remained in the infirmary. "I almost broke a scanner over his head today," Lara muttered. "Never knew it would be Eli who drove me to drink."

Hawke grinned. "So he's on the way to being healed?"

"Yes." A faint smile. "I have to keep him here because his new skin is so fragile, but he'll walk out with no scars in less than a week."

"You do good work, Lara." He kissed her on the cheek, then popped in to see Riley.

"No one else needs you today," the lieutenant said and pointed to the door. "Take advantage of it while you can."

Doing exactly that, Hawke went tracking his favorite prey. "Toby," he said, catching the young boy as he ran outside with a soccer ball in his arms, school having let out half an hour earlier. "Have you seen Sienna?"

Toby shook his head, his hair—not yet as dark a red as Sienna's—getting into his eyes. Hawke narrowed his own eyes. "When was the last time you had a haircut?"

Pushing back the strands, Toby shifted from foot to foot, his face flaming a shade perilously close to that of his hair. "Um . . ."

"Toby." Never before had Hawke needed to use that tone with the preteen who was so well behaved, it left his wolf a bit bemused.

"I don't like scissors," Toby blurted out. "Near my head, I mean."

"Walker's okay with this?" The Psy male wasn't the type to let things slide.

"Sienna kind of got me out of it."

That, Hawke understood. Sienna was fierce in her protectiveness when it came to Toby. Maybe too much so. Hawke understood taking care of those who were his own, but he also understood that a boy needed to explore and be proud of his own strength. "Come on, you're having a haircut today," he said, shifting his priorities because no matter the searing depth of his need to see Sienna, this young member of his pack needed him. "How can you get anything done if you can't see?"

Toby dragged his feet, but he obeyed. Hawke had him

dump the soccer ball in the backseat of the truck as he started it up.

"Where are we going?"

"To see Sascha." His wolf's curiosity about the baby was too strong for him to wait any longer, and he knew the empath would be happy to tidy up Toby's hair.

Except Toby went stiff at the idea, the scent of his distress slapping against Hawke. Stopping the truck at once, he reached out to rub the kid's down-bent head. "What's the matter?"

"I like Sascha. A lot."

"I know." That's why he'd figured the whole haircut deal would go down better with the empath's help.

Fisted hands on tense thighs. "I don't want her to think I'm a baby."

Oh. "Same with Riley?" The kid worshipped the lieutenant, who treated him like a much younger brother.

Toby's nod was hard and fast.

"Hmm. In that case, I'll have to do it." Driving to park the car deeper in their territory—and aware of Toby gaping at him—he had the boy get out, then rummaged around in the storage well until he found a pair of scissors in the first-aid kit. When Toby gulped, he pointed to the bed of the truck and said, "Sit."

The boy clambered up onto the tailgate, legs hanging off the edge and words tumbling out at high speed. "My mom used to use Tp to make me sleep when I had a haircut. I never liked it."

Happy to hear that the fear was a harmless remnant of childhood, not based on hidden trauma, he said, "We're not using the sedatives in the first-aid kit, so forget about it."

Toby's face fell. "Those look really sharp."

Reaching up, Hawke snipped off a bit of his own hair to test the blades. "Yeah, should do the trick."

"Uh-oh." Huge cardinal eyes. "You shouldn't have done that."

"Why?"

"'Cause every time you cut your hair, Sienna gets mad."

His wolf pricked up its ears. "Yeah?" He stepped closer.

Toby froze.

"Okay," Hawke said, having had enough experience with pups to understand logic wouldn't help right now, "close your eyes and scream as loud as you can."

"What?"

"Just do it."

Toby took a deep breath, scrunched his eyes closed . . . and screamed.

Wincing at the earsplitting volley of sound, Hawke snipped off the boy's far too long bangs in one cut, making sure not to touch the metallic blades to the kid's skin. "Not bad." It wasn't crooked in any case.

Toby's eyes snapped open. "Did you do it?"

Hawke handed him his hair. "What do you think?"

"I don't think anyone else will let me scream." A pensive statement.

"Well, as long as you don't mind looking like a prison escapee, I can do it."

"Okay." Toby beamed.

"How about the bottom?"

"Yours is longer than mine."

"You can leave it that length on the condition it doesn't get in your way."

Toby frowned, considered. Serious little man, Hawke thought, realizing he hadn't spent that much time with the boy. But man and wolf both liked him—Toby had a simple and deep kindness to him that Hawke knew would never disappear. The last vestiges of childhood fears aside, there was strength there, too. Hesitant yet, still growing, but when Toby came into his own, he'd make the pack proud, of that Hawke had not a single doubt.

"Cut it." A decisive statement. "I can have it longer after I pass my outdoor lessons."

Hawke was impressed. "You sure?"

A strong nod. Then Toby closed his eyes, inhaled. It took three screams and by the last one, Toby was laughing. So was Hawke. They sat on the tailgate afterward, eating peanuts from a bag Toby had had in his pocket. The nuts were crushed, but that didn't matter.

Hawke found himself reevaluating his opinion of the boy as they talked. Toby had the gentleness of an empath, but he saw everything—and he understood that the world wasn't always kind. Who better, after all, to know the dark side of the human heart than someone gifted with the ability to sense emotion?

But he was also a child.

"I'm thirsty," he said after crunching the last peanut.

"Me, too." Turning around, Hawke hunted through the first-aid kit and came up with a bottle of water. "Aha."

"You'll have to replace that or Lara will tell you off."

"Don't I know it." Taking a gulp from the bottle, he passed it to Toby.

Who copied his actions.

Hiding his grin, he grabbed the soccer ball. "Come on, squirt."

Toby's face beamed. "Really? Me and you?"

Hawke played the ball over his foot. "Move it."

"I'm coming!"

They spent over a half hour together, with Toby proving to be both nimble and intelligent as an opponent. Afterward, they finished off the bottle of water before getting back into the truck.

Toby did up his safety belt. "How come you didn't ask me stuff about Sienna?"

Hawke raised an eyebrow as he started the vehicle.

Toby shrugged. "I figured you were spending time with me to find out about my sister."

Yeah, the kid saw everything. "Maybe I thought about it," Hawke said, because he didn't believe in lying to his pack. "But turns out I like hanging out with you."

Toby's whole face lit up. "You mean it. I know."

Mussing the kid's hair, Hawke drove him home. He went with Toby to the practice field to ensure the boy's coach was aware Toby hadn't played hookey, and the kids begged him to stay. He was alpha. Caring for pups was instinctive. As a result, night had fallen by the time he was able to go after Sienna again.

And this time, nothing was going to keep him from his prey.

RECOVERED FROM COMPUTER 2(A)
TAGS: PERSONAL CORRESPONDENCE, FATHER, ACTION NOT REQUIRED

FROM: Alice <alice@scifac.edu>
TO: Dad <ellison@archsoc.edu>
DATE: November 12th, 1974 at 11:04pm
SUBJECT: <no subject>

Dear Dad,

I received a notice today terminating my access to the X
designation volunteers and "requesting" I cease my research. I'm a
scientist. I can't do that, especially when I'm on the brink of
discovering the answer.

   What worries me is that if I'm right, I may well be giving those
who seek to control the Xs a way to hold them hostage. The
promise of safety could be used as an "incentive" to force them to
act as psychic weapons—I wouldn't have worried about such a
thing a few years ago, but the Psy Council is no longer what it once
was.

   Call me when you get this e-mail. I can't get through to the dig.

Love,
Alice

Chapter 33

SIENNA WASN'T IN her room. Nor was she in the family quarters—but Walker was. The telepath jerked his head toward the corridor. Realizing the eldest of the Laurens wanted to have this conversation away from the kids, Hawke led them to a small, private alcove before saying, "I'm surprised you waited this long."

"There's a time and a place. This would be it." Holding Hawke's gaze in a way that not many men could, Walker said, "You will be good to her." Not a statement, but an order.

Hawke's wolf stirred. "Do you think I'd be otherwise?"

"If I did, you'd be dead."

It was Judd who'd been the assassin, but Hawke had the sudden, crystal-clear realization that when it came to Sienna, Toby, and Marlee, it was Walker who was more dangerous. "Understood." If he had a daughter, he'd kill any man who dared hurt her. And whatever their actual relationship, Walker was the closest Sienna had to a father.

She'd said as much to him when he'd asked about her father as they danced that night in the training room.

"I know his identity, but per the reproduction contract, his only involvement in my life—and Toby's—was biological."

"Did you ever feel the need to track him down, demand more?" he'd asked, unable to comprehend how a man could walk away from his children.

"No. I don't think Toby has either." There'd been no emotional distress in her tone, her next words explaining why. "We've always had Walker, you see."

Now Walker gave a clipped nod. "Then we're clear." Turning on his heel, he walked back to his quarters.

Hawke's wolf shook its head, staring after the Psy male with pale green eyes. "You told me you were a teacher in the Net."

The man looked over his shoulder. "I was. You never asked me who I taught." The door closed.

Deciding that conversation could wait, because whatever he'd been, Walker was now loyal to the pack, Hawke continued on his search. Sienna wasn't hanging out in the common areas. He checked Lara's domain next, discovered she'd been in an hour earlier. Starting to lose his temper, he shoved into his own place to grab a bite to eat before resuming the hunt.

The scent of autumn and spice in the air, in his every breath.

"You owe me a game," Sienna said, picking up a card from the deck she'd placed on the carpeted floor of the front room of his quarters. Dressed in jeans and that sexy-as-sin black shirt with those tempting snap buttons, she sat cross-legged on the carpet, her hair a sheet of dark fire licking down her back.

His wolf growled, bad-tempered because she'd outwitted him. "How did you get in?"

"It's not like you lock your door."

"No, because people don't waltz into an alpha's quarters."

"So, punish me."

He'd expected challenge, was caught by the wickedness. His wolf came to attention. "I might just do that," he said, prowling over to crouch down and nip at her lower lip.

A tremor silvered over her skin. "Is that it?"

Satisfying as it would've been to gorge, he decided to eat her up in small, luscious bites tonight. "For now." Rising, he went into the compact galley and threw together a plate. "Have you had dinner?"

"Yes."

Coming down to sit across from her, he fed her a plump grape anyway. As her lips closed on the ripe fruit, his wolf watched, fascinated. "Poker," he murmured.

"Of course." A husky answer.

He ate half a sandwich before speaking. "We have to have stakes."

Lines on her forehead. "For credits, you mean?"

Poor innocent baby, about to get fleeced. "Tut, tut, gorgeous. You know when you play poker with a man behind closed doors, there is only one acceptable currency."

Her mouth fell open. "You'd play for *that*?"

Enjoying shocking cool and collected Sienna, he took his time eating the other half of the sandwich. "Clothes, Ms. Lauren. What did you think I was talking about?"

She blew out a breath between gritted teeth. "Sometimes I really want to"—a frustrated sound—"bite you!"

He froze. "I might let you."

"I won't do it if you'd enjoy it."

Bad-tempered thing. His wolf liked that about her. "Let's play."

"I might not be Silent any longer, but I still have the perfect poker face." A smug smile.

It stayed on her face as she divested him of his socks—he'd kicked his shoes off earlier—his shirt, and his belt. That was when her concentration began to falter, her eyes flicking over his chest and back. Again. And again.

The wolf arched its back, preening for her.

And Hawke stopped playing nice.

SIENNA had seen Hawke unclothed before—it was impossible not to catch such glimpses since changelings came out of a shift naked, but pack protocol meant she'd always forced herself to look away. Even if she hadn't, those times, she'd been nowhere near this close.

His chest was taut with muscle, his abs washboard flat, his skin a warm, strokable honey lightly furred with silver-gold. She wanted to press him to the carpet and lick him all over.

"You planning to fold?"

She jerked up her head, almost dropping her cards. "What?"

"Time to show your cards."

Certain she had him beat, she laid out her spread. "Full house." Her eyes went to his jeans.

She was so busy imagining him naked, she almost missed the smile that flirted over his lips as he said, "Nice, but not good enough," and fanned out a royal flush.

Stunned, she stared.

"Strip, beautiful."

She went to pull off her socks, her skin shimmering from the impact of that verbal caress.

"Nu-huh." A shake of his head. "Shirt."

That snapped through the sensual fog. "But I let you take off your socks first!"

"Yeah, I didn't know you had a foot fetish. Shirt."

She glared.

"You reneging on the bet?"

Fuming, she began to unsnap the buttons of the black shirt.

Hawke watched her with predatory alertness. "You'll be cute dressed in just your socks."

The image made her fingers halt on the final buttons, but when he raised his eyebrows, she kicked herself back into gear, shrugging off the shirt before she could lose her nerve.

His groan made her thighs clench. "You're wearing a fricking tank top underneath!"

"Frustration's not so funny now, is it?" she said with a smirk.

A slow smile that made her stomach go twisty and tight. "So this is revenge?"

"Maybe." Her satisfaction lasted until she figured out that Hawke was a cardsharp. Heart in her mouth, she was certain he'd make her strip off the despised tank next, but he rubbed his jaw and said, "Tank with the socks—could be cute."

Nervous anticipation or not, she couldn't keep from stroking her gaze over his chest as she waited for the verdict. What would it feel like to touch him, to rub her—

"Socks."

"What?"

"Want me to change my mind?"

"No!" Getting rid of the socks, she dealt the next game since he appeared to be content with her playing dealer. Except it was impossible to concentrate with him lying on his back only two feet from her, one leg stretched out on the carpet, the other bent at the knee as he held his cards up above him. It was like being shown the most beautiful classic statue in the world and being told not to touch.

Her nails dug into her palms.

"Baby?"

Expecting more of the sensual teasing that had her melting from the inside out, she was surprised at the tenderness she caught in that wolf-pale gaze. "Yes?"

"Do you want to be naked?"

"I agreed to play the game." Sienna always kept her word. It was a choice she'd made after leaving the Net, a stance that defined her.

"That's not what I asked."

She could've lied to spare her pride, but that wasn't what she wanted between them. "I'm not as comfortable being naked as a changeling." She'd never been nude in front of anyone after the age of five, except in a medical setting. Those weren't good memories.

Hawke put down his cards. "Want to touch?" The sensual invitation sliced right through the cold echo of the humiliation that had been her yearly physical, when her entire body was inspected from head to toe to ascertain that she had no imperfections that might make her a less viable weapon.

"Yes," she said, her throat thick with raw *want*.

"Then I'm all yours."

Pushing aside the cards, she crawled to kneel beside him. "Anywhere?"

"As long as you don't indulge your weird foot fetish." A lazy smile that invited her to play.

It was an irresistible temptation. Leaning down, she kissed that teasing mouth. His hand immediately fisted in her hair, holding her to him as he tasted her with breath-stealing thoroughness. "Will you ever," she said, chest rising and falling as she attempted to take in air, "give me control in this kind of a situation? In a sexual context?"

"No." The wolf looking up at her. "Does that bother you?"

She put her hand on his chest, the tensile warmth of him a sudden, acute addiction. "I have to be in control of my power every minute of every day." It was impossible not to stroke him, not to sleek her hand over the light covering on his chest that was even softer than it looked. It made her wonder how it would feel against her nipples.

His hand tightened in her hair. "What just went through your head?"

"Figure it out," she murmured, because while she discovered she wasn't averse to handing him the reins in bed, she wasn't about to roll over either. "I want to touch now."

His chest vibrated under her palm, and she realized he'd growled. But the sound held no anger. It was more sensual, deeper . . . intimate. Thinking back to what she'd been doing, she realized she'd grazed one flat male nipple with her nail.

So she did it again.

Making that same rumbling sound, he tugged her down with the grip he had in her hair, and took her mouth again, his lips a possessive brand. She found herself on her back, with him heavy between her thighs a second later. When she pushed at his shoulders, he said, "You can still touch." A light kiss on the corner of her lips, his stubbled jaw scraping across achingly sensitive flesh.

"Not if you keep doing that." It was beyond impossible to concentrate with him so big and warm and aroused above her. "Hawke."

Something in Sienna's voice made Hawke's wolf go motionless. Bracing himself with his forearms on either side of her head, he looked into eyes of inky black. "You need a break?" He hadn't forgotten who and what she was, the demands her gift made on her.

Her hands smoothed down his chest.

It took teeth-gritting control not to order her to stroke those hands over the hard ridge of his cock. "Baby, that's not going to make me behave."

"You have to," she said, "because it's my turn. I need to touch you."

A cool statement, but he heard the very real frustration behind it. As evidenced by the last time they'd been together, frustration in bed could be fun—but not the kind he heard in her voice. Need stripped bare, the same raw touch-hunger that had had him in its claws before he'd allowed himself to indulge in her. She was right. It *was* her turn.

So he locked his muscles, dropped his head, hair falling around his face, and let her pet him. Remaining quiescent under her exploration was torture, hungry as he was to claim her. Yet the wolf grit its teeth along with the human, as if aware that this woman, while strong enough to survive a childhood that would've broken most, was also deeply vulnerable in certain ways.

"You're so beautiful." A husky murmur that was a rough stroke across his taut flesh. "Your chest hair, it's so smooth, so fine. Like the thinnest of pelts."

It was also highly sensitive. "Use your mouth," he found himself demanding as the leash slipped.

But Sienna didn't shy. "Oh, yes. I want to do that." While he was still trying to quiet his primal response at the unhidden delight of her response, she wiggled down a fraction and placed a hot, uninhibited kiss right above his left nipple. He bit back a very blue word, a sheen of sweat coating his entire body. As he knew, Sienna learned fast. Her next kiss included the scrape of teeth.

Hawke's growl raised every hair on Sienna's body. Shivering, she licked at him, taking the salt and heat of him inside her. Part of her couldn't believe she had her hands on him at last, that she was free to stroke and taste as she wanted. The rest of her wanted to gorge, her legs clenching around the sensual intrusion of the big body between her thighs.

It would be easier to reach all of him if she pushed him to his back, but first, she wasn't entirely sure he'd go, and second, being surrounded by him was . . . beyond pleasure. His thighs pushed against the insides of hers as the thick weight of his erection pressed through his jeans, just brushing against her. His arms were tense with muscle on either side of her, his chest above her, his hair falling sexily around his face as he watched her with a predator's focus. One who wanted to bite.

She tried to reach his lips, fell short. "Kiss me."

Leaning down without a word, he ran his lips across hers. It was a tease, made her attempt to rise toward him once more.

"Nu-huh." He shook his head. "Be good."

Trembling, she lay back down.

Her reward was a suckling kiss, teeth closing over her

lower lip, a languid release that made things low in her stretch tight. "I hope you like teeth," he said in that rough, deep voice that made her want to do infinitely wicked things.

"I like yours."

He settled himself more heavily on her. She felt at once caged and as if she would fly into a million pieces with the slightest touch. Panic fluttered in her throat, the shock of a woman who'd grown up in a prison of discipline and darkness. "Hawke."

"Shh." Kisses on her cheekbone, his forearm bracketing her head as he used his free hand to play with strands of her hair. Another kiss, this one on her nose. "We've got all night." A whisper of a kiss on the corner of her mouth. Another. "No need to rush."

Gentling her, she thought, he was gentling her.

The unexpected tenderness of him surprised her . . . undid her. Yet, even at this moment, there was no doubting the power of the wolf who prowled behind his eyes. "Did you always know you'd be alpha?" she found herself whispering into the intimate hush.

His expression changed, became touched with darkness. "I knew when I needed to know," he said at last, and though the words were unspoken, she understood he wanted her to drop the subject.

That was the one thing she couldn't do, though she knew her persistence might shatter the magic of this sensual moment. Touching him, being with him, it was only part of what she needed from this man. She couldn't have his soul, couldn't have the mating bond, but she'd fight for the rest of him even if it left her bruised and bloody. "What did the Psy do?"

"They broke my father." Clipped-out words. "It took them a week."

Bile burned the back of her throat. It was near impossible to disrupt changeling shields without killing or injuring the target, but given a week with a wolf who, in all probability, had been dosed with drugs . . . "I'm sorry."

"Nothing for you to be sorry about." His fingers tightened on her hip. "You didn't have anything to do with the experiment."

A chill over her skin, the first glimmer of horror. "Experiment?" She reached out to stroke his jaw, found it hard as stone.

"Enough. There's nothing there except blood and death." He thrust his hand into her hair. "What we are now, that's what's important."

How could he say that? The past had savaged him—he carried the scars on his heart to this day. "Don't," she whispered. "Don't shut me out like that." *Don't give me even less of you.*

Shaking his head, he moved as if to kiss her, to end the conversation . . . froze. "Sienna, your eyes, they're burning."

Jerked back to the cold reality of her life, she dropped into her mind, saw the storm of flame. It shouldn't have built to critical again this fast, shouldn't have incinerated her shields and poured into her eyes, a violent voracious thing that would consume everything in its path and search for more. Fear squeezed her throat, but she had no time for the ice of it. "I need to get out of the den. Now."

Chapter 34

THEY TOOK ONE of the all-wheel-drives as deep into the isolated interior of den territory as possible before Sienna said, "Stop." Tumbling out of the vehicle the second Hawke braked, she ran toward a small clearing surrounded by the tall bulk of dark green firs, her feet cushioned by millions of pine needles. "Step back," she ordered when Hawke caught up to her.

"You don't scorch the earth when you release your power," he said, the planes of his face a study in pure, implacable will. "You didn't burn me when you lost control as you came." He locked his arms around her.

"Let go!" It terrified her that she'd hurt him. "Please!"

His arms were immovable steel. "I trust you. Trust yourself."

"Hawke!" Energy poured out of her in a screaming rush. Acting on primal instinct, she threw a shield of cold fire around every part of Hawke that touched her a split second before she punched a massive pulse of the same fire into the earth. It rippled in an eerie wave of crimson and gold on the surface before sinking below the forest floor. *Beautiful.*

Then there was no more thought. Only the brutal cold of an X.

She didn't know how long the fire burned through her, but she would've crumpled to the ground afterward if Hawke hadn't been holding her up. Shuddering, she leaned against him only for the seconds it took her to get her legs working again. Then she shoved, surprising him into releasing her.

"You bastard! I could've killed you!" Shock continued to

shudder in her blood, fighting with terror-fueled rage for dominance.

"You're allowing fear to drive you," he responded, eyes grim with determination. "Ming's still in your head, keeping you in a cage. Break out and own your ability."

"That's a load of bullshit!" Never before had she screamed at anyone. Never before had she felt such bone-chilling fear. "You don't know anything about being an X! Have you forgotten I almost killed my own mother?"

"You were a *child*."

Her laugh was flavored with bitterness. "You have no idea what I can do." All this time, she'd been fooling herself that he wanted her despite knowing she was a monster. If he'd understood in truth . . . "You felt the intensity of what I earthed. Yet I can do this." A single flick of her hand and X-fire encased a forest giant that had stood for centuries.

Ash, fine as dust, rose into the air between one blink and the next.

"Now you know."

HAWKE gritted his jaw as Sienna swayed on her feet. "That was a singularly stupid thing to do." Grabbing her in a fireman's carry, he threw her over his shoulder.

"Put me down." A weak protest before her body went limp.

Worry tore through his veins, but he could feel her heartbeat, sense her breath. Focusing on that, he strapped her into the passenger seat before digging out his phone. "Sienna's unconscious," he said when Judd answered.

The other man took a second to reply. "She's fine. Her mind is intact."

Relief was a punch to Hawke's gut. "I'm going to strip her hide when she wakes up." Shutting the passenger door, he jogged around to the driver's side and switched the phone to the hands-free comm mode before beginning the drive back.

"It sounds," Judd said when Hawke finished relaying what had led to Sienna's collapse, "like she overloaded her psychic pathways."

Hawke frowned. "So she does have a safety switch." He'd

gotten the impression that conscious control was so necessary to Sienna because she had no built-in off switch.

Judd didn't reply long enough that Hawke's blood went cold. "What aren't you saying?"

"I think we need to have this discussion after you return."

Hawke's patience was nonexistent when it came to Sienna's well-being, but he saw the lieutenant's point. "We'll be there soon."

Judd met them at the infirmary, where Lara ran a high-tech medical scanner over Sienna and pronounced her in perfect health. Only then did Hawke nod at Judd to follow him out into the corridor. "Tell me."

"She's accelerating at an exponential rate," Judd said, pulling up a chart on the tiny datapad he carried in his pocket. "After she confirmed she'd been purging her power more often of late, I spoke to Walker to see if we could pinpoint any specific times or dates. It took me until just before the South American operation to realize it was Toby we needed to speak to—she allows him closer than anyone else."

White lines bracketed the former Arrow's mouth. "He knew before all of us. He's been making a note in his diary each time he feels she's about to go critical. Since she hasn't had any incidents, the logical conclusion is that she instituted a purge in each case." Judd turned the datapad so Hawke could see the screen.

The pattern was impossible to miss. It had been almost a year between Sienna's arrival and the first time she earthed herself. The next came after eight months. Then six. The last few had been mere weeks apart. Hawke's wolf rose to the fore, helping the man think with clear-eyed purpose. "Can it be stopped?"

"No." An absolute statement. "That's what makes her an X."

"Silence"—he forced himself to say that word, to consider that option—"kept her under some kind of containment."

"Only to an extent. She's the sole cardinal X ever born, according to our records. Even Ming was playing a game of Russian roulette with her. No one had any idea what would happen as her power matured."

"Does she know?"

"I think she doesn't want to know." Black erased the gold-

flecked brown of Judd's eyes, a rare indication of strong emotion. "The only way she can survive is to believe that she can
change the inevitable."

"Then we leave it at that." He could see Sienna growing
deeper into her skin day by day. No way in hell was he going
to cut her off at the knees. "You sound certain that it can't be
stopped, but is there any way to slow the progression?"

Judd shoved a hand through his hair. "I've been searching
for the manuscript I mentioned to you once."

"The dissertation on X-Psy?"

The other man nodded. "I've found no evidence to confirm
its existence, but I'm waiting to hear back from one final
contact."

Hawke's wolf caught the minute change in Judd's expression. "The Ghost. You don't trust him."

"Not in this. She's a weapon of infinite potential."

And the Ghost, Hawke knew, had an agenda that had nothing to do with peace.

EIGHT hours later, with the mountains kissed white-gold by
the morning sun, Hawke stood staring at the door that had
just been slammed in his face. "Sienna," he growled.

Silence from the other side.

He slammed his hands palms down on the flat surface
hard enough that she couldn't miss it. Waited. Still nothing.
Part of him—the part that made him alpha—wanted to rip
the door off its hinges, throw her onto the bed, and teach her
what happened to a woman who dared defy him. He wouldn't
hurt her. But he would bite her. *Hard.*

Strangling the primitive urge, he decided to walk it off but
changed his mind midway and headed to the garage instead.
The drive gave him enough time to settle so that he wasn't
feeling completely feral when he arrived at his destination—
after having made a small detour to pick up something.

Sascha laughed when he handed her the stuffed toy wolf.
"How did you talk your way past the sentinels?"

"Natural charm." He thought about kissing her on the
cheek but decided to cut Lucas a break.

"What're you doing here?" the leopard demanded, his

hands on Sascha's hips as they stood in the doorway of the cabin.

"I've come to meet my new girl," Hawke said, doing his best to look harmless. "Where is she?"

Lucas scowled, but moved out of the doorway when Sascha turned to press a kiss to his jaw. "Come in," the empath said, heading deeper into the cabin.

Hawke hung back long enough to stick out his hand. "Congratulations."

Lucas shook it. "Thanks." Jerking his head toward the bedroom, he said, "Sascha refuses to move the bassinet to the nursery yet."

"Just Sascha?" Hawke raised an eyebrow.

The snarl was quiet but no less powerful for it. "Do you want to see her or not?"

Hawke caught a delicate new scent hidden beneath the protective markers of a panther and an empath as soon as he crossed the threshold. Baby powder and smiles. The innocence of it made his wolf stop pacing, anger and irritation temporarily shelved.

Conscious of the instincts that had to be clawing at Lucas, he kept his hands behind his back as he peered down at the tiny creature in Sascha's arms, her curious eyes already as bright green as her father's. "Hello, sweet darling." It was impossible not to smile, not to fall in love a little.

Sascha nuzzled the baby with a gentle, maternal kiss before saying, "Would you like to hold her?"

Hawke glanced to Luc first. The leopard alpha nodded. "I'll tear your throat out if you even breathe wrong."

"Fair enough." Taking the precious bundle from Sascha, he cuddled the baby close to the warmth of his body. When she scrunched up her face, he laughed. "Yes, I am a wolf, little cat." Touching a careful finger to her nose, he was startled to feel tiny hands grip at it. "Look at that."

Fascinated, Sascha thought, looking from one man to the other. They were both fascinated. It hadn't astounded her in the least when Naya had wrapped Lucas around her finger, but somehow, she'd expected Hawke to last longer. But really, was it any surprise? He was alpha, too, had those same strong protective urges running through his blood.

The baby made a fussy noise.

Taking her from Hawke, Lucas held her against his chest, purring low and steady until their princess quieted in contentment. Sascha didn't know how she stood it, the love for her mate and child that filled her body. It was so visceral, so intertwined in every cell of her being. An impossible, huge thing that eclipsed all that had come before.

It threatened to blind her to everything else, but she was an E-Psy. And so, she caught the whisper of darkness in the man who was an alpha without a mate. Glancing at Lucas, she tilted her head. He scowled. She pursed her lips. Sighing, he said, "I think baby girl here wants to go for a walk."

Hawke exited first, with Sascha following Lucas out. He walked across the clearing until he was out of hearing range—if they kept their voices low. "You're worried about something," she said to Hawke, cutting to the heart of it.

Black thunder rolled across that harsh but beautiful face. "Stop doing that."

"I can't help it." She never intruded on people's emotions, but she could no more stop sensing them than Hawke could turn off his sense of smell.

Folding his arms, he leaned against the cabin wall while she perched on the window ledge a foot away. "What happened?" She prodded, because you had to with men so used to keeping everything contained. "Does it have to do with Sienna?"

"What makes you say that?"

"She's the only one who incites this reaction in you."

Hawke stared at where Lucas walked the baby. "She's refusing to talk to me."

"That shocks you." No, Sascha thought, that wasn't quite it. "It stuns you that she's able to hold out against you."

Hawke scowled. "You make me sound like an ass."

"Not an ass—just a man who rarely has anyone stand up to him." She felt the baby's searching mind, sent reassurance as she did a thousand times a day. "Tell me why she's not talking to you."

After Hawke finished, she said, "I see."

Pale eyes pinned her to the spot, his dominance a staggering wave. If she hadn't been used to living with Lucas, she might've wilted. As it was, she touched her fingers to his jaw and pushed a fraction. "Stop that."

The wolf continued to prowl behind that icy gaze, but he glanced away.

"Let me ask you one thing," she said, wondering if she'd be able to get through to him, this man who, from what she knew, had become alpha at an even younger age than Lucas. "If Judd told you to keep your distance, would you?"

He folded his arms, biceps pushing against the sleeves of his white T-shirt. "The two situations aren't the same."

"She's a cardinal, Hawke." Gentle words, but Sascha was a cardinal, too, and the statement held a piercing power as it settled on Hawke's skin. "If you're to have any kind of a relationship with her, you must accept what she is—ignoring her when she makes a decision about her own power is about as far as you can get from acceptance."

Hawke's wolf paced inside his mind, wanting to tear at her words with its claws. "I have to get back." There were a hundred things he had to handle today, but the most critical, he thought as he said good-bye to the leopard pair, would take some careful planning. There would be no more doors slammed in his face—of that much, both man and wolf were certain.

**RESPONSE FROM ESTES PARK POLICE DEPARTMENT TO
QUERY BY GEORGE KIM ON BEHALF OF PROFESSORS MAE AND
ELLISON ELDRIDGE: JANUARY 8, 1975**

We regret to inform you that Alice Eldridge appears to have
suffered a fatal accident during her most recent climb. A search-
and-rescue unit is attempting to recover the body, but it is lodged
so deep inside a crevasse that it may not be safe to proceed.
Telekinetic assistance has been denied.

Chapter 35

ACCORDING TO A packmate, Lara had headed down to the waterfall, but Walker found no sign of her when he arrived. In the end, it was the crimson of her wool coat that gave her away—she was sitting tucked into the trees, her face turned toward the wild fury of the water.

Knowing she'd catch his scent, he walked to sit by her side, his shoulder touching hers. "You have shadows under your eyes." He wanted to reach across and wipe them away, even knowing that to be impossible. When she didn't reply, he said, "Talk to me, Lara." He wasn't used to silence from the woman who had become his closest friend.

"I had an emergency call from one of the women this morning. She was three months pregnant."

Everything in Walker went quiet. "Something was wrong?"

"She had a miscarriage." She took a ragged breath. "There was no warning, nothing to indicate a problem. I keep a careful eye on the pregnant women, but I didn't catch this—" Wet in her voice. "I couldn't fix it."

He touched his hand to the wild energy of her curls. "Some pregnancies terminate without any apparent reason, you know that."

"Intellectually, yes. But . . . She's in so much emotional pain right now."

Stroking his hand down the stiff line of her spine, he rested it on her hip. "I saw Hawke in the infirmary with a young couple when I went to find you."

Lara nodded. "I called him in. He'll be able to help her

wolf to an extent, help her mate, too." She wrapped her arms around raised knees. "She's strong, healthy, will heal. I just hate that she's having to go through this hurt. I *hate* it."

Walker wasn't female, would never carry a child, but he was a father. "Yelene," he found himself saying, speaking a secret he'd never shared, "was pregnant with our second child when we got the rehabilitation order."

Lara sucked in a breath. "She lost the baby."

Of course she'd think that, this healer who worried so much about her pack. "The order was for everyone who bore Lauren blood. She'd already aborted the child by the time I came home." Everything else, he would have accepted, would have survived, but that act, it broke something inside him. Because even in the PsyNet, he'd worked with children. Dangerous, gifted children, but children nonetheless, and he'd done everything in his power to protect them. Yet—"I couldn't protect my child."

Hearing Lara's quiet sobs, he turned and took her into his arms, weaving his fingers into her hair. She buried her face against his chest and cried as if her heart was splintering. She understood, he thought, knew that it wasn't only his unborn child that had died that day. But . . . as Lara cried for the child he'd lost, as she gave voice to the grief he couldn't express, the tight knot of sorrow inside him began to unravel fragment by jagged fragment.

"I sometimes wonder," he whispered, the soft skin of her nape delicate under his palm, "what my son would've been like."

Lara's hand spread on the fabric of his shirt. "Tell me what you imagined." Her voice was raw with weeping, but her strength, it was an enduring flame.

It took him a long time, but as the water continued to thunder into the pool below, Walker held the warmth of her close and spoke of the son who lived deep within his heart and always would.

HAWKE nodded at Lake as he jogged down to the perimeter in the quiet of the hour before midnight. "Any problems?"

The soldier shook his head. "Spotted a couple of falcons

in the distance when it was light, but they stayed clear of den territory."

"Good." Hawke spent several more minutes talking to Lake, having had a heads-up from Riley about him. Intelligent, Hawke thought, and not only that, but he had the capacity to think outside the box. "Are you happy with your current duties?"

Lake took a deep breath. "If I had the choice, I'd prefer more complex tasks."

"Talk to Riley tomorrow," Hawke said, because he didn't want the talented young male getting bored. "He'll shift your duties."

"I understand we're at high alert after the recent events." An intent look. "I can wait until we're better situated to move things around."

"No. We're not going to allow anyone to stifle the growth of our pack."

"Yes, sir." Lake glanced down, back up. "I wanted to say something—about Maria."

"Go on."

"She's still pretty cut up about stepping off watch that time. If you could . . ."

Hawke's wolf liked the boy better for his request. "I'll take care of it."

"Thank you." A faint smile. "Sienna should be about five hundred meters to the north."

Hawke pointed south. "Go."

Lake left with a salute—and a grin.

Jogging along the perimeter until he caught the rich, vibrant scent of a woman who was well and truly under his skin, he drew in a deep breath of the cool mountain air and leashed his wolf. Demands would get neither man nor wolf anything when it came to Sienna. Neither would orders. This was about male and female. Hawke and Sienna.

He found her standing watch on a cliff's edge, keeping an acute eye on everything that passed. Quiet as it was, it took her the barest instant to detect him. "Would you like a report, sir?"

He narrowed his eyes at her tone, but where the alpha in him would've delivered a quick and lethal verbal response to anyone else, that wasn't the relationship he wanted with Sienna. "No, I'd prefer a kiss."

Back as stiff as steel, she said, "I'm working," but then, to his surprise, glanced back. "I heard about Ameline's miscarriage." Her expression was solemn.

The memory of his packmate's silent cries had his wolf wanting to lift its muzzle in a mournful howl. "She's hurting bad, but she's strong. So is her mate. They'll survive this."

"You sat with her?"

"Yes." Controlling the impulse to fist his hand in her hair, tug her close until he could breathe in the warm spice of her skin . . . until he could unwind on the deepest level, he focused on the land that was his home. The night was stunning, the velvet sky dotted with diamonds. "Do you wonder if the Council understands why we'd fight to the last breath to hold this?"

"Yes." Her own face lifted to the sky. "The psychologists will have done a full workup. But they won't believe you'd refuse to surrender even at the threat of massive casualties."

"Some things are beyond logic." Losing their home would rip the heart out of the pack—it wouldn't matter if they survived. "We both know that." He stroked his hand down the thick rope of her braid.

She jerked away, the truce over. "You ignored me."

"Yeah, I did. And I'm not sorry I did it." Maybe he'd been an ass, but he'd also been right—she *had* been shortchanging herself, had now learned that she could wield and direct the cold fire, choose her targets even at that level of pressure.

"Surprising." Sarcasm dripped off the single word.

"But," he added with a growl, "I won't disregard your views about your own abilities next time."

Sienna froze at the unexpected statement. "Not much of an apology," she said, scrambling to reorder her thoughts.

"That's because I wasn't apologizing."

Of course not. "Go away."

He tugged at her neat braid instead, unraveling it before she realized what he was doing. Gritting her teeth to stop from reacting, she stared out at the hush of the forest as he smoothed out the strands. "You have curls in here," he murmured from behind her. "Did you braid it while it was damp?"

That sneaky wolf charm was not going to weaken her defenses this time. "I'm working, in case you didn't hear me the first time."

Arms sliding around her waist, tugging her back against a warm male chest. "I've come to keep you company."

Reaching back, she pulled her hair out from between them. "I like being alone."

A quick nip of her ear. "Such a liar."

Folding her arms, she resisted the urge to kick back at him with a booted foot. "This patch is quiet," she said. "Lake wanted to run tonight, so I'm standing as sentry."

Hawke's arms came up to cross over her chest as he held her impossibly closer, his thighs on either side of hers. "That was one of my first tasks—sentry." His voice was quiet, full of memory. "The alpha started putting me on watch when I was nine."

"Nine?" Far too young, according to SnowDancer's own rules.

Hawke chuckled. "I was making trouble—had too much energy and nowhere for it to go. They tried running me to exhaustion, but I outlasted everyone except Garrick, and the alpha couldn't spend every day with me."

Sienna realized she'd relaxed against him, but she was too fascinated by this tiny glimpse into his past to worry. "Were you a good sentry?"

"No," he said to her surprise. "I couldn't stop moving long enough to keep watch." Another laugh. "So Garrick made me a messenger. I ran constantly along the perimeter, taking messages from one sentry to another, spending time with the soldiers, learning from them." Looking back, he knew half the messages had been created to give him something to do.

"It was the best thing Garrick could have done." The work had not only provided an outlet for his energy, it had begun to teach him the skills he would need in the future—as well as connecting him to the men and women he would one day be called upon to lead.

"This Garrick was a good alpha?"

Hawke thought of the slender black man who'd appeared about as strong as a willow branch—and who had fought like a gladiator for his pack. "Yes."

"Oh." Sienna paused. "I guess . . . no one ever mentions him, so I thought maybe he was a bad person."

"No." Hawke forced himself to speak. "They don't say anything because they don't want to hurt me." But it wasn't fair to the man, the alpha Garrick had been. "Garrick died fighting one of his lieutenants." The next words were stone fists in his chest. "My father."

Sienna's hands came up to close over his. "You said he was abducted, hurt. He was no longer the man you knew."

Hawke's mind filled with the memory of the agony on his father's face as blood poured out of his chest. He'd taken his last breath in his mate's arms, his hand held by his mortally wounded alpha as their already weak healer tried to save them both.

"Was your father the only one?"

"No."

"Your mother . . . she lost her mate."

He never spoke of his laughing, gifted mother and what it had done to her to lose her mate, not to anyone. "There's Lake, coming up now," he said instead of answering her question. "I think we should go for a run." A high-pitched whistle and Lake raised his hand to signal he understood.

When Hawke shifted to face Sienna, he saw her eyes had turned to midnight. "You're good at keeping a distance between you and a lover, aren't you, Hawke?"

He curved a hand over the column of her throat, stroked. "I haven't exactly been keeping my distance from you."

"There's more than one kind of distance." Not saying anything further, she took a black hair tie out of her pocket and pulled her hair into a sleek ponytail.

Her words disturbed both man and wolf, but his past wasn't why he'd tracked her down. "Come on, Lake's almost to us." Loping down the slope, he waited for her to catch up. They ran the watch at a moderate speed, which allowed them to take in their surroundings, confirm everything was as it should be. "Your need to purge the cold fire," he said, wanting to get that out of the way, "was that because of my touch?"

"No," she said at once. "I was aware it was building—just made a miscalculation as to how close I was to critical."

Hawke thought of Judd's revelation, placed it against Sienna's will. He knew where he was putting his money. "You fully recovered?"

"Yes."

"Good." Deciding to set the issue aside for tonight, he asked, "Who's your preferred partner on watch?" It wasn't a question from alpha to soldier, but man to woman. He wanted to simply be with her on this beautiful night, her voice brushing against his skin as they passed under the moon-shadow of forest giants.

"You won't believe me, but Maria." Sienna ducked under a branch, leaving a strand of ruby red behind.

He liked that she'd inadvertently marked their territory. "You're right, I don't believe you."

She wrinkled her nose at him. "Until the fight, we worked well together. We've actually kind of become friends since then."

"Yeah, I remember your buddies from Wild."

Ignoring his snarl, she pointed out a fleeing rabbit. "Lake is very serious—too much like me. I think we become too quiet together."

Hawke could see how that could happen. Sienna needed a wolf who was willing to play. Though of course, wolves weren't the only predators in this region. "Seen that leopard cub lately?"

"If you're talking about Kit, yes. I had lunch with him today."

He felt claws pricking at the insides of his skin as they came to a halt on top of another rise that allowed them to look out over the territory. "Lunch."

Most women would've either bristled or frozen at his not-so-subtle attempt at intimidation. Sienna showed how shockingly well she knew him by ambushing him with an unexpected bite on his lower lip as he bent to demand more information. She was gone before he could retaliate.

His wolf bowed its back in pleasure, happy to play with her at any time and delighted she'd initiated this game. Catching up to her, he shot her a look that promised revenge. Her response was pure cool-eyed Psy . . . except for the laughter hidden in that cardinal gaze. He was about to tug her to him, taste the laughter, when he heard something that had his wolf coming to a dead stop.

STOPPING at once when Hawke went motionless, Sienna shoved her amusement to the back of her consciousness. "What do you sense?" She kept her voice subvocal, in a range she could only just hear herself.

Not answering, Hawke angled his head to the left, narrowed his eyes, then arched his neck.

The eerie beauty of the howl electrified every tiny hair on her body. It seemed impossible that it was coming from a human throat, and yet she could see the reality of it in the corded strength of his neck. Responding howls came back to them over the air currents as the last echoes of Hawke's warning—and she'd learned enough about wolf harmonics to have figured out that that's exactly what it had been—died out.

"Let's go." Hawke set what was a brutal pace for her, leading them away from the perimeter.

He sent up another howl maybe thirty seconds into the run, waited only long enough to get a response from each of the sentries. But a bare minute after they'd begun to run again, he slammed her body to the ground, in the hollow created by the roots of a centuries-old tree, covered it with his own, and said, "Hands over your ears."

Stuttering blasts of noise sounded an instant later. She tried to turn, see where the bullets were hitting, but Hawke's body was too heavy, keeping her pinned. Hands over her ears as he'd ordered, she stayed in position and hoped with everything in her that Lake and the others in the strike zone had gotten under cover before the attack.

It seemed to go on forever, an endless hail of violence. The increasing level of noise indicated the offensive craft was getting closer—she was about to try to talk to Hawke, tell him they needed to move when the sonic boom of a massive explosion set her ears to ringing.

Chapter 36

A SECOND EXPLOSION followed on the heels of the first.

Hawke rolled off her an instant later. "Baby, you okay?"

She said, "Yes," through the buzzing in her ears, aware he had to be in acute pain, given the sensitivity of changeling hearing. "You?"

"Hurts like a bitch, but eardrums didn't blow." Getting to his feet, he hauled her up.

"W—" Her dazed brain rallied to make sense of the debris raining down from the sky only meters away. "We need to check the wreckage as soon as possible, in case they have a Tk cleanup squad ready to mobilize." The destroyed craft might yield information the pack could use to its advantage in the growing hostilities.

"Go," Hawke said to her surprise. "Do what you need to if Tks 'port in. I have to check on the others."

"Be careful."

Getting his nod, she took off. The debris was lumps of blackened and twisted metal at first glance, nothing of any use. Keeping her senses—physical and psychic—on wide alert, she did a crisscrossing grid search at high speed, hoping like hell the pack's air-defense systems had left her something to find.

As it was, she almost missed it.

It had to have been part of the hull, a tiny warped square that she glimpsed with the corner of her eye. Running back to it, she gloved her hand in a layer of cold fire before picking it up. Her ability protected her from the blazing heat coming off the debris, but it did nothing to affect her vision.

The single silver star on the metal fragment was as bright as platinum.

HAWKE made contact with Brenna as he ran, the sat phone's reception crystal clear. "Are the skies clean?"

"Yes—and the aerial-defense systems are rearmed and ready."

"Has Lara been notified?"

"She's on her way. Riley's coordinating everything. I'll patch you through."

"Casualties?" he asked as soon as Riley came on the line.

"No reports so far." Crisp, collected words. "But we've got some severe injuries."

"Why did it take so long to blow those bloody things out of the sky?" SnowDancer knew its weaknesses, had prepared defenses. "They should've been picked up before they ever got close enough to hit anyone."

"Same stealth technology they used last time," Riley said. "I've asked the cats to send in teams to secure the wreckage until we can spare the people—what we find could prove critical in modifying our detection systems."

"Were they hit?"

"No. The attack was focused on SnowDancer."

Seeing Lake's fallen body, Hawke said, "I'll call you back," and hung up.

The young soldier had taken a shot through his back, but he was breathing. "Go," he whispered. "I'm not going to fucking die and give them the satisfaction."

Good man. "Lara's on her way," he said, making the tough decision to take Lake at his word, check on the others.

It was a long night.

Lake had lost a lot of blood, but the bullet hadn't nicked anything major. Sam had been hit once, the bullet digging a channel across the side of his skull and knocking him out, but Lara assured Hawke the damage looked worse than it was. Inés had taken a bullet in the leg, Riaz had been hit in the shoulder, and a newly promoted Tai had fractured his left arm as he dived to avoid the bullets, while Sing-Liu had been hit twice, both bullets entering through her back to crush a path through her internal organs.

The small human woman was the most badly injured, alive only because her mate, D'Arn, had shoved his energy into her in an effort to keep her alive after he felt her pain through their bond. He'd collapsed where he stood in the den, but he'd kept her alive. It was now up to Lara and her team.

The DarkRiver healer, Tamsyn, worked beside Lara. She couldn't heal wolves, but as a qualified physician, she could take some of the burden by dealing with the less severe injuries. Riley and Indigo had the security situation under control, had made sure the attack left no gaps in their defensive perimeter, while the techs were combing through the wreckage. That left Hawke free to remain in the infirmary.

It was near dawn that he put his hands on Lara's shoulders and said, "Go to bed." All the injured had been treated and were now resting.

"I'm okay," she mumbled, cheek against his chest, "one more espresso and I'll be set. Where's Tammy?"

"Her mate carried her off an hour ago." Literally. "Now go to bed or I'll handcuff you to it."

"Kinky." But she didn't resist when he walked her to her room and pushed her in the direction of the bed.

Turning around when he was certain she didn't plan to sneak back out, he made his way to his own quarters and stepped into the shower. Dressed in sweats and a clean T-shirt afterward, he didn't crash, but headed to Sienna's, knowing she'd only returned to the den thirty minutes ago—she'd been on protection detail over the techs since the attack. Her strength made his wolf raise its head in pride.

She opened the door at his first knock and said nothing as he pulled off his T-shirt. When he nudged her into her bed, she went without argument. He curled himself behind her, nuzzled his face into the curve of her neck, and fell headlong into sleep.

LARA had fallen asleep the instant she stumbled facedown into bed, not bothering to strip, but her wolf nudged her awake what felt like moments later. "What?" she mumbled, feeling someone tugging at her shoes. "One sec—"

"Shh." A strong, warm hand on her hair. "Just getting these off." Another tug and her medical coat was gone, too.

"Kids," she mumbled, not able to find the will to move.

That big, callused hand stilled on her body. "They're with Drew and Indigo."

She tried to say that that was good, but exhaustion kicked her hard. Right before everything went dark, she felt Walker's lips on her temple, warm and firm. Wishful thinking. But it was a nice way to go into sleep.

NO, no, no, no, no, no, no, no . . .

"Perfect." Ming walked into the room to examine the pile of fine ash where there had once been a screaming person. "While your lack of control is problematic, I can't be less than pleased with the strength of your ability."

She was a monster trapped in a room with another. Maybe she should just burn them both up, end it all.

A vice around her mind, black and vicious, a reminder that her thoughts weren't her own. "Stop," she said, blood trickling out of her nose.

"Remember, Sienna," he said, the birthmark on the left side of his face the same color as her blood. "I own you. You are my creature."

A growl in the evil silence of that room, shaking the very walls.

As she watched, Ming began to disintegrate until he was nothing, less than nothing. The sight of it caused her such violent pleasure that when the growl turned into a voice and ordered, "Rest. I've got you," she snuggled back into a big, muscled body and surrendered to the wings of sleep once more.

SIENNA woke perhaps three hours after Hawke had come into her room. At the time, there'd been no need or time for words—though she had a vague memory of hearing his voice sometime in between. Frowning, she thought back, caught fragments of what might've been a nightmare, but there were no lingering remnants of terror.

Hardly surprising given the protective heat of the man who slept curved around her. Hawke's thigh was pressed demandingly against the softest part of her, his hand flat on her abdomen beneath her favorite old tank, his arm under her head, his face nuzzled into the curve of her neck—the reality of him was a sensual pulse under her skin.

Part of her wanted to turn around, to rub her face against the fine, silky hairs on his chest, but a bigger part was scared to shatter the moment, to have him wake and leave. She knew he'd have to go. He was alpha, and last night, the pack had been attacked. He'd given himself and his people a little time to rest and regroup, but morning had broken—everything would kick into high gear as soon as he rose.

A rumble against her back, his hand moving in lazy circles on her abdomen as he wedged his thigh more firmly against her. "Morning." That rough, male voice made her skin go taut, her face flush with heat that had nothing to do with embarrassment and everything to do with throat-clenching desire. She'd never woken up with a man tangled around her, never thought that when it happened, it would be *him*.

"Morning," she managed to say, readying herself for the loss of his presence. "I can make you coffee before you go." Yes, she wanted him to stay, but he was the heart of Snow-Dancer, being alpha as much a part of him as her abilities were of her. She'd never consider getting in the way of his loyalty to the pack, had understood even as a girl barely out of the Net that he was loved by many, needed by many. "I only have instant, but it's not bad."

"Not coffee," he said, kissing the curve of her neck. "Give me something sweet to take into the day."

She squeezed down on that slowly rubbing thigh, her body tight, hot. "What do you want?"

His hand moved, his fingers trailing along the top of her waistband. "To pleasure you."

"I—" She'd never stuttered in her life, but it looked like that was about to happen. Swallowing, she attempted to rearrange her scattered thoughts. "I don't know if I can handle it."

"We've played before." Another kiss. "You said that wasn't what made the cold fire spill over."

"No, it didn't."

"Then?"

"I'm not sure my control is good enough," she admitted, because while emotion didn't drive the X-fire, it did have an impact on her capacity to cage it. That was what Silence had given those of her designation—a cold, calm place in which to stand. "After last night I feel as if my emotions are on a hair trigger. I might lose my grip on my abilities if I . . ."

"If you?"

"You know."

Teeth nibbling at her shoulder, a wolfish tease. "Orgasm. I think that's the word you're looking for." His fingers dipped just below the waistband of her pajama bottoms, making her pulse jump. He licked over the spot on her neck.

She clenched around his thigh. *"Hawke."*

"Say stop and we'll stop." Words spoken against the flush of her skin, but they held a serious undertone.

It turned a key inside of her to realize he was doing exactly as he'd said he'd do—respecting her decision when it came to her abilities. "Not yet," she whispered, keeping a rigid psychic grip on the reins of the cold fire.

Murmuring in approval, he withdrew his fingers, shifting their positions until he was braced on his side beside her as she lay on her back. Throwing a leg over her own, he said, "Wouldn't want you to escape," as he bent to kiss her.

It was slow, lazy, as if he had nowhere to be, though she knew he had a thousand calls on his time. Curling her arms around his neck, she drank in the warm masculinity of him as he continued to play his fingers over her skin. "Yes?" he asked into her mouth when she broke off to catch her breath.

Her stomach held a thousand frantic, trapped butterflies. It scared her how much he made her feel—and that angered her. Sienna Lauren, cardinal X, was never scared. It wasn't who she was. "Yes," she said.

He chuckled, pressing affectionate little kisses on the corners of her mouth. "So stubborn." Another kiss, a little bite of her lower lip as he slid his hand a fraction lower. "Exactly like I like you."

She felt her abdomen quiver, was powerless to stop it. Gripping his arm with one hand, the other on his shoulder, she luxuriated in the sensation of the muscle and tendon of him moving under her touch as he drew more of those languid circles low on her navel.

Lower.

A gasp escaped her, smothered against the skin of his neck. He smelled of warmth and man and Hawke. Just Hawke. Always Hawke. So when he slipped his hand under the waistband of her panties to run his finger down the center of her, she arched her body toward him in instinctive response.

He liked that. She knew because he kissed her jaw, murmured, "You're damp. I can smell you, all luscious and ready. Makes my mouth water." His finger stroked back up, and then he used two to spear through her, trapping her clitoris in between.

SO responsive, Hawke thought as her body arched again, so sweetly responsive. It was all he could do not to pull down the pajama bottoms and panties she'd worn to bed with a faded red tank and lick her up like his own personal dessert banquet. The sole thing stopping him was the fact that he knew he'd have to rush it.

"That's it," he murmured against those lush lips he loved to kiss, to bite, to suck, "let me pet you. Let me please you." Circling one finger at the slick entrance of her body, he pushed in gentle demand.

Her hands clenched on him again, but he tasted no fear in her scent—only the earthy, intoxicating musk of feminine arousal. Still, he kissed and stroked and nuzzled until she relaxed, until she let him in. God, she was tight. Her cry was a breathy sound against his senses, her hips motionless for two long seconds before she began to shift them in experimental little moves on the intrusion of his finger.

He shuddered, kissed his way back up her throat to capture her mouth. "Damn, you're beautiful," he said when she gasped for breath.

Using his thumb to rub at the tight bundle of nerves at the apex of her thighs even as he continued to thrust in and out of her with his finger, he bent his head and very carefully bit her nipple through the soft fabric of her tank.

"Hawke!" Her body fractured around his hand, the slick heat of her such wicked temptation that he continued to stroke inside her as she trembled down from the orgasm, inciting tiny aftershocks of pleasure and indulging himself in the silken tightness of her at the same time.

Withdrawing his finger only when she moaned, her body limp, he cupped her with possessive intimacy and took her mouth again, nipping and licking and tasting. "Good morning."

That cardinal gaze was a soft, hazy black when her lashes lifted. "Good morning." Kiss-swollen lips shaping the words, the skin of her face marked red from the roughness of his stubble.

He should've been sorry he supposed, but he wasn't. He liked seeing his marks on her. Playing with the damp curls between her legs, careful not to touch her oversensitized clit, he simply watched her for long moments. His cock was a hard ridge in his sweats, his need painful, but no way in hell was he going to settle for a quickie their first time together.

Then she reached down to close her fingers over him.

Chapter 37

CHRIST. SLIDING HIS hand out from between her legs to press against the bed, he allowed himself to push into her touch. Once. Twice. "Enough." Grabbing her wrist, he pinned it by her head.

Lazy, sated eyes smiled at him. "You felt so hard and hot and—"

"You put your hand on me again," he warned, "I won't be satisfied with a few strokes." No, it would just take the edge off . . . and unleash the wolf.

Curving her leg over his hip, Sienna leaned up to kiss his throat. "Thank you for my orgasm."

His cheeks creased. "You're welcome."

Another kiss before she lay back on the bed, looking up at him in a way that said she'd glimpsed the harsh reality that had begun to force its way back into his mind.

"We're going into war," he said, releasing his grip on her wrist. "There's no longer any doubt about it."

An intent gaze, fingers stroking his nape in tender affection. "I think conflict has been inevitable since the instant the packs decided to stand against the Council on any level."

He took another kiss before changing their positions so that she lay on top of him, his hand on her lower back. *Skin*, his wolf insisted, *skin*. So he pushed his hand under the waistband of her pajama pants and panties to lie over the sweet curve of her butt. She jerked but relaxed almost at once. *Good.* He wanted her to get used to him, to his touch, to his body, since he planned to be indulging her, and indulging *in her*, on a regular basis.

"We didn't go looking for war," he said, caressing her with small, slow movements as he allowed himself a few more minutes of rest. "If the Council had left us alone, we'd have left them alone." Discussing such a critical issue with Sienna was not something he'd have considered even a few months ago, yet it now felt natural.

"They can't accept," she said, playing her fingers over his collarbone, "that you're a power in the world."

"That's always been the problem, hasn't it?" He placed his free arm under his head.

"Silence takes away everything else," she mused, "but power—there is nothing in the Protocol that prevents a hunt for more. In truth, Silence rewards those who are cold-blooded enough to go after it with single-minded focus."

Hawke tried to think of what it must be like to live in the PsyNet, couldn't imagine it. "I've heard people say the Net is beautiful."

"Yes—in the same way as a perfectly cut gemstone. Pristine and cold." Her hand stilled on his skin. "I didn't understand that while I was in there, but even then, I knew it was wrong for a mother to be parted from her child."

He heard the pain in her, slid up his hand to press against her lower back. "You loved her."

"She tried to save me, but she was a cardinal telepath with a secondary telekinetic ability"—a hitch—"and in the end, she couldn't save herself."

Hawke knew her mother had jumped off the Golden Gate Bridge, could guess at the scars the tragedy had left behind. "Did her shields shatter?"

A shake of her head, her cheek pressed to his shoulder. "She went mad. It happens with some strong telepaths, even under Silence. It's as if no shield is enough to protect them, as if other people's thoughts sneak in under cover of night and take up residence." A touch of wet on his chest, the taste of salt in the air. "Free," she said. "That's what my mother shouted as she jumped—that she was free. Everyone believes she spoke of Silence, but I know my mother would've done anything for silence. She wanted only to be free of the voices."

Such a pragmatic tone hiding so much pain. Such a slender body hiding so much power. Everything about Sienna was a contradiction. But on one thing, he wanted no doubt. "You're mine," he said. "Understand that." He'd meant to reassure her that she need never fear he'd abandon her, but her body was suddenly all tense muscle and bone against him.

"I'll never be yours until you're mine."

He fisted his hand in her hair, tried to make his response gentle. "I can't give you the mating bond, Sienna." He'd been honest with her from the start, had hoped she wouldn't make him hurt her this way.

"I know."

A taut silence . . . because what else was there to say?

But Sienna spoke again. "I don't think the attack means the Scotts intend a rapid escalation."

He didn't try to force the conversation back to the original topic, though the possessive heart of him didn't like the answer she'd given, no matter how unfair it was of him to demand more from her than he could offer. "Explain."

"It's part of the scattergun approach we talked about earlier." Self-possessed words, no hint of the tears drying on his chest. "The Councilors are well aware by now of how a changeling pack functions. They'll expect the attack to motivate you to evacuate your young, your vulnerable—and so they'll be ready with an ambush."

Hawke's heart went cold at the idea of the pups being hurt.

"The targeted strikes, the ships designed to evade your defenses—everything indicates that whoever is behind this has done their research," Sienna continued. "In my opinion, they've figured out that the best way to demoralize the pack to the point of no return would be to wipe out the young." Her words were cool, crisp, but he didn't make the mistake of thinking she didn't care. He knew how many hours she volunteered in the White Zone, how many of the pups called her "Sinna" and raised their arms for a cuddle.

But the fact that she'd seen that stomach-turning prospect, had the background to even consider it, was stark evidence of the darkness in which she'd grown up. She'd spent her childhood with a monster. And still she'd managed to retain her personality, retain her soul. He was so fucking proud of her.

Right at that instant, her phone beeped. Though she made

no move to answer it, there was no ignoring the fact that their time together had run out. "I better go," he said.

"Yes, of course." She scrambled up to sit on the bed beside him when he rose.

"In one hour," he said, getting to his feet and glancing at the old-fashioned wall clock she had to have found in a second-hand shop, "I have a lieutenant meeting. I want you there."

A startled pause, followed by a quick nod. "I'll be there."

Reaching over, he gripped her nape, kissing her deep and wet and again. "Next time," he promised, "I won't stop with just petting your sweet body."

Spice in the air, the taste of Sienna. "That assumes there'll be a next time."

"You should know better than to dare a wolf, baby." Nipping at that full lower lip he loved, he pointed a finger at her. "One hour."

NINE a.m. and decisions were being made. Judd, Riley, Indigo, and a bandaged-up Riaz, along with Andrew, Sienna, and Hawke, were physically present in the conference room that had been designed to connect the lieutenants to Hawke no matter their location. It took a couple of minutes to patch everyone else in. Tomás was the first to spot Sienna sitting unobtrusively to the side.

"Why, Sienna Lauren, as I live and breathe." A smile that held more than an edge of flirtation. "Aren't you looking pretty these days?"

Sienna, to her credit, retained her cool. "I saw you doing the chicken dance once, Tomás. It wasn't sexy."

That made Kenji hoot with laughter, Alexei flash a megawatt grin. Hawke's wolf was pleased to see that Sienna's face didn't go slack at the sight—most women had a hard time resisting Alexei, even when he wasn't trying to charm. "No time for play," he said, and the entire room snapped to attention. "We have the same two choices we did earlier this year. Strike first or wait for them to come to us."

"Strike first and we might have a slight advantage," Tomás said, dark eyes incisive, "but if we send out teams, we leave our territory vulnerable. Could be exactly what they want."

"Agreed." Judd's practical voice. "Aside from that, while the compound in South America won't be an issue, we don't know how many other operatives the Scotts have under their command."

"And," Riaz added, "we know they're coming. This assault was an attempt to get us to retaliate, squander our resources. They want to soften us up before they attack."

Matthias nodded from one of the comm screens, the rugged beauty of the Cascade Range visible from the window at his back. "Our previous strikes made sense at the time, but things have changed. I say we wait, we prepare."

"We need to check something else, too," Riley said from beside Hawke. "All indications are that they're focusing their aggression on SnowDancer and DarkRiver, but we need to make sure they haven't also got plans in place for the city."

"Any luck tracking down the weapons?" Matthias asked.

Riley gave a grim shake of his head. "No."

"Their past actions," Judd said, "would seem to suggest they won't destroy San Francisco, but given Henry's recent behavior, there's a possibility he and Shoshanna may be willing to sacrifice the city if it wins them the war."

Cooper agreed, his face set in hard lines as he looked out from the comm screen. "Fact is, they get us and the cats out, there's only Nikita and Anthony left to stand in their way. And neither has any significant military strength."

"Still," Drew pointed out, "it might not be a bad idea to scope those two out, see how many offensive Psy abilities they might be able to add to the mix. Even if it's a few powerful telepaths, they can help hold off the mental strikes of the other side. Anthony's people might even be able to predict some of the moves."

"I've already asked," Hawke said. "Seems war throws predictions off course because so many things are done in the heat of the moment. But he says every one of his foreseers, Faith included, are certain the violence is set to hit soon. Might even be a matter of days."

"So"—Indigo leaned forward—"we take a stand?"

Hawke nodded. "The more we spread out, the thinner the wall they have to breach."

"Far better to dig in and make them dig us out," Jem

agreed, her blonde hair dull in the cloud-drenched light in her part of the state.

"That leads us to another question." Riley tapped the twisted piece of metal he'd placed on the table when the meeting began. "According to our records, the single star is Kaleb Krychek's personal emblem. We decided he wasn't involved in this, but what if he's playing everyone for fools?"

They all looked to Judd. Who picked up the fragment of hull and turned it over in his fingers. "Kaleb is difficult to predict, but my gut says this is a deliberate attempt to implicate him, confuse the picture."

Indigo took the piece of debris from her fellow lieutenant. "Any way to confirm?"

"I asked Luc to call Nikita," Hawke said, still put on edge by the idea of any kind of a relationship with a Psy Councilor. But distrust aside, they agreed on one thing—this region was theirs, and they would hold it.

Glancing at Sienna, he gave a nod. "There's something else you all need to hear."

SIENNA had spoken to Councilors without flinching, grown up with an Arrow for an uncle, and had just spent the night with a wolf alpha. Yet her throat was dry, her tongue threatening to tie itself into a thousand knots. Because of Hawke. Because by bringing her into this, he'd tied his pride to hers.

With that thought came the sense of balance she needed. No matter what she'd said this morning, the truth was, she loved him, and in a way that wouldn't allow distance, not even if that distance would save her pain. He wouldn't, *couldn't*, accept her as his mate, but she would give him everything. It was the only way she knew how to be.

"Sienna," he said as she rose so everyone could see her, "tell the others what you told me."

She laid out her theory about the likelihood of an ambush targeting SnowDancer's most vulnerable.

"You sound very confident," Cooper said. It was the first time they'd ever spoken, though she'd seen him in passing when he visited the den. The jagged scar on his left cheek was a distinctive marker against his bronze skin, but it was the near black of his eyes that held her attention. "I respect your intelligence, but you're young and you're no longer in the Net."

She didn't shy, because if there was one thing she understood, it was war. More, she'd lived in the dark long enough not to discount even the most sickening of possibilities. The wolves had a primal core of honor they didn't realize, just didn't expect certain actions. "I know you're working on the assumption that it's Henry and Shoshanna Scott behind this," she said, "and they do appear to be the primary aggressors from what I've picked up. However, the strategy? It's pure Ming LeBon."

Judd shook his head. "Nothing points to Ming being involved. According to both Nikita and Anthony, he spoke against the Scotts on the Council."

Under normal circumstances, Sienna would've bowed to Judd's experience, but her uncle hadn't spent ten years with Ming, hadn't lived and breathed the Councilor's ideas of military tactics, hadn't seen the many faces he was able to wear with ease. "Henry Scott," she said, focusing on the facts, "has done a number of aggressive things over the past year, but he's never approached anything of this magnitude.

"Whatever happened to turn him aggressive, he doesn't have the training or the skill to pull off such a big military op without serious help." While she didn't mention it right then, she was starting to have the disturbing feeling that Ming had been involved in the previous incursions on SnowDancer land as well—in truth, he may well have given Henry a "guiding hand" for longer than anyone knew.

Jem spoke for the first time, frown lines marring her brow. "She's right. I've sort of made a hobby of keeping track of the Council—"

"Some hobby," Riaz muttered, scratching at the bandage hidden under his chocolate brown shirt—until Indigo reached over with a pen and tapped the back of his hand.

"Yeah, real scintillating stuff." Jem rolled her eyes and carried on. "A couple of years back, Henry was linked, in most cases, to things Shoshanna spearheaded. It's obvious that's changed, but I'm with Sienna. No way he's become a military mastermind all of a sudden."

Hawke turned those wolf-pale eyes to Judd. "We need more data from the PsyNet."

"Understood—but I can't go to my contact with this."

Having had a very interesting conversation with Judd a few months ago, where the Arrow had trusted him with the identity of the Ghost, Hawke wasn't surprised. The lieutenant had shared the name because he'd wanted Hawke to be able to understand some of his decisions without further explanation, to be able to filter his responses through the lens of knowledge.

"Not worried about me being compromised?" Hawke had asked, aware of the lengths the Council would go to uncover the rebel's identity.

"No. If they capture you, they'll kill you. Even Psy know not to mess with certain predators."

Now, Hawke said, "Do the best you can."

Glancing at Sienna, he saw her tense her shoulders, rise to interrupt the buzz of conversation. "There is," she said, "a foolproof way to figure out if my theory about their plans is correct."

Hawke glanced at Riley. "We got the manpower to hold the perimeter while we do this?"

"I can ask a few of the cats to cover. Riaz can do the same for me in the den since Lara's ordered him not to rip his stitches out on pain of healer wrath."

"Then," Hawke said, holding Sienna's gaze, "let's do it."

Chapter 38

IT WAS NOT wholly unexpected when Kaleb responded to Nikita's message by teleporting into her office only minutes later. When you were the most powerful Tk in the Net, such things required a negligible use of power. His gaze zeroed in on the twisted piece of metal on her desk before she could say a word. "I see," he said, taking a seat in the chair on the other side of the glass expanse.

The chair was positioned an inch lower than her own, meant to put visitors at a psychological disadvantage. Of course, none of them were Kaleb Krychek.

She watched him examine the metal, conscious that he could lie with such smooth ease she'd never pick it up. He might have been an ally of sorts, but she never forgot that the man across from her had been in the control of a true psychopath from a young age—there was no way to know what echoes Santano Enrique had left in his psyche.

"So," he said at last, "what do you think?" Cardinal eyes watched her without blinking.

"I think you're too smart to mark your assault craft with your emblem," she said. "I also think you're smart enough to do precisely that to throw us off the trail."

He smiled. It meant nothing, she knew, was a physical action he'd learned to mimic to manipulate the human and changeling masses. "True," he said. "All true." Returning the piece of hull to her desk, he looked out at the city through the plate-glass window at her back. "However, while the squad is mine, I do not yet own them."

"You don't need the Arrows." Notwithstanding his telekinetic abilities, Kaleb had independent command over hundreds of men.

"Still, it makes no rational sense to strike now when I could go in later with a force almost guaranteed to take control with very little destruction." Rising, he did up a button on his jacket, the material a deep navy featuring razor-thin pinstripes, the cut perfect. "The fact is, I don't want this city. That has never been my goal."

That, Nikita thought, was the most honest thing he could've said. Kaleb had far grander ambitions—he wanted to control the Net itself. Not taking her eyes off him as he gave a clipped nod before teleporting away, she reached for the phone. "It's not Kaleb," she told Max Shannon, aware the changelings felt more at ease dealing with her security chief.

But when she hung up, she didn't return to her work. Instead, she reached out with her psychic senses along an old and familiar telepathic pathway. *Your child. She is healthy.*

Yes, Sascha answered, though it hadn't been a question. *She is extraordinary.*

Half Psy, half changeling—that in itself made Sascha's words true, but Nikita knew that wasn't what her daughter meant. *You're not safe in the city.* Not with war lingering on the horizon.

It's home, Mother. A long pause. *Do you plan to leave this region?*

No.

A push along the telepathic pathway, and she realized Sascha was trying to send her something bigger than a direct thought. Aware her daughter's Tp was weak, she reached out with her own, "caught" the sending in a psychic grasp . . . and saw an image of an infant with cat-green eyes and skin of a smooth golden brown a shade paler than her mother's.

Sascha's child. Nikita's grandchild.

Chapter 39

HAWKE SPOTTED THE ambush from a ridge high above the isolated road that lay along one of the routes they would've used to evacuate their vulnerable. His wolf's anger turned cold, primal. There were some things you did not do even in war. "Will they be able to sense non-Psy minds getting closer?" he asked the male lying on his stomach beside him.

Judd gave a single nod. "You might be able to distract them by sending in a decoy—fill up a transport with soldiers."

"They can't tell the difference between immature and mature minds?"

"Not if they're running a general telepathic sweep." He lifted the binoculars to his eyes again. "I can make out the weapons. They're high velocity—" A dangerous pause before Judd passed the binoculars to him. "Twenty degrees to the left of the man in the center."

Hawke scanned twenty degrees, stopped. The cold-blooded bastards had a grenade launcher. "No mercy. They die. All of them." This war was not going to be fought with the lives of their young and their old. "Scotts, Ming, whoever the fuck is behind this needs to know we mean business."

"We eliminate the ambush, we give away the fact that we're not only aware of their strategy, but capable of predicting it."

Hawke's wolf was howling for blood, but both man and wolf had learned to think past the red haze of rage long ago. "It'll also get rid of ten of their men at this location, however many the others have found."

"Indigo's team has another group in their sights," Judd

reported on the heels of his statement, "as does Drew's. Riley's sector looks clean."

It was, Hawke had to admit, damn convenient to have telepaths in the packs. Sienna was paired with Indigo, Walker with Drew, Riley with Faith NightStar of all people. While the DarkRiver F-Psy was a noncombatant, she had the necessary telepathic range. Her mate was acting as her shield.

Because of that telepathic network, it took only minutes to organize the decoys, another hour to get the transports in position. None of the vehicles could be allowed within range of the grenade launchers—their purpose was simply to distract. In the interim, the changeling teams made their way down to just beyond the scope of the enemy's telepathic sweeps.

"Stay out of sight," Hawke told Judd. "They can't know we have a Tk on our side, not until it's unavoidable." Getting the lieutenant's nod, he said, "Everyone ready?"

"Yes."

"Time."

"Fifty seconds till the vehicles come into view, fifty-two till mobilization."

It was a hard, fast battle. That was the only way to win with the Psy, given their ability to obliterate minds with their psychic strikes. There were also no teleport-capable telekinetics in this group, which signed their death warrants.

Afterward, Hawke stood looking down at the bodies and felt nothing but a quiet, hard satisfaction. He wasn't a man who liked to kill, but these people had planned to savage Snow-Dancer's young. For that crime, death was the only penalty.

SIENNA had never seen the wolves move with such cold, sleek violence. The Psy units stood no chance. Part of her was shocked at the bloody reprisal, but it was nothing to the protective rage that had filled her when she'd seen the grenade launcher, understood the true malevolence of their intentions. For an instant, the X-fire had threatened to slip her grasp, but paradoxically, it was her protective drive toward the pups that had helped her get it back under control.

It was over in a matter of minutes, and as day turned to

night, she found herself walking through the den with a man
who had the eyes of a hunting wolf and hair of silver-gold.
Today, he'd not only spoken to her about pack issues, he'd
treated her as an integral element of SnowDancer's defenses.
Part of her was still waiting for the other shoe to drop, but at
that instant, for the first time, she felt like a partner in some
sense, not simply a young girl who wore her heart on her sleeve.

"The cats are holding off on any evacuations, same as us,"
he told her as they walked. "Right now, everyone is safer
within our protections."

"It'll be quiet," she said. "When the children are eventually moved."

Hawke's wolf hated the idea of a silent den. "It won't be
forever."

Sienna began to turn left as they reached a fork in the
corridor.

"No." He gripped her hand. "This way."

She didn't say a word, and neither did anyone else who
saw them along the way. A few days ago, they'd have been
teased, whistled at, and otherwise hassled in the most playful
of ways. Today, the mood was somber, everyone aware what
was coming. The corridors were emptier than usual, many
pack members having gathered in the common areas to talk,
take strength from one another. There was no one at all in
the corridor paved with river stones and painted with images
of wolves at play, in sleep, during a hunt.

Hawke knew why Sienna avoided this particular exit from
the den. She'd damaged the mural once by accident, her X-fire
acting as a laser to fracture a small area of the wall, destroy
the paint. "I was never angry with you for that," he said as
they entered the painted wonderland.

"This place . . . it's important to you." Her hand curled
around his.

Tugging her to a particular section, he said, "Look."

Sienna leaned forward. "It's a sleeping pup— Oh!" He
watched as she traced the second pup hiding behind the broad
green leaves, waiting to pounce. "I never noticed him."

"She hid a lot of things in the mural," he said, the ache
inside him an old grief. "It was meant to be an artwork that
made the pack laugh, linger, want to play."

"Speaking to the heart of the wolf." Dropping her hand from the wall, Sienna raised her head. "It was your mother, wasn't it?"

"Yes." His gifted, laughing mother. "She was a submissive wolf."

Sienna's eyes widened. "I just assumed . . ."

"I think it surprised my father, too." Inside, his wolf howled at the bittersweet memories. "He first saw her here. She'd flown in from a different sector, started the mural only hours earlier." Hawke could almost see her, her white-blonde hair tied back with one of those colorful scarves she'd favored, a streak of paint on her nose or across her cheek. "He came running through from the outside in wolf form with an urgent message for Garrick. And he just stopped."

"He knew straight away?" Wonder in Sienna's voice.

It made Hawke tighten his fingers on her own. "He said it was like being hit by a two-by-four." His father had always shaken his head at the memory, laughter creasing his face, lighting up eyes two shades darker than his son's. "He was covered in mud and he had somewhere to go, but all he could do was stare at her."

"What did your mother do?"

Hawke laughed, recalling the way his mother would always pretend to bare her teeth at his father when she told her side of the story. "She dropped half a tub of green paint on herself when he came racing in and had turned around to give him a piece of her mind when the air just went out of her. She was submissive, should've dropped her gaze, but she couldn't do it, couldn't break that connection.

"Garrick found them an hour later, her splattered with paint, him with dried mud turning his coat stiff. They were just sitting there, looking into each other's eyes. Their mating was complete, and it was one that held firm until the last." Until his father's death and his mother's heartbreak.

Unable to continue speaking of it, he tugged her out of the den and to the pool below the waterfall, its surface a frothy white from the crash of the water. Shadowed by the jut of the cliff above, the sandy area was a haven of privacy.

"This is a make-out spot," Sienna said as she finished clambering down. "Evie told me. I think Tai sneaks her here."

His lips tugged upward. "Why do you think I moved that rock at the top? It's a time-honored signal that the pool is occupied." The stresses of the day falling away under the caress of her responding smile, he took a seat on the ground. "Did you manage to see your family today?" He tugged her close when she settled next to him.

"Yes, I spent time with Marlee and Toby after we returned, but Walker was busy."

"Speaking of Walker," he murmured in her ear, "I saw him glaring at Lara a few minutes ago." Hawke had slipped away before either of them had seen him, certain the Psy male would take care of the healer. They'd had a few injuries today, and she was already worn thin after the events of the previous night.

"Walker doesn't glare," Sienna said, shifting so that she faced him on her knees. "He just *looks* at you until you obey."

Laughing, Hawke moved to bracket her between his thighs and touched his forehead to hers, oddly content. They talked of other matters, of Toby and Marlee, of Cooper and his new mate, until Hawke ended up lying next to her seated form, his arms crossed under his head. "It's good to have four lieutenants mated now," he said, his eyes on the rocky ledge above, but his attention on the compelling, textured scent of the woman by his side. "We'll need that stability in the leadership structure even more after this is over."

"May I ask about her?" A quiet, unexpected question.

The wolf was very much in Hawke's eyes when he glanced at Sienna. "Her name was Theresa, but I called her Rissa."

Rissa. It was strange to finally know the name of the ghost who owned Hawke's soul. "What was she like?"

"Sweet—in nature and in spirit." Hawke's hair slid over his forehead as he pushed himself back up into a sitting position, arms hooked around his knees. "Even as a toddler, she'd give her toys to other kids if they cried. I never saw her throw a tantrum, never saw her without a smile."

Sienna clenched her hands in the sand. It was becoming plain that Hawke's Rissa had been nothing like her. "It's why you're drawn to Sascha," she said, hiding her pain, hiding everything. "She must remind you of Theresa in some way."

"I guess." He frowned, shoved back his hair. "The thing

is, I don't know what Rissa would've grown up to be—she never had the chance to spread her wings."

"Yet you're certain she would've been your mate?" It just slipped out, that plea disguised as a question.

A pause. "That can't be altered, Sienna." Gentle words. Implacable words. "It's a knowing nothing can erase."

She fisted her hand against her abdomen in a vain attempt to hold the pain inside. "I can't argue with that," she said. "But the fact is, you never mated with her." They'd been too young to love that way.

"The wolf chooses only once." Curving his hand over her nape, he pulled her close, until his lips almost brushed her own as he spoke. "I can't change that, baby."

Gut-deep need drove her response. "That's a pretty excuse, don't you think?"

Eyes gone night-glow, dangerous and merciless. "Enough, Sienna." Squeezing her nape, he released her.

She wondered if he thought that was the end of it. "It tore your heart out when you lost her," she said, insistent because she had to be, because this was important enough to forever break her. "It devastated you when you were a child—is it any wonder that you refuse to allow yourself to be that vulnerable again?"

Rising to his feet, he strode to the edge of the pool, glanced back. "You can't talk the truth away, no matter how many words you use."

She got up, too, bracing herself against the dominant force of his personality. "I've seen the effects of the mating bond," she said, looking into that face shaped by adversity and determination, until he was a man few dared challenge. "I can understand why a changeling who'd been mated once would never, ever seek the same with anyone else."

"Then why the hell are we having this conversation?"

"Because *you weren't mated!*" Her voice rose in spite of her vow to keep this discussion tempered, rational. "Have you ever considered that it isn't the wolf stopping you from mating, but the human half?" The part that understood that to open himself up to the chance of a mate would mean opening himself up to the chance of the same soul-shattering pain.

"It's not a choice." He looked like he wanted to shake her.

Sienna wanted to pound at him with her fists, force him to listen, to see. "Bullshit! Drew *made* Indigo see him, Brenna fought for Judd, Mercy and Riley's relationship took years to grow, so don't you dare take the easy way out by saying it's all predestined! Don't be a coward!"

Chapter 40

SOMEONE HAD OUTTHOUGHT him, Ming realized, switching off the comm after a clipped discussion with Henry Scott. There weren't many people on the planet capable of doing that, especially when it involved military strategy.

Sienna Lauren was on the short list.

He'd suspected she was alive ever since he'd seen the report filed by one of Henry's men, flagging a curious psychic energy pulse inside SnowDancer territory. The description of that pulse hadn't sounded odd to Ming—it described the power of an X. While his team had failed to get the Snow-Dancers to admit to offering sanctuary to Psy defectors, today's events further strengthened his suspicions.

If Sienna *had* lasted this long, the girl had either figured out a way to circumvent the inevitable consequences of the X-marker, or she was about to go completely active. Since the former had never before been done, Ming was betting on the latter. Which meant everyone in the world would soon know if Sienna Lauren was alive. And Henry would get what he wanted after all—carnage on a scale that would dwarf anything the Council had ever done.

Chapter 41

GOD, SHE MADE him angry. Two hours after the confrontation by the pool, Hawke remained pissed at Sienna. Maybe he should've felt some softer emotion—perhaps even pity—because she was asking for something he couldn't give, would never be able to give. But the fact of the matter was, she'd made him steaming mad, and that was how he stayed. The only good thing was that driven by angry energy, he'd canvassed almost everyone involved in making sure the pack was ready for any further assaults.

Riley had a few things he wanted to double-check, but he'd already adapted the rotation schedule to take the injured into account—and Matthias was on his way to the den with a unit of skilled fighters, as well as a sniper team trained by Alexei. The group was flying in under the radar by hopping onto a private plane owned by Nikita Duncan. Even if the enemy realized Nikita was assisting the changelings, the plane's true ownership was hidden behind so many sub-corporations that no one would give it more than a cursory glance. Territorially speaking, the other lieutenants would cover Matthias's sector.

Indigo's novices were drilled and well able to provide the necessary support if needed, while Riaz had inventoried their weapons and pronounced that everything was in pristine shape. In the best news of the day, the techs had found enough in the wreckage of the Psy stealthcraft that they'd complete the modifications to the pack's air-detection systems tonight, plugging that security hole.

DarkRiver, too, had locked its defenses. Mercy's and Riley's work together meant that instead of doubling up, the packs would function as a single cohesive unit in any attack. According to Lucas, Nikita and Anthony had provided lists of their people who might prove helpful in any skirmish. The two Councilors would also utilize their own psychic abilities to assist.

"If it looks like the Scotts are going to hit San Francisco," Hawke said on the phone to the leopard alpha, "we position the Psy there." There was no way to evacuate the entire population of the city, which meant they'd have a higher risk of sustaining casualties.

"Are you sure?" Lucas didn't sound convinced. "Henry's going to throw his strongest at SnowDancer."

"We've got weapons and a sizable number of trained people." The leopards had charge of city security, but even they couldn't cover all of the vulnerable. "It might also free up some of my people."

"I'll have Vaughn work Anthony's and Nikita's people into the city's defenses, get back to you."

Everything, Hawke thought as he hung up, was either ready, or would be by tomorrow. Now, it was just a case of keeping an eye on the enemy and being ready to move when they struck.

There was no longer an "if."

"I think," Judd said to him a half hour later, as they stood watching a group of novices and younger soldiers complete the training run at night, "we should blow the South American compound soon."

Hawke tracked Sienna with icy focus—she didn't have a wolf's natural night vision, but she was doing more than fine with the night-vision lenses strapped around her head. "Movement?"

"They're approximately a day, two at most, from completing the runway. Weapons are being shifted into the hangar for loading."

Hawke knew Judd had rigged the hangar, so that wouldn't be a problem. "Jem sent in a report out of Los Angeles an hour ago," he said, frowning as Tai accidentally slammed into Sienna and they both tumbled into the mud below. Lara had healed the young male's fractured arm, the injury minor enough that it hadn't strained resources she needed to focus on the more badly hurt. "Looks like the Scotts might've gotten in more weapons and troops than we thought via the shipping routes."

"Means they won't be hobbled by losing the camp."

"No, but it will have an impact, and more important, there's a strong chance it'll spur them to strike. If we can get them to do that before they're ready, it'll be to our advantage." He tracked Tai and Sienna as they joined forces to get over a stubborn obstacle. "Push the switch when you think it the best time, just give us enough warning that we can hunker down for an assault."

Judd nodded at the training run. "You've factored Sienna into the equation?"

Claws raked along the inside of his skin, drawing blood. "I don't want her giving herself away unless it's necessary."

"But you're not disregarding her?"

"I'm not an idiot."

Judd raised a shoulder in a shrug. "It happens with predatory changeling males—you do tend to be protective."

"Look who's talking."

"Why do you think I fit in so well?"

Hawke called Sienna into his office forty minutes later, after she'd had a chance to clean up. "Here," he said, tapping a spot on the map and restraining the urge to snarl at the memory of the words she'd flung at him by the pool. "If there is an attack, you stand here, and you *do not engage* unless I give the order."

A crisp nod, no defiance. "You want to keep me as a surprise gambit as long as possible. I understand." Her words were calm, practical—as if they'd never had that fight.

His wolf peeled its lips back over predator-sharp teeth. "Pretending to be Silent, baby? Too late for that."

Flame, dangerous and hypnotic, crawled over the black of her eyes. "Would you prefer I act the part of a hysterical female so you can write me off?"

He gripped the edge of his desk. "Careful."

"Why?" A look that might as well have come from a pissed-off female wolf. "I'm not the one who seems unable to separate work and pleasure."

"Feeling bratty tonight, are you?" It satisfied some deep part of him that he'd gotten her riled up so fast—he would never allow or accept distance from his woman.

"Don't." An unexpectedly serious response. "Don't lessen my opinions by calling me a brat. And you know, don't call me baby either."

"If you think you can 'handle' me, Sienna," he said as the animal prowled to the surface of his mind, "you're looking at the wrong wolf."

"Can we get back to work?" Cool words that ruffled his fur the wrong way.

SIENNA didn't know how it happened. One minute, she was fighting off the blade of dissonance as she stared at the large, territorial map on Hawke's desk, with him on the other side, and the next, he had a grip on her waist and was pulling her onto the solid bulk of the desk with a speed and strength that left her breathless. She found herself kneeling on the dark wood, her hands on his shoulders what felt like a millisecond later.

"You can't just—" But his hand was already on the back of her head, and she was being kissed until she couldn't breathe. Gasping in air when he drew back for the barest instant, she tried to prepare herself for the next kiss . . . but of course, there was no way to prepare for Hawke.

He'd touched her with exquisite tenderness when he'd brought her to pleasure this morning, but at this instant, he was pure demanding wolf, nipping at her lower lip, sucking at her upper one, stroking his tongue inside her mouth until she knew she'd carry the taste of him into her very dreams. As for his hands, one fisted in her hair, the other gripping her hip—proprietary didn't even come close.

The temptation to submit was crushing. She'd wanted him for so long, and now that he'd given her the right to touch him, to hold him, she had to fight with her own hunger not to grab at the crumbs he offered. Maybe he was right, maybe they would never mate—but she knew, she *knew*, that this man with his beautiful wild heart was capable of giving far more than he was willing to risk.

Wrenching away her head, she twisted out of his hold using a trick Indigo had taught her and ended up on her feet on the other side of the desk. "Hawke, there's—" *!!* The wordless warning from the primal part of her brain slammed through her a fraction too late—he was already launching himself over the desk and toward her.

Instinct punched to the surface, and she found she'd formed a wall of cold fire between them. He skidded to a halt on the other side, then angled his head in a move that was distinctly not human, touched his finger to the fire. A hissing breath, those wolf-pale eyes meeting hers through the rippling sheet of crimson flame licked with yellow. "You burned me."

"Well," she said, shoving tangled strands of hair off her face as her heart thudded double-time, "you didn't seem to be willing to listen to reason."

Not giving her any warning, he thrust his arm through the cold fire. But she'd already doused it and was out the door . . . to run headlong into a very hard, very wide male chest.

"Hey there, darling. Careful now." Strong, unfamiliar hands on her shoulders.

Feeling Hawke exit the office, she took her chances and twisted around behind the solid bulk of the man she belatedly recognized as Matthias, all dark, dark eyes and rich brown skin shaped over a face that held hints of so many cultures, it was impossible to define him as anything but stunning. The big lieutenant gave her an odd look but shifted to intercept Hawke when he went to move around Matthias.

Saying a silent thank-you, Sienna took to her heels. It was self-preservation. In his current mood, Hawke might get her to agree to anything he wanted . . . even an existence in which she would forever be second best.

WALKER was on his way out of the infirmary after having had a late dinner with Lara, when he saw Kieran about to head in. The handsome young soldier carried a bouquet of colorful blooms.

"Are those for Lara?" He didn't move out of the doorway.

"Yeah. I thought since she's been working so hard, it might

be nice for her to have these in her office." A flashing smile. "Do you think she'll like them?"

Walker didn't have to think about his answer. "She won't be getting a chance to see them."

Kieran might've been human, but he'd grown up in a wolf pack. His gaze went flat with challenge. "How about we let Lara decide."

"No." Walker held the other man's distinctive gray-green eyes until Kieran jerked his head away.

"Fuck." Fingers crushing the slender stems in his grip, he thrust the bouquet onto Walker's chest. "You might be more dominant, but I will skin you if you don't treat her the way she should be treated."

As Kieran stalked away, Walker looked at the crumpled flowers in his grasp and considered why he'd felt compelled to keep the other man from getting anywhere near Lara. Kieran had only been trying to look after her in his own way. Except, Walker realized, he didn't want anyone else looking after the SnowDancer healer. Bringing her dinner when she worked late, making sure she got enough sleep, holding her when she cried, those were Walker's responsibilities.

. . . you don't have any other rights—you didn't want them . . . They belong to the man with whom I'll build a life, have children.

She'd been furious the night she'd thrown those words at him but that made them no less true. So . . . either he backed off right now, or he asked for the rights he'd once rejected. There was no guarantee she'd say yes. In fact, there was a high chance she would refuse, having moved on in her personal life.

His hands clenched around the already bruised stems in his grasp.

HAWKE growled at Matthias as he sensed Sienna disappearing down the corridor. "Get the hell out of my way," he said to the big lieutenant.

Matthias folded those arms, which were the size of small tree trunks, and sighed. "I'm only looking out for your dignity. Chasing women down the corridors is not done."

"I'll chase whomever I want." But the wolf's temper was retreating.

Matthias grinned. "Pretty little thing, your Psy. And fast. What'd she do to get you in a hunting kind of mood?"

"None of your business." Scowling, he jerked his head toward the office. "Since you refuse to leave."

Matthias ambled in. "Nice to be here, even under these circumstances."

"Your team?"

"Primed and ready to go." Matthias raised an eyebrow at the mess on Hawke's desk but didn't comment. "They know den territory, but I've got them doing a run to refamiliarize themselves."

"Good. Make sure they don't overdo it—I have a feeling the shit is going to hit the fan sooner rather than later, and I want them rested."

"I've told them an hour, no more." Smoothing out a wrinkled map after picking it up off the floor, Matthias put it on Hawke's desk with pointed care. "Alexei says his snipers are ready if we can set them in position ahead of time. They're not trained to get themselves through enemy fire yet."

Hawke nodded. "Riaz can handle that." The lieutenant was an excellent sharpshooter.

"Have you made a decision about the den?" Matthias asked, his expression now devoid of any humor.

"It can't fall." Even if SnowDancer survived, seeing the enemy in their home would savage them. "We blow it up if necessary."

"I'm not going to argue. No one will."

"Yeah, but let's make sure it doesn't come to that by kicking their asses."

As it happened, things didn't go quite as expected.

"Some kind of viral infection," Judd said to him the next day. "Eighty percent of the troops in the Pure Psy compound are down. From the medical chatter the techs were able to intercept, it looks like the bug's going to lay them out for three, maybe four days."

"Confirmed?"

"Yes. Henry's not playing us."

"We could hit the compound now," Indigo said when he

pulled his lieutenants—and Drew—together for a meeting. "Force Henry to move."

"Yeah, but we still haven't discovered the weapons cache in the city," Riaz pointed out. "This could be our chance. Henry's people might get sloppy because of the delay."

"If we don't find that cache," Judd said, "and they strike, what they have in there could give them a decisive advantage."

In the end, it was decided that since eliminating the compound now as opposed to later didn't give either pack any tactical advantage, they'd hold off and spend the extra time intensifying the search for the weapons. "If we do locate the cache," Riaz said, "the teams need to know not to let on."

Alexei was the first to catch Riaz's meaning. "If Henry doesn't realize the warehouse has been compromised, he won't hesitate to launch the assault even after he loses the Pure Psy compound."

"Yes," Judd said. "Riaz is right. Henry and his supporters won't mobilize if he feels they're at too much of a disadvantage."

That was not an option they wanted Henry to consider, because fact was, the packs couldn't remain at "red" status forever. It would wear out their people, leave them vulnerable when the assault did come.

"I'll brief our teams and the Rats, too," Indigo said, then glanced at Judd. "I meant to ask—can Tks 'port in with bombs?"

"Components, yes. Functional bombs, no. They're too unstable and tend to go off during the teleport."

"The vulnerable," Jem said to Hawke after Judd finished speaking. "You still planning to wait to evacuate them?"

Hawke nodded. "Less chance of Henry discovering their location and changing the focus of his attack."

"I've been talking with Mercy," Riley said as Jem nodded, "and we both realized that there's a last-ditch alternative if something goes wrong and we can't get the children and elders a good distance away." He pulled up a holographic map that showed the abandoned subway tunnels beneath San Francisco. "We get them down to the city—Rats will make sure the enemy never finds them."

Indigo shuddered. "Wolves inside those narrow tunnels? In the dark?"

"We can tell them it's an adventure." Riley's voice was pragmatic. "The elders will make sure the young ones are okay. And it's not dark. The Rats have a nice setup down there—better than you'd believe."

"My wolf's not a fan, but it's a good plan to have in hand," Hawke said, then looked around at his men and women. "We'll not only survive this, we'll come out of it stronger than we went in, because we have something the enemy can't imagine: heart."

RILEY waited until after Hawke had left the room with Andrew—who'd been told to make certain the alpha was the first to leave—before speaking. "I realize this isn't the best time," he said, "but we need to do something for Hawke." He told them his idea. "It needs to be finished before everything goes to shit. He deserves that much after everything he's done for the pack." They hadn't had time before, but the virus had just given them at least a three-day reprieve.

"He deserves a hell of a lot more," Indigo said to a round of nods, then grinned. "He'll fight better when he's not in such a bad mood anyway."

Matthias shook his head. "I dunno, feral and mean is how I like him." But it was clear he was joking. "Tactically speaking, we're set—so, hell yeah, we can take a few hours to complete this project."

"The pack's morale could use a boost, too," Riaz pointed out. "Once word gets out about this . . ." His smile was broad.

Judd rose to his feet. "It isn't a done deal, you understand." Quiet, solemn words.

"We know." Tipping back his chair, Riaz met the other lieutenant's eyes. "But we have to hope. None of us likes the alternative."

Loneliness, Riley thought, absolute and unending, that was the alternative. No life for any wolf, but particularly not for an alpha who'd given his blood, his sweat, and his soul to the pack since he'd been little more than a child. "Then we begin in an hour. I ordered the materials two weeks ago." Just in case.

Chapter 42

THE GHOST LOOKED down at what he'd uncovered. To say that it was an unexpected development would be a distinct understatement. The next question, of course, was what he planned to do with his discovery.

He could let things lie in peace. No one would ever know. Nothing would change. That might be to his advantage. After all, there was a reason for this secret, things the Council didn't want the world to know—but didn't want to lose either. He could take and use that knowledge for himself.

Hunkering down beside the long, rectangular glass box coated with over a century of grime, he considered what Judd would say when he told him there was no second Eldridge manuscript.

Chapter 43

HAWKE WENT LOOKING for Sienna after the meeting because he could do nothing less. He found her sitting cross-legged in the White Zone with a sniffling pup in her arms. "Shh," she said. "He didn't mean it. You know he didn't."

More sniffles.

She stroked her fingers through the pup's soft brownish fur. "Do you want to stay with me?"

A decisive nod.

Smiling, Sienna bent to kiss the top of that furred head. "Well, you can, but you know, I can't hide as good as your friends. I can't howl either." Her head lifted. "Look who's come to ask you to play."

The pup pricked his ears, raised his head. Another pup shuffled over, gave an inviting "yip," and nuzzled at his friend. As Hawke watched, Sienna murmured something to both of them, and the two pups touched noses before the one in her lap wriggled up and ran off with his playmate.

"You never talk to me as sweetly," he murmured, coming to crouch behind her.

A jerk and he knew she would've gotten up if he hadn't slid his legs to either side of her, locking his arms around her body. "Here."

Sienna looked down at the box on Hawke's palm and felt her frustrated anger crumble like so much dust. The box was open, and it held a small mechanical toy—a merry-go-round in motion, tiny lights flashing along the fluted roof and on the posts. There were five horses, each unique and painted in a vibrant splash of color. "This is one of yours," she said, knowing he wouldn't have had time to go to the toy shop.

"Now it's yours." A kiss on her neck as the toy wound down. "Take it."

Her nipples beaded against the cotton of her bra. "I can't." He was doing it again, razing her defenses to steal her heart.

Teeth nipping at the sensitive lobe of her ear, making her jump. "Don't you like it?"

"You know I do." She touched a careful finger to the detailed face of a black horse with a blue and gold saddle. "But it's yours."

He put it on the grass beside them. "I'll just leave it here then."

Stubborn, stubborn man. She knew he'd go through with it, too. "Why?" she whispered. "Why are you giving this to me? Why are you here when you're angry at me?"

A long, quiet breath, his arms hugging her against the muscled breadth of a chest she'd ached with missing last night. "I don't want to hurt you, baby. Never would I hurt you—but I can't give you what I don't have to give."

A single tear trickled down her cheek at that solemn statement raw with tenderness. Her heart, her damned vulnerable heart, had been his from the day she understood what it was he incited within her. She had no true shields against him. Never had. Never would. "Then give me everything else," she whispered, because while she could fight a ghost, she couldn't fight the truth in his voice. "Give me not only your joy, but also your sorrow, your hurt. Treat me as—" She hesitated, because the word *mate* was a painful wound between them.

"—as my partner, as mine."

"Yes." Maybe she would always be second best, but pride was no defense against the soul-deep need she had to claim him, be claimed by him. And if a part of her heart broke at the acceptance, she was old enough to put it away, where it wouldn't poison the life she could have with this man who was, and always would be, her one and only.

"My father's name was Tristan," Hawke said, the words rusty and cracked with age as he rose and pulled Sienna up with him to a more private part of the forest. She was right. They would never have the mating bond, but they could build their own, strong as steel and as unbreakable. "He was taken while he was on solitary watch in the mountains."

Tristan had been a lone wolf before he mated, but afterward, he'd preferred to remain near his mate, had grumbled about being away. Beyond the primal draw of the mating bond, his parents had *loved* each other and their son. Hawke had grown up petted and secure of his place in the world, but not spoiled, not with a lieutenant for a father. At four years of age, he remembered thinking, *That's who I want to be when I grow up.*

"My mother," he continued, despite the rock of memory crushing his chest, "felt something through the mating bond on the second day, so Garrick sent out a search party. By the time they found him"—found his strong, proud father—"he'd been missing a week, and it appeared he'd had a bad fall. He recovered from the wounds fast enough, but he came back . . . damaged." The only time Tristan had touched his son after his return from the mountains was as he lay bleeding to death on the snow. "He attacked Garrick two weeks later."

Sienna's hand spread out over his heart, as if she would shield him. "They programmed him to assassinate your alpha."

"Yes. He was the final one taken." That knowledge had maddened him as a boy—until he understood that his father had been a dominant, a protector, would've never wanted anyone else to suffer in his place. "There'd been trouble in the pack on and off for over two years. Pack members acting erratic, constant fights that led to deaths, men getting violent against their women." To this day, the idea of it agitated his wolf. "That isn't who we are, who we ever were."

"No." Sienna lifted up her head, such intense empathy on her face that it seemed impossible she'd once been Silent. "It had to do with the experiment, didn't it?"

He tightened his arms around her. "They wanted to see if they could erode the bonds that held a changeling pack together by pressing on 'key factors' until the pack imploded." The bastards had broken juveniles as well as adults, poisoned so many good men and women.

"It was designed by a small fringe group of scientists." In the end, that was what had saved SnowDancer, because the survivors had been able to cut off the head of the evil before the data was passed on to the higher echelons. "They weren't Council, but they felt free to treat us like lab animals because the Council at the time made it clear that that's what they considered us."

Sienna wrapped her arms around him in the fiercest of embraces.

Widening his stance, he tucked her impossibly closer. "My father, he went out saying 'fuck you' to the bastards." A grim smile. "During the fight, when another one of the turned tried to shoot Garrick, he shifted to take the bullet." It had been too late though, the alpha's injuries severe enough that their already weak healer had been unable to save him.

Sienna shook her head against him. "He must've been extraordinarily strong to fight the compulsion enough to do that."

"Yes." His father had clawed back his honor at the very end and, in so doing, taught Hawke to never, ever surrender.

"I am so proud of you." Tristan's final words to his son *as Hawke knelt beside him on the bloodstained snow, his hand gripping his father's in angry desperation.*

Then, as blood continued to pulse out of his chest, Tristan had met his mate's tender kiss, whispered, "Until the next life, my love."

"My mother, Aren, simply couldn't function after he died. She tried so hard, but one day, she went to sleep and didn't wake up." Always for him, the joy he'd felt in his parents' arms would be forever bound with echoes of pain, of loss.

Sienna, this Psy who'd lost her own mother, rose up on tiptoe and wrapped her arms around his neck in silent comfort, her cheeks tear-wet against his own when he bent to meet her halfway. Hawke had never cried for the loss of his parents. Not as a boy. Not as a man. Now, as he buried his face in a fall of silk as dark as midnight rubies, the wolf raised its head in a silent, mournful howl.

WALKER closed the door to the medical storage room behind himself and glanced down the packed rows. According to Lucy, Lara was in here somewhere.

"Walker?" A tumble of corkscrew curls as she leaned out from where she appeared to be sitting on the floor. "Is that coffee I smell?"

Wanting to smile at the greed in her voice, when smiling remained an act that didn't come naturally to him, he went down on one knee beside her. "What are you doing?"

"Inventory," she said with a groan, leaning her head against his chest. "I want to double-check we have all the essential supplies since we have a fraction more room to breathe."

He passed her the coffee, watched her drink. As always, it caused an inexplicable sensation in his chest to know that he was caring for her. "Enough?"

She nodded. "Thanks."

Putting the mug on a shelf above her, he fought the compulsion to thrust his hands into the silken warmth of her curls, pull her close. Lara was changeling, and changelings needed touch, needed sensual contact. The incident with Kieran had made him realize he didn't want any other man looking after Lara in that arena either.

"Walker?" Lara lifted a questioning eyebrow.

"Are you dating anyone right now?"

She went immobile. "No." Her answer hung in the air.

"I want those rights, Lara." If she said no, Walker had the sudden realization that he wouldn't back off like a civilized man.

He saw from the way she sucked in a breath that she understood the reference. "You already have most of those rights as my friend. What would change?"

He was no wolf, but he didn't need to be to understand the challenge from her changeling heart. It was instinct to drop his head, to tug at her hair and arch her neck, to take her lips with his own. He'd never kissed a woman before Lara—such things were simply not done in the PsyNet. He found, however, that he understood the mechanics of it quite well even after a single prior experience.

Lara's lips were soft under his, and they parted on a gasp when he ran his tongue along the seam. She tasted of a sweet femininity that was already tied to his thoughts of her, but there was a hint of something darker beneath, a deep vein of sensuality. It made him hunger. If, he thought, he planned to be selfish and keep her all to himself in spite of the fact that he wasn't in any way good enough for her, he might as well indulge.

Tugging her more firmly against him, he stroked his tongue to hers, felt her hands clench against his chest, her body strain against his own. He repeated the act, wanting to incite further caresses from her. This time, Lara moaned, a low, pleasure-drenched sound that made his erection tighten to a near-painful level.

When she pushed at him, he frowned but released her. Seeing she needed to gasp in a breath, he allowed her a moment, then took her mouth again. No wonder changelings and humans were so greedy with this act. It created the most decadent sensations, especially with Lara's fine-boned jaw under his fingertips, the little sounds she made in her throat humming over his skin.

She pushed again, and he would've stopped only long enough to allow her to draw in air again except that she put her fingers over his mouth. "Walker, stop."

He went motionless. "No?"

"No, I mean, yes. Wait." Shoving her hands through her hair, Lara took several rough breaths in an effort to get her mind back into gear. "I need to know exactly what you're asking for, what you're offering," she said. "No blurred lines."

"A permanent, exclusive relationship," he said without an instant's pause, his eyes locked on her. "Me and you."

"You have to be sure." She was so vulnerable to him that he could destroy her. "This isn't something we can come back from."

"I'm certain." An implacable look. "Do you need time to come to a decision?"

It would've been smarter to say yes, to allow them both to cool off. But she was a predatory changeling wolf with a man she'd craved for so long, a man who was offering himself to her in a way dominant men rarely did. She tugged him down with her hands in his shirt.

His mouth took control within seconds.

There was no knowing how long he might have kept on tasting her if there hadn't been a knock at the door, a yelled-out request for assistance. Her lips were wet when they parted, her breath coming in jerky gasps, his eyes translucent green in the low light inside the storeroom.

"What kind of flowers do you like?"

"Amaryllis," Lara had said in response to that out-of-the-blue question, and now, only hours later, what did she have on her desk but a vase of glorious blooms red as velvet cake and as luxuriant.

Swinging past the office, Lucy backtracked, whistled. "The quiet ones always have the best surprises up their sleeves."

Quiet. Yes, Walker was quiet. He was also a very fast learner. Her fingers lifted to her lips, dropped guiltily when she saw the clock and figured out she'd been mooning over the flowers for ten minutes. But she couldn't resist one last touch.

Walker had kissed her.

Walker had sent her flowers.

Walker was courting her.

"Lara."

She jumped as his voice came to life behind her, and knocked a crystal paperweight to the floor. The green and blue spiral, which Ava had brought back from New Zealand, smashed into at least five different pieces. "Damn."

"I startled you. I apologize." Hunkering down, he began to pick up the fragments.

Her hand went to his shoulder without her conscious volition, spreading on the flex of muscle. "I should've scented you but"—his head lifting, the look in his eyes stealing her breath—"the flowers are so beautiful. I was distracted."

All the pieces in his hand, he rose. "I can fix this for you."

"Don't worry about it," she said, her wolf quivering with impatience to know why he'd come. "Once broken, some things can't be fixed. I'd rather you spend that time with me."

It was only later, after he'd left her with a slow, deliberate kiss that curled her toes that Lara wondered if she'd prophesied her own heartbreak. Because Walker Lauren might've kissed her, might've given her flowers, might even be courting her, but there remained a deep reserve to him. The distance was a solemn reminder that strong, steady Walker's capacity to trust had been broken into far more pieces than her crystal paperweight.

HAWKE asked Sienna to move into his quarters that night, but she needed a little more time to accustom herself to . . . everything. To what she'd gained, what she'd never have, what the future held. So she asked him to sleep in her bed.

Emotions chaotic, her muscles tensed as he curled himself around her. But he kissed her pulse, said, "Sleep. I just want to hold you."

It took her an hour to obey, but when she did, she fell into a deep, dreamless slumber. She woke to find him gone, but he'd left a note commanding her to meet him for dinner at seven. Honestly, she thought with a smile, he couldn't help with the orders.

It was that smile she carried into the day, rather than a heart heavy with the echo of loss. The decision had been made and accepted. To rail against it would only poison the beauty of what existed between her and her wolf. After showering, she dressed and grabbed some breakfast before going to stand her shift on the watch rotation. The pack was on high alert, and Sienna never once dropped her guard, but except for the short period when Evie came down to join her for lunch, the day passed about as fast as the average tortoise.

Returning to the den at last, she helped Toby and Marlee with their homework, then went to her room to clean up and ready herself for dinner. Wrapped in a robe, she was staring into her closet when there was a knock on her door. "Indigo," she said, letting the lieutenant inside. "Did you need me for something?"

"Evie said you had a date with Hawke." At Sienna's nod, Indigo passed her a flat box she'd carried into the room. "A woman needs to pull out the big guns when dealing with a man like him."

Sienna opened the box after the other woman had left with a grin and a hug, to find a simple black dress with spaghetti straps and a hemline that would come to a couple of inches above her knees. Then she put it on. Lusciously soft and silky, the material skimmed over her body with such faithfulness, it appeared as if she'd been poured into it. Not only did it shape her behind, the bodice cupped and plumped up her breasts in the most sensual of offerings. All of it done with flawless elegance.

"I love you, Indigo," Sienna said, feeling sexy and bold and confident. Pairing the dress with delicate, heeled evening sandals, she dried and left her hair unbound. Hawke liked running his hands through it, and since he let her play with the thick silver-gold that fascinated her so, it was only fair.

The knock came just as she finished running the gloss over her mouth. "You're ten minutes early."

The wolf on the other side of the threshold stroked his eyes oh-so-slowly down her body. "You look bitable."

Her hand clenched on the door, because she knew full well he meant it when he said things like that. "You're dressed up." She'd never seen him in anything but jeans.

Tonight, he wore a black-on-black suit that threw the vivid coloring of his eyes and hair into shocking relief, the shirt open at the collar. But though he looked like he could've walked out of a spread in some fancy men's magazine, there was no hiding the predatory glint in that gaze.

Leaning forward without warning, he fisted his hands in her hair to take her mouth in a kiss that made it clear he considered her his. *All* his. Every inch of her. Her nipples went tight, her thighs clenching in a futile attempt to ease the ache in between. From the satisfied smile on his lips when he drew back, she knew he was cognizant of her arousal. It might've made her feel at a disadvantage, except that he made no move to shield his own response.

"Let's go," he said, taking a last little nip, "or we'll never get to dinner."

"Wait," she said as he tugged her out and pulled the door shut, "I don't have my purse."

"Won't need it." He began to lead her down the corridor, fingers intertwined with her own.

"Should we be going out when things are at such a critical point?" The military strategist in her was disturbed enough to fight her desire to have him all to herself. "If the Scotts manage to harm you—"

A finger pressed to her lips. "We're not going far."

Given his words, she wasn't surprised when he led her to his quarters, but she lost every bit of air in her body when she saw the table set with an immaculate white tablecloth, gleaming silverware, and long-stemmed candles, which Hawke lit before pulling out a chair. "Come here."

It was impossible to do anything but obey, particularly when he rewarded her with a kiss that had her breasts rising and falling in shuddering invitation. Pressing another hot, wet caress to the curve of her shoulder, he moved to take a seat, not on the other side of the table, but to her right. She knew why when he uncovered the first dish—a crisp green salad with curling red and orange tendrils of the bell peppers she loved so much—and lifted a fork.

Chapter 44

HAWKE LOVED HAVING her here, in his territory, all glowing skin and dark hair glimmering with hidden notes of fire. The wolf rolled in her scent, playful as a pup—but Hawke was vividly conscious of the spice-scented arousal that had grown ever hotter as the minutes passed. She hadn't rebelled against his feeding her, had in fact, insisted on returning the favor. But the dessert bowl had only one spoon, and he had it.

On second thought . . .

Throwing the spoon over his shoulder, he dipped his finger in the rich butterscotch ice cream, brought it to her lips. Her mouth formed a soft, hot vice around his finger as she sucked—then she brought her tongue into play.

Every part of him wanted to lunge at her, but he resisted the primitive urge. This night, it was about her. She'd given herself to him, and he wanted her to know that he understood the value of her gift, that he would never allow her to feel anything but cherished.

Removing his finger through lips that teased him with their luscious grip, he swirled it back in the ice cream and painted the curve of her mouth with the sweet treat before dipping his head and kissing it off. Her lips were cool from the icy treat, but they warmed up fast, her taste a lick of butterscotch and spice.

"I think," she said, hands clenching on the lapels of his shirt, the top curves of her breasts flushed and plump, "I've had enough dessert."

"Then"—he nipped at her lips because he loved the way her arousal spiked each time he did it, flicked his tongue over

the small hurt—"I guess it's time for mine." He felt the tremor
that shook her frame as he drew her out of her seat, knew it
wasn't fear. Sliding his hands down her ribs, he rested them
on the temptation of her hips. Anticipation turned her eyes
to midnight as he backed her out, kiss by slow kiss, from the
living area and into his bedroom.

Onto his bed.

"Mine," he said, moving around to the end of the bed
after placing her on the sheets, so he could circle his hands
around her ankles, tug her forward a couple of inches. "All
mine."

"Hawke."

"I like the way you say my name in bed." Lifting one
slender foot, he pressed a kiss to her ankle, then undid the
strap that held up her pretty sandal and dropped it to the floor.
Her foot curled under his touch, a delicate kittenish arch.
"Maybe I'm the one who's going to end up with a foot fetish,"
he murmured, lighting a kiss on her other ankle as he undid
the second sandal.

A laugh that sounded startled came out of her.

Pleased with himself, he took a playful bite of her little
toe as he flicked aside her shoe and raised his head. "Look at
you, aroused and sexy and in my bed."

No blush, no hesitation. Those passion-dark eyes followed
him as he shrugged off his jacket and threw it on the back of
a chair, before beginning to unbutton his shirt. His wolf
preened for her.

SIENNA clutched at the sheets, her body making small restless
shifts as Hawke's black shirt parted to expose a strip of masculine chest she wanted to rub up against in the most scandal-
ous of ways. When he tugged the shirt out of his pants and
finished unbuttoning it, her throat dried up.

There was something deliciously decadent about a man—
about him—in a partial state of undress. As if she'd caught
a glimpse of the forbidden.

Kicking off his shoes and socks without taking his eyes
off her, he prowled over to the side of the bed. "I like this
dress," he said, and it was a vocal caress. "Let's not tear it."

Putting one knee on the bed, he leaned down to kiss her, pure heated demand. "Turn over," he murmured after he'd melted her bones.

It probably wasn't the best of ideas to give him everything he wanted, but she had no willpower where he was concerned. Could any woman resist him when he was like this? Sienna didn't think so—of course, if any other woman did ever dare touch him, she'd fry the bitch in under a second.

"What just went through your head, hmm?"

She told him the truth, saw the wolf laugh, bare its teeth. "That's my girl." His hands flipped her onto her front. "You understand it's a two-way street?" Fingers pushing aside her hair to bare her nape. "Next time that baby cat puts his hands on you, he's dead."

"Kit is my friend."

"You can't have a baby cat alpha as a friend." A bite on her nape.

Oh, God. It was near impossible to think, but she found the will to reach back and pull on his hair. "Leave my friends alone or I'll be forced to get mean."

Licks over the bite, laughter against her ear. "I *like* you," he said, and she had the deep, deep awareness that it was the wolf part of him that had spoken with such delight.

The tug came an instant later, the zipper being lowered. Then . . . a breath of hot air against her spine, open-mouthed kisses along the skin bared by the parting metallic teeth.

Shivering, she arched for him, felt his fingers slip inside her dress to the curve of her waist. The roughness of his skin was a shock that made her moan. More kisses on her back before he removed his touch to tug down the straps. Instead of turning onto her back, she rose up a fraction and pulled the straps down off her arms, pushing the dress to her waist.

A big, warm hand on her ribs, curving up to cup her breast without warning. Crying out, she fell forward. It trapped his hand between her body and the bed—not that he seemed to mind. Squeezing and petting her with possessive heat, he dropped a rain of kisses over her shoulders.

"No," she protested when he removed his hand.

"I want this dress off." A couple of hard tugs and it was gone, leaving her dressed in nothing but the lace panties she'd bought months ago but never before worn. They'd felt too hedonistic, too sensual. That was before she'd started playing with an alpha wolf.

Pushing long strands of hair off her face, she turned her head to see said wolf straddling her thighs. He was still clothed, that unbuttoned shirt pure provocation, but his eyes had gone night-glow, his face taut with wild hunger. It was instinct to curve her body up toward him, to seek to entice.

His gaze flicked up to meet hers, and then he *moved*, gripping her jaw so he could take her mouth in a full-bodied kiss that was all tongue and heat and teeth as he slid his free hand under her body to close over the sensitive flesh of one breast, the hard push of his erection insistent against skin naked under fine black lace. It was at that moment, with his beautiful, hungry mouth on hers, his big, gorgeous body pressing down against her own, and his fingers plucking at her nipple that she realized she was in way over her head.

HAWKE knew it the instant Sienna lost her confidence, the instant she started to retreat. Rubbing his thumb over her nipple, he fought his possessive urges and gentled the voracious kiss. She was his. There would be only pleasure for her tonight.

It was difficult to break away from her mouth, to resist the temptation to squeeze and mold her neglected breast. Instead, nudging her onto her back, he nuzzled at her neck before rising to shrug off his shirt. "Touch me?"

Her hands went to his chest at once, petting him the way she knew he liked. It made him want to spread her thighs, settle in between, until he could rub his cock against the damp softness of her. She'd be so lush, so perfect. Instead, he allowed himself only a single lick to the tip of one tightly furled nipple—to her quivering moan—before beginning to kiss his way down her body.

Her fingers clenched in his hair.

Realizing she was attempting to keep him at her breasts, he smiled, retraced his steps. "This what you want, baby?"

She arched up off the bed when he took her nipple into his mouth, rolling the taut nub over his tongue. Sensitive, very sensitive, he thought, closing one hand over her hip, the touch of lace under his palm a sensual pleasure . . . but nowhere near as erotic as her naked skin. Releasing that nipple without biting—he'd save that for next time—he swirled his tongue around the other, wanting to drown her in pleasure, until she'd never feel the lack of the one thing he couldn't give her.

"Did you enjoy my mouth on your breasts?" he asked after resuming his downward journey.

"You know I did." Husky words, her hands shaping and caressing his shoulders.

Wanting those hands on every inch of his body, he pressed a kiss to her navel. "I like to hear." Her arousal was intoxicating this close to the liquid heat between her thighs, and he had to fist one hand in the sheets to rein himself back before he scared her. "Tell me if this pleases you." Skipping over the damp curls under the small triangle of black lace that teased rather than concealed, he kissed and nipped at her inner thighs.

A shuddering breath. "Yes."

Spreading her legs, he used a single claw to cut the sides of her panties. A tug later and they were gone. Every one of her muscles locked at the same moment, and when he looked up, her eyes were closed tight. His mouth watered to taste the drugging scent so rich and luscious against his tongue, but he wanted her with him.

Rising, he pressed a kiss to her stomach, to her chest, to her throat, to her lips. She opened to him without hesitation, dangerous and wild and Sienna. Only when her hips were undulating up toward him did he run his hand back down to the heat between her legs, caressing her desire-swollen folds with a single finger, his touch delicate. "You like this."

"Yes." A sigh, a roll of her hips as she searched for more.

He cupped her, stroking around the tight, wet entrance that had his cock jerking in the confines of his pants. She cried out into his mouth and gripped his biceps, but he drew away to kiss his way down her body once more. This time her eyes stayed open, and on him.

SIENNA had just barely enough presence of mind to check the cold fire. It was nowhere near critical after the most recent purge, and her reinforced shields were holding. That meant she could enjoy this night, enjoy being with Hawke.

Right now, she wasn't sure she'd survive what he intended to do, but oh, how she wanted it. Her body felt like a toy that had been wound up too tight, every part of her straining to reach for something she couldn't quite touch. "Hawke, please."

Wolf-blue eyes held her own. "Trust me."

"Always." There was no question of trust, never had been.

A wicked, wicked smile. "I told you it was my turn for dessert."

With that sinful statement, he pulled her legs over his shoulders and gave her a kiss so intimate, her mind roiled with blackness before sparking in a fever of crimson. She'd never known, never understood. When she'd read about it in the women's magazines, it had seemed like an act that would embarrass her. Right now, she wasn't embarrassed. She was eager and needy and so pleasured it hurt.

If the first level of dissonance had been in effect, she would've passed out from the pain, but though the sensations were beyond anything she'd ever known, there was no agonizing backlash.

Her wolf had no inhibitions, refused to permit her any either. "A little more," he said, spreading her thighs even farther to allow him better access to flesh swollen and flushed with passion. It made her hands clench on the sheets to imagine how he saw her. Slick and pink and open. Then he began to taste her in slow, wet strokes, one finger entering her in a prelude to the ultimate penetration, and her thoughts fractured into a long, shuddering submission.

She came to, to find a very satisfied wolf at her side. He was drawing patterns on the sweat-sheened skin of her navel with his finger. "How was dessert?" she asked, her throat a husky reminder that she'd screamed at the end.

A flash of teeth. "I plan to go back for seconds in a bit."

She sucked in a breath. "Bad wolf."

Sliding down his hand, he tugged at her damp curls. "Hungry wolf."

Right then, Sienna knew she was sunk. Absolutely and gloriously. "I want you."

Wolf-pale eyes gleamed at her from below a thick fan of lashes. "How much?" A tease and a dare in one.

Turning to push him onto his back, she kissed her way down his throat to bite at his pulse. His hand clenched in her hair, his muscles taut. He didn't stop her when she smoothed one hand down that beautiful chest and lower, to the top button of his pants. She had no idea when he'd gotten rid of the belt but she was grateful—her fine-motor functions were somewhat impaired after the way he'd eaten up his dessert.

Now, she lifted her head, bracing herself with one hand on his shoulder as she looked down to watch her other try to undo the button. He hissed as her fingertips brushed the thrust of his erection, every one of his muscles going so rigid, she'd have thought him in pain except that she'd felt the kiss of raw sexual pleasure, understood.

Frustrated because her fingers kept sliding off the stubborn button, she ignored it and slid her hand under his waistband. To touch hot, hard flesh sheathed in delicate velvet. Her breath rushed out of her, but her hand was being pulled away before she was anywhere close to satisfied, and suddenly, she was flat on her back with a wolf at her mouth, at her throat, at her breasts. He sucked her nipples into his mouth, hard and wet, possessive hands plumping up her breasts for his enjoyment.

She was used to the teeth by now . . . but not the way they made her feel.

Jerking, she went to wrap her leg around his waist, was halted by his hand on her thigh. "Pants," he muttered and rose off the bed in a lightning-fast move. A split second later, he was back, pulling her leg over his naked hip.

Sienna tried to push at him. She wanted to see, wanted to pet and caress that hard male body. But then he ran his tongue along the lower curve of her breast, and she lost her train of thought, her hands clenching on the muscled silk of his shoulders. "Kiss me." It was a needy whisper, and it was hardly out before he was there, one hand cupping her face while he braced himself above her with the other, his mouth teasing and playing with hers until she lost her breath, had to break the delicious contact.

"More?" the wolf asked.

She tried to suck in a breath. "You're naked."

A slow, slow smile. "So are you." He slid his hand down her thigh, shifting to stroke through the softest, most sensitive part of her. "So slick," he said, those eyes hot and hungry as he rubbed at the entrance to her body.

Her mind fogged over, her hips rising to meet his touch. When he pressed, she gripped his biceps and pulled him down, intent on tasting his mouth, his neck, any part of him she could reach as he breached her with a finger, adding a second with a slowness that made her shudder. He scissored them just as slow, stretching her tissues and rocking jolts of pleasure through her. Readying her, she thought through the haze, he was readying her body for his possession.

She could feel him against the inside of her thigh, knew the proud thickness of his erection would be nothing easy to accept. Lights flashed behind her eyelids as he used the head of his cock to tease her clitoris. Easy was not something that mattered. She just wanted him. Now. "Inside me." *Hurry.*

Hawke heard her, but he continued to pump his fingers into her, continued to kiss her—sucking at her lower lip, dipping his head to mark her breasts, her neck. "Not yet." He wanted her all but liquid with pleasure before he took her, because it was going to hurt. No way around that, even if the thought of hurting her in any way pissed him off. She was tight and hot, and he was a big man.

"Let me pet you some more." Sweat shimmered on her throat, and he licked it off, savoring the salt and spice of her. "I love your breasts." They were flushed pink from the brush of his jaw, the touch of his teeth. In a chair, he thought, biting at her lower lip when she ordered him to "Finish it!" He was going to take her in a chair the next time so she'd be astride him and he could play with those pretty breasts as he pleased.

Feeling her muscles clench around his fingers, he kissed his way back down her body again and spread her thighs, inhaling the erotic musk of her. His mouth watered, and since she was his and she was delicious, he decided it was time for seconds. It only took one long lick for her to shatter, but he kept going, using his mouth to pleasure her with flicks and nips and hot little sucks focused on the slippery nubbin of flesh at the apex of her thighs until her body went limp, aftershocks rippling over her skin.

When he prowled up this time, she watched him from beneath heavy-lidded eyes, her chest rising and falling in a rhythm that was pure temptation. "Are you," she gasped as he slotted himself against her, began to push, "like this"—a throaty feminine sound, her tissues liquid fire around him—"all the time?"

He wasn't thinking much anymore, consumed by pleasure, but he knew one thing. "For you—yes." Gripping her hip, he slid in another couple of inches, felt her nails dig into his shoulders.

But instead of pushing him away, she pulled him toward her. The leash snapped, and he buried himself to the hilt in a single thrust. Her pained gasp was muffled against his shoulder as her legs quivered around him. Yet she continued to hold him tight. Finding some semblance of civilized thought, he petted her thigh, nuzzled, and kissed until she began to move her hips—or attempt to in any case. He pinned her to the bed, and he had every intention of using that leverage for her pleasure.

One hand on her hip, he slid back out torturously slowly . . . then slid in the same way. Sienna's eyes flared open, held his. "Do that again." An intimate demand.

Teeth bared in a feral smile, he did. Then again. And again. Until she fractured around him, those tiny muscles squeezing so tight around his cock he almost came. He wanted to pound into her, to flip her onto her hands and knees, and to mount her in the most primitive of ways, but that could wait. Tonight, this, it was for her. So though his jaw hurt from how hard he'd clenched it, he continued to stroke into her slow and easy and again. And had the pleasure of feeling her body rise to meet his over and over.

This time, he allowed the erotic pulse of her orgasm to sweep him under, wring him dry. "Next time," he murmured in her ear as he collapsed, his heart a fucking drum against his ribs, "I'm not going to behave."

Chapter 45

TEN HOURS LATER, those rasped-out words had Sienna wondering just how very bad he could be, because if he'd been good last night . . . *Dear God*. Her body still bore the marks of his passion. The insides of her thighs were stubble-burned, and there was more than one bite mark on her breasts. Remembering how he'd taken her with such primal thoroughness made her skin flush, things clench low in her body. She wanted his teeth—

Thwack!

"Ouch!" She slammed up the long wooden staff too late to block Indigo's strike. "That hurt."

The lieutenant rolled her eyes. "Here I was trying for a love tap. Stop mooning about his wolfiness and start giving me some real competition."

Swiveling the stick, Sienna went for Indigo's legs. The lieutenant avoided the sweep, but the move put her slightly off balance. Then they were off. Indigo was too experienced for Sienna to take down, but she got in a few good licks, and by the time the practice session ended, her blood was pumping, her black athletic tank stuck to her skin.

"Thanks. I needed that," Indigo said, gulping down water. "What are you scheduled for now?"

"I have a free afternoon." Sienna opened her own bottle, took a long draught. "Thought I'd spend time with Toby and Marlee, do some work on a course paper at the same time."

Indigo's eyes gleamed as she put down the water and reached back to redo her long black hair into a tight ponytail. "You know anything of what's happening between Walker and Lara?"

Sienna began to buff her fighting staff with a towel. "What are you talking about?"

Indigo laughed at her fake innocent act. "They're not getting away with it, you know. Everyone's just being real polite and pretending not to notice they're kissing each other in dark corners."

Sienna's lips twitched. "My uncle would never be so common as to kiss a woman in a dark corner."

"No, must be someone tall, blond, and silent who looks exactly like him."

Sienna was still laughing at that dry statement when she went to join the children after a quick shower to wash off the sweat. However, she hadn't been at the family apartment long before she got a call from Riley.

"Sienna, I know you're meant to have the afternoon off, but can you accompany Mariska and three of her techs up to check on the hydro station?" he said, referring to the "green" system that used the natural power of the water crashing over the mountains to supply the den's power. "The plant is secure, and I've got Drew heading up with the team, but he should have backup, just in case."

"Of course, but I'm with Marlee and Toby. Can you—"

"It's not even a question, sweetheart. Bring them over— they can hang out in the senior soldiers' break room off my office."

Knowing the kids loved spending time in the hub, which saw a constant rotation of the pack's dominants—with more than one willing to pull up a chair to chat to a couple of "pups"—she said, "We'll be there in fifteen." It actually took closer to twenty to get everything sorted, but she left her brother and cousin competing with each other to tell Riley their latest news.

Drew was waiting for the team at the exit—or more accurately, he was kissing Indigo and smiling all the while. They'd been laughing before they kissed, Sienna thought, remembering Hawke teasing her as they lay in bed. She'd felt it when he smiled as he kissed her. It had been more wonderful than she could've imagined. "Ahem," she said, lips curving at the memory. "At least find a dark corner."

Indigo shot her a laughing look. "Touché." Another kiss

before she headed down the corridor, a woman with long, long legs and a body that moved with lithe muscular grace. "Don't get shot," were her parting words to her mate.

"Too scared of you to dare!" Drew called out, then grabbed some of the techs' gear. "Let's go, boys and girls."

HAVING spent the day with Matthias's and Alexei's teams to make sure they were comfortable with the terrain and aware what their duties would be in a combat situation, Hawke was more than ready to take some time for himself. Thanks to his people, he could.

Waylaying Sienna as she headed to her quarters after returning from the hydro station, he tugged her down to the garage. It was tempting to lick up the taste of her, but if he put his mouth on those lush lips, they wouldn't make it any farther than his bedroom.

"Where are you taking me?" she asked once they were on the road, the light diffuse as the first whisper of night touched the Sierra. "Am I being Psynapped?"

His wolf laughed. "We're going to play."

It should've sounded silly, Sienna thought, when there were so many other things to worry about, but there was no denying that the constant state of battle-readiness was an unrelenting tension at the back of her mind. Last night had been a sensual respite, one that had left her more alert and aware today. "Play isn't a waste of time, is it?" she said out loud, having never quite understood that until this moment.

"The wolf has decided that that question doesn't deserve an answer."

It made her laugh. "What's the game?"

"Wait and see."

Half an hour later, he brought the vehicle to a stop deep in den territory, the area so dense with trees that he'd had to punch up the hover drive and get creative in his driving. As he set it down, she peered out at the small cabin hidden amongst the firs. "It looks new." So new the area was still littered with wood chips.

"The lieutenants in the den banded together with the senior soldiers and started to throw it up." He shook his head.

"Apparently the other soldiers got wind of it and wanted in. It took them twelve straight hours with a revolving crew and by the end . . . seems almost every able-bodied adult in the den had something to do with either building the cabin or making sure it was furnished."

She heard the stunned joy in his voice, felt her heart clench. "They love you." *Just like me.*

"Yeah." Shaking his head, he got out and jogged around to open her door. "I'd have torn into them for spending time on this when we're so close to war, but Drew tells me the project boosted morale back to normal levels, so . . ." He pulled her from her seat. "This is ours," he said, leaning down to rub his nose against hers. "The area's off-limits to the pack when either of us is in the vicinity."

Sienna stood on tiptoe, her hands on his shoulders. "Just us?"

The bright slash of his smile echoed her own. "Just us."

It was an incredible gift. She loved SnowDancer with every beat of her heart, would die to protect the people who'd become her own, but being able to be truly alone with Hawke for even a few hours, a few minutes—she had no words for the force of her joy. "Let's go explore."

Laughing, he followed at her heels as she ran up the two small steps and crossed the porch to push open the door, flick the manual light switch. "Oh, it's wonderful," she said as the cabin was bathed in a soft glow. The entire place was a single large room, except for an alcove at the back fitted with a wooden sliding door.

There was a kitchenette off to the left, with a table and two chairs tucked in neatly under the window. To the right was a fireplace set with an eco-friendly laz-fire, in front of which lay a fluffy white rug Sienna could already feel plush and decadent against her skin. The rest of the available space was dominated by a huge bed with a wrought-iron headboard. Her eyes widened.

"Hawke," she said, "why are there fur-lined handcuffs hanging from the headboard?" Stepping closer, she saw— "They're too big for my wrists." *Oh.*

Hawke made a growling sound low in his throat. "Probably Drew's idea of a joke."

"No," Sienna murmured. "Drew told me to never, ever talk to him about sex. As far as he's concerned, I'll be a virgin until I'm a hundred, same as Brenna."

Unhooking the cuffs, Hawke brought them to his nose. Sniffed. "Son of a bitch." His grin was half-amused, half-feral.

"Who?"

"Figure it out. Who do you think is sitting at home laughing his ass off at the dance you've led me?"

Sienna paused, considered all the people who cared about Hawke *and* who'd dare pull a prank like this. "Lucas," she said. "It was Lucas."

"Damn cat must've snuck in here after the crew left." He fiddled with one cuff, smiled as it made a snick of sound. "What do you know—they tighten up fine for smaller wrists."

She didn't trust that look. *"Hawke."*

"Come here." A command, for all that his voice was soft, his eyes hooded.

She swallowed, took a step back. "Um . . . perhaps . . ."

"Scared, Sienna?" Thick, silver-gold lashes lifted to reveal those impossible eyes, the eyes of a husky or a bird of prey.

"No." It wasn't fear that caused her heart to beat a staccato drumbeat against her ribs, her blood to turn molten.

Hawke smiled . . . and she realized he was stalking her in slow, steady steps. Twisting, she saw she was about to back herself into a corner. She jerked left, expecting him to stop her. When he didn't, suspicion licked through her veins. "I'm glad you're going to be reasonable about this," she said, never moving her eyes off him.

"I like your hair." That wild gaze stroked over her. "Put it down for me."

"I don't think that'd be a good idea." It was instinct to disobey him, to challenge him.

"I disagree."

Her hair tumbled around her shoulders before she so much as sensed him shift position. He was crouched on the bed, on the other side of the room by the time she realized what he'd done. A very satisfied, very male smile flirted with his lips.

Playing with her, she thought, he was playing with her.

And tonight, there was no leash on the wolf.

"You think you're so smart," she said, inching to her left again as he reached back to pull off his T-shirt with masculine roughness. The door was only a few steps away.

T-shirt on the floor, he angled his head in a way that sent his hair sliding over one side of his face. "I think you should take off your top."

"Try it and I'll—" She shot up a column of cold fire between them, making him come to a skidding halt, his nose a bare millimeter from the flame.

He bared his teeth. She grinned . . . and took off, slamming the door shut behind herself as she dropped the wall of flickering red and gold. Something crashed hard on the wood as her feet hit the earth and her instinct was to turn around, check he was okay. But that wasn't the game. And she was nowhere near wolf-fast. He was breathing down her neck in seconds.

But she was an X. A cardinal.

She blocked his way using her abilities until he fell back. Chest heaving, she came to a halt, bracing herself with her hands on her thighs as adrenaline thumped through her. God, but he was fast. Never had she seen anything or anyone move with that kind of speed. *Dangerous man. Her man.*

Having caught her breath, she rose to her full height. But even with her every sense on alert, she didn't have the slightest inkling he'd circled around on her blind side until she turned to find herself staring into eyes gone night-glow. "Pretty, pretty Sienna."

Gripping her wrists before she could summon the cold fire, he tugged her close, shattering her concentration; his chest was a gorgeous, touchable distraction. There wasn't even a hint of sweat on him. It should have been annoying, but she was far too fascinated by the smile flirting with his lips to care. "My Sienna."

The absolute possession in his voice didn't scare her. "Yours."

A short, sharp nip at her neck. She shivered with pleasure, before twisting away from him using a move Indigo had drilled into her until it was second nature. She wondered if the wolf lieutenant had known this day would come. Hawke smiled at her, a delighted predator. Then he lunged.

She scrambled backward, only to feel him brush past her and into the forest.

The game was on again.

Taking off in the opposite direction, her night vision ample in the early evening light, she began to laugh inside. This was *fun*. It was only a couple of minutes later that she felt him pacing her in the trees to her left. Heart pumping hard and fast, she raised a wall of X-fire and disappeared in another direction, muddying her scent by using every trick in the book. It wouldn't work of course. He was an alpha, his senses acute, and—

A bouquet of wildflowers in her path.

Laughter bubbling out of her, she picked them up, put a cherry red bloom behind her ear. Taking the rest in hand, she looked up. And realized he'd herded her back to the cabin.

To the bed.

Butterflies in her stomach. Because she understood his words from last night now, knew that he'd been on his very, very best behavior. Tonight . . . tonight she'd be tangling with the dominant, wild heart of him.

Creeping up to the cabin, she tried to locate him in the dark shadow of the trees.

Silence.

Taking a long, deep breath, she made a run for it. Her feet left the ground midway through the journey, and she barely had time to utter a short scream before he dumped her on the bed, the wildflowers scattering around them as he braced himself above her, all playful smile and wolf eyes. "I win." A sharp nip to her lower lip. "What's my prize?"

Chapter 46

OH DEAR GOD. She was melting into a pile of goo. He was big and beautiful and impossible . . . and hers. He was hers. Not as she'd once imagined he would be, but this bond that continued to grow between them? It was as strong, as precious. "I'll brush your hair for you."

He blinked, thought about it. "All right."

Delighted, she waited for him to get off so she could rise. He stayed in place, his gaze never moving off her lips. She parted them, felt his breathing change. "Hawke?"

"I'll get you the brush."

She hadn't even managed to catch her breath before he was back over her again. "Here."

Taking the brush, she reached up to push one hand through the thick silk of his hair. It was cool, soft, stunning. A wolf's pelt given human form. "Beautiful."

"More." He dipped his head, allowing her to run the bristles through the strands. A low growling sound of pleasure accompanied her first stroke, and he lowered his body a fraction, so she could feel his weight against her legs. "Harder."

Obeying, she ran the brush through his hair over and over. "You're closer to your wolf than any other changeling I've ever met." It told her so much.

"I am as I am." A wolf's answer. It had no time for over-thinking things. "Open your mouth."

She dropped the brush. "Wh—" His mouth took hers.

The kiss was hot and deep and all kinds of sinful, his hand closing gently around her throat to hold her in place as his tongue played with hers and his thigh rubbed against the arousal between her legs. When he let her breathe, it was only for the barest instant before he was taking her again. Her hands clenched on his shoulders, muscle and tendon flexing so powerful and hot under her touch.

"Sienna," he murmured against her lips. "Smart." Another bite to her lower lip, this one softer. "Strong." His body settled heavily on her own, his erection a demanding hardness between her thighs. "Mine."

When she used her nails on his back, he growled and dipped his head to suck on the pulse in her neck, making her body arch. Or attempt to. He was too heavy to shift. Fisting one hand in his hair, she breathed in the scent of him and knew that tonight he'd demand more than surrender, more than submission. He'd demand everything she was, then ask for more.

"Your heart's fluttering like a bird's." A lick over her pulse.

It took concentration to find the words, to put together a coherent sentence. "This is only my second time, you know." Then she used her mouth on the strong cords of his neck.

He liked that, his chest rumbling against her. "I'll make it good for you. You know I will." Arrogant and sexy and tender, he braced himself on one arm, running the fingers of the other down her front, over the buttons of her shirt. "I don't like this."

The shirt tore down the middle.

As she sucked in a startled breath, he pressed an open-mouthed kiss to the bared flesh of her abdomen, his hand stroking under and around the torn shirt to spread over her lower back.

"Hawke."

Sliding his hand around to the front again, he moved it in slow circles over her navel. "Hmm?" Another kiss, this one on her breastbone. "Does something hurt, baby?"

She shook her head. "Kiss me."

A wolf-sharp smile before he gave her exactly what she wanted. A kiss that tore her wide open with its sensual tenderness and reformed her anew. She nipped at his mouth this time, and he paused, gave her a *look* out of eyes slitted until she could only see a strip of wolf-blue. "You bit me."

"I say it's fair play." She tapped her own lower lip. "You've done it more than once."

He growled low in his throat, splaying his hand over her ribs. "Bite me again."

Undone, she did. Then, deciding to play as wild as her lover, she dug her fingernails into his shoulders and gripped the taut tendon of his neck between her teeth. He froze above her, his entire body tense with expectation.

She bit down hard enough to leave a mark before releasing him.

He snarled at her—but she wasn't fooled. She'd seen the wolf laughing in his eyes. "I marked you," she said, smug.

His hand closed around her throat. "Maybe I'm mad at being marked up."

"Are you?"

His answer was to move his hand, place it over her breast, her bra no protection against the primal heat of him. "I know where I'm going to mark you. Again."

Feeling her flesh swell under his touch, she said, "What if I don't like being marked up?"

"Tough." A blur of movement and her bra was in so many shreds around the bed.

Sienna rose toward him in wicked invitation. He made a deep rumbling sound in his throat that peaked her nipples to tight points, and then his lips were on her soft flesh, marking, branding, tasting, and sucking. Thought scattered, sensation crashed. Thrusting her hands into his hair, she held on for the ride of her life.

HAWKE tried to pull himself back, knowing Sienna wasn't equipped to handle everything even after last night. He couldn't do it. He'd waited too long for her—wolf and man wanted her with feral ferocity. "If you need to stop me," he forced himself to say, lifting his head to meet her gaze, "do what you need to do."

Cardinal eyes gone black with desire locked with his own. "Are you planning to hurt me?"

He growled. That was a question that didn't need an answer.

"Then why," she murmured, "would I want to stop you?" Her hands tugging at his hair, pulling him up so she could seduce his mouth with a hot, drugging kiss. "Give me everything." A whisper. A command.

He didn't take orders from anyone . . . but for her, he'd make an exception. Closing his hand over the erotic invitation of her breast once more, he squeezed, catching her responding cry with his mouth. Under his palm, her nipple was hard, pebbled, pure temptation.

Breaking the kiss, he made his way back down her throat, nipping at her pulse because he liked the way that made her body flush with heat, the sensual musk of her deep and earthy. It drugged his wolf, intoxicated the man. Flicking out his tongue to tease the taut bud of her nipple, he smiled as her abdomen quivered under his palm.

He bit her next.

She jumped but didn't seem to mind his teeth there. But it was when he began to suck with hard, long pulls while plucking at her neglected nipple that she moaned, her hands clenching in his hair. Filing away that piece of knowledge for future reference, he scraped his teeth over her nipple.

Her entire body jerked.

Switching hand and mouth, he rubbed his thumb over the nipple he'd left wet and throbbing, then settled down to give the other one the same treatment. A rumbling sound of sexual pleasure rolled up from his chest as her ankles locked at his back, merging with her throaty little cries.

When he lifted his head, her breath was jagged, her skin bearing the marks of his loving. But she was very much with him, his smart, sexy Psy. Raising her fingers, she played them over his lips, laughing when he tried to nip at them. Then she growled at him. Delighted, his wolf leaned down to press kisses along her jaw, down the line of her throat.

Her scent was so decadent, so rich. Autumn and spice and steel. He rolled it around himself, happy because as of last night, that scent was intertwined with his own, not to be erased as long as they remained lovers—which would be forever. No negotiation. No "out" clause. "Do that again," he murmured, grazing his teeth along the outer curve of one of her breasts.

A shiver across her flesh. "I *need*."

Nuzzling his way down to her abdomen, he pressed a kiss

on her navel, his tongue tasting the perspiration-damp heat of her skin. "Let me satisfy you." He forced himself to go slow, to not rip off the rest of her clothing. Instead, he gave her time to fight, to get away if she needed to as he broke her hold on him to slip off her shoes, then moved to undo her jeans and pull them down her legs, along with her panties.

But she stayed in place, her pretty legs sleek against the skin of his jaw as he threw the clothing off the side of the bed and rubbed his face against her.

"Oh." A short, shimmering sound, her hands fisting in the tumbled sheets.

Intrigued, he rubbed his jaw against the soft skin of her inner thighs once more. Her legs clenched around him, her scent a wild perfume. Wanting to lick it up, he rose onto his knees, spreading her thighs in front of him as he did so. His stubble had marked her soft skin, and he wasn't the least bit sorry.

Stroking his hands down her calves, he felt her socks. Chuckled. "I think we'll leave these on."

She rubbed one socked foot on his thigh. "Shouldn't sex be more serious?"

"Baby, which pack have you been living with the past few years?" Leaning down, he kissed the side of her knee before shifting down to lie between her legs.

"Hawke?"

He stroked her legs up over his shoulders. "What do you need?"

THE husky question, asked in a tone that said he'd give her everything, anything, melted Sienna from the inside out. "You're beautiful."

Her wolf looked up, his eyes reflecting silver in the lights that stroked them both in soft gold. "I like hearing you say that. Tell me again after."

"After what?"

"This." Sliding his hands under her buttocks, he lifted her to his mouth and then he—

The scream was torn out of her. It didn't stop him, and oh, she was grateful. As he sucked and bit and tasted, she realized he'd been holding back last night in more ways than one. If that had been the dessert, this was the full-course meal.

When he stroked his tongue through her quivering flesh, she lifted herself up to his mouth for more. "Shameless," he teased, letting her feel the edge of his teeth. "Just the way I like you." She got more. A lot more.

Her brain hazed over. Legs crossing at his back as he ate her up like she was the most exotic delicacy prepared for him alone, Sienna surrendered to the rolling waves of pleasure, the breakers crashing over her in a wash of ecstasy so hot and sweet, it made flames lick up along her skin, a splinter of dissonance spear down her spine.

The pain was negligible—and it shouldn't have been.

That worried her, but only for a second, because Hawke raised his head with a final, lingering lick, and moved one hand up to play with the flickering red and yellow of the cold fire. "It doesn't burn."

It took massive effort to find enough brain cells to put together an explanation. All she got out was, "No."

Rubbing his jaw against her navel, Hawke moved to press kisses along the insides of her thighs. "No more," she found the will to say. "Can't take it."

A chuckle that held total male satisfaction. "What if I want to play?"

"I'll kill you," she threatened.

Laughing in a way that told her the primal heart of him was very much in charge, he shifted up her body even as he slid his hand down to cup her with breathtaking intimacy, using one finger to stroke the excruciatingly sensitive entrance to her body. She arched into the touch, and when he bent to take her mouth, she took his in turn. His body was warm muscle and heavy weight on top of her. And his chest . . .

She rubbed against the fine, soft hairs that covered the ridged plane, her nipples tingling with sensation. When he pushed a finger inside of her, she bit down on his shoulder. He growled, holding her head against him as he stroked that finger in and out in a maddening rhythm.

Insane, she thought, he was going to drive her insane. Releasing her grip on his shoulder, she grabbed his head between her palms. "Now."

The wolf looked out at her. "In a minute." He inserted a second finger, parted them inside, caressing her in the most intimate fashion.

"Hawke." She could feel an orgasm approaching again, knew she wasn't going to be able to fight it.

Of course he didn't back off. He petted her even more outrageously. She fell hard—and came to rest in his arms, her entire body so limp with pleasure that the idea of moving was not even to be considered. But when he kissed her, she found she had just enough energy to return the long, lazy tangling.

A stroke inside her, and her tissues quivered at the realization that his fingers were still lodged within. "Sorry," she murmured, "going to sleep now."

A sexy, sexy laugh. Raining a line of hot, wet kisses down her throat as he withdrew his fingers, he spread her legs. It came to her that he was wearing his jeans, that she had on the remains of her shirt. "Clothes."

"Hmm." A momentary coldness and then he was back, hot and hard and very, very aroused.

She sucked in a breath as he pushed in with the blunt head of his cock, her fingernails digging into the skin of his shoulders. It still wasn't comfortable, but oh, the rough friction felt good. Pushing one hand into his hair, she undulated her pelvis toward him, welcoming his possession. He shuddered, taking a hard grip on her hip. And then he thrust.

She jerked, tried to process the sensations, realized there was no managing this.

His hand clenching and unclenching on her hip, the bare kiss of claws. It made her shiver, meet his gaze. "Yes," she said, seeing the unasked question in his eyes, this wolf who'd given her pleasure upon pleasure.

It was like snapping the leash.

Untamed and infinitely hungry, he moved over her, in her, with a hot power that had her crying out, her body going tight around the velvet steel of him. Clawing at his back, she felt his muscles bunch under her touch, his body a creation of raw beauty and wild strength.

Reaching behind himself, he pulled one of her legs off his

waist, bent it to the knee, and pushed it wide, spreading her for his possession. His next thrust went so deep it reverberated through her very being. The last thing she remembered was feeling the kiss of claws along the side of her knee as he growled and sank into her in a rush of scalding heat.

Chapter 47

HEART PUMPING LIKE a rapid piston, Hawke raised his head after the orgasm that had almost ripped him in two to look down at the woman who continued to hold him inside. Possessive thing. Nuzzling at her as she tried to open heavy-lidded eyes, he stroked his hand down her thigh and said, "Again."

Her response turned the air blue.

Smiling against her skin, he took a lazy bite out of her breast, licking over the mark that was already fading. He'd just had the best orgasm of his life, and he felt like he had more energy than he knew what to do with. As for his body, it was more than ready. Remaining seated in her snug channel, he stroked and petted as he checked to make sure he hadn't inadvertently hurt her with his claws.

There were no cuts, no injuries. The wolf relaxed, content to play now. When she bit him on the arm—*hard*—the instant he flicked a finger over her clit, he lifted his head. "Still sensitive?"

"Yes, so don't even think about it." Hazy, desire-drugged words.

Moving his hand, he smoothed it down her leg instead, teasing his fingers over the soft skin at the back of her knee. "Hmm." It was a pleasure all its own to pull out of her tight sheath, especially when her lips parted in a wordless murmur of reluctance.

Pleased with every single thing about her, he flipped her onto her stomach before she could object and slid right back in to the hilt. Her moan was deep, her hands fisting on the sheets. He knew she'd liked it—he could feel her pleasure in every delicate tremor of her internal muscles. "At my mercy," he said, bracing himself on one arm as he ran his free hand along the curve of her spine.

Her hair, that silky ruby red fire, tangled with his fingers, made him think of the darker curls between her legs. Blood humming with remembered pleasure, he flexed his cock inside of her, felt her roll up toward him. It caused his entire body to throb. So he did it again. She responded.

It was a long, lazy loving this time, filled with hot scents and the quiet murmur of lovers lost in each other.

LARA straightened her hair in the mirror for the thousandth time and checked in with Lucy via the comm.

"Don't worry," the young nurse told her. "I've got everything covered. And I know you're only next door if we have an emergency."

"Sing-Liu—"

"Is fast asleep, her mate curled up around her. Take advantage of this time—you won't have any free time soon if things go the way everyone thinks they will."

Knowing the nurse was right, she nodded and signed off. Then she slid her hands down the front of her simple black wraparound dress, tucking her curls behind her ears, knowing they'd pop right back out, and called her best friend, Ava. "How do I look?"

"Gorgeous, hot, and delicious."

Lara's lips twitched. "Thanks."

Ava's eyes turned solemn. "He came to you, Lara, so the man's earned brownie points in my book, but it doesn't alter who he is."

"I'm not so sure," Lara murmured. "I see beyond the shield now, Ava, and the man I see? He's capable of giving me everything I need and more." She had to hope, to believe that she could get Walker to see that, too.

"In that case," her best friend said with a wide smile, "lock the door and kiss his brains out."

Lara pressed her hands to her stomach at the idea of it. "I better go. He'll be on time."

He was.

She drank in the sight of him as she opened the door. "Hi." Dressed in jeans and a crisp white shirt with the sleeves folded back to the elbows, he looked calm and contained and distant. She wanted to muss him up so badly she had to curl her fingers into her palms to restrain the urge.

Entering when she stepped back, he closed the door behind himself. His eyes lingered on her face, on her curls, before sweeping down the front of her dress, back up. "Why are we watching a movie, Lara?"

"I—it's what people do on a date?"

"Do you want to do that?"

Unable to read anything on that calm face, in those steady eyes, she said, "We're alone. We can do whatever we want."

"In that case, I'd like to kiss you." Reaching out, he curved his hand around the side of her neck.

"Oh, well . . ." Her lips parted of their own accord, and when he dipped his head, she could do nothing but stand on tiptoe, her hands tight on his shoulders.

He raised his head far too soon. "The sofa will work better," he murmured and lifting her into his arms, carried her to the seat.

She found herself sitting on his lap moments later, one arm around his neck, the bottom part of her dress having split to reveal a dangerous length of thigh. It might've embarrassed her, except that Walker's eyes were trained on that bared flesh, and all she could think was that she'd die if he didn't put one of those big, capable hands on her.

"I," he said, tugging the two parts of the dress farther apart, "don't know much about intimacy."

"No?" It came out husky. "You're doing just fine." So fine her heart was going to beat out of her chest at any minute.

"Do I have permission to touch you, Lara?"

Of course he'd ask. He was Walker. He took nothing for granted. "Any and all skin privileges you want," she whispered, wanting no mistakes on that score.

Light green eyes met hers for a blazing instant before he closed the callused roughness of his hand over her calf, ran it up to cup the back of her knee. "So soft."

Shivering, she reached down to tug at his hand. "It's sensitive."

He didn't move. "Does it hurt?"

"No. The other kind of sensitive." The kind that had her nipples peaking against the soft fabric of her dress.

"Then I'll touch you there again later." Sliding that hand up over her thigh, he flattened his other over her spine.

When he didn't make any other move, she looked up, met his gaze. "Walker?" He was a dominant, notwithstanding the fact that he didn't wear a wolf's skin. Men like that didn't hesitate once they had permission.

"This"—a squeeze of her thigh that had her stomach tensing—"isn't the only kind of intimacy, is it, Lara?"

Always, he surprised her, this man. "No," she whispered, stroking her fingers up over his nape and into his hair.

"Will you tell me about your parents?"

Her heart twisted into a thousand knots at the quiet, powerful request. This wasn't how she'd imagined the night would go. It was a thousand times better. "You know my father is Mack, the senior tech in charge of the hydro plant."

"And your mother is Aisha," he said at once, "one of the chief cooks."

"Yes. They're wonderful." Smart and loving and devoted, both to each other and Lara. "Though my mother despairs of my cooking skills."

"I know. Aisha's the one who makes up the plates I bring you." A spark of unexpected humor in that stunning green. "We get along very well—possibly because we're in agreement on the fact that bullying you into taking care of yourself is not only acceptable, but necessary."

It startled a laugh out of her to think of her vibrant, chatterbox of a mother and thoughtful, intense Walker as conspirators. "I wondered how you knew all my favorite dishes!" Wolf happy at the knowledge that the people she loved liked each other, she feathered her fingers through the hair that brushed his nape. "What about you?" she asked, so content in this moment that it hurt.

"Though the births were spread out over fourteen years, Judd, Kristine, and I were full siblings," he said, running his fingers over her thigh. The caress made her suck in a breath, but she didn't push for sexual skin privileges. Not now, when Walker was opening up to her in a way she'd never expected. "It made logical sense since the combination of maternal and paternal DNA kept creating high-Gradient offspring."

"It sounds . . . but I guess that's the way it is in the Net."

"Yes. My daughter was conceived by the same method."

But not brought up in the cold, Lara thought. Marlee had *always* been a child confident in her father's protection and love, even when they'd first defected. "You're a good father, Walker," she said, placing her free hand on his cheek. "You understand children."

Shadows moved across those rugged features. "That's why they put me in charge of the telepathic children drafted into the Arrow Squad."

Lara wasn't shocked. Part of her had always known he'd been no ordinary teacher. Linking her arms around his neck, she leaned her head against his shoulder and said, "I'm here."

As the minutes passed, Walker relaxed against the sofa, his hand smoothing up and down her back. Then he began to speak, telling her of being taken from his classroom as a twenty-two-year-old barely out of college and assigned to a school that offered intense one-on-one sessions to its students. "Ages four to ten," he said. "I didn't know then that the children were apprentice Arrows, but I saw at once why they'd been segregated, understood that they needed dedicated training."

Lara didn't know much about Arrows, but she knew Judd had been one, and so she could guess. "Their strength was dangerous."

"Yes." He tugged her closer, his hand rubbing the sensitive skin of her thigh. "I had no problem with my reassignment, with helping the children harness their abilities."

She nuzzled at him, the act affectionate, nonsexual. "Something changed."

Leaning into the tiny kisses she brushed over his neck, he said, "Day by day, I began to see the light go out of my students' eyes in a way that was more profound than could be attributed to the Protocol." The hand on her back slid down to clench on her hip, hard enough that she knew he wasn't aware of it. "Then I began to notice how many of them missed a day or two for medical reasons."

Lara's eyes burned, her healer's heart able to guess what was coming.

"Arrows are taught from childhood not to feel pain," he continued. "The easiest way to do that is to put them through such excruciating pain that the mind learns to shut it out. The side effect, of course, is that it turns them into merciless killers."

Lara swallowed her tears. "Judd."

"As a Tk, he had a different teacher in a different location. His name was wiped from the family records, and according to the PsyNet he no longer existed." The people who had sired Walker, Kristine, and Judd had signed away their rights to their child when he became too difficult to handle. "I had no idea where he was until he was old enough to skirt the psychic safeguards of his trainers, locate and teleport to my apartment."

Walker thought of the first time he'd seen his now teenage brother, glimpsed that same dead expression in Judd's eyes that he saw daily on the faces of the children he taught. The only thing that had kept him going was that *Judd had come home*. Even after everything they'd done to him, he had come home.

Lara's hand curved gently around his nape. "He came to you, not your parents."

That she understood the words he didn't say, couldn't speak . . . "We had no connection to them beyond our biology." Fisting one hand in her springy curls, he anchored himself to the present. "Defection wasn't something we even considered at that time. There was nowhere for us to go, the Council was so powerful." All he'd been able to do was ensure that his brother knew he hadn't been forgotten, would *never* be forgotten.

Then history had begun to repeat itself with Sienna, and it was the final straw. "Lara, I need you to know"—because he didn't ever want her to look at him and wonder—"I never hurt a child in my care." He'd risked everything to teach his students telepathic tricks they weren't permitted to know, and then he'd taught them how to hide the knowledge. It had been the only weapon he could give those small, vulnerable minds.

"Oh, Walker, I know you would never harm a child. I *know*."

The unswerving conviction in her voice, it destroyed something hard and dark and ugly inside of him, sanded away more and more of those jagged edges. His lips were on hers before he knew he was moving, the warm strength of her a benediction he'd never expected.

SIENNA didn't realize anything was wrong until after Hawke fell asleep, having first exhausted her into limp incoherence. When she'd recovered after that second loving to complain that she hadn't gotten a chance to explore his body yet, he'd laughed and promised that she could have her turn—after he got the edge off.

"Pretty long edge," she'd gasped ten minutes later, hair falling around her face as he slid into her from behind for the second time.

That had earned her a kiss on the back of her neck, his fingers curving down to flick the tight bundle of nerves at the apex of her thighs. "You have no idea." A knowing touch circled her clit as she quivered from the shock of his first caress. "See that chair? Having you astride me is next on my list."

The rough greed in his voice had sent heat rocking over her body, a darkly pleasurable sensation. However, this, what she felt now, was uncomfortable, as if her body was boiling from the inside out. Wiggling out from under Hawke's arm, she muttered, "Bathroom," when he would've stopped her, and made her way to the private alcove at the back of the cabin. Throwing water onto her face, she wiped it with a towel, but her skin continued to burn.

That was when she looked in the mirror.

And stopped breathing.

Her eyes were gold—blazing, flickering gold. Swallowing, she tried to quiet the panic that had her pulse in her mouth. The second level of dissonance hadn't kicked in, so whatever had caused this, it didn't indicate a dangerous loss of control. With that reassuring thought, she went within her mind, ready to reinforce the shields that contained the buildup of X-fire. To find them burned out. *Oh, God.*

The lines of dissonance programming had literally been buried under an avalanche of power. That should've been impossible—the pain should've blanked her into unconsciousness long before it got to that stage . . . except she was an X. A cardinal. No one knew how her power functioned, not in truth.

Connected as the events seemed, she knew the collapse wasn't as a result of the emotional impact of the previous two nights—her response to Hawke had been wild and dark and passionate long before they'd shared intimate skin privileges. "Calm," she said out loud. "Calm." When she had some kind of a handle on herself, she began to rebuild that which had been burned away . . . only to watch as the cold fire began to devour it at almost the same instant.

Horror filled her veins, speared through her mind.

But at the center of it was a cold, clear understanding.

She'd thought she'd beaten the X-marker, but all she'd done was corral it—there was no way to *stop* its progression. Her periodic purges had acted as a pressure regulator, but that regulator was no longer big enough. The power had grown in an exponential cascade over the hours she'd slept, until it was a massive beast shoving at her shields, wanting out.

All indications are that your power develops in erratic and unpredictable surges. At some stage, the surge will overwhelm.

She'd forgotten Ming's prediction, or perhaps she hadn't wanted to remember it. In this, the bastard had proven right. "No panic, Sienna. *Think*." Pacing in the confines of the bathroom, she realized the first thing she needed to do was earth the cold fire, buy some time.

It took her five minutes to sneak outside without waking Hawke, and she was convinced he didn't rise only because he could scent her and knew she was safe. The instant her bare feet hit the forest floor, she punched her power into it, the ground burning with phantom flames for almost a minute before the X-fire soaked into the earth.

Yet when she looked into her mind, she saw that by morning, the buildup would be close to critical once more. The cold fire was voracious, and it wanted to consume everything in its path, but that wasn't the most terrifying truth she saw inside the conflagration of her mind. Synergy, the catastrophic crest of an X's power, wasn't just possible, it was highly probable.

There was no going back once an X hit synergy.

Glancing behind her at the cabin, she rebuilt a second layer of shields before walking back inside. Her eyes had returned to normal, and so she allowed herself to stay with Hawke, to sleep in his arms this night.

One last night.

Chapter 48

MORNING CAME TOO soon, and along with it, the harsh reality of the inevitable consequences of the amplification in her power levels. She was grateful for Riley's early morning call seeking to talk over a security issue with Hawke. It gave her an excuse to keep the discussion on martial matters on the drive back, a topic she could handle even with her concentration fractured.

Her luck ran out when they reached the den.

"You okay?" Fingers gripping her chin, wolf-blue eyes piercing her through and through. "Did something I do last night—"

"No," she interrupted, wanting nothing to tarnish the memory of that wonderful, impossible, beautiful night. "I guess I'm just . . . processing." Not a lie.

A slow smile. "Here's something else for you to process." His kiss burned her with a far more welcome fire than the cold that licked through the psychic pathways of her mind. But she couldn't remain in his arms forever.

"Okay," she said, pacing from wall to wall inside her quarters. "Time to think." She couldn't do anything about the buildup of power, not here, not now, but she could get the hell away from those who had no idea how close they were to an armed and deadly weapon. Once at a sufficient distance, she'd have more room to consider her options, work out solutions.

In spite of the practical, positive nature of her thoughts, her heart was a lump of stone, terror crawling a thousand spidery fingers in her mind. Though she'd earthed it only hours ago, her power was already at over sixty-five percent. There was no escaping the cold, hard truth that there would come a time when she would turn into a living torch, her body spilling over with too much X-fire to allow even the faintest illusion of control.

He isn't my mate.

Pain roared through her chest, but for the first time, the idea of never having that bond with Hawke didn't tear her heart in two, but saved it. If he had been her mate, the shock of her violent death might've been lethal. "Thank you," she whispered to whatever unknown deity had given her that priceless gift.

The LaurenNet, her family, they would be safe. Judd and Walker were strong enough to hold Toby and Marlee in the network after Sienna was gone. *If she was less selfish, she'd cut her link to the LaurenNet now, allow her mind to starve to death.* "No," she said, hands fisted. That cold voice was Ming's, the voice of a man who'd only ever seen her as a thing to be used.

But she was a sister, a niece, a cousin, a friend, a pack-mate . . . a lover. Suicide would forever haunt those she left behind—Sienna knew that better than anyone. And, even though the odds appeared impossible, she'd never been the giving-up type. She'd fight to the bloody, bitter end to live.

Less than twenty minutes later, she'd packed a small bag and was ready to depart, her power levels having punched up to hit seventy-nine percent. Seeing Hawke was out of the question, no matter how much it hurt her not to go to him—he'd know, and she couldn't afford for him to stop her.

Toby. Marlee.

Her sweet, gentle baby brother, a boy who'd already lost his mother, would also know, but she'd have chanced that to hug him tight if she hadn't been so afraid her power would go unstable while she was still in the den.

Walker would protect him, she thought, fighting back tears because they had no place here, in the most crucial battle of her life. Walker would lay down his life for Toby. So would Hawke, Judd, Riley, Indigo, Drew, Brenna—so many people loved him. Sunny-natured Marlee would reach him even if everyone else failed. And she could 'path him later when she was at a safe distance, make sure he wasn't afraid, that he knew she loved him.

Hawke isn't a telepath.

Her eyes glanced off the phone she was leaving behind because it contained a tracking chip. She wouldn't be able to contact him if she failed in her last desperate attempt to contain her power, wouldn't be able to tell him the secrets of her heart. But he'd know—how could he possibly not know how much he meant to her?

The physical act of leaving was easy. No one had any reason to stop her. She didn't make any detours until she was well past the lake. Then she began to run, raising a wave of X-fire at her back. The intensity of it would erase the scents on the ground, in the air. Hawke might still be able to track her, but she had a head start and the most painful incentive to get as far as possible from those she loved. She would not murder them, would not become the monster Ming had trained her to be.

An hour later, her power hit one hundred percent.

HAWKE was speaking to Riley about Alexei's team of snipers when Toby ran up to them. The boy was so well behaved that the instant he grabbed Hawke's hand and tugged, he had both men's immediate and total attention.

"Sienna." Toby sucked in a breath, his face red, his chest heaving. "She's in trouble."

Hawke's wolf went predator-quiet. "Where is she, Toby?"

"I don't know." Stark terror in the skin stretched tight over his skull. "Her star is like ice in our Net. But there's fire inside." Trembling voice, a sheen of wet on his eyes. "You have to help her."

Hawke took Toby's face in between his palms, captured the boy's distraught gaze with his own. "You did the right thing coming to me. I'll find her." Always. She was his.

Toby gave a jerky nod. "You gotta go. I think she's running away."

No way in hell.

"Riley."

"I've got him." Riley put his hand on top of Toby's head.

"Go," both man and boy said.

He left, fury beating in every pulse of his blood. Did she really think he'd let her go? That he'd lie down and accept the fact that she'd cut and run? If she had, she was going to get a nasty surprise when he caught up to her. Because Hawke was feeling all kinds of mean.

A single question and he knew she hadn't checked out any of the vehicles. Which meant she was on foot. He shifted to wolf form mid-run, following her scent out of the den and to the lake. Anger had his wolf digging its claws into the earth, but worse was the jagged sense of betrayal. How dare she do this? How dare she think to isolate herself in this way? They were going to have the mother of all fights when he caught up to her.

Which he would do, very, very soon.

Sienna was smart, but she wasn't wolf, wasn't alpha. He lost her scent at the lake. It didn't matter. Because he knew her. He also knew this territory like the back of his hand. Cutting across the land with the speed of a predator infuriated with the woman he'd claimed as his own, he planned to head her off in under three hours.

SETTLING them in the break room off the infirmary, Lara made Toby and Marlee cups of hot chocolate, and handed out cookies. "Sienna will be fine," she said, ignoring the tear tracks Toby furtively wiped away, and hoping her words weren't a lie. "Hawke's gone after her." Hawke always ran his prey to ground. *Always.*

Marlee scrunched up her nose. "I bet he was mad."

Toby nodded to his younger cousin. "Yeah, Sienna's in big trouble."

They began to discuss whether they wanted to swap their cookies.

Startled, Lara looked up to meet Riley's gaze. The lieutenant gave a single satisfied nod before leaving the children in Lara's care—though Lara wasn't certain they were as sanguine about the situation as they appeared, especially Toby. But, having dealt with more than her share of boys, she didn't fuss. Instead, she moved around to fix the ribbon on Marlee's braid. "Did you tell your dad what was happening?" Walker would want to know as soon as possible.

"Uh-huh." Marlee nodded. "He was helping Riaz with the older kids far away. He's coming home though." Eyes identical to her father's pinned Lara to the spot when she finished with the ribbon. "Ben says you smell like my dad."

Lara hesitated, glanced at Toby . . . to see no surprise on the boy's face. Of course not. He was empathic, had to have picked up the undercurrents long ago. "Does that bother you?" she asked both children.

Toby just shook his head, but Marlee dunked her cookie and took a bite before saying, "No, Dad needs someone to cuddle him, too." A brilliant smile. "And me and Toby, we think you're pretty great."

Wanting to smile at the idea of anyone cuddling Walker, Lara pressed a kiss to Marlee's cheek before moving over to pour Toby some more hot chocolate. "You need anything else, sweetheart?"

Toby looked up, a quiver in his lower lip that he bit down to still. "A hug."

"Oh, Toby." Going to her knees, she embraced him tight. "We won't permit her to handle this alone. We're Pack."

A small hand brushed over her own as Marlee patted Toby's back. "Don't be sad, Toby. Hawke won't bite her *very* hard for running away."

Toby's eyes went huge as he drew back from the hug . . . and then he started laughing, turning to wrap one arm around his grinning cousin's neck to tug her to his side.

From the mouths, Lara thought, her own lips twitching, *of babes.*

SWEAT was trickling down Sienna's back, her face, pasting tendrils of hair to her temples when she crested the rise and found herself two meters from a very pissed-off wolf. "No," she whispered. "You can't be here." In the hours since she'd left the den, she'd realized that there was no way to turn back the psychic clock, no way to escape the inevitable. The only thing she could do was make sure she didn't take anyone else with her. "Go back."

The wolf snarled, lips peeled back to display razor-sharp canines.

It was difficult to stand her ground when all she wanted to do was go to her knees, wrap her arms around him, and ask him to make it all right. But even Hawke couldn't fix this, fix *her*. "I'm close to a lethal breach," she said, breath coming in ragged gasps. "You have to leave."

His response was to pace around her in a slow, predatory sweep. Dropping her pack, she swigged from the bottle of water she'd refilled at a stream an hour ago. "Stop trying to intimidate me and listen, you stubborn wolf!"

Pale eyes dared her to continue.

She folded her arms. "I'm not being melodramatic or a diva or a child." The time alone in the wide-open spaces of the Sierra had given her room to breathe, quiet the nascent panic to cold reason. "My power is amplifying at an exponential rate. I could go active at any time—in the bedroom, at the infirmary, in the *nursery*."

Hawke walked over to stand right in front of her, his ears pricked, his body motionless. She wasn't surprised in the least when he shifted in a storm of light and color. When it passed, he towered over her, his anger as feral as it had been in wolf form. "You. Left. Me."

It was the last thing she'd expected him to say. "It was for the best." He had her scrambling backward before she realized it. Her back hit a tree trunk. "I'm dangerous. I—" His mouth on her own, his hand gripping her at the nape as his body pinned her against the tree.

She should've resisted, but how was she supposed to exercise restraint when he was everything she had ever wanted?

Seventy-three percent.

Time, she had time enough to love him. Rising on tiptoe, she gripped at his waist as she met him kiss for kiss, breath for breath.

When he reached down and ripped open the button-fly of her cargo pants, she kicked them off after toeing off her boots. Her panties were in shreds an instant later. She shifted her grip to his shoulders as he lifted her up, wrapping her legs around his waist. And shuddered, her every nerve sparking with near-painful need as he claimed her with a single primal thrust.

But even wild with possessive fury and animal need, he remembered to brace one arm around her lower back, the other around her shoulders, so she didn't get pounded into the rough bark of the tree. Then he took her, kissing her with such ferocious demand that she could do nothing but give him everything he wanted.

"You left me." A husky accusation against her ear.

"I'm sorry. I'm sorry." Fisting her hand in his hair, she kissed him in ragged apology—she couldn't say she wouldn't do it again. That choice had been taken out of her hands the instant she'd been born an X. "Love me."

"Always."

THEY sat in the silver-green shade of the tree afterward, its branches shimmering in the sunlight. Sienna had managed to knot the top of her cargos across her hips, though they hung precariously low, while Hawke sat unashamedly naked, with her in his lap. His chin lay on her hair, one muscular arm around her shoulders, his free hand heavy on her thigh.

Head on his shoulder, she traced her fingers through the soft hairs on his chest. "I thought I'd beaten it. I thought I'd be the X who survived, but I was just fooling myself. I should've looked more carefully, should've realized—"

"You had no one to teach you," he said with changeling fierceness. "You're doing the best you can in a wilderness no one knows how to navigate."

"I never said," Sienna murmured, "but part of me always thought we'd find Alice Eldridge's book on X-Psy and that it would have all the answers. Stupid, isn't it? But I guess even an X can believe in fairy tales." Her hand fisted against him. "I can't go back. I'm not safe." Never would be safe.

"Then we stay up here." An absolute statement.

She'd never felt so cherished, so wanted, but she allowed herself only a moment to revel in the joy of it. "No. The pack needs you."

Hawke's hand slid up to her hip. "Pack is built on the bonds of family, of mating, of love. You come first. You always will."

Tears burned at the backs of her eyes. "You are their heart,

Hawke." Especially now, with Henry and his fanatics about to launch an assault.

"As you're mine." Reaching up to stroke the tangled mess he'd made of her hair, he released a breath. "When Rissa died, part of me broke. Even at ten, I knew I wasn't just losing my best friend, I was losing part of myself."

"If I could bring her back for you, I would." In an instant, even if it meant she would have to watch him love another woman.

"Shh." A shake of his head that said she didn't understand. "Rissa's death, her life, shaped me. She'll always be a part of me, but I haven't been the boy she knew for a long time. *You*—and only you—hold the man's heart."

Sienna froze. "You mustn't say that." They'd never have the mating bond, but this, what he was giving her, it was as precious, as binding. As painfully beautiful. "You mustn't."

"Ah baby, you know I do what I want." Rubbing his chin on her hair, he squeezed her hip. "Man and wolf, we both adore you. No way am I letting you go after the hell you've put me through over the years."

He was teasing, but she couldn't find any laughter inside of her. "I don't know how to stop this"—an excruciating, angry helplessness—"how to survive it." But she would find a way to send him back. Because SnowDancer needed him now, more than ever, this man with a heart so big, he'd held a broken pack together and made it strong again, a man who'd given sanctuary to the enemy . . . a man who'd loved an X.

Chapter 49

JUDD RETURNED FROM checking out a warehouse the novices had fingered in the city to find Walker waiting for him. His brother had wanted to tell him the news about Sienna in person, and now they leaned against one of the huge glacial rocks that littered this region, their backs warm, their blood chilled.

"Hawke's with her," Judd said, and it wasn't a question.

"Has your contact found anything?" Walker asked in a tone so devoid of emotion, it would've been easy to believe he cared nothing for Sienna.

The same man, Judd thought, had taken a near-broken teenage boy into his arms and told him he would always, *always* be family. The fierceness of that quiet declaration had given Judd an anchor in the midst of utter darkness, given him the will to survive. "I have a meeting with him tonight."

"What are the chances?"

"I don't know."

Three hours later, in the otherwise empty nave of an old, abandoned church he got his answer. It was a devastating one.

"There is no second manuscript," the Ghost told him.

A bleak gray invaded his mind. "Are you certain?"

"Yes. Alice Eldridge had an eidetic memory. According to the records I was able to unearth, she burned her research notes on the X designation when it became clear that Silence was inevitable. The implication is that she did so in an effort to stop the Council using her research in ways it was never meant to be used."

Judd didn't need the other man to spell it out. "The only remaining record was in Eldridge's head."

"Yes."

It was the final staggering hit. "We're going to lose Sienna." A cold, hard rock in his chest, the knowledge that he wouldn't be able to keep the promise he'd made to Kristine, wouldn't be able to keep her daughter safe. "There's no way to halt the buildup of cold fire once an X reaches this level."

The Ghost considered this, considered, too, what would happen if Sienna Lauren did survive. An X was power. A cardinal X was power without limit. She was a wildcard he couldn't control, one that might disrupt all his meticulously laid plans.

Then he looked at Judd, at the fallen Arrow who had walked with him even knowing what and who he was, who had kept his secrets. The Ghost knew nothing of friendship, but he understood loyalty and fidelity. He also understood that sometimes, plans needed to change—and that change could be used to a smart man's advantage.

"Come," he said to Judd. "I have something to show you."

Judd followed him down into the crypt, keeping enough of a distance between them that he was never in any danger of seeing the Ghost's face.

"Why do you do that?" the Ghost asked. "You know who I am." Perhaps the only one who did. Even Father Xavier Perez, the third part of their curious triumvirate, had never made the connection.

"If I am ever taken," Judd said, his words those of a man who knew danger could come as a silent shadow in the dark, "my mind is set with triggers that'll erase your name from my memory banks at a single mental command. Images are more difficult to remove."

So he'd made sure he didn't have any images to erase. "You could've ruled." For all of Judd's power, the Ghost had never before considered that possibility.

"It would have killed what remained of my soul."

The Ghost couldn't recall ever having had a soul, didn't know if he even understood what it was. "There," he said, pointing to a shadowy corner of the old and musty crypt.

Judd went motionless as his telepathic senses registered an unknown mind. "Who?" And what had the Ghost done?

The rebel leaned against the crumbling brick wall. "I don't think you'll believe me if I tell you."

Unable to detect any movement from the corner, Judd retrieved a slender penlight from his pocket and walked over to find a dust-coated glass box sitting neatly in the corner. It was about six feet long, a couple of feet deep if that, had fixtures that denoted a number of missing cables. Noticing someone had wiped away the sticky coating of dust near the top, creating a tiny window of clarity, he angled the cutting brightness of the light toward it.

A face looked out at him from within.

It was that of a small, fine-boned woman of mixed ethnicity. Her skin was a pallid brown, her eyes tilted up at the corners even in sleep, her skull smooth. Her hair had been shaved off, he realized, though there was no evidence of any electrodes ever having been attached to her skull. "Who?" he asked the Ghost once more.

"There is no second manuscript," the Ghost said, walking to stand beside him, "but you have no need of it. I've brought you Alice Eldridge."

HAWKE had made Sienna promise to stay in place when he left to get supplies. She'd broken that promise. But since he'd found her again before he got too grumpy and hungry, he didn't snarl as he said, "Put up the tent," and rolled the compact package to where she lay flat on her back, staring at the soft gray of the evening sky. "It's your punishment."

Clearly exhausted, she glared at him. "Do you never run out of energy?"

He pushed up the sleeves of his sweatshirt. "I'm alpha. Right now, I'm a hungry alpha who wants to take a bite out of you for making me run the extra miles. Put up the tent."

She sat up but didn't touch the tent. "Go bite yourself."

So, she was feeling pissy. That was fine with him. He liked it much better than the defeated pain he sensed had come close to breaking her earlier today. "Actually, I'd prefer to use my teeth on softer flesh." He was reaching out to snag her when flames erupted along her back, in her hair. "Sienna!"

She slapped up her hands. "I'm fine, I'm fine. Don't touch."

It was sheer hell to obey the order. He hauled her into his arms the instant the lick of red and yellow disappeared. "How bad?" he asked, seeing the pain at the corners of her eyes, knowing of the second layer of dissonance now.

"Bad. But not the dissonance. As soon as the power builds to a certain level, the dissonance either disengages or some-how short-circuits." Her throat moved as she swallowed. "And it's building faster and faster—I earthed after you left."

He felt a lingering sense of ice—cold enough to burn—against his palm as he ran it over the silk of her hair. "Sienna, can the X-fire burn you?" His wolf wasn't pacing anymore, its focus, the same focus that had helped a fifteen-year-old boy hold together a shattered pack, acute.

"That's how Xs usually die, and if it reaches that point, then there's no predicting how far the resulting explosion will spread." Her smile was tight, painful. "It's why we're consid-ered the most perfect weapon on the planet. An X can 'scorch the earth,' eradicating all that came before, but the damage to the environment is minimal. Much like after a real fire, the earth bounces back stronger and healthier—and the ag-gressors have a clean slate on which to build their own em-pire."

He saw through the rational speech. "What aren't you saying?"

"Ming had a theory—that if I could somehow purge my power on a level I can't achieve with the earthing, I could initiate a restricted burst from the nascent buildup that would consume only me." Her eyes met his. "If the flames ever turn blue . . . it means he was right. *Promise me* that you won't come near me if that happens."

"Come on," he said instead of giving her a promise he knew he wouldn't be able to keep. "Change of location."

"Where are we going?" She grabbed the tent.

"Nearer a lake I know of up here. If all else fails, I'm throwing you in there."

"I don't know if that'll work—X-fire isn't like normal fire."

"Better than turning into a human torch, don't you think?" Turning, he went to touch his fingers to her jaw, felt his heart stop when she met his gaze.

Her eyes, those startling cardinal eyes, were drowning in

shimmering, lethal gold kissed with crimson, and in them, he saw time running out at an inexorable pace.

JUDD didn't know who was more surprised, him or Lara, when he teleported into the infirmary with Alice Eldridge's frail body in his arms. But she threw off the shock to run to him at once, grabbing a scanner off a counter as she did so. "What do I need to know?" she asked as he placed the scientist's naked form on the nearest bed.

"Cryonic suspension," he said, head still ringing in disbelief.

"Impossible." Lara put down the scanner, picked up a pressure injector, and pressed it to Alice's neck. "No one has ever been brought back from suspension with their mind intact. Even the Psy made it illegal over a half century ago."

"She was suspended before that, when the experimentation was at its peak." It had been a time of chaos and change when Alice Eldridge had been taken—probably on the orders of a schemer in the Council superstructure who'd had some vague idea of waking her up later when things had calmed down and she could be properly debriefed.

But no one had ever come to wake her, her existence submerged by the wave of Silence that had swept across the Net. Perhaps the architect of her abduction had been killed, perhaps he'd simply forgotten her, but whatever the cause, the result was that Alice had slept undisturbed for over a hundred years in a small facility deep in the Balkans. A facility that ran on solar power, but that had had no gatekeepers or personnel for decades, was listed as a storage warehouse. One so small and unimportant that it was continually pushed down the list when it came time for inspections and renovations.

Judd had asked the Ghost how he'd found it.

The other man had looked at him with those eyes that held nothing of humanity. "I found it because I go where no one goes. There are places in the Net that belong only to me."

Now, Judd shook off his tiredness over the dual teleport and told Lara everything he knew. "She was found in an experimental chamber created by a scientist who was considered to be on the verge of unlocking the secret of cryonics."

"If he had, it wouldn't be illegal now," Lara muttered as she fitted a tissue-thin computronic skullcap over Alice's head and walked around to the control pad at the end of the bed to scan the readout.

For the hundredth time, Judd tried to sense if Alice's mind was active and came up against the same unexpected shield that had obstructed his earlier attempts. "He was a telepath, had a psychotic breakdown in which he destroyed his lab and all associated records before killing himself and his family." Perhaps that was the reason her abductors had abandoned Alice Eldridge—no one knew what chemicals the scientist had used to induce suspension, much less how to reverse the state.

Lara slammed a fist down on the control panel. "Shit," she muttered, staring at the woman who lay so lifeless on the bed, "just, shit."

Judd had never seen that expression on the healer's face. "How bad?"

"That's the thing—I don't know. It's not like they teach us this at medical school." She leaned forward, hands clamped around the edges of the panel. "I need Tammy and Ashaya."

"Who first?" He could do one more dual teleport.

A moment's pause. "Ashaya. She's not a medic as such, but she's a scientist—and she can discuss the situation with Amara."

Ashaya's twin, Judd knew, was insane. No one trusted her, and she couldn't be allowed in the den, but there was no discounting her brilliance. "I'll get Ashaya," he said. "You call Tammy, have her drive up." The teleport to Dorian and Ashaya's house wasn't difficult, since he'd been to the location before. He had enough energy to bring the M-Psy back before he slid down the wall and to the floor of the infirmary.

The two women ignored him as they worked over Alice, with Tamsyn arriving seventy minutes later. Sometime in between, Brenna found him, just like he'd known she would.

"Sweetheart," she said, kneeling down beside him. "You're about to flame out."

He gave a slight shake of his head. "Not over the threshold." But he was slurring his words, so he leaned against her when she sat down beside him . . . and then he was stretched out with his head in her lap.

The last thing he remembered saying was, "Walker, find him." His older brother had a way of seeing to the heart of things, would know whether or not they should tell Sienna what had happened when there was a good chance Alice Eldridge would never wake. Even if she did, there was no guarantee she'd be able to tell them anything—the Ghost had found data that suggested she may have asked an E to wipe that part of her memory clean.

SIENNA scraped a kick by Hawke's ear as the stars turned into glittering beacons overhead. "You can't stay up here," she said as he made a fluid move to avoid the blow. "You know that." No matter how well prepared his people, how well drilled, they were changeling, were wolf—without their alpha, the pack would be lost, rootless. More, she understood his wolf needed to stand in the line of fire, to be SnowDancer's first line of defense.

He danced out of the way of her strike. "You can do better than that, baby." Blocking her next kick with his hand, he pushed up until she had no choice but to flip and come down hard on her feet. "I won't leave you up here alone."

When he'd suggested a bout of hand-to-hand sparring, she'd figured she might as well accept since she wasn't going to sleep. Now she knew his cunning plan—to exhaust the argument right out of her. But they both knew she was right. "I'll be fine," she said after her teeth stopped vibrating. "I have supplies." Taking a moment to catch her breath, she decided it was unfair he had that lickable upper body on display. "Put your sweatshirt back on."

His eyes gleamed wolf-blue in the night. "Come closer and make me."

Her lips twitched, though she'd thought the cold fire had seared the laughter right out of her heart. "Maybe I should take off my own top."

A smile full of teeth. "Maybe you should."

Laughing, she set her feet for another attempt at taking him down. "Talk me through the pack's defensive plans." If she managed to hold off synergy, then she might yet be able to assist SnowDancer.

Moving with lethal grace around her, Hawke spoke, listened when she asked questions or made suggestions. There was a perfection to the moment that made Sienna think: *Yes, this is it. This is who we're meant to be together.*

If she could have, she would've frozen time at that instant, but second by second, minute by minute, the stars would dim, the sky would lighten—until dawn streaked a brilliant explosion of color across the Sierra. As brilliant as the cold fire inside of her, voracious and violent.

"Sienna, your eyes."

"I know." Stepping a small distance away, she let the flames pour out of her and into the earth in a storm of wildfire that was an impenetrable wall between her and her wolf.

Chapter 50

HAWKE HUNG UP the sat phone feeling as if he'd been punched in the chest by a granite fist. Sienna glanced back at him from where she sat on the edge of the lake, the early morning sunshine dancing over hair as black as the heart of a ruby. "What is it?"

"A dead woman come back to life." When he told her what—*who*—Judd had brought home, hope flared a shiny new coin in her eyes for a single bright second.

It turned dull almost as fast. "There's no knowing if she'll ever wake," Sienna said, "much less if she'll come back whole. I have to stay up here."

He'd thought he could leave her, could sacrifice his heart for his pack, but now that the moment had come, man and wolf both rebelled. "No," he said, going to crouch by her side. "You're heading down with me."

"Hawke, you promised you'd listen to me about my ability." A firm reminder, but the fingers on his jaw were a caress. "I know what I am. I know the destruction I'm capable of—don't make me kill those I love."

"You're able to monitor your power levels, know when you're about to go critical." He'd watched her leach off the violence of her ability twice more during the night, the flames seeming to flicker out over the lake itself.

"We can't gamble on that."

"You can move closer to the den." He wasn't used to losing. However, Sienna's iron will was one of the things that had first drawn him to her. "No." Rising to her knees, she put her hands on his shoulders, no stars in her eyes. "But I won't go any farther from this point."

He stared at her, the wolf attempting to dominate her into acquiescence. Even when he said, "Promise?" there was nothing of acceptance in it.

"Cross my heart."

Hauling her against him, he branded her with his mouth, his lips, his breath before leaving with a single, furious command. *"Stay alive."*

WALKER knocked on Lara's office door that afternoon, wasn't surprised to find her still dressed in the clothes she'd worn yesterday, black shadows under her eyes. This time, he didn't berate her for not taking better care of herself. Instead, he drew her into his arms, held her for a long moment before allowing her to pull back. "Eldridge?"

Lara's gaze was bleak. "The scans detect brain activity, but that means nothing if we can't figure out a way to wake her. Ashaya and Amara came up with a chemical cocktail, which we shot into her a few hours ago, but so far there's been no change."

Walker knew both Judd and Sascha had been attempting to get through the strange shield around Alice's mind in an effort to nudge her to consciousness on the psychic level. Walker, too, had tried. To no avail. And now— "I have to leave."

Lara touched him in that wolf way, stroking back his hair, sliding her hand over his pectorals as if to smooth his shirt. "Why?"

He bent toward her, making it easier for her to "pet" him as the wolves called it. "Hawke wants me with the children when they evacuate." The SnowDancer alpha's face had been drawn in harsh lines when he returned to the den this morning, but he'd given the order to evacuate with a crisp, clear focus, as he had so many others.

According to Judd, who'd be back to full strength by tonight, surveillance at the South American compound was showing a rising level of activity as Pure Psy's people began to recover from the virus. The runway would be complete by tomorrow morning, which meant the compound had to be taken out of the equation tonight at the latest, before any of the weapons-heavy transports took off.

Everyone agreed the children needed to be gone prior to that. Because once SnowDancer blew the compound, the war began. There was no hope of peace. Both Nikita and Anthony had attempted to reason with Henry in a last-ditch effort to halt hostilities. The other Councilor's response had been to try to assassinate them on the psychic plane.

"Of course," Lara said, hand settling on his waist. "You're the perfect choice—the kids will listen to you and feel safe at the same time."

Her immediate support of him made an unexpected warmth uncurl in his abdomen. "Drew's promised to spy on you for me and report if you're not eating."

"The sneak will do it, too." Her smile faded too soon. "It's a hard thing to ask of you right now, isn't it? To leave her?" She wrapped her arms around him.

"Sienna would be the first to tell me to go," he whispered into the softness of her curls, numbing the pain permeating his chest at the thought of the girl he'd never been able to protect. The only thing he could do for her now was to ensure those she loved were safe. "She'd do anything for Toby and Marlee."

Lara kissed him, hot and giving and possessive in a way he'd never have expected from her before he'd truly known her. Sliding his hand under her hair, he tilted her head, indulged in the wild sweetness of her for a moment out of time.

"I'll contact you as soon as we know anything," she said when they parted, her lips wet, her eyes determined. "We'll keep working with Alice."

"I know you will." A piece of him threatened to shatter, a piece that bore Sienna's name, the name of a girl who was as much his daughter as Marlee. "Take care of yourself, Lara." Because she owned a piece of him, too, a broken piece she'd somehow soldered back together and that bore her mark now.

He couldn't say the words, had spent too long in Silence, but he'd learned other ways to speak. Taking the paperweight she'd knocked off her desk out of his pocket, he put it in her hands. "It's fixed. As long as you don't mind more than a few scars."

Tears in her eyes, she pursed her lips, shook her head . . . and held the paperweight to her heart. "I love you, Walker."

He left with those words held to the most secret part of him, but rather than joining the evacuation, he went up to where Sienna sat beside a wide, blue lake that mirrored the mountains with such perfection it seemed there was no sky, only an endless vista of jagged peaks touched with snow. When she flew into his arms, he held her tight. And watched the cold fire of an X lick at her hair, over her spine. She wrenched away, her eyes dry of tears, her voice resolute. "I have to earth."

He would've waited, would've done anything he could for the girl he realized had become a woman of courage and strength, but he knew she didn't want him to see her like this. So he walked forward, cupped her face, and pressed his lips to her forehead. *Fight, sweetheart, fight.*

As he turned away, he felt the earth shudder under a pulse of raw power and knew that if he looked over his shoulder, he'd see nothing but a column of wild yellow and brilliant red, a woman consumed in flame.

HAVING confirmed that the warehouse the novices had found in the city held the weapons cache, SnowDancer blew the South American camp at midnight.

Stealth planes flew over the city at three a.m.

Pure Psy operatives began to appear along the Snow-Dancer-DarkRiver perimeter an hour later, pouring out from craft that landed just out of range of the anti-aircraft weapons over changeling territory, most covering the remaining distance on foot, while a front guard stood ready for teleportation.

The intruders were loaded up with so many weapons that had the changelings been relying only on their physical strength, the battle would've been over before it began. As it was, Alexei's sharpshooters, along with those trained by Dorian and Judd, were in prime position to pick off those attackers who were teleported in. And the changelings had extraordinary night vision.

The enemy learned quickly and began to teleport in farther from the perimeter, inside DarkRiver land. But the leopards knew that land like the backs of their hands, and while their people were all in the city tonight, they'd laid out a welcoming mat—a number of the aggressors fell victim to their traps. And this time, there was no question about the enemy combatants' allegiance. They wore the emblem on their shoulders.

"A black spiderweb." Matthias's voice came into Hawke's earpiece. "That's Henry Scott's symbol."

Not unexpected but it was always nice to have confirmation. "If the enemy hits you with a psychic blow," he told his people as they prepared to engage, "aim at their heads. If you don't have a shot, turn around and run like hell until you get out of range." Changeling shields were strong, but they weren't impenetrable. "I need live soldiers, not dead heroes."

A chuckle from the line, his wolves ready for battle.

Then Henry Scott teleported in onto the perimeter, surrounded by an armed guard so thick, it was impossible for anyone to get a shot in. The Councilor held up a hand.

Knowing time and the wind would only help his people pinpoint the locations of the Pure Psy teams, Hawke gave the order to listen.

"This," Henry said, "is your last chance. Surrender and I will let you walk away."

Hawke's wolf wanted to rip out the man's throat, but it was better to let the bastard talk, find out as much as they could. "Now why," he said from his position behind a slight rise, "would we want to do that when this is our land?" Their *home*.

Henry Scott's voice was ultimately reasonable. "You've been caught up in the middle of a political situation you have no hope of understanding. It's in your best interest to give in."

"What do you say, boys and girls?" Hawke murmured into the mike worked into the collar of the thin black bulletproof vest he wore over a long-sleeved T-shirt of the same color.

The howl started at one end of the line and was carried from soldier to soldier, until it reverberated around the mountain. Hawke's wolf peeled back its lips. "Go!"

* * *

HAVING had a telepathic report from Judd as well as a call from Hawke on the sat phone he'd left her, Sienna had earthed herself and double-checked her power reserves. The chance of an unpredictable spike remained, but since that wouldn't matter if the people she loved were dying when she could've saved them, she took the risk of heading down.

She reached the combat zone just as hostilities began, the hairs on the back of her neck rising at the sound of the wolf howls singing through the air. Tempting as it was to detour, to glimpse the battle, she made her way directly to the spot Hawke had pointed out on the territorial map what felt like months ago. There was a pair of night-vision lenses waiting for her, along with a tiny key on a thin silver chain.

If you want to know what this opens, stay alive. —H.

"Hello, wolf." Placing the chain around her neck, she slid on the night-vision lenses and began to scan the combat zone.

It was automatic to search for that vivid mane of silver-gold, distinctive even through the color distortion caused by the lenses. But she couldn't see it anywhere. Her heart stopped beating at the thought that he'd been hit, was down, and then she realized—every single SnowDancer in human form was wearing a knit cap over his or her head.

Yes, of course. The enemy would never know which one was Hawke, giving them no specific target. "Come on," she said, whispering encouragement though she knew they couldn't hear her, "we can do it." That was when she spotted him, though his hair remained covered, his face turned away. Still, she knew the way he moved—a human wolf. *Her* wolf.

HAWKE saw several of his people fall, knew they'd been hit with a psychic blast. Racing out to the one closest, he pulled the male back out of range with a grip on his bulletproof vest, then went back to retrieve another, a woman. Around him, more SnowDancer soldiers were doing the same, as others fought off the Pure Psy operatives targeting those trying to assist the injured.

There was no doubt that Scott had a massive advantage with his telepaths and telekinetics, but from the looks of things, the Tk unit was beginning to tire from the troop movements—which meant SnowDancer didn't have to worry about missiles being lobbed at them without warning, though the techs had prepared for that eventuality by placing a number of interception units along the defensive line.

The changelings had also evened out the field with preparation, the choice of *when* to fight, and the knowledge of home ground. Enemy soldiers who tried to teleport in behind Snow-Dancer's defensive line found themselves caught between layers of wolves arranged up and down the mountain.

Not all of those wolves were changeling.

Good, Hawke howled to the feral wolves that treated him as alpha. *Watch. Hold.*

The wolves howled in unison in response, and Hawke saw the enemy freeze for a fraction of an instant. Then the crashing noise and blood-soaked scent of battle started again. Contrary to Hawke's expectations, Henry Scott remained on the field. The Councilor stood in the center of that tight guard, his eyes closed—Hawke realized the man was using his considerable psychic abilities against the changelings at the same time that he saw a shot coming straight at a soldier.

"Drew, duck!"

Drew slammed flat. His gaze was annoyed when he raised his head. "I swear to God, if I get shot again, Indigo will strangle me." Obviously irritated by that, he turned around and took out the man who'd come after him just as Snow-Dancer's aerial defenses ignited an incoming vessel, causing everyone to run for cover from the falling debris.

Scrabbling up beside Hawke, Drew put his back to a tree. "That should remind them to keep the hell out of our skies," he muttered, then pressed his finger to an ear. "I've got info coming in from the Rats—Henry's operatives are landing all over the place in San Francisco."

TEIJAN and his people were used to being forgotten, being shoved aside. They were Rats, accustomed to living Below, where the world couldn't hurt them. But the DarkRiver cats had seen them, had treated them as sentient beings capable of giving something back. As for the wolves—well, the Rats remained leery of them, but there was no arguing that Snow-

Dancer had always held up its end of the bargain. More than one Rat had been pulled out of trouble or given protection by a wolf who was otherwise a stranger.

"It's home," Zane had said when Teijan had told his people what might be coming and offered them the option of leaving. "We stay and we fight."

Now, they did just that.

Having worked with DarkRiver over the past couple of months to connect with the cats' network of human and non-predatory changeling shopkeepers in Chinatown, that connection spreading out through family and business contacts like an ever-growing tree, the Rats had a flow of information coming in not even the PsyNet could beat.

They knew where Henry Scott's people were landing, their numbers, the approximate type and number of their weapons within seconds of each landing. All that data was routed at once to the DarkRiver teams in charge of holding the city as SnowDancer held the mountains.

The tactical split showed a massive amount of trust from both packs—because some of that mountain land was DarkRiver territory, and if San Francisco fell, then Henry Scott's army would have the perfect location in which to dig in and throw assault after assault at the wolves. Both parts of the defense had to hold if they were to win this battle.

"A new team's rappelling down near Russian Hill," Teijan reported to Clay, "and a bigger one has surrounded Nikita's building."

Clay's voice came through peppered with the sounds of gunfire. "She said she didn't need backup, but—"

"Wait." Teijan swore low and hard. "Nikita doesn't like people poaching on her territory. Fifteen attackers just went down with exploding brain syndrome." There was no other way to put it—on the video feed coming through a street camera, Scott's people fell where they stood, their brains leaking out their ears.

The survivors wisely decided to get the hell out of Nikita's zone.

Teijan smiled, switched connections. "They're coming your way, Vaughn." He had, he decided, developed a sudden soft spot for Nikita Duncan, especially given that Psy loyal to her were also feeding information into the Rats' network.

Catching a new piece of data, he switched connections again. "Lucas, I've got jet-choppers flying into SoMa. You need to be prepared for aerial attack." Connected as he was to the communications systems, he heard the DarkRiver alpha say, "Judd, can you deflect?" just as the assault craft began to drop small, high-impact bombs.

"Got it."

On the screen, Teijan watched the bombs arrow back to the jet-choppers, turning them into spectacular fireballs.

"Holy fuck," Zane muttered from where he was holding contact with the wolves. "It kind of freaks me out that this guy's been in the region the whole time without us knowing."

Teijan had met Judd Lauren earlier that day, had to agree with Zane. "At least he's on our side." Pulling up screen after screen of information, he patched in the telepaths and telekinetics supplied by Nikita and Anthony. "Full unit heading through Chinatown to DarkRiver HQ. Ensure the guards are shielded against mental attacks."

"Understood. Message communicated to all Tp units in range."

Zane tapped a screen. "Enemy's ignoring the bunker," he said, referring to the third subbasement of a building owned by DarkRiver on the outskirts of Chinatown but held under the name of an unrelated corporation. Right now, it was home to the leopard healer and her team, as well as the mate of the DarkRiver alpha, their child having been taken to safety by the evacuation team. "Would you have your mate in a war zone, Teijan?"

"Yes," he said without hesitation. "The alpha pair *must* always be part of a fight. Sascha's safe in the bunker. Pure Psy has no idea it exists." If there was a breach, Teijan had a team standing by to whisk them out and away through the tunnels. "Whoa!" He punched a fist into the air as Judd "Freaking Scary" Lauren reversed a missile right into a stealthcraft, turning the night sky incandescent.

But the sweet moment was cut short an instant later as Zane ripped off his earpiece, clapped his hand to his ear. "Oh fuck, something bad just happened in the mountains."

Chapter 51

AGONY HAZED THROUGH Hawke's brain. And he realized that Henry Scott might just have outthought them after all. "Brenna," he said into the mike, "can you block that?" It was almost impossible to speak.

Brenna's voice came out garbled, and he went to switch to a better channel . . . when he figured out it was his hearing that had gone, blood dripping down the sides of his face from violently ruptured eardrums. Unable to figure out what she was saying, he scanned the combat zone. A large number of his people were down, hands clasped over their ears. Others remained standing, but it was clear their balance was shot.

The only ones unaffected were the human members of the pack. In front of him, Kieran pushed aside a packmate in the line of fire and took on an attacker in hand-to-hand combat, while a reinjured Sam, his shoulder bearing a field dressing, dragged SnowDancer after fallen SnowDancer to safety. But there weren't many human packmates. Not enough.

Henry's men weren't even bothering to shoot anymore. Instead, they were walking up to dazed and bleeding wolves, and smashing them in the backs of their heads. Prisoners, Hawke thought as he shot down as many of the enemy as he could, Scott wanted prisoners. To torture? For experimentation? It didn't matter. No SnowDancer would ever suffer as Hawke's father had suffered. He kept on shooting, covering those soldiers darting out to drag in unconscious or hurt packmates. But even with an alpha's strength, he was no longer as fast or as effective.

His people continued to fall under brutal crunches of bone.

They had one last weapon. His wolf had scented her on the air currents, the autumn and spice of her as vivid to him as the blood that saturated the air. The only problem was, he didn't want to use her that way.

SIENNA dug her nails into the pine needle–strewn earth. They were falling onto their knees one by one, her friends, her family, *Hawke.*

Energy rippled through her body, a massive buildup of X-fire that would need to be earthed soon—or used in combat, as it was meant to be used. "Hawke, I'm here," she whispered, not knowing whether to intervene or to wait for the signal as agreed. If she entered the conflict at the wrong moment, she could ruin everything.

Suddenly afraid that there would be no signal because Hawke was dead, she spread out her telepathic senses in a desperate search. Her mind recoiled from that of another powerful telepath, but Henry Scott had sensed her. She saw his eyes flick open as he searched for the unfamiliar mind.

"Please," she whispered as the attackers began slamming their weapons down on SnowDancer skulls. "Use me." *Let me do this.*

Her breath was a razor in her chest when a howl—broken, the cadence all wrong—lifted into the air. It didn't sound like it should have, but she understood.

It was time.

Abandoning any attempt at secrecy, she walked out onto the night-cloaked battlefield bathed in the crimson and gold shimmer of cold fire. The enemy might have been Silent, but they went pale at the sight of her. An instant later, they began to shoot. She would've taken evasive action . . . except the flames around her repelled everything, melting the bullets down to nothing, reflecting the lasers back at the shooters.

It was then that she realized Judd couldn't have acted as the failsafe. No bullet would've gotten through. That wasn't the scariest part—her link to the LaurenNet was shielded by cold fire even Sienna wouldn't be able to breach, the ultimate defensive measure from a martial mind. But that was no longer an issue. She knew what to do now, and she would do it after the battle was done and her pack was safe.

Angry and sickened at the sight of the broken and hurt SnowDancers around her, Sienna spread out her arms, palms facing the sky. And the fire with the cold, cold heart touched the enemy, and they weren't there anymore. She aimed the most powerful wave at Henry Scott, knowing he'd try to get his men to teleport him out.

The bastard screamed high and shrill before he disappeared. She didn't know if he was dead, but she did know the attacking force should've retreated at the sight of her. Yet bullets continued to fly, now aimed at the fallen changelings.

No.

Something arctic and dark and deadly rose up inside of her as the X-fire emerged in a straight line on either side of her body, cutting the enemy in the way in half and cauterizing the massive wounds with such flawlessness, it appeared the men had fallen into two neat pieces. The rest of them were trapped beyond the wall of voracious flame, but they continued to shoot. And then her mind, a huge, vast, endless thing that saw and heard every sigh, every heartbeat, caught the whisper of more of them coming down through the mountains. They'd slipped in past the defenses when the sonic weapon took out the changelings as well as the feral wolves, and now they thought to flank them from behind.

"Traitor!" The word came from the throats of those in front of her and she knew them then. Pure Psy. Zealots. They would not back down.

Very well.

The cold, dark thing inside of her shoved aside all else . . . and the flames began to feed. Screams filled the air, filled her consciousness, filled the sky. The monster inside of her, she thought with a small part of the endless vastness that was her mind, had seized control.

The problem was . . . the Psy weren't the only targets in the vicinity.

HAWKE pulled his injured out of range of those Pure Psy operatives who'd been trapped on this side of the divide when

Sienna created that bladelike wall of X-fire. It was clear the enemy would not surrender, but trapped as they were, he offered them one final chance. The response was a hail of bullets, so he gave the order. When it was done, he checked on his people. Most were staring shell-shocked at Sienna as she blazed in a storm of crimson and gold, her hair flying in a terrible breeze, her eyes caverns of pure, raw power.

At first the wall of cold fire, it had touched the enemy alone, but now it changed shape, became a wave that rippled outward in both directions, growing ever closer to the injured and bleeding SnowDancers.

Ignoring the pain of shattered eardrums barely begun to heal thanks to his strength as alpha, he screamed, "Sienna!" as he ran to her, even knowing she couldn't hear him inside the inferno that consumed her, until it poured out of her eyes, her mouth, her every pore and every cell. The cold burn of it hit him a meter from the quickly creeping edge.

He knew she'd told him not to do it, that the X-fire would kill him the same as anyone else if she wasn't in conscious control. But he had to stop her, had to save her. If she took the life of even one SnowDancer and survived to witness what she'd done, it would break her.

"Baby, you better be in there!" Running back, he got a racing start and jumped through the flames, expecting to fry. Instead, he slammed into her body, his arms going around her, but she didn't go down—as if the cold fire had rooted her to the earth.

Her eyes, those eyes filled with red and gold, so stunning, so lethal, seemed to see him for a second, and he was almost certain he heard, *Forgive me*, deep inside his head before a dark, endless something grabbed his mind, punching through with such savage force that it brought him to his knees.

Shoving aside the throbbing pain as the shock of the impact vibrated through his body, he raised his head and looked out through the wall of X-fire, saw the flames lick out and over his people at a speed not even a wolf could outrun.

No.

It spread, a crackling wave of wild color over the injured, over those that stood guard, over the sentries and into the forest, going endlessly in every direction until his people were consumed by it. Until they burned up in it, so fast and hard that there were no screams. Only a terrible, endless silence.

"No, Sienna, no," he said, rising to hold her to him in a futile attempt to get through to the woman behind the vast dark of ravenous power. She'd come to save them, but what was inside of her, it had broken free, and now she killed the very pack she'd wanted to protect. His wolf knew what he had to do, but he couldn't snap her neck, couldn't erase her.

God help him, he couldn't, not even to save SnowDancer.

A minute, an eternity later, the flames blinked out, and Sienna sagged in his arms.

"Sienna." He was shocked by how very light she was, how very fragile. "Don't you dare leave me."

When he raised his head, he looked first toward the Pure Psy side, unable to bear what he'd glimpse on the other. *Everything*—the enemy, the trees, the grass, the rocks—was gone, smears of ash barely visible even to his night vision. Agonizing pain in his heart, he turned. And saw. "Oh, baby, I understand." So smart, his Sienna, so aware that his wolf would know each and every one of his people, feral wolves included. "There's no need for forgiveness, you hear me?"

Her eyes flickered open for an instant, and they weren't the night sky of a cardinal. They were a startling, amazing gold untouched by crimson. "A hundred years," she whispered. "That would've been nice, don't you think?"

"This isn't over yet."

"The LaurenNet link remains protected," she said, and he had the impression she was talking to herself. "Strange. But it doesn't matter." Gold melting to blue in her eyes, she pushed him hard without warning, ending up sprawled on the earth. "I love you." Blue flame licked up that wild tangle of ruby red, the scent of burned hair sharp and acrid.

Man and wolf both realized what she intended to do, said, *FUCK NO!*

Using the doorway she'd opened when she punched into his mind, the wolf shoved wild changeling energy into her, bowing her back, snapping her eyes open again, and shutting off that lethal blue flame. "What have you done?" A question filled with horror as the violent snap of the mating bond brought him to his knees beside her.

* * *

IN the middle of a San Francisco street under siege from two
Pure Psy units, Judd clutched his head. "No," he whispered,
and then there was no more thought.

HOURS away, in a protected safe zone in the middle of a different mountain range, Walker Lauren's mind went blank as
something crashed into him so hard, he didn't even have a
chance to alert the other guardians. *The childre—*
    Meters away, Toby lay slumped on a tabletop, while Mar-
lee crumpled off her chair and to the floor.

IN the den, the command center was thrown into chaos as
Brenna fell where she stood. "Judd!" Mariska yelled, slamming to her knees beside Brenna's limp body. "Find out if
anything's happened to Judd!"

HAWKE allowed Lara to heal him first after it was all over,
because without him, she would collapse under the weight of
the injured.
    "Where's Sienna?" she asked him after she finished heal-
ing the remaining damage to his eardrums.
    His wolf hated the answer he had to give, the choice he'd
had to make. "I had Drew take her up to the lake in the
mountains. She's unconscious." He didn't know what other
mated pairs saw through the bond, but he saw rippling crimson and gold, their bond so raw and new it was a painful ache.
    Right now, the X-fire was a placid pool, the battle had
drained Sienna at such a deep level. But it would grow
again—colder, stronger, more voracious. When it did, the
bond would give him enough warning that he'd be able to
take his mate deep into the lake, far, far below the surface.
Where he'd hold her as the cold fire consumed them both, its
destructive fury dampened by the water. The stone walls of
the den, far thicker and stronger than the rocks Sienna had
neutralized, and reinforced with titanium plates in places,

would protect the pack if the water and the distance weren't enough.

"Walker and the kids?" Lara's eyes were haunted when they met his.

He touched his hand to her hair in wordless comfort. "In the same state as Brenna and Judd. Do you want everyone moved here?" Judd had been taken to the bunker in the city, while the others remained in the safe zone.

"No." She began to heal a female soldier whose brain was swelling inside her skull. "It's probably better if we don't move them, since we have no idea why they collapsed."

"The cats will come up to help once they take care of their own injured." DarkRiver had taken far less damage, would hold the city and the perimeter against any opportunistic attacks until SnowDancer was functional again. "Take anything you need from me," he said, his wolf torn between his duty to the pack and his need to be with Sienna.

The only thing that soothed him, that allowed him to hold his focus on channeling pack energy into Lara, was that Sienna wasn't alone. Everyone in the combat zone had seen what she'd done. Everyone understood the price she would pay. No one would leave her alone in the dark.

It was over five hours later when Judd staggered into the infirmary, supported by Clay and Vaughn. Since Lara, exhausted, needed a break anyway, Hawke sat her down with an order not to move, before turning to Judd as the other male braced himself against a bed. "Brenna?" the lieutenant asked, his voice raw. "My family?"

"Unconscious, but otherwise fine." Hawke pushed him into a chair when the former Arrow threatened to topple over. "What the hell happened to all of you? Did Henry—"

But Judd was shaking his head. "You."

Hawke frowned, looked at Vaughn. "Did he hit his head when he fell?"

"Mating bond," Judd muttered. "Shoved the balance—" It was the last thing he said before he slumped.

Clay caught him before he would've fallen off the chair, and together with Vaughn got him into a bed in the same room as Brenna.

"The sonic shockwave was heard as far as the city,"

Vaughn told him afterward, "but it wasn't strong enough to incapacitate."

"Do we have enough people to cover in case they come back?" He knew Riley had been liaising with the cats, but he hadn't had a chance to talk to the lieutenant.

A nod. "WindHaven falcons are sweeping over the area now—it was a good idea to hold them in reserve. Rats have city intelligence covered."

Before Hawke could ask anything else, Vaughn clamped a hand over his shoulder. "Look after your people, Hawke. We'll handle it."

Trust, Hawke thought, came in many forms. A baby in his arms. A surge of deadly flame licking over his people. A leopard guarding the gate. "Go."

THE first thing Judd did when he managed to pierce the veil of consciousness at dawn was to check his mate and family were fine. The second was to find Alice Eldridge's bed, which had been pushed into a quiet corner of the hectic infirmary. She lay as silent and lifeless as ever, her secrets locked inside her mind.

Judd had a conscience. He also knew he might've been tempted to tear Alice's mind apart in a search for answers if it would save Sienna, but whoever had taken Alice had done something to her. Her mind was sewn up so tight it was better protected than that of most Psy—the problem was, Alice's shields had been locked into place. The only way to penetrate them without a very specific telepathic "key," now lost in time, would be to kill her.

Exhausted, his head in his hands as he leaned his elbows on her bed, he almost missed the beep on the monitor above the bed. Then it sounded again. Jerking upright, he searched for Lara, saw Hawke carrying the healer into the office where she had a sofa. From the protective way the alpha held her, it appeared she'd lost consciousness, unsurprising given the number of injuries SnowDancer had suffered.

"Alice," he whispered, turning to clasp his hand around the woman's thin one as he kept an eye on the electronic readout above her head.

Her eyes fluttered open. So deep and intense was the brown of her irises that it was difficult to distinguish pupil from iris even when she focused on Judd's face. Her lips parted, as if she'd speak, but her throat emitted no sound. Squeezing her hand, he reached over to snag some ice chips off a trolley to wet her throat.

"Arrow," she said in a hoarse whisper, but there was no fear in her, only defiance.

"Former." Perhaps he should've waited, but he had to get the information while she was conscious and lucid. "We need to know if you discovered anything about X-Psy that would help save one about to go critical."

Confusion. "X?"

"Cold fire," he said. "X-fire. *Remember.*"

Not even a glimmer of recognition and he knew the Ghost had been right. Alice had asked for her own memories to be erased. It had to be the reason why she'd ended up in cryonic suspension rather than assassinated, her abductors needing time to work out how to retrieve the data. However, he refused to give up—she'd been in stasis for so long. There was no knowing how it had affected her mind. "The burning ones," he said, using every key word he could think of. "Fire. Flame. Synergy."

An instant of piercing clarity. "Find the valve."

Chapter 52

HAWKE FELT EVERYONE in the infirmary sag with relief when the first of the healers from the other sectors arrived. They'd asked to come before the conflict, but SnowDancer couldn't risk putting all its healers so close to danger. But now, they were needed, and nothing could keep them away.

It cost him, but he didn't leave until the healers pronounced that the injured had been stabilized enough that he could take a break. He headed straight for the woman who was the beating heart of him. The tent Drew had rigged over Sienna's unconscious body was empty, their packmates having left when they sensed his approach.

It was as if she'd been waiting for him.

"No." It was a whisper so quiet, even most changelings wouldn't have heard it. But Sienna was Hawke's, had always been his, whether she'd known it or not, whether he'd accepted it or not.

"Yes," he murmured, dipping his finger in a bottle of water and rubbing it over her lips. "Yes."

A shake of her head, but her lips parted, searching for more. He trickled some into her mouth, making low, deep sounds of encouragement in his throat. "Come on now. Open those pretty eyes for me."

"Dark."

He didn't know what she meant by that, but driven by his wolf, he leaned down to nip at her lower lip. "Hawke," he said. "That's the word you need to be saying."

Lines formed between her eyebrows.

"Hawke," he repeated, squeezing her hip. "Hawke."

"Hawke." It was a sleepy murmur as her eyes flickered open. That cardinal gaze displayed a wild burst of unadulterated happiness for one stunning instant before it was wiped away by shocked horror as she scrambled up into a sitting position. "What did you do?" A mental door slammed shut with such force it shot pinpricks of light behind his eyelids.

Snarling, he gripped her jaw, "Don't you dare try to block me." His wolf began to batter at the wall it couldn't see but could feel, tied as they were by the mating bond, a bond that would never allow that kind of distance.

The barrier broke in an avalanche of emotion, tangling them up until he could sense her in every part of him. Taking in a shuddering breath, he clasped her head between his hands and said, "Try that again and I'll paddle you."

Her eyes narrowed. "Don't you talk to me like that."

The laugh came from somewhere deep inside him. "Good morning to you, too, sunshine." Then he kissed her. And kept on kissing her until she bit down hard on his lower lip. "What?" he growled.

"Air."

The gasp gave him the impetus to rein himself back. "Judd said your family is okay." Hawke hadn't asked too much more, especially when the former Arrow told him what Alice Eldridge had said before lapsing back into the same comalike state she'd been in since entering the den.

REMEMBERING the wrenching sensation that had torn at her before she lost consciousness, Sienna closed her eyes and stepped out into what should've been the LaurenNet.

It wasn't.

She blinked, shook her head.

"Sienna." Lips on her jaw.

She thrust a hand into his hair. "Stop distracting me." Yet she turned her face toward his, taking just a little more in spite of the dread that knotted up her throat—and giving, too. He was changeling, touch essential to his happiness. "The LaurenNet is gone."

His head snapped up. "What?"

"Shh." She touched psychic fingers to the sparkling wolf-blue and flame-hued rope that connected her to Hawke—*oh, God*—but tempting as it was to focus on the beauty and terror of it, she moved on, spreading her psychic senses.

She found Judd first, linked as he was to Hawke. Bonded to him was a mind Sienna was used to seeing in the Lauren-Net, though it wasn't Psy—Brenna. Judd was also connected in a wholly different way to another mind she recognized: Walker. She, too, was connected to both Judd and Walker, and all three of them had direct links to Toby and Marlee.

However, those weren't the only minds in this web.

Nine other minds, strong and wild in a way she couldn't explain, speared out from the central core that was Hawke, spokes on a wheel. A tenth mind was held closer to his own in a more protective way. All were fortified by natural shields it would take savage force to pierce—a stab of pain, of memory—and not a single one was Psy. A number of other minds connected outward from the spokes.

"I can see Lara, see your lieutenants," she whispered, amazed by how "messy" this network was, so many intertwined and crisscrossing connections. "Indigo . . . I know her. She's sparks and strength and *life*. And Drew, bonded to her so deep and strong." Her heart smiled. "That must be Cooper's mate." Even here, he was protective, her mind tucked close to his.

"Riley. I know him, too." He was the calm in the midst of the storm, the rock on which every one of them depended. "Strange," she whispered, seeing how the most powerful bond Riley had disappeared into nowhere. "Mercy."

Strong, slightly rough fingers on her jaw. "Everyone is safe?"

"Yes." She touched psychic fingers to the bond that was Lara's. It wasn't like the others, and she knew on an intuitive level that the tie between alpha and healer had its own set of rules, as would the links between the lieutenants and the healers bonded to them. So complex. So glorious.

"Sienna."

Opening her eyes, she met those of a wolf. The LaurenNet, she thought, had held Judd even after Hawke blood-bonded him, because the neo-sentience within the familial network had known they couldn't survive without him. But what

Hawke had done on the battlefield had tipped the balance—
and tied as the family was to one another, Judd and Sienna
had wrenched everyone into the SnowDancer Web.

"Good." He kissed her hard. "Now explain to me what the
hell you thought you were doing turning yourself into a human torch!"

Outraged by the accusation, she almost forgot what she'd
been going to say. Almost. "You idiot!" She pushed at his
shoulders, didn't manage to move him an inch. "It was *safe*!
I was wiped out; the flames would've consumed me alone."
She'd known after the X-fire slipped her grasp—cold, such
cold inside of her—that it was the only way to ensure she'd
never again cause that kind of carnage. "Why did you stop
me?"

"I took what was mine."

"What I did"—*sheer, unrelenting horror*—"might've
wiped me out for a short period, but I'm *not* stable, Hawke."

"You wanted me to watch you burn? Fuck that!" The wolf
stared out at her, arrogant and insulted and furious.

But she wasn't about to back down. "Yes! You should've
let me decommission the weapon." That was what she was,
how she should be treated. "Cut it," she ordered. "Cut the
mating bond." She'd already tried to do it, found she
couldn't—it wasn't a Psy construct, followed no rules of psychic power that she knew. "Cut it!"

"I'm changeling, baby." A growling statement. "I couldn't
cut it if I wanted to."

"I'll do it," she said, shivering with panic. "There must be
a way. I'll have to go into your mind and—"

His face was suddenly in hers. "Try it."

Flinching, she went to do just that, because she *would not*
hurt him, hurt any of them . . . and found she couldn't. He
was inside her, her mate—that impossible, beautiful word—
and the idea of violating him was anathema. "I'm sorry." Her
shoulders slumped. "For what I did before."

Bloated with power, she'd torn through his shields and
into his mind on that field of battle in a final, failed attempt
at saving her packmates even as she incinerated the enemy.
Hawke's wolf knew each and every one of his people, every
inch of his land, every one of the wild wolves—she'd thought

to keep them safe by "showing" the cold fire that they weren't to be touched. "How many—"

"You hurt *no one* in the pack." A ruthless tone that forced her to listen. "Not a single singed hair aside from your own, you extraordinary, crazy, beautiful woman."

Her lower lip shook, and then she found herself being wrenched forward into a crushing embrace, her face buried in his neck, her arms gripping at him. "I was so scared," she whispered, because she could admit that to him, to her wolf, who saw her through to the very soul. "Everyone's safe?"

A pause. "We have a number of injured. Lara collapsed earlier, will get up in a while, start again. The healers from the other sectors have begun to arrive."

She recalled the sickening crunch of bone as Henry's men smashed weapons into the backs of skulls. "Will it be enough?"

"No." The harsh truth of an alpha. "But we won't give up as long as they're hanging on."

"Is there—" She swallowed the huge lump in her throat. "My friends?"

His arms clenched around her. "Tai's critical. So is Maria."

No, no. "Evie's heart will break." And Lake. Strong, capable Lake. He loved Maria with a tenderness that seemed to gentle even her reckless spirit.

"No surrender." Unrelenting. Inexorable. "Never do we surrender."

"No surrender," she echoed, then took a long, shuddering breath.

"Does the word *valve* have any specific meaning to you on the psychic plane?" he asked, and when she shook her head, he told her what Alice Eldridge had said.

A sound of sheer rage escaped her mouth, and then she was punching her fist over and over against his chest. He let her expel the bitter anger, held her when she lay breathless against him. "I almost wish we'd never found her," she said, her chest rising up and down as she tried to gasp in air. "I told myself not to hope, but I *did*." A tiny secret part of her had been convinced the scientist would wake with the answers just in time to save her.

Other men might've given her pretty words of comfort, lies that meant nothing, but Hawke, he spoke to her martial mind, talking through the battle. "We weren't prepared for that sonic weapon." His tone told her that wouldn't happen again. "But because of you, we held the mountains."

"The city?" she asked, her voice hoarse.

"Leopards held it. A bit of structural damage but limited injuries thanks to the Rats, Judd, and Anthony's and Nikita's people. The Pure Psy operatives who survived turned tail and ran." He stroked his hand down her hair, long and slow and again. "I can feel the cold fire along our bond."

"Yes." The battle had only wiped her out for a time. It had done nothing to change the fundamental truth of the power amplification. "It's at fifty percent." And it was frigid, until it froze her bones. "It feels stronger." Darker. More cruel. Fear curled around her throat, tight as a noose. "Can we get farther away from the den?"

Hawke didn't question her, simply said, "I know a good spot."

They'd just stepped out of the tent when the power inside of her surged in a violent rage. Her knees locked, then gave out. She would've crumpled to the grass if Hawke hadn't clamped his hands on her upper arms as the X-fire threatened to shove out of her very skin.

"No." Even this deep into the mountains, the den was too close. Her friends, her family, her pack was too close. "Hawke, I can't hold it." Panic beat in her throat. "If I breach, it'll consume everyone in the vicinity." Her power had grown even more vast, even more voracious, would move out for miles in every direction.

Stone, steel, plascrete, nothing would stop its ravenous pulse.

Then she saw the scorching yellow and blazing crimson begin to divide and separate into pristine rivers inside her mind, in preparation for a final catastrophic merge. "I'm about to hit synergy!" Turning her into a human bomb of incalculable destructive power, one that would obliterate any trace of two packs called SnowDancer and DarkRiver, of a city called San Francisco, of a mountain range called the Sierra Nevada . . . and keep going.

If you ever go supernova, Ming's arctic voice, *the continent on which you stand might cease to exist.*

Ming had been wrong, she realized in that moment when her power was so pure, so clear. There was no *might* about it.

A warm male hand gripping her own, ripping her from the horrifying understanding of just what she was. "The lake," her wolf said.

She ran beside him. "It might blunt the impact." Part of her knew it wouldn't be enough, that even the deepest part of the lake couldn't contain the tidal wave of her power, but she had to believe. Then she felt an unexpected psychic burn inside of her, saw that the cold fire was eating away at her network shields, would soon pour out into the SnowDancer Web in a violent storm. It had never before threatened to penetrate a psychic network—but she'd never been this close to synergy.

Fear twisted knives of ice through her heart as they hit the water. "Hawke! The X-fire is spreading on the psychic plane. I can't cut my mental bonds, but you can—"

Wolf-blue slammed into her eyes. "Don't you dare ask me to hurt you. *Don't you fucking dare.*"

Pain ripped her in two, the world already tinged crimson and gold, and she realized her eyes were drowning in X-fire. A single tear trailed down her cheek as the frigid water reached her thighs. "I'll burn out your mind."

He continued to swim farther into the lake, pulling her along. "The others?"

The water hit her breasts, soaked into her chest, into her bones. "The web"—she kicked her legs in an attempt to help him—"will collapse without you." He was the center, the key. Had her family been part of it longer, they could've built failsafe bonds, but as it was, the web was a wholly changeling construct, created by ties of blood . . . Hawke's blood. "The changeling members won't suffer any ill effects.

"Walker and Judd"—she gasped past the cold that consumed her—"will be able to drag the children into a smaller LaurenNet." She 'pathed Judd a warning. Her sweet Toby, and smart, funny Marlee remained unconscious, a small blessing.

"When you die—" The words wouldn't come, and it had nothing to do with the fact that her body was in the coldest, deepest part of the lake. "When you die," she forced herself to say, "the psychic shock will tear me from the web, regardless of the links to my family." He'd become her anchor in every way and losing him would destroy her, ending her life and the threat of synergy. "We should dive just in case, but once separated from the web, I won't be a danger anymore."

Her wolf cupped her face, nothing but a wild devotion in his touch, in his voice. "Then what's there to be scared about?"

It broke her heart, that he was hers. "I love you." *I'm sorry.*

A caress down the mating bond, an untamed kiss that she knew was her wolf before he said, "Forever," and dived with her in his arms, the water closing over their heads in a sheet of sparkling blue.

Cold. So, so cold.

It was the last thing she had physical awareness of before the crimson and gold collided to create an inferno that poured over and through her shields with a vicious strength she could never hope to control. *Hawke!* It was a telepathic cry as the flame seared down the mating bond, turning it into an incandescent ribbon.

His arms clenched around her, shocking her back to the world for a single instant before she was wrenched to the psychic plane once again. She watched in horror as the rapacious tempest of her power surged into Hawke. Instead of burning out his mind, it encased it . . . and continued to spread out on the bonds that tied him to his lieutenants, their mates, the healers.

It wanted all of them.

No! No!

Chapter 53

THE FIRE RACED along the familial bonds, too.

First it hit Judd. Then it hit Walker. And held. She knew both men had risen to consciousness, were shielding to the limit of their strength to save the children as well as Brenna, but she also knew they'd fail. The power continued to pour out of her, surge after surge after lethal surge.

For a blazing instant, the SnowDancer Web was the most beautiful thing she had ever seen, a brilliant gold and crimson network lit with pure raw energy. It spoke not of death, but of life. But of course, that was a lie. Even as the minds of Hawke's lieutenants blazed a terrible red, Walker and Judd finally broke.

WALKER knew the moment before Sienna's strength overwhelmed him that he was going to break. Reaching out with his telepathy, he knocked both drowsy children back into unconsciousness. They wouldn't feel any pain, have any awareness of going into the final good-night.

Lara.

A single, painful thought before there was no more time. The brutal energy of an X shoved into his mind. For an instant, it was a thing of beauty, such unadulterated power that he was staggered by it. If only there was a way to harness this.

Then it rammed into his final telepathic shields, burning them to ash as the wave crashed. He had a moment to glimpse the web and think that the power was arrowing itself to him, as if he was some kind of lodestone. The flame—*so cold, so violent*—shoved into his psychic core a second later.

Death had never felt so exhilarating.

In the physical world, he went to his knees, his vision flame yellow and bloodred, but on the psychic plane, his telepathic reach was magnified a thousand times over for a gleaming instant, and he had time to be grateful that he hadn't been born that way, for a man was not meant to know the world's secrets.

He waited to die, to feel the frigid burn of an X's touch, but the power continued to pour through him. Gritting his teeth against the impact of it, he reached out to touch a telepathic hand to the children, found them unconscious but unharmed. That was when he focused his psychic eye beyond the avalanche of power. And saw something so incredible, it would've brought him to his knees if he hadn't already been on them.

The strange twisting motion at the center of his mental star, it had nothing to do with children, nothing to do with telepathy. It blazed diamond bright as it spun at phenomenal speed, acting as a filter for Sienna's energy. The destructive potential was trapped, eradicated, the rest returned to the network. The interconnected threads of the web continued to burn, but second by second, the vicious red was fading into a shimmering gold . . . until at last, there was no more raw power.

Walker's mind blinked out.

IT wasn't until two days later that everyone was functional enough to have a rational discussion. They met in the main conference room, the lieutenants from around the state coming in via comm feeds. Cooper's mate stood by his side, while the others in the SnowDancer Web, as the Laurens were calling it, took seats around the conference table. The only ones missing were the children, and the healers from the other sectors—they'd decided to head back home, leaving Lara as their representative.

"That was some trip," Tomás said, breaking the ice. "Holy hell, I was on speed for two days. I swear I ran patrol nonstop for thirty-six hours."

"We healed everyone," Lara said, flexing her fingers, her voice too jerky, too fast. "Everyone in the infirmary, everyone in the pack that we could find with even the slightest injury. Anyone have a sore back? Scratches?"

Beside her, Walker did something Hawke wouldn't have expected from the quiet, contained Psy. He put his hand under Lara's hair, curving it around her nape. It was a very changeling display of possession—a signal to every other male in the meeting that Lara was now off-limits.

Hawke's wolf approved.

"I had sex," Drew said with a grin. "Lots and lots and *lots* of sex."

Indigo threw a balled-up piece of paper at him, but she was grinning. Catching the paper, he said, "Hey, no use in good energy going to waste."

Everyone chuckled, the atmosphere nothing like it would've been a few days ago if they'd been talking of Sienna's power. "So," Hawke said, playing his fingers through his mate's hair, "it looks like we all got a boost."

"She acts like a mini-reactor," Walker said in that intense, contained way that had everyone paying attention. "Her power is infinite."

"So we're going to keep getting mega-hits like this?" Tomás's dark brown eyes sparkled as they landed on Sienna's down-bent head. "Not that I don't appreciate it, sugar, but it did make me 'hyper,' according to my mother."

"Toby hasn't slept for two days and counting," Lara said. "He outran his changeling friends—he thinks it's wuuuuuunderful. His word."

Sienna spoke for the first time. "I think that was a one-off," she said, twisting her hands under the table where she thought Hawke couldn't see it. "Walker and I have been talking, and our theory is that it was because I was trying to contain the power and it built up to a critical mass. If I release a steady stream of it, it'll boost your energy levels without having a discernible impact like it did this time around."

Leaning over, Hawke nipped at her ear. She turned bright red. *"Hawke."*

"No one is angry at you, Sienna," he murmured. "Look at them."

He saw her raise her head, glance around, felt the staggering relief that poured down the mating bond. When she turned and reached up to pull his hand from her hair, bring it to her lips, he was undone, his wolf her slave.

Looking away from her only when she put his hand down on the table, her fingers tangled with his, he found the others had begun to speak amongst themselves, giving him and Sienna privacy. "It's clear that Walker acts as a filter . . . a valve," he said during a lull in the conversation.

Matthias looked troubled. "What if something happens to Walker?"

"We've been talking about that," Sienna spoke up, a confidence in her voice that had been missing earlier. "The helix appeared in Walker's mind around the time my mother was pregnant with me, so there's a chance one of the other Psy in the network would develop the ability."

If they were right, she'd explained to Hawke, the implications were astounding. It meant the neo-sentience in a psychic network didn't only organize the network, it could *influence* it on the individual level. Which, if the rumors about the current rot in the PsyNet were true, led to some very disturbing suppositions.

"However," Sienna continued, "we're not relying on that. Now that we know what Walker's mind does, Judd thinks he can train his own to mimic the effect. It won't work anywhere near as well, and the power surge will be a *lot* rougher—"

Matthias cut her off. "It'll work." A fierce smile. "That's the important thing."

Kenji glanced at Walker. "Does it take anything out of you?"

"No." Walker tapped a finger on the table. "In fact, I've never felt more alive. For the first time in my life, I'm making complete use of my abilities. The valve runs automatically in the background, so it won't interfere with my normal duties."

Jem stared at the Psy male. "Wow, I never heard you say so many words in a row before."

That made Tomás and Drew burst out laughing. Alexei, Cooper, and Matthias were a tad more restrained, but even they had grins on their faces. Hawke's wolf laughed deep within. His pack, his mate. All here. Life was good . . . except for the fact the Psy Council now knew that not only Sienna, but the entire Lauren family, was alive.

WALKER kept his hand on Lara's lower back as they exited the meeting room. "Do you have patients?"

"No. I healed everyone, remember?" A sparkling look from those tawny eyes. "*Everyone!* Even the ones who were dying. I was super-healer. Or okay, super-healer with super-healer assistants. Did you know Tai kissed Evie right in front of Indigo? With *tongue*. And Maria baked everyone cupcakes."

"You're still power-drunk." It made sense. From what they'd learned over the past few years, it appeared that there was *always* a neo-sentience in any psychic network, and even the most embryonic one would've understood that the healers needed the power more than anyone else. Except that there'd been so much energy, giving Lara and the others extra really hadn't been necessary. "How many fingers am I holding up?"

Lara giggled. Slapped a hand over her mouth. "I'm so happy—all those injured, healed. I actually ran out of people. Too bad Alice Eldridge isn't a wolf or I could've woken her up. Elias is kinda mad I found him and fixed him up without leaving even a teeny-tiny scar that he could brag about. When are the rest of the juveniles coming back? I bet you they'll give me something to heal."

Hiding his laugh at the rapid speech that reminded him of his daughter—who was attempting to break the world skipping record in the White Zone—he nudged her in the direction he wanted her to go. "Tomorrow."

"Oh, good."

As she slid an arm around his waist, he said, "Drew said he had lots of sex. Want to do that instead?" He needed to claim her on a fundamental level, to touch and stroke and caress and know that she had come out of the flames of war unscathed.

Lara's head snapped up. "Now?"

"Yes."

She grabbed his hand as if to drag him along behind her. "Hurry up."

"Wait," he said as they reached her quarters, "are you too power-drunk to give consent?"

Lara recited the periodic table back at him. "See, all my faculties. Now can we have sex?"

"Yes."

Her breath turned jagged when he nudged her back into her quarters and locked the door behind himself. Those big eyes didn't get any smaller when he unbuttoned and stripped off his shirt, then kicked off his shoes and socks. As he took the belt out of his jeans, she sucked in a breath, walked forward.

And bit him.

Right on his pectorals, sinking her teeth deep enough to leave a dark red mark. It snapped what control he'd maintained, and he found himself picking her up and throwing her on the bed. She got up as if to get away, but he'd been in the pack long enough to know her wolf was playing with him. Pulling off her shoes, he tore off her jeans and panties with a lack of finesse that might've worried him if Lara hadn't been making low, needy sounds in the back of her throat.

"Take off your sweatshirt." It was an order.

One she obeyed with shaking hands.

"The bra."

It was gone an instant later. However, instead of lying back, she stretched out on her hands and knees in front of him, looking up with a distinctively wolfish look in her eye. "I'll be gentle." Solemn words that made him want to smile. "I know you're a virgin. Psy don't have sex, do they?"

"No." Intimate touch was forbidden in the PsyNet. "But I think I have the concept figured out." Surrendering to temptation, he stroked his hand down the curve of her back.

She arched into the touch, her skin shimmering with heat. "Are you teasing me?" A suspicious look, even as she rose up on her knees to tug open the top button of his jeans.

"A little." He bent down to nuzzle at her, biting her gently on the earlobe as he'd done that night in her apartment when they'd talked and done so much more.

She shivered. "You remembered."

He remembered everything about her, from the way she made those tiny sounds when he licked his tongue across hers, to the way she pushed her breast into his hand when he pinched her nipple. "On your back," he whispered, because the need in him was a demanding thing, one that wanted to brand, to claim in a way he'd never before experienced or understood.

Obeying without argument, she braced herself on her elbows, looking at him with those brilliant eyes as he shucked his jeans. Her gulped-in breath was a caress across his senses. Taking a grip on her ankles, he spread her thighs. "Who do you belong to, Lara?" he asked quietly.

"You." It was a whisper. "Only you."

He wasn't surprised to feel her inside him, inside his very heart. Of course that was where she'd be—it was the only way to make sure he could protect her. Lara was one of the most vulnerable people he had ever met. She had the capability to face down even Hawke if she thought the alpha was causing himself harm, but by that same token, she'd cut out her own heart and give it to him if it would keep him going. Walker wasn't sure how she'd survived this long without someone to watch out for her.

"Walker . . . did we just . . ." Shocked words, rapid breaths.

Chapter 54

HE MOVED UP the bed to rise over her. "Lara?"

"Yes?"

"Let's have sex first, talk later." He might've been Silent once, but that man was long gone. The one who remained was holding on to his control by the skin of his teeth.

Hands on his chest, shaping and petting. "Okay."

When he reached down to caress the slick heat between her thighs, she grabbed his wrist. "Let's skip the foreplay this time."

"Okay." Spreading her thighs, he stroked into her, going slow because she seemed too tiny to take him. The heat of her was a sensual jolt that threatened to wrench the reins from his grasp. He'd thought about sinking into her tight grasp, thought about exploring this beautiful body with its soft curves, but never had he realized the savage impact of this act.

Mine. It was a primitive thought.

Right then, she locked her legs around him and thrust her body up at the same time.

Lara cried out as the aggressive heat of Walker slammed home inside of her, clutching at his back in a vain effort to find an anchor. Her mind was awash in shock and wonder, her body buzzed. She parted her lips to speak, found the words stolen by a demanding male mouth that set her free only long enough to ask, "Does it hurt?"

"So good." She bit at his jaw, and he reacted the way he always did when she did that.

He took over her mouth, licking and tasting and demanding . . . while moving in her, slow and deep, one callused hand on her hip to pin her in place. Having hungered for this most intimate of skin privileges for so very long, she met him kiss for kiss, touch for touch, but it was crystal clear she'd never be the dominant in bed.

Her wolf had no argument with that. She was a healer. She needed a mate who was strong, able to care for her as she cared for others. Kissing at his neck as he reached down to cup her buttocks, to angle her for a deeper penetration, she felt her entire body clench. "Walker! *Please.*"

His next strokes were hard and fast and possessive, his kisses the same. Pleasure rippled over her in waves and then crashed, breaking her into a thousand splinters. She held him to the end. Never was she letting this man and his heart go. Never.

IT was after the third round of sex—yes, she was sore, and no, she didn't give a damn—that Lara worked off enough energy that her brain started to function on any level other than the sensual. Snuggling close to Walker, who lay on his side beside her, stroking her curves with those delicious hands, she kissed his chest, licking up the salt-laced taste of dark water and snow-dusted firs.

Her wolf snuggled up next to him, too, bathing itself in the radiance of the mating bond. It was strong and steady, just like the man who was her mate. "You know this is for life, right?" she asked, half-afraid he'd want to back off now that the buzz was gone.

"Yes." He stroked his hand over her butt. "The mating bond will make it easier to keep an eye on you."

"Walker."

He switched positions so he leaned over her. *"Lara."*

Oh, she knew she was going to have trouble with him—but damn if she wasn't looking forward to it. "Can you see us in the web?"

"Yes." A satisfied smile. "It's rearranged itself so you're by me. Where I can shield you."

"I never knew you were this possessive."

Her answer was a slow, hot kiss that had her rubbing

herself against his thigh. Before he could take over, she pushed him to his back and rose to straddle him. Those distinctive green eyes lingered on the modest swell of her breasts with such carnal intent, her toes curled. When he reached up to touch her, explore her, he did so with such intense focus she felt as if she was the most intriguing thing he had ever seen.

He pinched her nipple in precisely the way she'd whispered she enjoyed that sultry night in her apartment. "Lara?"

"Yes?" It was a trembling question.

"Teach me more of the foreplay you like."

She was a changeling, sensuality in her blood—and yet his blunt request had her breathless. "I like everything you do to me."

"In that case"—he flipped her onto her back again, spread her thighs—"I think we should explore the concept of oral sex."

Her brain hazed over. And stayed hazed.

Because once Walker Lauren put his mind to something, it didn't budge—and the man did not leave any task unfinished. "Hmm," he said after the orgasm left her a quivering mass of female flesh. "Let's do that again now that I know what I'm doing."

Now that he— "Touch me and die." Grabbing those big shoulders, she hauled him up.

"No more oral sex?" A quiet, sexy smile she knew only she would ever see.

Her entire body melted. "Oh, no. Yes to more oral sex." Pushing him onto his back, she slid down his body.

Her mate, she learned, knew some very interesting words.

JUDD had gone to Xavier's to pass over a data crystal encoded with information relating to a woman his friend had been searching for, for years, but as he waited for Xavier to finish speaking to someone in his office and come on out, he found a black-garbed male taking a seat on the moonlit back steps next to him.

He wasn't surprised—he'd expected this from the instant his family's cover had been blown. "Hello, Aden."

Aden looked out at the kitchen garden behind the church. "I did not expect to find you so near a place of worship."

"Have you come to kill me?"

"Those are my orders."

"Since I can teleport, that means Vasic is nearby."

Aden looked at him for the first time; that face with its high cheekbones, olive skin, and uptilted eyes was that of the quintessential Arrow. Cold. Without any indication of a man behind the mask. "Vasic was taken off Jax when you were," he said without warning, referring to the drug that turned Arrows into killers.

"Did it help him?"

"He says there was nothing left in him to save."

Judd's eyes went to the emblem on the shoulder of Aden's uniform, a single star. "Kaleb didn't give the order."

"Ming." Aden turned back to look at the garden. "He doesn't understand us, never has, though he once wore the badge of an Arrow."

Judd leaned forward to brace his arms on his knees. "I broke the code. I left the squad."

"To save an X." Aden echoed his move, unusual from a Silent Arrow. "Silence was meant to save the Xs, save all of us who don't fit into the normal world."

"It's failed, Aden."

"Yes. For some at least." A long pause. "The Council no longer exists, though the populace doesn't yet realize it. The factions are already forming behind the scenes."

"You're talking about a civil war." One that would devastate the Net.

"Perhaps it's been inevitable since the instant our race chose Silence."

Yes. "How long?"

"There'll be a small lull as each faction gathers support . . . months, Judd, not years."

Bells rang somewhere in the distance, and they both went quiet.

"Has Walker ever told you he had me as a student?" Aden asked after the echoes faded.

Judd shook his head. "He doesn't speak about his time in the squad's schoolroom."

"What he taught me . . . tell him it has saved the life and sanity of more than one Arrow."

Judd thought of his brother's brilliance at telepathic deceptions, without which they would've never escaped the Net, and wondered just how Aden had utilized those skills. "If you need me, I'll stand beside you."

"You exist. Sienna exists. It's enough. You not only survived, you've found happiness. I don't understand the emotion, but I know it's better than the dark. So do the others."

Hope, Judd thought. That was the word Aden couldn't find. "What will you do?"

"Silence is falling." No change in the tone of his voice, nothing to betray the scale of what he was talking about. "We will watch, wait, and fight the war when it comes."

Judd didn't ask on which side Aden and the Arrows would stand. He knew.

DIZZIED by the turn of events that had left her with decades, maybe a century left to live, Sienna was more than grateful when Hawke took her to the privacy of their cabin. She found herself being kissed an instant later. She wanted to nip at those firm lips, even knowing it would be a very bad idea. Might just get her devoured. "Wait, I—"

"No talking," he said, a bare millimeter between them. "Skin privileges first."

"Talk first." She dug her nails into his chest.

Picking her up, he pinned her to the wall, her legs around his waist. "Okay." Clever hands opening the buttons of her shirt, a sexy mouth on the skin of her throat and the upper curves of her breasts.

"Hawke." It was a moan, her fingers in his hair.

"You don't need these, do you?" Her jeans and panties were torn into fragments moments later, his hand cupping her with heated possessiveness as he kissed the life out of her.

"Off." She pulled at the sides of his shirt, heard a button ping to the floor.

He refused to help her, more interested in playing with her slick flesh, in teasing and tormenting the breasts he'd bared by cutting her bra with a claw. But Sienna had claws of her own. Putting her lips to his ear, she said, "I want to rub my breasts against your chest."

She was on her back on the bed with breathtaking speed, a naked Hawke above her moments later. He snapped his teeth at her. Laughing, she did the same. And then she pulled him down and did exactly as she'd demanded.

Her wolf let her play, played with her, and it wasn't until they were lying on the rug in front of the fireplace—Hawke dressed in a pair of jeans barely buttoned, her in his shirt— nibbling at a tray of food that Sienna plucked out the key she wore around her neck. "What does this open?"

Rolling to his feet, he went out to the vehicle to return with a small metal box that he placed beside her before resuming his previous position. Knowing the wolf wouldn't give her a clue, she slid in the key and unlocked the box. Lined with blue velvet, it was empty.

Strange how she understood. "For the memories we'll make." Her throat grew thick, and though she knew there was a chance his answer would break her heart, she had to ask the question she hadn't dared to until this moment. "How did we mate?" *Had the events on the battlefield pushed him into it? Did he regret it?* She couldn't speak those fears aloud, but they lived in her heart, bleak and painful.

HAWKE glanced up at Sienna and knew that he held the balance of power, that what he said next would affect the remainder of their life together in the most profound of ways. He could answer her question without giving anything away, without tilting that balance. Or he could make another choice, one that took them beyond lovers, beyond mates, and to a true alpha pair.

"You were right," he said and saw a storm of emotion in those extraordinary cardinal eyes.

It would've been easy for her to smile, to accept the admission at face value, but that wasn't who Sienna was. "About what?" she asked, watching him with an expression that had turned a little guarded.

His wolf wasn't surprised. Sienna had her own scars, and

it would take time for those to fade. Hawke was okay with that—because he was planning to be there for the long haul, ready to battle any nightmare that dared touch her. "About the mating bond." Rising up into a sitting position, he braced one elbow over a drawn-up knee. "It wasn't the wolf holding me back.

"When Rissa died," he said, giving Sienna this last secret corner of his heart, "it was like having a part of me ripped out. I didn't speak for a month, didn't do anything but sit by her grave." Boy and wolf, they'd both kept hoping that if he wished hard enough, Rissa would come back. "It took me a long time to accept that she was gone, that the only thing I had of her was the hole she'd left inside me."

Sienna moved close enough to curve her hand around the calf of the leg he'd raised, her eyes inky black. But she didn't interrupt, this woman who understood him in ways he wasn't sure he understood himself, who'd forced him to face the cold, hard truth of the lies he'd told himself over the years. That didn't make it any simpler to rip the scab off this wound—hell, he was alpha for a reason. Vulnerability wasn't a sensation he enjoyed.

It made his next words rough, almost harsh. "It was easier to believe that my shot at mating died with Rissa than to risk that kind of pain again." Thrusting his hand into her hair, he shook his head. "Except I never had a prayer when it came to you. You're in my every breath and every thought, intertwined so deep inside me that love's not a strong enough word—you have my devotion, your name branded on my soul, my wolf yours to command. A hundred years? It'll never be enough. I want eternity."

Tears, slow and quiet, ran down Sienna's cheeks.

He wasn't finished. "You have the power to tear me to pieces, to wound me so deep and true that I'll never recover. What Rissa's death did to the boy I was? You have the ability to do a thousand times worse to the man I've become. Some part of me knew that was a possibility from the instant you walked into my life—so I tried to keep you at arm's length even as I demanded everything you had. I was a coward."

"Hawke, no." On her knees in front of him, she shook her

head in open distress, wiping away her tears with the backs of her hands. "I should've never said that."

"You called me on my bullshit," he said, raising his other knee and bringing her in between. "Made me mad as fucking hell, and it'll probably do the same in the future when you do it again. Fair warning."

Her lips lifting up at the corners in a shaky smile, she twined her arms around his neck. "You mean you're not going to become tame and well behaved now that we're mated?" Tiny kisses on the corners of his lips, on his cheeks, on his jaw. "Damn."

Leaning into the affection, he allowed her to soothe the sharp edges within. "I can pretend if you want." He petted the sweet curve of her behind, naked beneath the tails of the shirt she'd commandeered.

A husky laugh. "I wouldn't know you." Her next words were solemn, her expression intent. "I know we had an agreement about no alpha stuff between us while we were courting. But that's going to change. I accept my rank, and I'll continue to take orders from those who are more senior. But never you."

She continued to speak before he could interrupt, her hands moving to cup his face. "I'm yours. No limits. I'll give you everything you ask, anything you want, except this one thing—obedience because of rank. You will never be my alpha. Not in public, not in private. You're Hawke to me. Just Hawke. Do you understand?"

His wolf shuddered, relaxed as he bent to touch his forehead to hers. "Understood and accepted." *Mine*, he thought, *mine*. For the first time in his adult life, he had someone who was his—and with whom he could engage in a way he couldn't with any other member of his beloved pack.

They sat like that for a long time, his wolf peaceful on a level it hadn't been since he'd picked up the mantle of leadership at fifteen. And that wolf, it wanted her touch, too. He shifted without telling her, heard her gasp. But when the wolf laid its head in her lap and closed its eyes, her fingers clenched, soft and possessive in his fur. Content, he slept.

*   *   *

SIENNA sat stroking the silver-gold pelt of the huge wolf who slept with his head in her lap, her heart filled with a depth of wonder and joy she couldn't comprehend. The words he'd given her, the power he'd given her . . . she hadn't expected either.

I love you beyond life. It was a thought sent down the mating bond, and when the wolf seemed to sigh, it was clear some part of him heard her. That bond was so deep, so visceral, she knew there would never be another for either of them if one died. The changelings were right—*mating* was only once and forever.

A silent tear touched her cheek . . . a tear for Rissa. If Hawke ever wanted to visit the girl who had held his heart as a boy, Sienna wouldn't stop him. Rissa's ghost had been laid to rest—what remained were memories that should be cherished and held close. In a way, she thought, Rissa belonged to both of them now, as did her mother, Kristine. Pieces of the past that had shaped them, made them, brought them to this moment.

A moment in which she caressed a wolf who'd held together a broken pack through sheer grit and determination. It wouldn't be a simple or easy life, she thought, her lips beginning to curve. He'd try to dominate her, of that she had not a single doubt. But he would also love her with every powerful beat of that wild changeling heart.

. . . you have my devotion, your name branded on my soul, my wolf yours to command. A hundred years? It'll never be enough. I want eternity.

No, not simple or easy.

Vivid and dangerous and extraordinary, that's the life she'd have with her wolf.

When that wolf raised his head, she smiled. "Hello."

He shifted, and suddenly, she was being kissed by a naked man who scrambled her brains. Gasping in a breath as he scooped her up in his arms to throw her playfully onto the bed, she laughed. "Is the edge off yet?"

"Ask me again in a month or so." Then he pounced.

It was a long time later, her skin shimmering with aftershocks of pleasure, that she frowned and said, "What's your full name?"

Hawke's wolf flashed in his eyes, the ice blue glittering with the same amusement that had his cheeks creasing. "What brought that on?"

"I refuse to be your mate and be in the dark." She stroked her palms up over the temptation of his chest, her breasts tingling at the memory of how hard and beautiful he felt pressed up against her. In spite of his earlier words, he'd let her play with his body, stroke the rigid heat of his cock, learn him with her mouth.

Of course, that hadn't lasted long. When she'd complained, he'd promised to let her use the handcuffs on him next time. Sienna couldn't wait to hold him to that promise, to taste every muscled inch of him, but first things first. "Tell."

Leaning down, he nipped at her jaw, a quick, affectionate bite that had her jerking. "No distracting me," she complained, rubbing her foot over the back of his calf, the hairs on his legs crisp and rough, a sexy caress against her skin. "I want to know."

His chuckle vibrated through the palms she had on that resilient flesh. "If you're sure." Another small bite before he whispered it in her ear.

She blinked. *"No."*

He growled, but it was playful. "Don't you like it?"

"It's beautiful, you know it is." Perfect for him. "But then I have to ask about your first name. It doesn't seem very wolfish—especially considering the age and significance of your last. Was it a family name?"

He shook his head. "My mother had decided on a name if she ever had a boy, long before she met my father, regardless of the fact that Hawke wasn't any kind of a name for a wolf." He settled over her, a heavy male blanket. "When they mated, she decided to take her mate's surname, which was one of the oldest, if not *the* oldest, in the pack, but she refused to change her mind about her son's name."

Sienna heard the echo of deepest love in that statement. "Your father accepted it."

"He adored her." A simple answer. "Plus he figured any son of his would soon handle anyone who hassled him over his name—he was right." The arrogance was pure male wolf.

Charmed, she kissed a line up his neck. "In your mother's

defense," she said, unable to stop petting him, "it's a gorgeous, unique name."

"Just not meant for a wolf." He bent into her caresses. "Honestly? I like that they both gave me a name."

She did, too. "What about me?" she asked. "Do I take your last name since we're mated?"

"Do you want to?" A tilt of his head, the wolf watchful but not demanding.

She considered the question with care, thinking of who she'd been, who she was now. "Yes," she said at last, "but I'd like to keep mine, too." As with Hawke, the past was gone, but it had left an indelible mark, could not be forgotten. "It's a part of me."

Lips against her own, a wolf's kiss. "That works fine for me . . . Sienna Lauren Snow."

Continue reading for
special deleted scenes from

Kiss of Snow

BRENNA and JUDD

Author's note: I love the intimacy of this scene, but I felt the information conveyed here about Sienna had come through in other parts of the book. This scene also offers another glimpse into Judd and Brenna's relationship, but as they already had one fairly major scene, I decided to delete this one (much as it hurt!).

Judd arrived home to find his mate curled up in wolf form on a plush rug in the living area of their quarters. Going down on one knee beside her, he ran his hand over her back, her fur gloriously soft beneath the roughness of the guard hairs. Her eyes flicked open in a burst of wild welcome, and then the air was colored in the brilliant sparks that denoted a shift.

Even after all this time, it still stunned his heart when she did that, when she allowed herself to be so very, very vulnerable to a Tk who could conceivably disrupt the shift on a fatal level. The fact he'd cut out his heart before doing that wasn't the point, not when Brenna had once been terrorized by a telekinetic.

As soon as she was kneeling warm and naked in front of him, he slid his arms around the sweet curves of her body and bent to rest his forehead against hers. Everything in him sighed in relief, in surrender. Home. He was home.

Brenna ran her fingers through his hair, over his shoulders, again and again. Petting him. Never had he imagined he'd experience such intense emotion, this wild joy that made him feel as if he had a wolf inside him, too. It was that emotion that had him speaking his heart as he looked down into eyes of brown cut with shards of blue.

Extraordinary eyes.

Of a survivor.

Of his mate.

"I want this for her," he said, his voice harsh. "I want her to know this kind of happiness." Like a telekinetic Arrow, an X lived a life defined by the violence of her gift. Softness, tenderness . . . those weren't things they ever dared to dream could be theirs.

Brenna cupped his face, her hands warm and silken. "He's a good man, Judd. If they get together, you never have to worry he'll misuse her in any way."

"I know." Judd's trust in Hawke was that of a lieutenant in his alpha—absolute and without reserve. "But it hurts her, what she feels. I hate seeing that." He'd tried to protect Sienna as an Arrow, teleporting in to see her without Ming's knowledge, but in the end, she'd always been alone in the dark with a monster. "I wish I could save her the pain."

"Oh, sweetheart." Kisses on his jaw. "We didn't exactly have an easy courtship." Cupping his face again, she claimed his mouth, sweet and hot and wet. "Anything worth winning is worth fighting for."

WALKER and LARA

Author's note: This was originally written as a continuation of the date scene in chapter 47. While it no longer lines up perfectly with the final scene, it offers a small glimpse of what went on that night between Walker and Lara.

Lara is seated on Walker's lap on the sofa as the scene begins.

A change in those pale green eyes. "No rushing, Lara."

She brought her hand up to stroke his jawline. "I thought you didn't know what you were doing?"

"You're teaching me." Turning his head when her fingers brushed his lips, he sucked one gently into his mouth for a slow, hot second.

It made her whimper.

In response, he leaned forward to nuzzle a kiss to her throat. "You smell . . ." The sound he made was beyond masculine, low and deep and so very Walker.

Oh, God.

"Teach me what else you like." That big hand stroked up to the back of her thigh, higher. The instant she quivered, he repeated the stroke on the exact right spot.

Another kiss on her throat, his jaw brushing against her. He'd shaved before he'd come to her, she thought, his skin smooth under her touch as she wove her fingers into his hair. She loved the feel of his stubbled jaw against her, but the small sign of care, of tenderness, undid her.

Leaning down, she nipped the top of his ear.

His hand clenched on her thigh. "Again."

She did as he demanded, tugging lightly with her teeth before letting go. On her thigh, his hand squeezed once more before relaxing, the roughness of his skin an exquisite caress. "Do you like that, too?"

"Yes," she whispered, because this moment, it was quiet. Secret.

When he lifted his hand from her thigh, she wanted to moan in disappointment, but then he ran it over her breast and she clenched her fingers in his hair, the thick strands raw silk against her palm.

Walker had never thought he would one day have a lapful of warm, curvy woman in his arms. And that it was Lara . . . Unable to quite process the depth of what she aroused in him, he stroked his hand down her ribs, to the sensual swell of her hips.

Any and all skin privileges you want.

The wolves, for all their liking for touch, didn't offer such a thing lightly. It spoke of complete trust on Lara's part. Moving his hand back up, he curved it under her breast. Her nails dug into his nape, a tiny bite he hungered to experience on other parts of his body, sensual touch a new territory—one he planned to explore only with this woman. "I want to see your naked breasts."

Heat flushed over her skin, but she didn't say a word as he moved his hand to the top of her dress and tugged, pulling the fabric aside to reveal a lacy black bra that barely covered her nipple. His pants, already tight, were suddenly highly uncomfortable. "Show me." It came out hard, almost cold as he fought the force of his need, but Lara, this woman who understood him, didn't seem to mind.

Lifting a hand to her bra, she tugged down the cup so it framed her breast, offering herself to him. He bent his head and took. Tasted. Indulged. The sound she made when he sucked and rolled her nipple over his tongue had his hand returning to push up under her dress to close around the sleek softness of her inner thigh.

"*Walker.*"

"The other one," he murmured, then realized she'd gone still. "You're uncomfortable."

A husky laugh. "No, just the way you look at me . . ." Raising her hands with those whispered words, her body soft with welcome, she pulled away the dress and the bra until he could lick his way around her nipple before tugging it between his teeth. Her thighs clenched on the hand he had between them, squeezing tight. Listening to her body, he shifted that hand until his knuckles brushed against the delicate lace of her panties.

A little cry that did unknowable things to him.

Increasing the pressure, he felt her body tighten and then she was tugging up his head with her hands in his hair, her lips seeking his in feminine desperation. He kissed her the way he'd learned made her melt, licking into her mouth as he pressed her closer to him with the hand he'd braced on her lower back.

She shuddered, pressed hard against his knuckles. "Walker . . ."

He was no expert lover, but he knew how to listen, how to put together pieces of data—so he rubbed his knuckles against her. When she whimpered and strained impossibly closer, he deepened the pressure once more. Her cry was gasped out, her body quivering as she fell into him.

Trust. Such absolute trust.

Shifting his hand down to her thigh, he smoothed it over her knee, then back up. And since it was so easy, he leaned down and bit her ear like she'd bitten his. She jerked, smiled against his neck. "No fair." A soft, intimate murmur. "I'm helpless."

He kissed the line of her throat, running his mouth up to tug at her earlobe with his teeth . . . and felt the ripple of shocked pleasure that rocked her. "Is this what the juveniles call 'making out'?"

"Yes." Gasping in a breath, she laughed. "What do you think?"

"There's a high level of frustration involved." His erection felt as if it would snap in half.

"That's part of the fun." Nuzzling at him, she said, "I can do something about that frustration," and it was an offer both intimate and warm.

Every muscle in his body went tense—he'd fathered a child, but until Lara, he'd never before touched a woman . . . been touched by her. Yet now he held a beautiful, sensual woman in his arms and he wondered how he had ever survived without her touch. "Show me," he said, his voice lower, rougher than he'd ever heard it.

A fox-bright gaze, small tempting kisses. "I love your voice." Sliding her hand down his chest, she tugged at his belt. She'd just undone the top button of his pants and was unzipping him when his erection jumped at the brush of her hand. Walker grit his teeth, but it was too late. The single touch after a lifetime in the cold shattered him, ripping pleasure through every cell of his body.

Perhaps he should've been embarrassed, but with Lara petting and kissing him, all he felt was . . . He didn't have the word, but he knew that no one had ever made him feel like this. "Sorry," he murmured, luxuriating in her caresses.

"Now that we're both relaxed"—a wicked smile—"want to do it again?"

SIENNA ambushed by DREW

Author's note: This was how the second scene in chapter 16 originally ended. However, much as I enjoyed seeing Drew again, I decided the pace of the story was better served by a shorter, tighter scene that ended with Sienna's memory of her first meeting with Hawke.

"Do it." A hand on her head, snapping the thread of memory.
"Drew."

"Morning, sugarpie." Reaching over, he snagged another muffin for her.

"Stop with that nickname." In spite of her scowl, she had no resistance to his smile—or the blueberry-and-white-chocolate treat he held out. "Thanks."

Pouring himself a big cup of coffee, Drew grabbed a muffin for himself before sitting down across from her. Freshly showered, his brown hair looking closer to black, he was clearly wide awake. "Do you have an early shift?" she asked.

"Indy did," he said. "While I'm intellectually and physically opposed to getting up before the civilized hour of noon, sneaking kisses while I walked her to her post was too tempting to resist."

Sienna felt a pang of longing, wondered what it would be like to be adored with such open joy. "What're you doing in this section?" she asked, hoping Drew wouldn't pick up on her desolate mood. "You're one of the smug-mateds now, you know."

Grinning, he tapped her on the nose. "Came to see someone else, caught your scent."

Her responding smile was genuine. "I'd better go." She polished off her milk. "Have to get down to the eastern perimeter."

Drew rose as well. "Want some company?"

"You have time?"

"For you"—an arm flung around her shoulders—"all the time in the world."

Her usually infallible antennae didn't start to twitch until they'd reached her watch position. "So," Drew said, lean-

ing against the proud might of an ancient fir that brushed
the dawn-streaked sky, "it seems I'm going to have to kick
Hawke's ass for whatever he did to put that look in your
eyes."

That was when she remembered Drew wasn't only playful
and affectionate, he was also—according to the scuttlebutt
she'd picked up—the pack's tracker. "He'll wipe the floor
with you," she said instead of answering the implied question.

"Only if I fight fair. You know sneaky is my preferred
method. Plus I know a certain former Arrow who'd be more
than happy to provide backup."

Sienna began to walk the perimeter, hoping if she kept
this light, he'd drop it. "No need to do any violence on my
behalf."

"Oh, I disagree." Easy words as he fell into step beside
her. "Little sisters have to be looked after."

Halting, she stared at that handsome face with its lake blue
eyes so bright and shrewd. "Don't you dare pull the overprotective big brother act with me." Having witnessed him and
Riley with Brenna, she was well warned.

"It's not an act." A teasing smile but there was an edge to
it. "He hurt you."

"*Drew.*" Walking over, she touched her hand to his heart.
"Don't do anything, please. It would be . . ." Agonizing. "Just
don't. Please."

Drew closed his hand over her own. "Hey, of course I
won't do anything if you feel that way about it." Shadows
darkening the lake blue. "But you know you can come to me,
right? Anytime?"

She nodded, but this was the one thing she couldn't talk
about with anyone. Not without tearing open her heart, ex-
posing vulnerabilities so deep, they held the potential to
destroy her.

MARLEE talking to WALKER

*Author's note: This conversation is from one of my earlier
drafts of* Kiss of Snow. *Because of changes in the ensuing
drafts, it doesn't slot neatly into a particular chapter.
However, as you'll see, a certain aspect of this scene did
make it into the book in the form of the conversation Lara
has with Marlee in chapter 48.*

It was his daughter with her gap-toothed smile who took him
to task. "Daddy?"

"Yes?" He carefully sanded the edge of a tiny table, a piece
of furniture for Marlee's dollhouse—her dolls had apparently
decided they "must" have a dining room.

"How come"—a crunchy bite of pear—"you don't kiss
Lara like Uncle Judd kisses Aunt Brenna?"

Walker froze. He knew full well his daughter was intelligent, but this—"Why are you asking me that question?"

She swung her legs from her seat on his workbench and
took another bite of her fruit before answering. "'Cause Ben
says you smell of Lara and grown-ups only smell like that
when there's kissing." A breath. "But I said you weren't kissing her and he said you probably were in secret, so I was
wondering how come"—a second breath—"you didn't just
kiss her like normal?"

A little dazed, Walker leaned against the bench beside his
daughter, the miniature dining table forgotten. He didn't tell
her that Ben was wrong. There had been no kissing—but he'd
clearly spent enough time with Lara that their scents had
become intertwined on some level. So, he asked a question
he'd never thought he'd ask his child. "Does my spending
time with Lara bother you?"

Toby, the boy he considered his son, was an empath, would
instinctively understand that Walker needed Lara in a way
he might never be able to articulate even if he accepted it; but
Marlee had always been a daddy's girl.

Now, she frowned. "Why would I?" She offered him her pear.

He took a bite, gave the rest back to her. "I never want you
to feel as if I'm not paying attention to you."

Marlee beamed. "Yeah, but if you mate with Lara, then I'll have a mom like Ben does!"

His heart stopped. "You miss having a mom?"

"I guess, a little." She kicked off her shoes before leaning into him when he put his arm around her. "The mom I had before, she wasn't a *real* mom. I think Lara would be—we're not her kids, but she cuddles me and Toby and Ben and the other pups. Sometimes she tells us off if we're naughty." A guilty glance up from under her lashes. "But she's nice."

None of that, he thought, was a surprise, because Lara's heart was as big as the Sierra. "I'm not sure if I'm what she needs." He didn't realize he'd spoken aloud until Marlee said, "Ben says his mom likes it when his dad brings her flowers. Did you get Lara flowers?"

No, he hadn't. And still she gave so much of herself to him, had become the one person with whom he could speak of anything. A friend, he called her, knowing he was tying her to him, keeping her from forming relationships with other men.

Selfish.

But he also knew he wouldn't step back, wouldn't set her free. Because sweet, competent Lara had made long-dormant parts of him come to painful, brittle life.

INDIGO and SIENNA in conversation

Author's note: In Play of Passion, *Indigo makes a promise to herself that she'll warn the woman who becomes Hawke's prey. This scene, intended for one of the early chapters, was written as a fulfillment of that promise. In the end, I decided the book worked better if Indigo's support of Sienna came through in a more subtle way, but this scene (though it doesn't slot neatly into the final book) shows just how strongly Indigo cares for the young woman Sienna has become.*

Sienna was on her way out of the den that night, having put Toby and Marlee to bed after helping both with their homework, when Indigo walked up to her. "Going somewhere?"

"I just needed to get out." Her skin felt too tight, too full, her psychic energy shoving to escape—something Walker had spotted as soon as he'd returned home a few minutes earlier. "Thought I'd go for a walk." When she was alone, far from the den, she'd earth herself, expending the buildup of power the only way she knew how.

"I'll join you."

Sienna nodded. In spite of her edgy state, she wasn't yet ready to free the monster within. "The waterfall?" It was a little farther than the lake that was her usual spot of choice, but more likely to be empty.

"Perfect."

Neither of them spoke again until they reached the rocky edge of the waterfall. Sienna took a seat with her legs hanging over the side, her face kissed by the occasional cool spray carried by the wind.

The water was inky black today, except for where it foamed at the bottom, the roar of the fall another piece of the tapestry that made the Sierra Nevada so very magnificent. There was peace here. Sienna knew that. She just couldn't quite capture it, couldn't quite make it affect her the way it should. Always, inside her, there was chaos, a tumult of energy that hungered to live, to experience, to explore.

"So," Indigo said, coming down to sit on her left, long legs hanging over the edge beside Sienna's, "listen up."

Sienna knew that tone of voice. "What did I do now?"

Indigo's lips quirked. "Nothing. Believe me, that surprises me, too."

Sienna should've been offended—maybe a year ago, she would've blown up at the wry comment. But she'd grown up in that year. "I wasn't that bad."

"Puh-leeze, you're still the reigning champ of trouble with the trick you pulled that turned every drop of water in the den bright purple."

"Nontoxic dye," Sienna said, making a mental note to share Indigo's assessment with her accomplice, Evie. "And the kids thought it was awesome." She'd never have done anything that would've scared them.

"Uh-huh. Then there was the time you told all the juveniles you could read their minds and that you were spying on them for Hawke."

"That wasn't such a good idea in the end," Sienna admitted. "I think some of them are still wary around me."

Indigo snorted. "You have your group of troublemaker friends. Tai I can understand, but how the hell did you rope in Evie?"

"Mind control. Obviously." Sienna met the lieutenant's laughing gaze, told a quiet truth. "Your sister's heart is so full of goodness, it makes me scared for her." Like Toby, Evie had no badness in her.

Indigo's expression gentled. "Yeah, me, too. Which is why I'll kick Tai's ass bloody if he hurts her in any way, shape, or form."

Sienna thought of what Tai had said to her about Evie, knew Indigo wouldn't have to make good on that promise. "Did you want to talk to me about how I messed up by stepping off watch?" Her stomach knotted because Indigo was someone who mattered, whose opinion Sienna deeply respected.

"I trained you, Sienna. I know you have been beating yourself up about that since the night it happened." Indigo leaned forward, turning her face into the fine mist coming off the waterfall. "You were always harder on yourself than I was."

I have to be. Failure was simply not an option, not for an X. "I'm sorry," she said, not voicing the harsh truth she'd learned to live with over the past year. Before that, she'd let it strangle her, and her resulting anger had further accelerated her rate of decline. No more. "I know it reflects badly on you if I stuff up."

Indigo put a hand on her shoulder, squeezed. "We all make mistakes. And you're paying your dues—far as I'm concerned, it's done with. When do you finish in the kitchens?"

"Two more days."

Indigo nodded. "The thing I wanted to discuss with you has to do with Hawke. Specifically"—the lieutenant met her gaze—"you and Hawke."

Sienna stopped breathing, her mind catapulting her to the shocking heat of his touch that night before he left the den.

All that maleness so close to her, all that barely contained power. "What about me and Hawke?" she managed to say.

Indigo's unbound hair whipped off her face in the wind generated by the waterfall, baring the clean, strong lines of her face. "I promised myself I'd warn the woman who became his prey."

Sienna gripped the wrist of one hand with the other. "I'm not."

"No," Indigo agreed, and it was a stab to Sienna's heart. "Not yet."

Sienna jerked up her head. "What's that supposed to mean?"

"It means you have a problem, sweetheart." The term of affection was accompanied by a shake of her head. "That big, gorgeous wolf is going to shut you down the instant you step out of line—because he can."

"There's not much I can do about that, Indigo. He's alpha." The ultimate law.

Indigo's jaw firmed. "Find a way." A cool statement as she reached out to tap Sienna's temple. "That brain has gotten you into more trouble than most of the other young ones combined. Put it to work on the problem."

Sienna rubbed her fingers over her wrist. "But—"

"Quiet. Listen." Angling her body, Indigo spoke directly to her, those brilliant eyes night-glow in the dark. "He *sees* you. Maybe it pisses him off—"

Sienna sucked in a breath.

"—but you want him pissed off."

"I don't think so," Sienna muttered, thinking of how lethal Hawke could be in that kind of a mood. She was still smarting from the way he'd torn a strip off her hide after that idiotic fight with Maria.

Indigo ignored her. "When he does come after you, *fight*. Fight for everything."

Sienna closed her hand over the jagged edge of the rocks. "He touched me the night before he left for the mountains." The secret spilled out of her.

"Good."

"No." Unclenching her hands from the cold bite of the rocks, she went to shove her hands into her hair before remembering she'd braided it. "He hasn't made even a token effort to find me since then."

Indigo frowned. "Look, I don't know if I should be telling you this, but what the heck—you're going to need all the help you can get."

A sick feeling bloomed in her abdomen at the warning in Indigo's tone. "What?"

"He's sexually hungry," Indigo said bluntly. "And since he's a stubborn bastard, he might try to work it off with another female."

Sienna felt a cold, cold rage burn within her, an icy thing that had her heart turning rigid in her chest. It took conscious effort to wrench back the fury, to quiet the responding violence of her ability.

"Makes you mad enough to kill, doesn't it?" Smiling, Indigo pulled back several strands of hair dancing across her face. "Then make sure he doesn't have the chance to see anyone but you. However, that's not the issue."

"No?" It came out almost soundless, her brain hazed by darkest red.

"Have you been with a man, Sienna?"

A whip of heat slicing clean through the cold rage. "It's not—I'm not—I—" She clamped her mouth shut, tried again. "It's different for Psy." She'd been trained against all physical contact. It had taken her years to get to the point where she was able to allow someone she trusted close enough for a kiss.

"I know. That's why I'm asking, and you just gave me your answer." Indigo blew out a breath. "I think it's time we had a birds and bees talk."

Sienna wanted to dig a hole and crawl into it. Scrape the dirt over herself for good measure. "I had that in my first year of health class."

"Not that talk. The talk about how predatory changeling males can get when they're on edge. You, of course, will have to multiply that by ten since Hawke is alpha and hasn't had sex in months at the very least. So listen up, and take notes."

ABOUT THE EMPATH

*Author's note: This scene, from one of my earlier drafts,
tells you a bit more about Zia, the empath mentioned in
chapter 13. It also reveals more information about
Hawke's father, the majority of which was later rewritten
into other scenes in* Kiss of Snow, *so this particular scene
wasn't so much totally deleted as redistributed throughout the book.*

*Sienna and Hawke are lying in bed as the scene opens,
Sienna's arms braced on Hawke's chest as she looks up
at him.*

"Zia was one hundred and twenty-seven years old." The
woman had been as wrinkled as a raisin and as tiny as a child,
but he'd never seen her sit still. "I didn't understand what she
was when I was growing up—I knew she was Psy, from before Silence, but I never really thought about it." He'd been a
boy, with a boy's happy self-absorption. "I just figured she
was a telepath if I ever did think about it."

"She would've been an adult when Silence was imple-
mented." Sienna's tone held pure fascination. "The things,
the changes she had to have witnessed."

"Yes."

A thoughtful frown before she lay her head back down on
his chest. "Her life must've held such sadness."

"I realized that when I grew older," he said, "but at the
time, she was one of the elders and I was a kid." A kid with
two loving parents and a girl who was his best friend. Then
Rissa had died and his father had started to act in ways that
had scared Hawke's wolf on an elemental level. "Zia," he
continued, "was the first person who actually sensed that
something was very wrong in the pack. At first, I don't think
anyone really paid her too much attention." If they had . . .
But the clock could never be turned back.

Sienna nuzzled at his neck, as if she knew how the memories clawed at him. Cuddling her closer, he continued, "But
then a number of the pack—including my father—started to
behave so erratically it was dangerous, and Garrick began to

listen to Zia. It was too late by then though." His father's bloody rampage as he cut down the others who'd been compromised had already begun.

"I'm sorry, Hawke."

"I've come to terms with what happened. It helps that my father fought to the bitter end. He couldn't stop himself from harming Garrick, but he stepped in the path of a bullet for him." His angry pain had been tempered with time, until he could remember the man who'd loved him with such fierce loyalty, and forgive the one who'd broken.

"He died in my mother's arms. Zia told us later that his mental shields had been so compromised, they'd collapsed—as if his brain was lying cracked open to the elements, his skull gone." He thought of the pain his father must've suffered as he tried to fight the compulsions, the horror of knowing he was acting without honor, but being unable to stop it. "All in all . . . we lost a quarter of the population in the den before the bloodshed ended."

Wet heat on his chest and he realized his tough, unbreakable Psy was crying. "Ah, baby," he said, shifting until he was braced over her. "It wasn't you," he said, able to read her thoughts for all that he was no telepath. "It could never be you."

She shook her head. "I could've been one of them."

"Never. You have your mother's heart." He kissed her cheeks, sipping at the salt of her tears. "We survived." The remaining seniors and elders had held SnowDancer together until he turned fifteen. They hadn't been able to give him any more time—because a wolf pack without an alpha could not grow strong, could not heal. "I'm going to love you now, Sienna."

A smile that held too many years, too much knowledge. "Not as much as I love you."

It began with a kiss and ended with him holding her as dawn lit the sky, knowing that he couldn't hold back the coming of the day.

JUDD about ALICE

Author's note: While this scene is powerful, I deleted it because I felt Judd's need to help Sienna, his commitment to doing everything he could for his niece, was already clear. The timeline of this scene doesn't tie perfectly into the final book, so keep that in mind as you read.

Ten hours after Judd had brought Alice Eldridge into the den, she showed not the faintest sign of consciousness. He met Lara's eyes across the woman's unresponsive body. "I can attempt to breach her mind."

Lara's expression grew troubled. "Even if you're able to do it without hurting her, I can't allow you to invade her privacy that way."

Judd had no such compunctions, because if they couldn't stop the cascade of Sienna's power, he would have to put a bullet through her heart, end her life. They'd decided on that the day they defected, and it was a promise he'd hoped never to have to keep. "It's Sienna's life on the line."

"And you'd do anything for her." Lines around Lara's mouth, pain in her words. "So would I. But Judd, to violate one woman to save another?"

Judd knew she was right—but he also knew he'd cross far worse lines to save his sister's child. But Sienna wouldn't buy her life at the cost of Alice's, and so he couldn't act on the dark impulse. "Sascha," he said, his mind clearing for a second. "She may be able to sense something without causing harm. I'll get her."

Lucas almost killed him when he teleported directly into the cabin, the DarkRiver alpha's claws a bare quarter of an inch from his throat. "Shit." Judd froze.

"I should gut you," Lucas said, the leopard very much in his gaze. "Jesus fucking Christ, man!"

Judd didn't dare move until the other man dropped his hand. "I apologize." He should've never entered the cabin—if he'd been thinking straight, he wouldn't even have come close. "I came for Sascha."

The empath walked out of the bedroom, Naya—so small, so vulnerable—cradled in her arms. "What do you need?"

When he told her, her eyes turned to pure midnight. "It's really her?"

"Yes." Alice Eldridge's research had been erased from the web, but there were still a few scattered photos of her, mostly on dusty sites kept by conspiracy theorists—but not even their theories came close to the reality of the strange life and "death" of Alice Eldridge. "Will you come?"

Turn the page for a special preview of
Nalini Singh's next book in the
Psy-Changeling series

Tangle of Need

Coming June 2012
from Berkley Sensation!

RIAZ CAUGHT A flash of midnight hair and a long-legged stride and called out, "Indigo!" However, he realized his mistake the instant he turned the corner. "Adria."

Eyes of deepest blue met his, the frost in them threatening to give him hypothermia. "Indigo's in her office." The words were helpful, but the tone might as well have been a serrated blade.

That did it. "Did I kill your dog?"

Frown lines marred her smooth forehead. "Excuse me?"

God, that *tone*. "It's the only reason," he said, holding on to his temper by a very thin thread, "I can think of to explain why you're so damn pissy with me." Adria had been pulled into den territory during the hostilities with Councilor Henry Scott and his Pure Psy army a month ago, had remained behind to take up a permanent position as a senior soldier. She had fought with focused determination by Riaz's side, followed his orders on the field without hesitation.

However, off the field?

Ice.

Absolute.

Unrelenting.

Frigid.

Folding his arms when she didn't reply, he stepped into her personal space, caught the subtle scent of crushed berries and frost. A strangely delicate scent for this hard-ass of a woman, he thought, before his wolf's anger overrode all else. "You haven't answered my question." It came out a growl.

Eyes narrowed, she stepped closer with a slow deliberation
that was pure, calculated provocation. She was a tall woman,
but he was taller. That didn't seem to stop her from looking
down her nose at him. "I didn't realize," she said in a voice
so polite it drew blood, "that fawning over you was part of
the job requirement."

"Now I know where Indigo learned her mean face from."
But where his fellow lieutenant's heart beat warm and generous beneath that tough exterior, he wasn't sure Adria had any
emotions that registered above zero on the thermometer.

Adria's response was scalpel sharp. "I don't know what
she ever saw in you, but I suppose every woman has mistakes
in her past." The slightest change in her expression, the tiniest fracture, before it was sealed up again, her face an impenetrable rock face.

Scowling, Riaz was about to tell her exactly what he
thought of her and her judgmental gaze when his cell phone
rang. He answered without moving an inch away from the
woman who was sandpaper across his temper, rubbing him
raw with her mere presence. "Yeah?"

"My office," Hawke said. "Need you to take care of something."

"Be there in two." Snapping the phone shut, he closed the
remaining distance between them, forcing Adria to tip back
her head. "We will," he said, realizing those striking blue
eyes with an edge of purple had streaks of gold running
through them, beautiful and exotic, "continue this later."

That was when Adria's cell phone rang. "Yes?" she answered without breaking eye contact with the big, muscled
wolf who thought he could intimidate her.

"In my office," Hawke ordered.

"On my way." Hanging up, she raised an eyebrow at Riaz
in a consciously insolent action. "My alpha has requested my
presence, so get out of my fucking way," she said with utmost
sweetness.

Eyes a brilliant dark gold that were more wolf than human
narrowed again. "Guess we'll be walking together."

Not giving an inch until he stepped back and turned to
head to Hawke's office, she walked in silence beside him,
though her wolf bared its teeth, hungry to draw blood, to bite

and claw and mark. Damn him. *Damn him.* She'd been doing fine, coping after her final separation from Martin. That had been a bloody battle, too.

"You'll come crawling back to me. Maybe I'll be waiting. Maybe I won't."

Adria bit back a raw laugh. Martin didn't understand that it was over. Done. Forever. It had been over the night a year ago when he'd stormed out of their home, not to return for four months. The truly stunning thing was that he'd had the gall to be shocked when she'd told him to go find someplace else to sleep and slammed the door in his face.

"Cat got your tongue?" An acerbic comment made in a deep male voice that ruffled her fur the wrong way.

"Go bite yourself," she muttered, in no mood to play games. Her skin felt too sensitive, as if she'd lost a protective layer, her blood too hot.

"Someone should bite you," Riaz muttered. "Pull that stick out of your ass at the same time."

Adria growled, just as they reached the open door to Hawke's office. The alpha looked up at their entrance, unhidden speculation in blue eyes so pale they were those of a wolf given human form. However, when he spoke, his words were pragmatic. "You two free to go for a drive?"

Adria nodded, saw Riaz do the same. "What do you need done?" Riaz asked.

"Mack and one of his trainee techs went up to do a routine service of the hydro station," Hawke told them, "but their vehicle's not starting, and they've got components that need to be brought back to the den for repairs."

"No problem," Riaz said. "I'll take one of the SUVs, pick them up."

Even as Adria was thinking the task was a one-person job, Hawke turned to her. "You're now one of the most senior people in the den." His dominance was staggering, demanding her wolf's absolute attention. "I'd like you to get reacquainted with the region, given that you haven't spent an extended period of time here since you turned eighteen."

She nodded. Ranking just below the lieutenants in the hierarchy, senior soldiers were often called upon to lead, and as a leader she had to know every inch of this land, not just the section she'd been assigned to during the battle. "It'd be better if I do it on foot."

"You can explore in detail later on." Hawke pushed back strands of hair that had fallen over his forehead, the color a distinctive silver-gold that echoed his coat in wolf form. "I want you to have a good working knowledge of the area as soon as possible." He handed her a thin plastic map. "The trip up to the hydro station will take you through some critical sections—and you have certification in mechanics, correct?"

"Yes." It had been an interest she'd turned into the secondary qualification all soldiers were required to possess. "I'll take a look at the vehicle."

"What about the replanting?" Riaz asked, his voice clawing over her skin like nails on one of those old-fashioned chalkboards the pups liked to draw on. "Felix's team have enough security?"

"They're fine." Walking to the territorial map on the stone wall of his office, Hawke tapped a large cross-hatched section below what had been SnowDancer's defensive line in the fight against Pure Psy. "Felix's volunteers and conscripts"—a sharp grin—"are planting the area with fast-growing natives, but for now, it's so open it's easy to monitor, especially with the cats sharing the watch."

Adria thought of what she'd seen on that battlefield filled with the screams of wounded SnowDancers, the cold amber and red of a flame so hypnotic and deadly, and wondered at the cost paid by the young Psy woman who held all that power—and their alpha's heart. "What are the chances of another Pure Psy attack?" she asked, intrigued on the innermost level by a relationship that appeared so very unbalanced on the outside, and yet one that was as solid as the stone of the den.

It was Riaz who answered. "According to Judd's sources, close to nil. They've got worse problems."

"Civil war," Hawke said, shaking his head. "If he's right, there'll be no avoiding the impact—so we make sure we're prepared to weather any storms."

Nodding in agreement, she left the office with the man whose very scent—dark, woodsy, with a sharp citrus tone— made her skin itch. "We should get some food." The drive wouldn't be quick, plus Mack and his tech, who had probably not planned to be up there this long either, would be hungry.

"Should be something in here," Riaz said, walking into the senior soldiers' break room.

They worked with honed efficiency to slap together some sandwiches and were ready to go ten minutes later. Clenching her abdominal muscles as she got into the vehicle with Riaz, Adria told herself to focus on the route, the geography, anything but the potent, masculine scent of the man in the driver's seat . . . because she knew full well why he incited such violence in her.

RIAZ drove them out of the garage, and into the mountains, very aware of the cool silence of the woman with him. The more time he spent with her, the more he realized how unlike Indigo she was, in spite of the superficial similarity of their looks. One of the reasons he'd always enjoyed the other woman's company was her up-front nature—Adria, by comparison, was a closed box with Do Not Enter signs pasted on every surface.

He understood that. Hell, he had his own "no go" zones, but with Adria, it was armor of broken glass that drew blood. "This track," he said, doing his job because personality clash or not, he knew his responsibilities, "is the most direct route to the hydro station."

"Not according to the map Hawke gave us." A quick, penetrating glance. "So what's wrong with the other road?"

Man and wolf both appreciated her intelligence, something neither part of him had ever doubted, even when she was slicing into him with her verbal claws. "Sheer cliff face right in the middle." Making two tight turns, he continued onward. "Meant to delay any aggressors if they ever get that far."

Adria didn't say anything for several long minutes, studying the map and their passage into the mountains. "I'll need to request another senior soldier go with me on some of my exploratory trips, so I don't miss things like that."

"I'll take you," Riaz said, because damn it, he was a lieutenant, even when it came to a prickly piece of cactus like

Adria. "Indigo made sure I was familiar with the details after I came back from my posting in Europe. It'll be good for me to go over the knowledge."

Adria blinked, taken by surprise. "I appreciate it." It was the only thing she could say without giving everything away.

Riaz snorted, his hands strong and competent on the manual steering wheel as he navigated a particularly steep embankment. "About as much as you appreciate a root canal, but whatever your problem with me, we have to work together."

Setting her jaw, she focused on the view beyond the window—of the most magnificent scenery on this earth. Summer was fading, though autumn hadn't yet arrived, and the land was swathed in dark green, the peaks in the distance touched with white.

A flash of movement.

"Who's that?" She jerked forward to watch a big tan-colored wolf race across a meadow to the left, chasing a sleek silver wolf she immediately recognized. "He's being rough with Evie." Fury boiled in her blood. "Stop the car."

Riaz's chuckle held pure male amusement, fuel to her temper. "That's Tai, and Evie won't appreciate the interruption, Aunt Adria."

Biting back her harsh response, Adria glanced at the two wolves again, saw what she'd missed at first glance. They were playing, all teeth and claws, but with no real aggression to it. Just as Riaz turned a corner, cutting off the view, the two wolves nuzzled one another and Adria realized Tai and Evie weren't just playing, they were courting. "She's too young." While Indigo was very close to Adria in age, Evie was much younger.

"She's still a wolf, an adult female wolf," Riaz said, pushing the car into hover drive to negotiate a damaged section of the road. "You might have forgotten, Ms. Frost, but touch is necessary for most of our kind."

Her hand fisted, that nerve far too close to the surface.

A year.

It had been a year since she'd been in a sexual relationship, a rawly painful kind of isolation for a wolf in the prime of her life. But she'd been handling it, until Riaz and the raging storm of a sudden, visceral sexual attraction that terrified her.

"If we're throwing stones," she said, protecting herself by going on the offensive, "I'm not the only one who prefers a cold bed." Riaz was a highly eligible male—the fact he'd taken no lovers was a point of irritation with the women who wanted nothing better than to tussle with him. "Maybe that's why you're such a prick."

Riaz's snarl was low, rolling over her skin with the power of his dominance. Wrenching the wheel, he brought the SUV to a stop on the side of the road. "I've had it." Turning off the engine, he turned to her. "What the *hell* is your problem with me?"

"Drive," she said, almost ready to crawl out of her skin with the need to rip off his T-shirt and use her teeth on all that hot, firm muscle. "Mack is waiting for us."

"He can wait a few more minutes." Golden eyes that were no longer in any way human slammed into hers. "You've had a hard-on for me since you transferred to the den. I want to know why."

Gut twisting, she snapped off her safety belt and pushed open her door to step out into the cold mountain air. The chill did nothing to cool the fever in her blood, the need ravaging her body, threatening to make her a slave when she'd finally found freedom. Desperate, she concentrated on the majesty of her surroundings in an effort to fight the tumult inside her. In front of her lay tumbled glacial rocks, huge and imposing, beyond them the dark green of the firs that dominated this area. Above it all was a sky so blue it hurt.

The slam of a door, followed by the thud of boots on the earth shattered her fragile attempt at control, and then Riaz was standing in front of her, blocking the view. "We are not leaving," he said, his skin caressed by the sunlight that gilded his hair a gleaming blue-black, "until we work this out."

Feeling trapped, suffocated, she shoved at his chest and slipped out to stand beside the car rather than with her back to it. "I'm not the only one who has a problem. You've been picking at me since the day I was pulled into the den."

He growled and the rough sound rasped over her nipples, wrapped around her throat. "Self-fucking-defense. You took one look at me and decided you hated my guts. I want to know why."

Jesus, Adria thought, how had she gotten herself into this? "Look," she said, deciding to back down before her wolf took control and she found herself feasting on male lips currently thin with anger, "it's nothing personal. I'm generally a bitch." According to Martin, she was one with a stone heart.

"Nice try"—a harsh laugh that held nothing of humor— "but I've seen you with others in the pack." He took another step toward her, invading her space and her senses.

Hell if she was going to allow him to walk all over her. "Get out of my face."

"You sure you want me to?" he asked, a dangerous look to him. "Maybe the reason you react like a hissing cat around me is because you want me even closer."

She sucked in a breath.

Riaz's eyes widened.

Look for

Angels' Flight

A Guild Hunter anthology
by Nalini Singh
Coming March 2012
from Berkley Sensation!